FALLOFF

FALLOFF

A novel by Robert Flanagan

Book III of The ASA Trilogy

Connemara Press

Yellow Spring, West Virginia

<www.connemarapress.org>

authorHOUSE®

AuthorHouse™
1663 Liberty Drive
Bloomington, IN 47403
www.authorhouse.com
Phone: 1-800-839-8640

First published by AuthorHouse 11/17/2011

ISBN: 978-1-4670-7294-6 (sc)
ISBN: 978-1-4670-7295-3 (hc)
ISBN: 978-1-4670-7296-0 (e)

Library of Congress Control Number: 2011919175

Printed in the United States of America

Book cover and dust jacket by Liam M. Flanagan

Acknowledgments

Every author, whether fledgling or hoary master of his art, and will admit it or not, must, in honesty and with a sense of humility, acknowledge the master writers who have gone before. In "acknowledgments" in *Involuntary Tour* and *Dragon Bait*, books I and II of this trilogy, I named some whom I credited with inspiration. I will add nothing further. I find most modern/current writing insipid, uninspiring, and too filled with obeisance to the abhorrent practices of political correctness. If this is my failing, so be it. It is a fact.

Yet again to the No Name Writers of Winchester, Virginia, whose evocative revelations still hold sway, though our regular association has faded into the mists . . . my great appreciation.

And, as before and always, my primary respect and thanks to the serving military forces in this country who have kept us all free to do what we will, however we may manage. Without their sacrifices, all else would be meaningless, and would already be lost to memory.

Some segments of this book have appeared in various publications:

Throughout this and the other two books of the trilogy, many segments derived from real happenings and have appeared as subjects of my newspaper columns weekly in the *Hampshire Review*, Romney, West Virginia. As columns about real people and events, they bear the imprimatur of essays, though not so formal as that may sound.

> Elements of several chapters appeared in various issues of *phoebe*, the literary journal publication of George Mason University in Fairfax, Virginia, in the 1970s and '80s.
>
> Segments of several chapters appeared as short stories in my book, *Peripheral Visions*, a collection of short fiction. Mountain State Press, Charleston, 2003.

Dedication

"The ASA Trilogy," the full work comprising three novels, is dedicated to a once-extant and formidable military intelligence organization, the U.S. Army Security Agency. For a more expansive comment in this vein, see "Dedication" in book I of the trilogy, *Involuntary Tour*, Robert Flanagan, AuthorHouse and Connemara Press, 2009.

Author's Note:

The "Author's Notes" in book I, *Involuntary Tour*, yet pertain. To avoid confusion in sequencing of scenes, please **note carefully the place/time** sub-headings in each chapter, as well as some internal shifts within chapters, hi-lited by use of three asterisks ***. Chapters and internal segments are delineated to provide clear tracking of the story.

Contents

Prologue

Fort Ord, California: January 1960

The change of military services had gone more smoothly than he might have hoped, remembering all those Marine admonitions against things Army. Enlisted into U.S. Army service in the belief he had the option of military intelligence, Winter had been taken in by the recruiter in Sacramento. "Man, you are lucky. I've just had a committed enlistee injured in a car wreck; he can't be inducted until after he leaves the hospital and treatment. His A.S.A. slot is available."

"A.S.A.?"

"Army Security Agency."

"What do they do?"

"They're like the other spooks, M.I. people. Military Intelligence, Counter-Intelligence and so-on. All the same game. Better grab this slot. If you wait for the C.I., it might take weeks to get the board set up for your pre-induction interview. Gotta convene a lotta guys in civilian clothes, you know."

Winter would come to understand the disparity in the recruiter's ambiguous promises; the recruiter probably believed what he was saying. No one outside the cloistered ranks of ASA knew what that lot did.

But now, here he was, in the system, waiting it out at Fort Ord for orders. Having prior service in the Marines, and out of service only briefly, Sixth Army command specified he might avoid Army basic training if he passed the Army infantry trainee graduation field test—the same display of military skills demanded of personnel graduating Army basic training at Fort Ord. Watching some of that lackluster performance while on a duty detail, he couldn't bring himself to call it Boot Camp, nor come close to equating it to Parris Island's gentle ministrations.

He'd breezed through the test along with five others: two prior Marines, two soldiers who'd been out of service for a short period, and one confused coastal guarder. He remembered all his General

Orders, could read a map with the best; his military bearing, drill, and general knowledge of the military world sped him through the process. By eleven hundred hours, he was back in the Snack Bar in Casual Company area. No basic in his future; standby for orders.

There was no one among the casual personnel with knowledge of ASA, so there was no source of information about ASA schools, assignments, or duty. By the recruiter's assessment, Winter most likely would be going to Fort Devens, Massachusetts, for training . . . but in what? Or as what? He was complacent, though, with the knowledge that he was now in a military intelligence career field. Grunt work was likely behind him for good.

Down the coast from where Nickie and toddler Jeremy waited in Everett, Washington, he was in the same time zone, and timed his regular evening phone calls to catch Jeremy before his bedtime. And Nickie would be winding down then. Tired as she must be, he could hear the longing in her voice, trying to be interested in his progress through a new world, but more concerned with when they would be together again. At the end of an unsatisfying conversation, both hung up feeling lower than before the call. Unwanted dread of the calls built in his mind.

* * *

After passing the infantry competency test and while awaiting orders, casuals were allowed passes. A few took off for Monterey, Seaside, or Carmel; there were good words about all these venues. Some soldiers were bold enough to head for L.A. and Hollywood, but only if they had access to a car. Without a personal vehicle, transportation was a bitch.

Among the soldiers in casual status was one Army holdover, a Latino named Guiterrez, home town Palo Alto. He had a car through some chicanery enacted when he reenlisted. He asked Winter and a couple others if they wanted to go to Salinas, over in the valley, out the back side of the post. Salinas, a sizeable town centered in the midst of California's farm country, had a large immigrant population, supporting many Mexican bars and restaurants.

Why not? Good as anywhere else as far as he was concerned. Guiterrez was married, but the questing look in his eyes told Winter that might not make a difference. Three of them went.

After a short ride across post, they followed a back road to the Monterey-Salinas highway, turned east and found the agricultural town within minutes. The first notion was food. Guiterrez, having drunk two beers in the car en route, persistently lobbied for chili beans.

"I want some real cheeli beans, not that starchy, phoney shit they push in the mess hall. Le's find some cheeli beans," he growled, playing his aculturation card. They left the car on the street, a derelict piece of junk which no one would consider stealing.

After checking the menu in three restaurants, Guiterrez insisted none of them had ". . . *real* cheeli beans." He continued drinking from an open can out on the street. Winter looked about, scanning the streets for a cop or MP. What he did not need was a brush with the law, especially now he was in this spook outfit where everything, it was implied, depended upon a clean security background check: no fag history, no shaky political affiliations. *No* criminal record, not even a parking ticket.

Winter and a Colorado Arapaho Indian named Marcus Tall Pony pulled Guiterrez off the street and away from his Grail of legumes with the implicit suggestion of femininity. Passing a bar with its door ajar, they could hear soft music playing, and saw a number of females inside. There were only a couple of guys, by their haircuts likely also GIs.

Inside the snuggery, giving it its name, The Hearth, an open fire burned on a built-up brick hearth in a round, stack-vented fireplace in the middle of the floor. Easy chairs surrounded the fire, and soft lighting revealed the ample presence of women. The three soldiers settled in, noticing as they did that the other pair of soldiers they'd first seen were now leaving, arguing and remonstrating with their hands as they departed. Place looked chic to Winter; he wondered what their problem was.

No one came to serve them. Order at the bar.

Tall Pony invested in vodka, maintaining that it was all myth about Indians—that they couldn't drink—then quickly proved the verity of the damning judgement. Guiterrez stayed with beer, but switched from the 3.2 available on post to Dos Equis, a premium Mexican beer. Winter ordered one, too.

The three sat, drank, and relived their indenture in Casual Company. Guiterrez already had orders and would be leaving in two days for Fort Monmouth, New Jersey. Tall Pony was being held up on a "medical thing," as he referred to it. Winter, watching him slugging down the vodka, suspected he knew what the thing was. And Winter now knew where he was going—Fort Devens—but not when, and not for what. It left him with a hollow feeling.

Glancing about, Winter commented on the lack of other men in the bar. Lots of women. A couple of dancing pairs moved sluggishly about the tiny floor beyond the glow of the fireplace, but both pairs comprised two women. A tiny flag went up.

After a couple of beers, Winter decided he'd had enough. Looking about, he focused on a tall, broad woman of remarkably even and lovely features. Watching her with a sense of pleasure in the way she moved, he noted her hand, playing over her equally attractive female partner's ass. The flag became a red signal rocket. He turned to say something to his companions, but missed his chance when Tall Pony lurched to his feet, muttered something about "quim" and made for the bar where he addressed himself to another bar chick.

"Get the fuck out of my face, dog breath. You look Indian. How!" she said scathingly, raising one hand with the middle finger extended. "Can't you read sign? Look around, asshole. Go back to the barracks and play with yourself, thinking of this body." As she said it, she thrust a pair of 38-double-Ds at Tall Boy.

Even Guiterrez, as drunk as he'd managed to get, could read *that* sign. The three soldiers, moving as one, sidled out of the lezzie bar and sought out the car, disgusted on two levels. The persistent lack of viable chili beans was a distant second.

Going back over the mountains to Fort Ord, Winter forgot the bar, still mulling the quandry of his orders and the related when, where, what. Fort Devens, OK. Massachusetts . . . a helluva reach for a Mississippi boy. Alien spaces!

* * *

In 1960, on the rare news broadcast that dealt with the subject, any reference to that particular part of the Orient was to Indo-China. And such mention *was* rare: Indo-China, six years after the French debacle, was yet a quiet backwater.

chapter one

Fleeing G.o.D.

Tan Son Nhut/Sai Gon, Viet Nam: December 1968

"Gawd a-mighty!"

Specialist Four Abel Axelson, Duty Non-Commissioned Officer at Davis Station, had made scant record of anything that had occurred thus far in his tour of duty on Christmas eve, but the distant mortars got his attention, distance being relative. And he was still pissed that, as a Specialist-4, he had been put on the Duty NCO roster where only E-5s and E-6s normally were allocated to such lofty indignities. But he was on the list for promotion to SP5 and the First Shirt snickered when he told him, "Just gettin' you *ack*-li-mated, boy. Gonna be a lot of these now."

Indulging a mood both flippant and irascible, Axelson made an entry in the duty log when the mortars stopped dropping into the edge of Gia Dinh, miles away. *Stopped.* No one would ever know why this negative happening warranted notice; he had not logged the onset of incoming. But overtaken by events so soon after, no one ever asked. The Duty NCO had not finished documenting the distant absence of mortars when the rockets found Tan Son Nhut.

The VC rocket cadre, likely not seeking targets of the louvered board billets—shanties that resembled tall chicken coops—were after the tactical aircraft beyond the fence. But the first rocket hit the hooch at one end of a row of like structures that served as billets for the 224th Radio Research Battalion (Aviation) enlisted troops, as well as Headquarters troops of the 509th RR Group. Some of that mixed command of soldiers, for once, counted themselves lucky to have been at work in the unlikely night hours.

A second 122-millimeter rocket of the best Urals steel plowed into the middle of the road that separated Davis Station from the Vietnamese Ranger training area. No one home there, either, and in that persistently ravaged road, the crater was scarcely noticed.

The third and last rocket got close to the VC's likely target, striking a Conex in the middle of a stretch of Conexes lining the corrugated metal fence between the flight line and the 509th billets. The 146th RRC's aircraft were nearby, but remained untouched.

Conexes, large shipping containers made of steel, roughly 6 by 8 by 12 feet in size, resembled an a-cubical hut. Some boasted greater dimensions. After serving as containers for supplies and equipment shipped to the battle zone, instead of being returned to the continental US containing damaged equipment, spent artillery brass, battle-damaged tanks, trucks, and other vehicles as intended, they were often used for storage or utility space by the holding unit.

The rocket-stricken Conex in this instance belonged to the 146th Radio Research Company (Aviation.), and was used for storing mechanics' tools occasionally; aircraft engines less often, when one had been pulled for maintenance or upgrade; and POL—petrol, oil, and lubricants—in small quantities. On the quiet December morning when this particular Conex was struck by the Slavic thunderbolt, it held only parts of two different Vietnamese mechanics' tool sets and a case of automotive engine oil, likely stored there as the first step in a progressive theft. Considering there were no casualties from the barrage of three rockets and the aforegoing mortars, the Commanding Officer of the 146th felt pretty good, losing only one Conex.

By the time the After-Action Report was completed two days later, along with peripheral paperwork delineating material-fiscal losses, the CO was not so happy. Itemized as "Destroyed by enemy action" in the unfortunate Conex—the items' presence sworn to by two sergeants, a warrant officer and a major—and claimed for replacement, was a list of supplies that would have required a full size hangar to contain them: two aircraft engines, rotary—one 450 hp Pratt & Whitney R-985 for the DeHavilland RU-6A, the 224th's standard "Beaver" single-engine ARDF aircraft; and, though no one could explain the anomaly, one T53-L-7 turboprop, one of two engines for the OV-1 Mohawk, along with one 3-blade, reversible-pitch propellor for that engine.

The 224th did not own, fly, or even like Mohawks. Wiser counsel prevailed, and the T53 and prop were removed from the list. Also itemized were five "tool sets, mechanic, aircraft-complete"; four wheels—three aircraft main wheels for the U-8, and one Jeep spare; 61 "blanket, Army, wool"; bed linen, 74 sets (complete: two sheets, one pillow case ea.); 19 "parachute, emergency"; seven cases of "bug spray"; and in an adventurous departure, two cases of frozen steaks, though no one attempted to explain how the Conex had come to be equipped with temperature control refrigeration.

The well-undocumented storage facility become known as "the million-dollar Conex," bringing smiles and guffaws across the four Corps. Visiting personnel expressed interest in visiting the site of the $1M Conex.

Captain Bannister, down from the 144th, leaned against the metal fence, admiring the full extent of destruction involving the Conex. With Chief Warrant Officer-Three Gardena, also of the 144th, they speculated how they might arrange such an unfortunate event on their ramp at Nha Trang. At the sound of irregular footfalls, they turned to stare out toward the open airfield.

A PFC clad in olive-drab T-shirt, torn-off fatigue trousers, and un-tied jungle boots jogged by at the edge of the taxiway. Beyond the PFC moved a Jeep driven by a sergeant, the vehicle geared down and pacing the PFC's exhausted strides. As the PFC shambled past the two officers, they heard his plaintive cry arise from a core of despair, "I hate this fuckin' place!"

If the two bystanders had not agreed with the plaintiff's position statement, being officers they would have been obliged to bring administrative action against this unseemly behavior. They turned back to considerations of the defunct Conex.

* * *

Hearing a rumor there were incoming 058 manual Morse intercept operators somewhere in the pipeline, Winter, at the request of Lieutenant Mabry after their return from Plei Ku, had visited 509th's personnel section.. Piltdown Pilot had requested Winter look over the list and see, first if he knew any of the Morse ops, and if so, might any of them offer help in PP's recruiting for LAFFING EAGLE. Winter's mind was on CRAZY CAT, but being somewhat unemployed, awaiting transfer, he agreed to help. The new year was still a few days away, and nothing would happen until after. But these new guys all came directly from school, Winter had heard. He was unlikely to know any of them.

The personnel clerk he asked about the new personnel regarded the warrant officer with a blank stare of disinterest and never answered. The hubbub of typewriters, shouts, ringing telephones, curses, and the overriding din of hammering by two stockade rats, awaiting courts-martial and spending their detention pointlessly pounding nails into boards, killed the possibility of ever running the rumor of fresh ops to ground. But Sergeant Fantz, standing nearby, said, "That's the first of 'em, Chief," pointing to a soldier standing before another clerk's desk.

When Winter turned, he was startled to see a soldier he recognized, and not one fresh from school. Billy Ray Damson, wearing SP4 rank. Damson had soldiered in the 3rd RRU with Winter in 1965, and had been at that time an SP5. That time together in Viet Nam four years before had been of minimal contact. Though SP5 Damson had tried to transfer into the Air Section where Staff Sergeant Winter was NCO-in-charge, it never happened. At that time, and for a change, the Air Section had been fully staffed. And though they worked in related sections, there had been little contact between the two men, who had an even longer history.

Now Damson was here, and in the mix of emotions and memories stirring him, Winter realized that, despite his lack of warm and fuzzy feelings for Damson, the man *was* qualified. He was even a *good* 058, had performed well in that role. He'd be a shoe-in for Air this time. Chucklin' Chicken was coming, already looking for ops. He walked over to break the ice, and to engage the assignments clerk in the possibility of such a deal for Billy Ray Damson. But, his mind a-swirl with conflicting memories, Winter felt no great hope about recruiting this soldier for LAFFING EAGLE, though he was technically competent.

For Winter had known Damson before that Viet Nam 1965, assignment. Asmara in 1961 had been their first encounter in the Army, a relationship that had not progressed well.

* * *

Asmara, Eritrea (Ethiopia); February 1961

On Valentine's Day, a levy of new Morse operators arrived in Asmara from Fort Devens in Massachusetts and Vint Hill Farms Station in Virginia. They were assigned out to the four tricks in short order. One, PFC Billy Ray Damson, found himself on DELTA Trick where, like any new man, he ordinarily would have been assigned a bunk in one of the DELTA Trick squad bays. But due to a temporary housing crisis, he was given the empty rack in Room 31 in BRAVO Trick's area. That assignment was also temporary, the clerk had assured the room's other occupants.

Rooms were reserved for SP5s, NCOs who did not have quarters off-post, and when circumstances permitted, the odd lesser grades, especially SP4s who were "old timers," men who'd been at the 4th USASA Field Station for more than a year and were nearing the end of their 18-month tour. Winter, by virtue of prior service and having made SP5, shared Room 31 with two other trick workers. The room held an empty bunk after Mellinson was shipped to Landstuhl Army Hospital, Germany, for the witch doctors to tease his schizophrenia. The empty bunk made for a measure of luxury in an environment of normally congested living conditions.

It provided slack space for the on-going poker game, then running for seventy-some-odd days; the room had acquired the risqué title of "Club 31." The bunk was handy for the occasional drunk who couldn't make it from the game back to his proper area—some as distant as the far end of that same third floor hallway, or more challenging, another floor of the building.

So when Damson dragged his duffel and B-4 bags into Club 31, looked about, and settled onto the unmade top bunk and occupied the unused wall locker with contentious arrogance toward the poker players, it set a bad precedent. Several of the players glanced at him between drawing cards, checking, calling, or raising; some tried to make small talk—"Hi, New Man. Where'd you come from?"—and checked his nametag for identity. Their efforts garnered small returns. They quickly ignored new guy, went back to drinking and cards.

When SP5 Winter came in at midnight from an eight-hour Swings trick, Damson was asleep in his new-found bunk. At one point in the foregoing evening, the new man had made a pointless appeal for the gamesters to "Keep the noise down!" after a particularly exhilarating outburst. Afterward, aware that he had fallen among chronic miscreants, he kept silent.

Later, after some weeks of little-to-no communications with the new loner, Winter discovered that he and Damson were both from Mississippi; further, they had lived close together in the same town, and had started school at the same time in the same class. It quickly emerged that they had known one another, were close friends and playmates in those best-forgotten days and here, half a world away in Eritrea (Ethiopia), they took up the friendship.

But it was short-lived. After a few days and a few drinks together, both men realized they had nothing in common, did not care for the other, and thus went back to enforced strangerhood, sharing the same room.

* * *

Tan Son Nhut, Viet Nam: December 1968

Winter paused to reflect on that earlier history, thought about his meager contact with Damson in his first Viet Nam tour, and decided there were too many question marks for him to recommend the man for Piltdown Pilot's menagerie.

December was disintegrating ever faster. Christmas had already done its worst. Signs of general paranoia emerged as the season inched toward year's end with Tet to follow. The question and the fear in every mind was: Would Tet '69 be a repeat of Tet '68?

A calm appraisal could have dispelled those fears. The Viet Cong, despite frenzied media assertions to the contrary, had effectively been destroyed as a viable fighting force in the '68 Tet uprising, which didn't rise up as expected, but did bring into common parlance the word "Tet."

Foremost in Winter's mind was his upcoming transfer north to Cam Ranh Bay, not some rippling fear of charlie. Sai Gon and III Corps had worn him quite thin. He was ready for change. The continuing standoff with his wife with its burden of oppression, and missing his children— even any word about his children— made him hunger for change.

The rift between him and Nickie was eight months old now, originating one dark night last April on a winding road in the Austrian Alps, when he, belatedly, informed her that he'd received orders for return to Viet Nam for a second tour. Badly wounded at the end of his first tour, Winter had been at great pains to convince Nickie that he would not be at such risk a second time. Having suffered every pain with him in the follow-up to that wounding, she held no fondness for the news which offered only the opportunity to re-live that time—or worse. Over the following months, after receiving orders at Bad Aibling in Bavaria, the split between them had taken firm hold. By the time he'd left her and the two boys on the Mississippi Gulf coast, in a new house where they would await his return, his marriage bore no promise of survival.

But he had good friends at Tan Son Nhut, here in the 224th/146th; they had helped his acclimation to solitude. Though he was shortly leaving them, no doubt he would make new allies up the coast. It was the military life.

He didn't realize just how much he anticipated the move until CWO Ito pointed out to him that evening in the lobby of the Newport that Winter's conversations these days invariably worked their way around to Cam Ranh Bay. The two were seated on the distressed sofa that formed the bulk of lobby furniture, awaiting time for the Circle-34 mess to open for the evening meal. Their conversation, lacking new inroads in culture, turned on Winter's mention of transfer.

"Cam Ranh. Cam Ranh. Winter Man, you're beginning to sound like a bleeding draftee with orders for Hollywood. It's not as if Cam Ranh is out of the warp zone, you know. Gotta be threats there like anywhere else in country."

"That's monumentally perceptive of you, Mister Ito. No doubt you're right. But the mission's attractive. Being back in the Ops end of things, instead of riding around country like a disenfranchised Ichabod Crane. I miss Ops. I've never been out of Ops since I joined this man's army . . . except for schools. Operations is my thing." He let it sit and fester as Ito said nothing. Then added, "Besides, the living can't be bad. I mean, anyplace where the bar stays open twenty-four-seven doesn't leave much to long for."

"That is such bullshit. You're not even a heavy drinker. And there's no downtown, no coochie bars, no poontang."

"Coochie bars? Poon-tang? You forgetting your officerly vows, inscrutable one? How can your little Oriental mind even conjure up those terms?"

"You're right," Ito smirked. "And I'm wrong. There *is* a *ville*. Just across the bay, or around the peninsula, whatever. Dong Ba Thin, right on the doorstep."

"Dong Ba Thin. S-two has nothing good to say about that place."

"Well, so what if it's the illicit substances capital for all of Two Corps? Gotta be some cooze in the woodwork."

Winter cleared phlegm from his sinuses and spit. "You'll never catch my virgin ass over there—for cooze, for dope, for liberty. They got nothing I want."

"Well, it's a choice. I may."

"May what?

"May venture into Dong Ba Thin. Not for substances, you understand; merely to avail myself of feminine game. If any."

Winter gave him a look of astonishment. "When do you figure you'll get T.D.Y. to Cam Ranh to pull liberty in Dong Ba Thin?"

"This 'liberty' you keep on about . . . is that something like a pass? I mean, pass is an Army term and you may not be familiar with it, stuck as you are in the 'fifties Marines' mindset."

"Yeah, yeah. Carry on. But don't forget what the Marines did to your people on Iwo."

This left-handed slight had become a standard put-down Winter imposed on Ito, despite that Ito's *people* were American citizens.

"There. Now you've done it. Again. That's all right, Kemo Sabe. You know—" he said, and Winter prepared for the comeback. Ito caught him out. "—it's sad to go off to war without a song. We don't have a song."

Grasping the direction of Ito's mind, despite his non-sequitur, Winter responded with a scoff. "Hell, we got lots of songs, if you care for rock-and-roll," knowing Ito's disdain for anything approaching that atonal cacophony. He added, "Now, Korea. Korea's the place we had no song. Bet you can't think of a single song that's associated with the Korean set-to."

"Was there a theme song in 'The Bridges of Toko-Ri?' For 'Nam, I could make a case for Tony Bennett. 'I Left My Heart . . .' is as close as anyone gets to Viet Nam's song. And Paul Mauriat's put out a few I like. Instrumentals. And I can stand C.C.R. Besides," Ito paused dramatically, "I won't be coming up to Cam Ranh on T.D.Y." Letting the statement hang, he pulled a sheet of yellow, flimsy teletype tearsheet from his pocket, unfolded it and handed it to Winter, "I got orders. Today. Transferring Chief Warrant Officer-Two Frederick Ulysses Ito to the First Radio Research Company, (Aviation), effective oh-one January in the year of our Lord, nineteen hundred and sixty-nine."

Winter sat forward, began to rise, then slumped back onto the torn sofa. He could not respond and sat, staring blankly at Ito.

He suspected it was all a ruse, cooked up by Ito just to confound Winter. Until the adjutant assured him, the night before their flight north, that Ito was indeed transferrring along with Winter.

The Lost Soul from Con Son Island, Lieutenant Gorby, staggered through the lobby, again, asking the world at large, "Were you there?" Winter thought he himself might be caught in a time warp; he never encountered Gorby except for the lieutenant's lamenting passes through the Newport BOQ lobby. When was it? Last night? Two nights ago? Neither could he account for the young officer's erratic gait. He was not drunk. He never drank at all when he came up from Con Son to the big city; of course, there, on the island, chances were. . . .

"Were you there? Were you there when they mortared my TOC?"

He didn't stop on his way through the lobby. Neither warrant officer made any move that could be construed as motive for holding him up. He ricocheted on toward the elevator. Gorby had never been on a firebase or LZ, never walked patrol, never been out of the Capital Military District except for his time in Con Son, and assuredly had never been in a Tactical Operations Center. His madness, or whatever delusion he embodied, took a purely self-deceiving posture.

Watching Gorby fall into the elevator when it came, Winter did not see Damson until the specialist walked up behind him, visible only as *someone* in the edge of his vision.

"Mr. Winter," Damson said, saluting sloppily.

Bound by oath and protocol, Winter stood and returned the salute. Crisply. "Billy," he said cautiously, "how you doin'?"

"O.K. Just wanted to be sure Lieutenant Gorby got inside all right. I drove him over from the club." There was no expression on Damson's face: the words could have been a recording.

Ito drifted away without contributing to the stark militarism of salutes.

Winter, nodding Damson ahead of him, walked away from the table-desk where a new warrant officer sat, wearing the blue and gold brassard, reading the Duty Officer Manual. A few days before, upon Damson's arrival in country, Winter had considered the possibility of asking him to move finally into an aviation billet in LAFFING EAGLE, but bending to caution, had not done so.

"Would have asked you this the other day, Billy Ray, when I first saw you, but we weren't alone." Winter continued quietly, "How come I last saw you in nineteen sixty-five you were wearing Spec-5 stripes, and now you're a Spec-4? Pulling duty driver and such shit. I think I even heard somewhere you'd made staff sergeant." Given Damson's contrariness, Winter was not sure he expected an answer.

And when he got one, it wasn't what he wanted to hear.

"Yes, sir. I'm going at this Army thing a bit different now, since they saw fit to send my young ass back over here. I'm working my way *down* the ladder, lookin' to make P.F.C. any day, now. Then, one more step and I'll be a blessed private."

There was a tense silence.

Winter looked for humor in the man's answer. There was none evident.

"And why . . . why might you want to be a private, for God's sake?" He still expected a punch line.

"Hell, Mister Winter. You know anyone . . . any single soul on earth with less worries than a private in the Army? He don't even have to decide what to wear or to eat: the Army tells 'im. How to think, what to say and who to. All good shit! And I'm already here in The 'Nam. What more could anyone ever do to me? An Army private, in Viet Nam—what more could any asshold load on me? Unless I asked for Air. And I'm unlikely to do that." He held his stance in silence a moment, and when Winter didn't respond, said, "Chief," gave a sloppy salute, and went out the door.

The new warrant duty officer watched Winter across the table, too far away to have heard.

Winter and Damson's relationship eight years earlier in Asmara had not been the stuff of lasting friendship. Their childhood did not come into it. He had no clue to the man's deep-seated anger.

Winter shrugged, said, "What the fuck? Over."

The duty officer leaned forward. "Whut'd ya say, Chief?"

Winter trudged after Ito toward Circle-34, not looking forward to having to tell Piltdown Pilot that any further head-hunting exercise on his part had gone for naught. And he would not know until too late that Damson's words on the Air Section were not etched in stone.

* * *

Winter flew with Smiley the next morning, testing a modification to the navigational system. The Nav-Aids never got a chance to function. The U-8 began losing oil pressure in the starboard engine in climb-out, and crept back into the landing pattern immediately, Smiley with one hand on the switch to feather the engine, both of them pointlessly gripping the parachutes they sat upon, though neither bothered to strap one on. The universal conviction held by all flying personnel of the 224th was that if they should have an emergency, have to bail out and pulled the D-ring, the sight that would meet the jumper's eyes would be a dense cloud of moths, fluttering skyward from the chute pack. There was no backup chute.

After an uneventful landing, and after Smiley had worked out his frustrations to his satisfaction by kicking the U-8's tires into submission, they walked to the club and drank with the 146th ops not on today's manifest, and a few mechanics who, it was rumored, couldn't find the flight line. It was a slow day.

In an unexpectedly strange turn of events, there was little action through the last days of 1968. Around Sai Gon, at least. Elsewhere, making headlines, the 1st Marine Division initiated Operation TAYLOR COMMON in Quang Nam Province, I Corps, and was thoroughly kicking ass. But locally, quiet city, though, the question was becoming more prevalent in polite conversation: would the '69 Tet season, anticipated in about a month, be a re-run of the '68 follies?

* * *

Except for the ARVN guards in the Viet army vehicle parking compound between the Newport BOQ and 3rd Field Hospital, firing their rifles into the air at midnight along with ten thousand other cloud-killers across the city, there was little excitement as the New Year moved forward to encompass the war. Wondering how many civilians and GIs, both Viet and American, were injured or killed by the spurious barrage of spent ordnance falling from the sky, Winter waited out the tag end of 1968.

On Armed Forces Radio on New Year's morning, a gushing of late but persistent Christmas carols was interrupted with the depressing news that by the previous night's witching hour, the number of US dead in Viet Nam had risen to more than thirty thousand. A figure almost as depressing as the carols. Winter retracted the cynical thought, raised his canteen cup and toasted Morning Report entries with one swallow of tepid water that tasted of iodine.

* * *

Winter had not realized how much bigger the Otter aircraft was than the old, trusty Beaver. The Otter RU-1A was another DeHaviland-of-Canada aircraft commonly in use in Viet Nam by the US Army, including a couple in the 224th Aviation Battalion. He'd logged hundreds of hours in the Beaver, but this U-1 was a whole other world. Looking around the spacious cabin, he reckoned they could fit nine or ten troops in here, with equipment; or in another measure, install up to four or five collection positions. Sufficently noisy,, it seemed quieter than the Beaver, though it mounted a much larger engine turning a bigger prop.

Ito, not yet accustomed to the common frailties of flight in Viet Nam, looked about suspiciously. He and Winter had the entire cabin to themselves, except for a mound of unidentified material covered with canvas and strapped down in the bay made open by removal of seats. The exotic nature of the private flight, chauffered by a lieutenant colonel with an agenda, did not seem to resonate with Ito. Every slight turbulence, every engine hiccup or slipstream of smoke from a cranky cylinder, was regarded by him as potential crisis. Winter said to him, shouting over the invasive engine noise, "You'll stop sweating the petty shit after you've flown a few missions."

Not considering that a positive endorsement, Ito said, "How do you figure that, O mighty warrior of the skies?" Ito's Oriental eyes opened almost round enough to allow vision. "Don't you hear all those fucking things breaking, failing, going wrong with this plane. Listen."

"It's not the stuff you hear that's going to kill you. It's any one of a million other silent causes. No way 'round it. But you'll come to love the flying life."

"Your ass! Uncle Sammy makes me do this shit; he don't make me like it."

"Don't you just hate that? Remember, what goes up—"

"Are you always like this, Winter? In the air? Man, I don't think I ever want to fly with you again. On missions or whatever."

"Not to worry, Little Yeller Chief. You be a controller. I be a controller, albeit the head controller. There be only one controller per flight. We'll probably never fly together again . . . more's the pity."

Ito responded, "You're harsh, man. Can't you see I'm suffering here?" Winter could see that Ito's skin was a sallow shade, appearing drained from his normal hue. An open invitation.

"When I first went to sea in the Marines," Winter said, "the old Navy chiefs used to ensure that the first day out when we hit rough water, the galley would serve up the greasiest food in the locker: pork chops, eggs floating in grease—"

"*Get away from me, asshole!*" Ito shouted, stumbling up from the wall-rack seat, searching for the relief tube. Winter wondered if there were bathers on the white sandy beaches skirting by beneath the aircraft. At six thousand feet, details were indistinct.

Something reminded him of times in his past, and he blanked out the rest of the flight north, thinking of Nickie and the boys on such a beach. Preferably, one near them on the Gulf Coast. But even feeling put-upon by his stubborn wife, he still wouldn't want her on the beach beneath a puking Ito. This was the year he was going home. When he recognized a haunting corollary—this leaving of G.o.D.—he felt a suspicious flutter in his stomach. The Sai Gon-Tan Son Nhut netherland depicted as the Garden of Delights did not translate.

Leaning his head back on the seat webbing, Winter found the playful allusion to "Garden of Delights," for some inexplicable reason, put him in mind of his brother, Larry. Had he chosen to look over at Winter at that time, Ito would have been curious about the look of despair that settled on his friend's face, though his closed eyes betrayed nothing.

chapter two

CRAZY CAT

Cam Ranh Bay, Viet Nam: January 1969

Deep in slumber, Winter basked in the unfamiliar chill of delicious air-conditioning, until two Phantom F-4s launching in tandem brought him back. His head erupted from the pillow, eyes wide. A split second before the instant of breaking ground, the two strike aircraft's afterburners cut in and the barely separated booms wrote finish to dreams. Despite similar conditions back at the Newport BOQ at Tan Son Nhut, and thinking he'd mastered the trick of blanking out aircraft thunder, the assault, surely from the next room, brought him upright on the edge of the bunk. In the taut edginess of disrupted stupor, he dropped his feet to the flip-flops and in one continuous movement was out the door in his skivvies.

By the time he pulled the door shut, preserving the precious cold, the launch thunder was fading, moving off like a summer storm. From outside his ground floor room, he could not clearly see the strip, merely a hint of white concrete as a nimbus, dazzling in the early sun.

He was billeted on the opposite side of the building from the Sandman Lounge, aka "the Sandbag." As the Sandbag kept non-union hours, living anywhere nearby meant minimal sleep, whether aircraft were launching or not. Only hardcore drunks chose quarters on the same side of the building with the Sandbag, and then with good cause: usually, so that when they became post-carousal casualties, they might crawl to their bunks with minimal scuffing of knees.

Winter, emerging from one netherworld to another, returned to his room, grabbed fresh skivvies, towel and shaving kit, and headed for the upstairs, center-building latrine and claimed an open shower stall. He closed his eyes against the sting of cold water, and when the unheated shower had dispelled most of the fog, he thought ahead to another non-flying, boring day.

Boring was no incoming. Boring was business as usual. Boring was good!

Winter-New-Guy was consigned to a cycle of training to prepare him for the unfamiliar aircraft. He had flown the one mission as observer before his transfer, but essentially as a passenger, without true aircraft or mission responsibilities. Had the mission suffered an emergency, he would have been shepherded through procedures by some terrified and sweaty guardian angel. Now came learning aircraft systems, fire and loss-of-power emergency conditions, loss of communications, enemy ordnance damage, bail-out procedures, escape and evasion. Beyond that, it got really hairy.

And a mode of operations unlike his ARDF experience must be addressed.

His first day in Jernigan's command, the CO told him, "The mission of First R.R. is different from what you're accustomed to. I know you know the four ARDF companies of the 224th and their mission. There will be changes you'll pick up over time. But for now, you require certification as a Controller so that Chief Voskov might wend his merry way toward The World. You have to learn the bird." Get certified as Controller . . . *and* get the go-ahead from Arlington Hall, as Major Jernigan had promised. Wheels within wheels!

Naval Air Facility, wherein dwelt and served the 1RRC, was a tiny world of its own making which Winter had yet to come to terms with. Plopped down on what was essentially an Air Force base, NAF sat sedately in the midst of the huge, sprawling coalition of bases and sites of feverish activity that framed the US presence on the peninsula. The NAF commander, a Navy captain, insisted on treating his land-bound facility as he would an aircraft carrier. The only advantage Army personnel saw to this quirky mindset was they were pretty well assured they wouldn't run aground.

Winter thought of his 1958 deployment on the U.S.S. Antietam, and equated that anxious experiment in nation building to this current state of being. There seemed little to compare. A constant undercurrent of life on NAF proceeded without regard to the ever-present war. The major threat, popularly stated, was that the peninsula would calve off from the mainland like an iceberg and sink under the weight of the materiel of war accrued at this central logistics mecca.

Training classes for Winter, Ito, and two new linguist operators were conducted by the Mission Operations Officer, 1LT Kerwyn, not to be confused with the Flight Operations Officer; sometimes by any one of several flight engineers; and by the Maintenance Officer, CW4 Bramwell Surtain The lessons were concentrated, hurried, and many, and presented over a compressed three-day period.

Winter early made the acquaintance of CW4 Surtain when absorbing the class on Aircraft Systems. Surtain did not frequent the Sandbag, the Navy mess, or anywhere else about NAF, so far as Winter had observed, and he'd not encountered the pilot previously.

The senior aviator entered the room and strode quickly over, introducing himself to Winter and Ito. "Bram Surtain. Welcome aboard, gentlemen. Enjoy your stay with us." He abruptly turned away and went into instructor mode before the small cluster of students. Except for his clearly descriptive, well-presented class on the maze of aircraft intestines, Surtain's brief welcoming words were the most Winter would hear that officer speak for weeks.

Surtain missed being handsome by a wide mark, but with gray hair that complemented a darkly tanned face and the dew-lapped visage of a middle-aged hound, there was about him something comforting. Older than everyone else in the First—a thing Winter could not know, but surmised—Surtain was yet a fit man. He was solidly built, like the hard-working Smith County carpenters who roomed weekdays at his mother's boarding house in Jackson when he was growing up. Shaking the pilot's hand was like gripping a lug wrench: hard, strong, though never offered as a challenge. He appeared a genial man, serious about his vocation.

Master Aviator wings were evidence he'd been driving

airplanes for at least fifteen years; but based on his weathered appearance and the deep-carved crow's feet about his eyes, it was likely much longer. Only later, after he'd flown missions with Surtain, and himself taken on new, additional duties, had he learned of the pilot's experiences in World War II and Korea as a Marine aviator. Then Winter got the whole picture. What he learned took nothing away from the pilot's uncalculated but comforting persona, but enhanced it. As an aviator; as an officer, as a man.

After three days Winter was finished with the classroom curriculum and deemed qualified to fly missions as Controller. A multi-faceted role, the Controller did in fact control the mission: he controlled assignment of targets, directed employment of the operator-linguists, was responsible for the hard-copy product and for its eventual consignment, and to fulfill the mission, performed many other, ill-defined tasks as they arose. He did not control the aircraft.

Kerwyn assured him, when he queried his status vis-à-vis the European hold for clearance, that Arlington Hall had given him the green light. He promptly put himself on the manifest for a mission.

The mission aircraft, P-2V "Neptune," was old; most had been built about the end of the Korean War, and acquired for this mission by the Army from the bone yard of military aircraft relics in the Arizona desert. ASA's piratical plundering there in the dry, desert air of Tucson, elicited two possible aircraft solutions to ASA's unique needs, only one viable—the P-2. The P-2 had only one foot in the grave, while the other option—World War II's long-defunct B-17—was solidly dead and moldering in Davis-Monthan's graveyard. Some P-2s, in various configurations, were still flown by the Navy; others had migrated to their final rest to fulfill the Navy's on-going conversion to the P-3 "Orion." But because the Navy still flew the bird, there were extant spares and replacement components in the Navy inventory. And many experienced Navy instructor pilots had P-2 experience, so that the Army could be assured of training in the plane from people who had really flown it. The hard-pressed Army systems people, offered a choice between *dreck* and shit, opted for the Neptune.

Lieutenant Kerwyn filled in the grievous history. "The six P-2 Neptunes the Army selected from the airplane junkyard were given a lick-and-a-promise in the hydraulics. Tires, dry-rotted in the boneyard, were replaced. Engines were de-Cosmolined, and airframes checked for damage. Holes were closed; metal and fabric replaced; and major efforts expended to make the six selected craft air-worthy, within reasonable limits. But mere flight integrity does not guarantee mission effectiveness. "

Though Kerwyn's little monologue bordered on pedantic, he knew his history.

He continued, adding food for thought for the others, a death sentence for Ito. "The electrical systems remain forever problematical, and though much of the communications equipment was replaced, the units of replacement were also old. Overly abused. Most came from warehouse and depot maintenance shop shelves. These shortcomings often lead to aborted missions. But the Army loves a challenge, and so . . . the Army brought the Neptunes here to Viet Nam." Winter had begun to notice a proclivity for word-building among the instructors in 1RRC.

At every revelation of the fragile nature of their mission aircraft, Ito's eyes rolled in panic, seeking an out. "Aww, man. This is bullshit. These things're not even designed for flight; they're for Crash Crew training."

Kerwyn assured them the CRAZY CAT operation had been in country for a year-and-a-half, and none of the aircraft had yet fallen from the sky.

It *was* true, Winter was told by an ex-operator, that one pilot had made a dog's breakfast of a landing at Tan Son Nhut by overshooting the field, an act normally disastrous. But it was only technically an incident: everyone walked away. The bird was resurrected and flew again.

Staff Sergeant Bokh, one of the flight engineers, told them about the Easter Exorcism of the previous April, but even that story, bordering on myth, spoke to the airplane's durability.

Bokh, himself a question mark of middle age, was a staff sergeant who had come to the Army from the Air Force, accumulating in the two services, twenty-two years of active duty. And still just an E-6; there was a subliminal warning there, but no one pursued it. The man was, as Ito put it, ignorant as dirt. That may be in some realm, Winter replied, but from what he'd personally observed, Bokh was a skilled aircraft mechanic, and oddly gifted with a loquaciousness of speech. When he talked about planes or flying, he was graphic, well spoken, at times approaching erudition. Confident in his facts, he cut through the hems and haws, the "like"s and "you know"s that plagued the garden-variety airplane mechanic in speech. The tale he told was history for Winter and the two linguists; for Ito, it was agony of an unparalleled order.

"On Easter Sunday, nineteen sixty-eight, not yet a year ago," Bokh lectured, "one of our dainty aircraft—tail number 131531—suffered the indignity of an enemy thirty-seven millimeter, triple-A shell through the left inboard beavertail, on the trailing edge of the port wing, just above the jet. The perforation caused the loss of several square feet of metal, and hazardly destablized flight. The round barely—but entirely, I have to say—missed the Rube Goldberg-like fuel distribution pipeline that spreads like ganglia through the innards of these fuckers." Implying terrors without spelling them out, his distinct patterns of speech setting him apart, he had the attention of the linguists and Winter. Ito appeared stricken.

"Passing through the wing, the round exploded just above and tore several holes in the port wingtip fuel tank We felt the explosion more than heard it. Yeah, we—" he answered the unasked question "—I was flight engineer on that mission. Captain MacWirt aborted the mission and we made Cam Ranh without having to bag it, or getting our feet wet. You'll recognize the bird. She's the one with a Purple Heart painted on each side of the fuselage, just below the cockpit." Bokh scratched his balding head, replaced the greasy fatigue cap, blinked into the silence, and melted away.

Winter wanted to ask him what a beavertail was, but wouldn't call him back or chase after. Better to keep his new-guy ignorance to himself. May be best he not know, anyhow.

* * *

After tossing and turning through another restless night, rehashing in his mind the letter he had received from Nickie just before leaving Sai Gon, Winter rose early. Through a shower and shave he pondered: What had she meant in the Thanksgiving card, that her next letter ". . . would offer a resolution." What resolution? The phrase upset him; made it sound as if he'd not done everything in his power to find a solution. But then he thought, Don't whine! At least begin to talk. Was that what she would offer? He just hoped she'd stop this *poor abused me* bullshit. And when, if ever, would he receive this prophetic solution?

He made early noon chow. Take-off was scheduled for 1315 hours; plenty of time. He was grateful, for he enjoyed indulging in the Navy mess's menu. NAF mess had an enviable reputation throughout the war zone, consistently receiving accolades as "Best Mess in Southeast Asia." Personnel of all ranks, all services, made extra effort to take meals there. A Navy warrant officer ran the mess, keeping a cold eye on budget, sanitation, even ambience, but primarily—quality of food. The mess officer, known only as Mister Watts, was rumored to spend at least eighteen hours a day in the facility. His varied menu, a notable departure from service messhall norms, placed NAF mess in a category without competitiion

Following lunch, Winter strolled back to the Army area with several enlisted linguists scheduled for that day's mission. They filed into the supply shed for flight gear issue. Winter felt a slight surge of excitement, as this was his first time through the full pre-flight process. His first, and only, previous flight had been hand-crafted for him by unknown benefactors.

Winter stared at the pile on the counter before him, then pawed through it until the clerk indicated by a disapproving stare that New Guy was out of line. Noting the clerk's sour look,

Winter, in a puckish mood, said, "A simple 'Fuck you!' will suffice, specialist." The supply clerk looked pained, and began reading from an inventory sheet, leaving Winter and the ops to locate and identify issue items.

"One pistol, semi-automatic, Army, caliber forty-five, model nineteen eleven-A-one . . ."

Winter, feeling like he was back in the supply line first day at Parris Island, responded, "Check. Serial number—"

"Don't need the number, sir. The forty-fives are all excess to needs, not inventoried."

Winter looked the question at Sergeant Bokh, waiting to draw his gear. Bokh responded, "Means we got them through some kumshaw handoff. Trade or what-not. Probably got a case of them from the Green Beanies, who don't have to account for them. They issue them to Popular Forces, Nungs, and other strange beings. Serial numbers are not recorded anywhere."

"Ah hah!" Winter nodded at the supply clerk. "Check . . . and . . . two clips of ammo, seven rounds each," Winter amended, ejecting, examining, and counting the rounds.

The clerk glared at him again. Winter was definitely encroaching on private turf.

"Next item—" the clerk grated, and it was a first for the warrant officer— "one blood chit, serial numbers as given on—"

"*Blood chit?*" Winter began pawing through the remaining items in his pile looking for a piece of paper.

The clerk smirked, pointed with a dirty finger to a piece of cloth partially obscured by other items: "There. That white silk cloth chit, a document, printed in fourteen languages-dialects," he said, and added, smoothly defining its function: "That's a promissory note . . . on your ass, sir," he gloated, "offering financial reward to anyone who aids a downed aviator to return to our lines . . . or brings back his body. Every crewman on the mission gets one, but only for each flight. Gets turned in with other items, post-mission. You're signing for serial number two six dash five oh five."

"Uhh, check," Winter said hesitantly, thinking of the

implications. The clerk read out a quick litany of other serial numbers, each responded to by one of the mission designees.

"Next. One radio set, emergency, A. N. dash U. R. C. eleven . . ."

"Check."

". . . and one battery B. A. dash thirteen fifteen slash U."

"Check. Uhh, wait-a-minute. Just a goddamned minute. Date of manufacture on this thing, this battery, is February nineteen fifty."

"Yes, sir. That's one of the new ones." The clerk made as if to read on.

"You mean you're passing out twenty-year-old batteries for us to depend on if we go down?" He was unsure if, as a new guy, he was being racked up by the snotty supply clerk.

"Yes, sir." The clerk segued smoothly to other features. "Radio's U. H. F. range, two hundred forty-to-two hundred sixty megahertz." There was no apology, no excuse in his voice.

"But the battery—"

"The battery's good for twenty-four hours continuous operation. If you're alive to use it." He made an ugly sound that sounded dismissive. "Inoperative batteries can be returned to the manufacturer in Tarrytown, New York"

Winter stared the question.

"Yes, sir. That's what I mean." He moved on. "Sir, we gotta launch mission."

Winter looked about. No one else seemed concerned; they had already undergone their baptism of fire. He turned back to the antsy clerk. "What about maps?"

"Well, there are your flight charts, of course, in the pilots' carry-ons, and then the maps in the emergency kit. Which is the next item." He neatly avoided explanation. "One pouch, canvas, emergency, air crew, with sealed contents." He looked pointedly at Winter. "Serial number one ess one one niner alpha niner eight."

"Yeah, check. So what's sealed in the kit?"

"Sir, could you ask another crewman later. I've got to finish issue. Besides, we've never had to use one." He began reading other kit serial numbers.

"Sure. Never mind."

"*Ba mui lam,*" the clerk muttered, stressed by having to deal with another FNG.

Winter looked at the small, dark green canvas-covered kit, some 4 by 7 by 3 inches, and laid it aside with the other checked items. "You're right," he replied. "Crazy."

The clerk looked startled when he realized Winter had understood him. They went on through the few remaining items.

"You have your own helmet already, right, sir?" the supply clerk directed at Winter.

Winter still carried the helmet he had been issued at battalion. He wasn't fond of the Gothic lettering spelling out some irrefutable truth in ancient German, but he used it. He had intended to design a more compatible headpiece, something *deliberate*, perhaps, not hinky, but he'd not gotten around to it. He knew he likely never would.

"Check."

* * *

Winter dragged the assortment of issue items into the briefing area. For the most critical of all emergency devices, a knife, Winter carried his old Marine Kabar. Some crew signed for Navy-issue emergency utility knives with the cutting edge of a biscuit.

"Goddammit! Is there no end to this crap?" Ito demanded, though issue seemed finally done. Despite his reservations, Ito was to share Winter's flight; he did not anticipate a fun time.

Winter said, "Just one thing, if you'll take a suggestion, Fred. I learned on my first tour to carry what might be your best survival tool—cash! I never had to use them, but American dollars are best. You just have to decide what denomination will best serve you."

"How's that, oh prescient one?"

"Most officers choose fifty-dollar bills. Safest. They're substantial reward you can pay out without creating inflation in an area." He did not spell out that the use of such funds would come only after crash and/or bailout. "Too much cash offered, you could be signing your death warrant."

"That's cute. Anything you can add that will further make my day? "

"No, really. The Zips can claim a reward by turning over a body, so if they suspect you have more money, they might arrange your immediate, albeit highly lamented demise. Some find twenties serve them best. And for those who can afford it—certainly you, my lavishly funded Oriental ally—hundred dollar bills. C-notes. But beware the appearance of lucre."

Winter hesitated, but Ito had no comment.

"Ultimately, everyone carries what he believes best . . . and what he can afford."

"Enough said," Ito grumbled.

"Well, not actually. Some pilots and crew carry gold or silver coins sewn into the lining of flight suits or vests. Usually South African *Krugerrand*s. Some use Swiss and French gold and silver coinage as blithely as Lebanese bankers," he finished in a sententious tone. "I don't go that far," he added lamely.

"I see, and is *that* finally it?" Ito looked as if he could use the relief tube.

"Well, there's the vest. Another permanent issue item, Air Force grey, worn over the flight suit . . . a multitude of pockets allows you to carry additional stuff with easy access. It comes with some issue items: a red-lensed blinking emergency light, several dye markers, and several packets of shark repellent—called seasoning by the crews—all issued as part of the vest."

"Thanks for that, Winter."

"What?"

"That fucking 'seasoning' comment. Does wonders for me, you asshole."

Content with Ito's asperity, Winter continued. "You got pockets for personal items, like a pocket knife, cigarettes, lighter, comb, candy bars, additional ammo, back up batteries, centerfolds—anything you're willing to lug around and live with."

"How much of all that am I to believe, you fucking sadist," Ito begged.

chapter three

Borin' Holes

Cam Ranh Bay, Viet Nam: January 1969

"Winter, you're flying this one as Communicator. Nothing to it. Sit across from me— I'm on the Controller pos—so you can observe me. Mine's the job you'll be doing after today. I got three days left in country. This is my swan song," CW3 Voskov crowed.

"Come on, let's hit it." He hoisted his load and along with his Communicator, Winter, the three pilots, crew of five operators, two aft-station watches, flight engineer, and one silent, evasive individual dressed in unadorned, new, tiger-stripe fatigues, walked across the short stretch of blistering aluminum panels to the aircraft. The U/I visitor later occupied one of the two aft station observation seats and never spoke to anyone during the flight.

Approaching the aircraft, Winter noted the Purple Heart painted below the cockpit and glanced at the tail number. Oh, great! Naturally, it just had to be -531. Like many who flew, he was subject to myths and illogical legends, and could become suspicious, even argumentative, over the most banal superstitions. But a close exam revealed no damage where the 37mm had penetrated the wing—no damage, *per se*; some of the wing panel was newer than the rest. He gave over his concern to a burgeoning interest in his new world.

The weather was mild: comfortable breeze off the ocean, temperature Winter estimated likely no more than 110° F. on the strip. He noted a stench of remarkable complexity drifting determinedly across the narrow strip of peninsula.. He tried to analyze its composition: take three parts Asian stock, add one shot of JP-4 jet fuel, blend with one jigger of *nuoc mam* in the making, add a pinch of sour brass, a reeking whiff of urine, a dusting of blistering, salt-encrusted aluminum, garnish with a whiff of napalm, and serve over alien Occidentals. Serves thousands.

As they approached -531, Winter said, "I heard the temperatures can reach 140° in one of these parked birds."

Voskov nodded at a prime-mover-towed blower cart, drawn up beneath the starboard wing, as if to dispel Winter's concern; a flexible hose the size of small town drainpipe connected to the aircraft. Despite the enticement of cold air blown into the bird, making it habitable, the crew remained on the ground, clustered in the narrow shade under the wings.

Standing idly, awaiting launch, Winter asked the senior linguist about the emergency kit.

"Well, sir, it's got most anything you'd ever need, so they tell us. Useful, should anyone find himself down in Indian country. Let's see, there's a signal mirror to attract flying aircraft, some small colored silk panels, same purpose, and a couple of tiny flares. There're fish hooks, fishing line, small pair of scissors, small cutting blade, two needles and some thread. Waterproof matches, a tiny compass, and several variable-length, stout cords. Standard Boy Scout outing shit. Then . . . oh, yeah, tetracycline antibiotic tablets, water purification tablets, APCs, salt tablets, a small tube of antibiotic cream . . . uhh, band-aids, bandages."

"Sounds formidable. What about maps? The supply weenie said it contained maps," Winter pursued.

"Oh, yeah. Little suckers. 'bout the size of a girl's hankie. Printed on silk. Don't know if you could find your way outta the parkin' lot with one, though. Map scale's infinitesimal: land mass depicted runs from the South China Sea to the far side of Burma in about six inches."

"It's obvious the kits are packed by machine. We were warned never to open one of them, unless we were down and in a world of hurt. There is apparently no possible way to re-pack everything into the kit." Winter sounded a note of disbelief.

"You can believe that, Chief. Ask Lieutenant Billingsgate; he demonstrated that to skeptics. Once, in the briefing room, when the Ops Officer was late for pre-flight, the lieutenant was whiling away the dead time and opened his kit. Just to 'satisfy his curiosity,' he said. You'll notice now, if you ever fly with him, that he carries a spare helmet bag, full . . . and not with helmet. It's the contents of his emergency kit. Supply won't accept it back, unpacked. For the rest of his assignment, the major says he has to carry the emergency inventory loose in the bag. We figure if he ever has to hit the silk, that shit will be spread across all four corps."

"My excitement knows no bounds," Winter muttered.

While the two talked, the three pilots, individually, had stalked cautious circles about the aircraft, overlapping one another's inspection zone, checking for flaws. Anything obvious that might hinder safe flight. They looked closely in engine nacelles, popped hatches, ran their hands over esoteric parts as if blessing them. Voskov, not a pilot, nevertheless emulating their concern, kicked the tire on the starboard main landing gear. Apparently satisfied with whatever furtive signal he received from the action, he led the crew onto -531 without further simulations.

Two pilots emplaned up the wheel well through the hatch by the forward landing gear; the rest of the crew used the bomb bay doors aft. There were no steps for the bay. Winter, following Ito and his linguists, thrust his equipment, pistol-holster-belt, and classified document container through the hatch, then hoisted himself up on the flanges. Thirteen crew and the one silent passenger comprised a moderate load on an aircraft that, with special mission configuration and full fuel load, could exceed 80,000 pounds.

Everyone on the crew, except the two pilots and flight engineer up front in their allotted seats, took ditching stations on the floor, backs braced against stanchions and firm paneling. When the pilot signaled by hand that he was ready for ignition on the recip engines, the dolly-mounted blower was disconnected and pulled away. The interior of the cramped aircraft took on the pleasant atmosphere of a Turkish bath, the smell even more intense. Winter and crew were immediately suffused with sweat. In the time it took to start engines, bring all systems on line, contact ground control, get taxi instructions, and begin taxi, the crew suffered humidity saturation.

Assuming a position in the queue of fighters, bombers, recon ships, transports, tankers, and administrative aircraft in the run-up area, and paying lip service to stray helicopters who didn't seem to follow any rules of the road, the P-2 lumbered into line where the crew prayed for a quick launch. But aircraft controllers had to contend with Air Force, Navy, Army, Marines; Air America, Indochine Air Lines, Air Vietnam and other CIA fronts; U.S., South Vietnamese, Australian, French civilian aircraft; airliners of commercial lines, and lease-haul for the U.S. government—anything with flight potential that could struggle its way to the end of the strip.

Finally, when Winter felt all hope gone, it was -531's turn and began its roll. With the two jets burning, they were quickly airborne. Immediately after takeoff during climb-out, the P-2 was flushed with rushing air. As systems settled down and the aircraft gained altitude, the incoming air became frigid. From languishing on the ramp in tropical swamp conditions, the air crews quickly found themselves shivering with the cold of space, enclosed in sweat-soaked flight suits.

Minutes after takeoff, jets shut down and flying only with the power of the recips, they settled on a northern track. Some 17 miles out from Cam Ranh they passed Nha Trang, huddled in a rainy haze a few miles to the west. Voskov reminded Winter to run his radio checks. The Communicator checked his prompt sheet for the callsign, then stared down at the azure sea below as they skirted the coast, watching light surf rush shoreward below.

Winter, having earlier brought the radio up on-line, now keyed the mike and called: "Outhouse two two, this is Cat's Paw five-three-one. Radio check, how do you copy? Over."

Nothing. White noise stretched into aggravating presence.

Voskov, listening to Winter through the intercom, glanced at his watch and grumbled, "Assholes probably not back from lunch downtown." Winter knew little enough about the politics of soldiering up here in the north, so far from the flagpole. In some ways he envied the operator who was billeted there in the beautiful seaside resort of Nha Trang. But now calling Cam Ranh home, Winter had no complaints.

"Outhouse two two, this's Cat's Paw five-three-one. How copy? Over."

Sharp click. Loud hiss of non-silence.

"Uhhh, Cat's Paw, this is Smokehouse one-niner. Outhouse two two is out of service at this time. I receive you five by. How me, over?"

"Uh roger, one-niner. I copy you five by five. I have no traffic. Over."

"Cat's Paw, roger. Negative traffic here. Over."

"Roger. Cat's Paw out."

"Smokehouse out."

"That's all it usually amounts to," Voskov's gravelly voice echoed through the intercom. "I only flew one mission when we had traffic for them, or them for us. The signal is always five-by. Well, almost always. Sometimes, in monsoon season . . ." he tailed off.

* * *

Winter saw nothing of note in the hour-and-a-half up the coast, offshore along the South China Sea. He began memorizing the pattern, passing Nha Trang, the ragged peninsula of Ninh Hoa, the fighter strip at Tuy Hoa, and in succession, Song Cau, the larger Qui Nhon, Vin Loi almost lost in a fold of coastal debris, Tam Ky, and finally Da Nang. With Da Nang in visual contact, -531 banked to port and took up a new heading inland to establish operational orbit. He knew it would become familiar enough in the months ahead that he might lead tour groups.

Today's mission was to fly a racetrack orbit along the South Viet Nam-Laos border, frequently passing over now-abandoned Khe Sanh. A year ago the Marines were hunkered down there under 'round-the-clock saturation shelling, rockets, and mortars, as well as perimeter probes and other indiscretions. Enough of that shit and you're tempted to sell cheap, Winter remembered. But, no! Not the goddamned Marines. There were Sandbag tales of flying missions while the Khe Sanh quadrille—a run-up to Tet—was on-going, and he was not displeased he had missed that entire dance.

* * *

Five-three-one reached the target area and maintained their presence in place for the next eight hours. Winter watched and learned. Mission operators were linguists, ASA specialists trained to listen to, understand, and transcribe Vietnamese language. In many ways a full year's training in the language might be overkill for the mission, Winter thought. The radio signals targeted by CRAZY CAT were Vietnamese language voice transmissions, all right, but the traffic consisted of four-number coded groups, spoken by the broadcaster. Each four-digit group was repeated to ensure reception, a gift for anyone listening who then had two chances to copy the traffic. Within a half hour, Winter felt confident he could copy that traffic himself. And his greatest accomplishment in Vietnamese language was to order a *Ba-mui-ba*.

Winter found his role as Communicator a snap. Utilizing dead comms time in random band search, he sought and found targets to aid the ops. He performed some dupe copy to check his quality later on the sheets to be returned to Cam Ranh. On the five assigned positions, ops recorded the groups by hand on unlined paper on a clipboard. They passed the finished pages to the Communicator, who transmitted them to the ground over secure radio. Winter followed suit. After a couple of hours engrossed in the process, between reporting priority traffic, both ways, and aiding the Controller when necessary, Winter realized that as an old Morse operator, accustomed to copying manual Morse targets up to 35 words a minute, these vocal groups seemed to drag. First mission and he had a lock. Voskov punctured his balloon when he said that all Controllers and most Communicators performed as well.

The lengthy mission had ceased producing intelligence when

the aircraft commander called back on the intercom and asked Voskov if there was any need to extend the mission. Given a negative the pilot announced, "OK, boys and girls. Pack 'em up. We'll be on the ground in lovely Da Nang in two zero minutes. God willing and the creek don't rise."

Winter followed with his eyes and listened as Voskov went through end-of-mission procedures, collecting every sheet of copy, blank paper, instructions, mission documents, or translation aids at the positions. The Controller carefully checked each sheet of paper: if it was not support documents brought from Cam Ranh, thus being returned to Cam Ranh, and if it displayed any markings at all, it went into the drop package, a classified pouch, twice inventoried, bundled, and sealed with proper classification markings. Everything else went into Voskov's mission bag, a serious, old leather briefcase of grand dimensions and extensive wear. Voskov reckoned it had served some Spanish knight as a wallet.

Inside the flap of the bag, Winter saw burned into the leather, readable only when the clasp was undone and the flap folded back, the unofficial but endemic motto of the Army Security Agency. It was the first time he had seen it written outside a secure area: "In God we trust; all others we monitor."

"It's your responsibility as Controller to be wedded to this mission bag," Voskov said solemnly. "You're responsible for the security of its contents in every move and placement between shutting down the in-flight mission—as now—and handing it over to the security people back at Cam Ranh Bay when your mission's concluded. The drop pouch is also the Controller's burden, but you shed that when we touch down at Da Nang and meet the courier. Once signed for, it then becomes his problem. But never, under any circumstances, turn over the pouch without getting the courier's signature on your log. *Never!*" His face suggested he might have done so at some point in a hazy past.

When they went into the pattern for Da Nang, Winter saw below him along the swooping black curve of the ocean, a busy pattern of tracers, both red and green. The aircraft was making a great deal of noise: flaps grinding down, hydraulics working, varicam slamming back and forth, engines straining, the two jets kicking in for the landing. To his silent, questioning lift of eyebrows, Voskov looked out his porthole window and answered Winter, shouting, "Marble Mountain. The Marines catch shit there just about every night. Get used to the view." He sat with the mission bag on his lap, both arms protectively around it.

When they touched down, it was quiet on the field, and the Marble Mountain Marine do-si-do on the far side of the promontory was a mere whisper. The pilot and courier from the 8th ASA Field Station at nearby Phu Bai were waiting when Winter and Voskov dropped through the bomb bay doors.

"Stash," the warrant courier pilot said to Voskov, "what happened? Ops sent us over here more'n two hours ago. Said you'd aborted the mission. Would be here early."

"Do we look aborted? That's—" Voskov looked at his watch "—twelve hours and five minutes already. It's almost oh-one-thirty. We have yet to fuel up, and another hour or more down the coast, deplane, debrief, and turn in issue before we can hit the rack. Abort, my ass!"

"Well, why'd they send us over early? We wasted two solid hours," the pilot whined. His courier, a quiet Spec 5 carrying an old M-14 rifle, said nothing but reached for the mission bag and clipboard proffered by Voskov. He signed with a jerky flourish, and turned with the package back toward the RU-8 parked nearby..

"Hey, don't know, sport. Not my call. We didn't abort. We're here on time. I've completed my mission responsibilities by giving your man the bag . . . and to tell you the truth, Rupert, I couldn't give a Raggedy-Ann fuck if you wasted a month's leave. What would you've been doing if you hadn't flown over early? Winning the war on your own?" He turned away from the startled pilot, mumbling, "Shit! Now ain't that something." He crawled back up through the bomb bay and disappeared.

It was warm and humid on the strip. After the crisp atmosphere at altitude and ozone-smelling air, the brief downtime was not refreshing. Winter watched a fuel truck hose up to -531, and heard the pump start immediately. He walked about the aircraft, peering out beyond the pattern of blue runway-taxiway lights, but could see nothing. No one seemed alert in the entire area. He knew that had to be wrong, but wondered about sentries. When the whine of the fuel truck pump soon shut down, Winter headed toward the hatch. They only required a partial fuel load; home was little more than an hour's struggle down the coast and the extra fuel was in case they got held in the landing pattern over-long..

* * *

When they landed at Cam Ranh Bay, the pilot taxied to the Navy ramp and shut down. When the crew deplaned and shuffled to the Ops building, were debriefed and turned in their issue, mission integrity came apart. Some, like Winter and a couple of the linguists, headed for the messhall. At 0310 they were offered a cornucopia of the previous day's leftovers.

Voskov and others headed for their rooms. The three pilots departed for the Sandbag with ribald invitations for accompaniment. Only during this flurry of dispersal did Winter realize the silent passenger in the tiger-stripe fatigues who had begun the flight with them, was absent. Though he hadn't noticed on the last leg of the flight, the stranger could not have been aboard when they left Da Nang.

He didn't dwell on it. Strange, elusive and irreconcilable specters drifted throughout the landscape of Viet Nam. They all might well have been cast in a bad production of "Terry and the Pirates."

* * *

Winter leaned in the door at the Sandbag where Bimbo Billingsgate immediately greeted him. "My man, my man. Well, how you likin' it, good buddy? The P-CAL, I mean." There were five more bodies injected into the space which easily held three.

Another FNG question. Was there no end? "And what's Pee-

CAL, Bimbo? 'lighten me, I'll let you know if I like it or not." Winter could do nothing but respond to this trivia.

"P.C.A.L. Pussy Cat Air Lines, my man. You've no doubt encountered our logo . . . that swave and de-boner kitty straddling Pegasus, hurling lightning bolts . . . that's us. So, how're you likin' it here, flying these antediluvian pieces of shit, livin' high on the hog with squid chow and nurses and our kimshee-breath allies?"

"Pussy Cat Air Lines? Uh huh, " Winter said. "And there must be at least a half-dozen T.W.A.s in country. Back in the Third, we were the first to call ourselves Teeny Weeny Airlines. Then it caught on. Other flying outfits stole the name. We were also called Terribly Wretched Assholes, and a few other unflattering titles unworthy of repeat."

"You got it. Matter of recognition. Sometimes I have to get out my wallet, check my military I.D. or my Albanian driver's license, just so I know for sure who the hell I am this month," the lieutenant agreed happily.

"Give the man a break, Bimbo. He hasn't had his first drink," Major Nichols growled.

"San Miguel. A cold one, if you please," Winter said over the lieutenant's babbling, playing off the standing joke of Lieutenant Billingsgate's willingness to drink anything, hot or cold, anytime. Billingsgate was the standard by which activities at the Sandbag were measured.

As the murmur of variegated discussion rumbled on, the drinkers spoke loudly to make themselves heard over the heroic but doomed efforts of the overworked air conditioner. The Sandbag's only door stood open whenever the bar was open, and the old Carrier window unit, mounted high up in the outside wall among playmates and hats and pithy epithets, tried valiantly to cool the entire outdoors of Southeast Asia. The air it produced inside was only marginally cool; its primary output was a steady, broad stream of condensate that kept the patio flooded.

Winter tipped the chill, beaded San Miguel Export up and worked in one-third of it. After the first swallow, he exhaled and began scanning the walls, poring over the incredible display of naked women, military aphorisms, and various unlikely subjects. He had made it a regular task, knowing it would take him the rest of his tour just to read everything there was to read on the hallowed walls. He quickly fixed on one of the aviator series he'd not read before:

OBSERVE, THEE, THY NEIGHBOR'S SPINNING
PROP, ELSE SHALL IT CAST THEE DOWN
TO HELL IN DISPARATE PIECES.

"Well, that's some kinda Mickey Mouse shit."

Concurring, turning toward the loud voice behind him, Winter looked out onto the "patio," a euphemism for a slab of uneven concrete poured by a work crew of drunken SeaBees as payment for an invitation to share the Crazy Cats' bar. A major in khakis sat on one of the broken lawn chairs scattered over the patio, and it was an indication of how drunk he was that he didn't seem to notice or to mind the precipitous tilt of the chair. He also was obviously not paralleling Winter's thoughts on the wall-mounted edict. The major was going on strongly to one of the CRAZY CAT officers, whom Winter had yet to meet, about how he had used up a three-day, in-country R&R to come up to the First so that he could fly a couple of missions, so that he might understand the mission and thus be available, should he be called upon, to help write the 509th Radio Research Group history.

After the war.

Assuming that the war ever got to an "after" posture.

Recognizing the ploy, Winter turned back and said to the XO, "You know, Major, of course, that the major—" he nodded at the loud voice outside "—wants to fly with us for one reason, one reason only. To get himself an Air Medal. I just heard him say that he planned to fly two straight missions, back-to-back. If he's lucky enough to get two full missions, he will have enough hours for a medal. Two straight thirteen-, fourteen-hour days for a piece of ribbon. Jeez-us!"

"Don't tell me, Chief. Group lets these pukes come up here, knowing that's their only aim. I can do nothing about that." He raised his shot glass and threw down a viscous concoction that looked dangerous. It was obvious he couldn't care less about the medals game.

Winter wouldn't let it go. "I've heard officers and NCOs at Group talking straight out about finagling straphanger time to earn a medal. Doesn't speak much to the value of the award to all these guys who have to fly the missions, day after day after day, good weather or bad, pushing their luck in these crates . . . and after all that, they get the same medal. Don't seem right, does it, Major?"

The Major was an old hand at ignoring junior officers, though. He demonstrated that facility just then.

Winter stood at the bar for a while longer, during which time two of the drunks in the corner drifted away. Coming up on oh-five-hundred. He mostly listened, some of the chit-chat going over his head as it referred to events which had occurred before he arrived, or about pilots and others who had finished their tours and moved on. He listened to a broken gripe session by Mister Phillips, complaining to the XO something about the "major's fear of flying." He didn't know which major was referred to, but thought it unlikely it would be the clown on the patio who had, by this time, emigrated to beddy-bye. The XO didn't seem comfortable with the discussion, and cut Phillips off. They talked then about important things: beer and cars.

Avoiding his room and restless sleep, Winter re-read epithets on the wall. The most prominent sign was writ small in an olde Englishe font and was framed and hung behind the bar:

The landlorde of this ordinary shall permit no licentious gathering of unknown strangers, being detrimental to goode order or likely to become a charge upon the community; nor knowingly harbor in house, barn, or stable any rogues, vagabonds, thieves, sturdy beggars, masterless men or women, pore folk, and other wrong doers, upon penalty of review in the County Courts, incarceration in the local prison, delegation to the stocks for a period such as shall be sette by the Court, or whipped. Drunkards who habitually indulge shall be committed to penury, shall be disenfranchised, and weare about his neck, and so hang upon his outwd garment a D. made of redd cloth & set upon white, to continue this for a yeare; he shall, upon first offense, render to the Court the sum of 1s, and for the second offense, 5£, and afterward to be punished by the Court as they shall deem meet.

"Who's the eighteenth-century enthusiast who unearthed this?" Winter asked. No one answered. Many drinkers had never read the proclamation, essentially the rules of a good public establishment. If Brenner weren't freezing his ass off in the Alps, Winter would suspect it to be his work. Elegant, though, by whoever. *Whom*-ever.

Goddamned Brenner.

When he'd tried every delaying tactic, even reluctantly reexamining that last letter from Nickie from every possible angle, and was finally left at the bar with only one drunk, an enlisted Airman from the other side of the field who was cutting Zs with his head in a puddle of beer, Winter was forced into action. He issued himself an old Marine order that concluded his day and said it all: "Stack arms, Winter-san," and ambled off to his room.

The room was pleasantly cold; he was convinced he could hang meat in here. He looked across the common interim space, between his so-called *room* and that of the other officer who lived in similar style. Bracken was snoring above the steady, low hum of the air conditioner. The two occupied, in essence, a suite: two individual spaces with a common space between. When the incoming Army troops had inveigled the SeaBees into constructing internal dividers to suit their tastes—in exhange for pallets of highly prized plywood—they had divided entire buildings, internally wall-less, first into rooms—really suites— then each such suite into three distinct spaces without internal doors.

The door from outside opened into the neutral area, flanked by the two "rooms." An air conditioner, refrigerator, reading lamp, cushioned chairs or sofa, shelves, coffee tables, all the trappings of civilization were located in the neutral space. As much as could be wedged into this minuscule *family room.*

The household appliances, paid for by occupants, were acquired in the Phillipines whenever one of the aircraft was flown there for a regular maintenance-cleaning program. Soon after he had settled in with comfort, Winter began feeling he was having an unduly soft time of it, for a war. He thought of grunts hunkering down in muddy, snake-infested holes they had to dig themselves, ceiling open to torrential rains, insects, and other pleasantries in the jungle.

But he couldn't do anything about that. He tried not to think about that. Best be thankful!

Suit up. Climb aboard antique airplanes and go off, boring holes in the stratosphere. But he was assured their mission was critical. Third MAF and 24th Corps seemed to appreciate their efforts, relying on the CRAZY CAT intel sometimes before their own integral product.

Winter pulled off his flight suit, only partly dried after standing half in, half out of the Sandbag for a couple of hours. He took guilty pleasure in the feel of frigid air flowing from the common space into his own, though he immediately broke out goosebumps all over. He shucked off the wet T-shirt and skivvies, pulled on fresh, dry underwear, and sat down on his bunk.

The light had been left on, a small reading lamp he must have forgotten to turn off yesterday when he left for the flightline. Or the hooch maid had left it on. He slid to the end of the bed where the gooseneck of the lamp curved over his pillow and sat, staring at the wall for a moment, then shifted his eyes to the family picture on his footlocker. Nickie. Jeremy. Adam. He reached for the collection of Dostoyevsky short fiction. Mutual suffering: the opiate of the masses.

chapter four

Der fliegende Holländer

Cam Ranh Bay, Viet Nam: February 1969

Flying out of Cam Ranh Bay was a mixed bitch. Little America where the R&R flights departed, where the South China Sea rolled in as green and foamy white as it ever was found to be in the Orient; where inbound beer was stacked in Overland containers and on pallets covering an area the size of Rhode Island, and the PX carried more brands of cameras and stereos than Stan the Dealing Man. But mission flights averaged thirteen hours, and in a vehicle dad would not have allowed you to ride in.

The night after Winter's initial mission flight, and not on that day's manifest, he joined other n'er-do-wells on the patio outside the Sandbag and let San Miguel set the pace for tales of wars known and unknown. Ito was there, in his cups to a reasonable degree. So, too, Bimbo, the XO, a Navy pilot without rank or nametag whom Winter did not know; others came and went. Finally driven by the direction of general comments, Winter related his own take on his first tour, following some unacceptable commentary by those not in Viet Nam at that time. He told them how in 'sixty-four the war, which was not really a war, had meandered along in its on-again, off-again fashion. The San Miguel influence blessing him with an elegance of recital he'd seldom known, he covered all bases. How in Broddard's and The Peacock Restaurant, in the San Paulo and the Golden Junk, a steak, fried rice, salad, and a beer was a buck-fifty; in the San Francisco and The Blue Moon, The Casino and others, *Ba-mui-ba* was still twenty-five cents a bottle, and Carling Black Label in the club on the base was a dime. The market was blatantly in the bear.

It had been a world removed from the increasingly grim rigors of a daily grind that was becoming a war, yet wasn't a war but something less. For most of the sixteen thousand troops in

Viet Nam, it was a five-day, forty-hours-a-week, semi-conflict. This general commentary did not include advisers who lived closer to the realities; Special Forces who served out their time in border compounds and remote, fortressed camps where the war was rapidly coming of age faster than elsewhere; and a few others such as Navy Seals, in whatever murky depths they found themselves, several breeds of spook, and helicopter pilots—these played the game for real.

But for the majority, when the day was over, or the week, the soldier showered off the dirt and sweat and mosquito repellant, dressed in civilian clothes, and took a taxi down town Sai Gon to forget about viper-green fields of rice and water buffalo that made noise at night in the bamboo like a clumsy sapper squad. Out of mind were the long, rumble-buck gunship flights that got better when a sampan refused to heave-to on the river in reply to the Americans' incomprehensible Vietnamese phrases, and the gunners jacked a belt into the machineguns and played at a one-way conflict. Afterwards, invariably, those days needed forgetting. The restaurants and bars helped.

Given the political intrigues crafted without consultation of those who did the bidding, there was no solution. A metaphor was offered—falling short of a corollary, but instructive—the military, instead of being handed a military objective (the reason for their very existence, the focus of their indoctrination and training) were herded onto a careening bus racing wildly down a blind mountain road, and found the bus had no brakes, indeed, no driver. But the bus, a self-perpetuating force, must not even consider stopping, even were it possible..

* * *

Nobody in 1964 forgot the so-called war; it was there . . . out there, beyond the perimeter. Just off the back street, just across the wrong bridge. The men who lived in the barricaded worlds of Tan Son Nhut and Bien Hoa, Can Tho, Nha Trang, Plei Ku and other centers were awakened nightly by the sound of heavy artillery. But the shells were mostly outgoing, falling in the distance. Remote villages became the spoils of midnight brawls. Battles were fought, soldiers died, sometimes in large numbers. For the most part they were Vietanamese soldiers. And lots of Vietnamese civilians. Occasionally, American advisers became casualties; Special Forces and helipcopter crews had their losses, and the Australians. But overall, US casualties were light.

Rarely did bad things happen to the odd American civilian who belonged to some nameless, faceless organization, men who slithered in and out the back doors of embassies and met for drinks on the veranda of the Continental Palace Hotel and the upper levels of the Caravelle. These men played a game of their own, not relegated to any set of rules or in observance of any constraints; the ends were often rucked-up gamesmanship. These were men who swung more power than they should for the time and circumstances. Still, for all their assurances about objectives and goals and a desire for immortality by affecting the lives of nations, they could not stop or reverse the tide of events either. And some of those died.

The Vietnamese died wherever they were committed by incompetent or ill-advised or communist *agent provocateur* leaders. American advisers, for the most part, died in jungle or rice paddy engagements, sometimes in booby-trapped vehicles and hooches. Special Forces, the elite of American ground forces, extremely competent in their chosen roles despite the bombast and sensationalism attendant upon their creation, were active in hit-and-run tactics with their native charges, notably so in the hills and mountains along the Laos and Cambodia borders. They were forced into playing a nasty game of one-upsmanship for the allegiance of scattered, stone-age tribes and possession of the lands and hamlets of these primitive peoples, and there those elite troopers died.

* * *

Winter tried to convey to his audience the overweening sense felt by the participants—at that time in 1964-65— that their exploits, however challenging or demanding, would never garner for them the kind of accolades and admiration enjoyed by, say, the 101st Airborne for their exploits in the Ardennes, the Marines going up Mount Suribachi, bomber pilots over Ploesti, or submariners in the Suragao Straits. Viet Nam was then, at best, a back-water war. And they'd known it at the time.

As if to rub in the fact of uniqueness as conflict, troops were called upon for ambiguous and unrelated-to-the-war tasks. Third RRU provided personnel as guards for the dependents' grade school on the road just before Gate 2 at Tan Son Nhut. These children were dependents of military and government employees who had brought their families to Viet Nam with assurance that it was a stable assignment. And when guerilla activity began to increase, and personnel were encouraged to ship their dependents back to CONUS, their refusal, mired in misconceptions and a total lack of understanding about what they were engaged in, created a need for protection. ASA troops, whose job was intelligence; had a fair grasp of the techniques needed to carry out their primary duties. They had no training in, no knowledge of, and little interest in acting as school crossing guards. But they could be spared to guard dependents and teachers whose continued presence was ill advised, but was also a political chip in a dangerous game of politics. Hell, Winter insisted, even back then, it had all been nothing but politics. But they lost no children.

And there were individual oddities. Once, in a perplexing little vignette that may or may not have had anything to do with the war directly—no one in the unit would ever know— Staff Sergeant Winter was ordered to the Tan Son Nhut base chapel as one of six NCO pallbearers in a memorial service for a Military Intelligence sergeant who had blown his own brains out with a .45. The dead man was from up-country, somewhere in Two Corps in the sideshow of conflict around Da Lat, working with Vietnamese Rangers. Winter, indeed none of the RRU personnel, knew the man. Nor was he ASA. How did 3rd RRU get roped into that gang-bang? he asked.

The most interesting observation Winter could make about the depressing episode was the uneasiness of the officiating chaplain, a Catholic major whose discomfort was no doubt brought on by the distasteful occasion of suicide and a conflict of two diverse doctrines regarding the burial: that of the Church and the Army. The Church was much harsher in its judgements.

* * *

To try to fill in the gaps of their understanding, exhibited by the clueless questions about *How could you be in a war and not be at war?* and similar questions never to be fully explained, Winter related how base-bound soldiers at random intervals learned of boobytrap casualties, though these were almost invariably in the boonies, up-country or down. An exception had occurred shortly before he had arrived in country when two 3rd RRU soldiers were killed, sitting in the bleachers at an off-duty softball game. An explosive device under the seat took them out. Early stages of a war without front lines.

Normally, beyond an occasional chopper crewman wounded, or less often the loss of an entire aircraft and crew—more often than not from non-hostile causes—Tan Son Nhut remained a relatively calm bastion of security in a countryside seething with political radicalism and guerilla extremism. The days were hot; the nights the same. Humidity stayed near the hundred percent mark for weeks at a stretch. Tempers frayed around the clock.

As he told it, Winter felt the immediacy of his recall, as if it were yesterday. There was simply no way to convey such vivid impressions on soldiers who had not been a part of it. And it was true, he had to admit, that in this environment, this privileged existence here at Cam Ranh Bay, he was finding it harder to bring back the polarization of that weekday war, weekend beer bust.

Taking stock of his own loquacious tirade, and slowing the intake of San Miguel, Winter shut down on a more personal tidbit. Knowing Ito's unease with anything to do with flight, he made an admission he'd never related to anyone.

"Fred, every time I flew a mission back then, every time I climbed up into a U-six, a U-eight, hell, a U-one, though I only did that once . . . every time, every flight . . . I got airsick. I didn't always toss my cookies, but I got nauseous. Queasy. Wasn't the flight. Or fear, I'm pretty sure. It was that turbulent air that bounced our small planes about like a wood chip on surf. If you find flight on these big, ugly honkers disquieting, at least it's fairly stable. And we fly high enough that we're less affected by updrafts and heat risers. Thank God, I don't have that to contend with this tour. Now that I've left that G.o.D. behind," he smirked.

But Fred Ito, in his advanced state of inebriation, and maintaining his basic skepticism, found no comfort in Winter's reported misery.

* * *

Everyone on the patio knew that CRAZY CAT arrived in country in 1967, and almost all that original complement of personnel were now gone. As he thought of it, Winter realized that was about the time he made warrant officer, and at that time in Rothwesten, he'd never heard of the strange outfit with their resurrected cast-off Navy aircraft, cross-trained pilots, depending entirely upon linguists for their intel collection efforts. But the job for new-in-country CRAZY CAT crewmen quickly settled in: brief, equip, launch, fly two boring hours up the coast and in on a radial from Da Nang to Laos, then work the racetracks and figure-eights along the border and over Khe Sanh where the Marines sat and waited and dodged incoming as their due. Eight hours on-station, ground fire like you'd expect at 9500 feet when charlie deployed Russia's gift of .51 caliber machineguns. But thank God! charlie had no aircover.

Then, set down in the hot unfragrant murk of the flare-lit impact area of Da Nang, drop the courier bag, re-fuel, launch and flutter home to another uncontested landing. Debrief. A few drinks. Hit the sack.

It was a living back then.

It was a living now.

* * *

In mid-February, boring holes in the sky of Eye Corps became the objective de jour of every straphanger in the 509th when a mission crew discovered the Flying Dutchman.

Or when he found them.

A couple of months previously, the 224th had experienced a Captain Hendrick Van der Decken as XO in the First RR. A career aviator with eleven thousand log hours, he'd transitioned into the P-2, enhancing the rumor that he had right seat time in the Wright biplane, but this was one bird he'd not flown. At North Island he scared the instructor pilots onto sick call, insisting on navigating purely by instinct, relying on no instruments, a decidedly hazardous route to pension, so thought the Navy IPs. By the time he'd reached 'Nam and the First, he had a reputation as a barnstormer whom none of the other pilots wanted to fly with, let alone the spook mission crew who mistrusted airplanes and airplane drivers anyhow. Only one flight engineer, Specialist Five Goodge, apostolic with bad hearing and terminal halitosis, would willingly mount to the sky with Captain VD. Thus an unlikely but unholy partnership was born.

The Group Chaplain, ever responsive to the need of troops for spiritual comfort in the face of enemy action, was equally aware that only twenty-five air hours—two sorties with the First Rah Rah—could garner him an Air Medal. He flew one mission with Van der Decken, and in a moment of lucidity, insisted the pilot resort to more conventional techniques to navigate them home when they were lost over Cambodia, uninvited, their unwelcome presence noted by angry pseudo- neutral AAA gunners. Captain VD's blasphemous response to the sky pilot and ". . . all he stood for" quieted the Chaplain. But God's local rep was a lieutenant colonel; he took assaults on his faith with a much more sanguine air than he did on his rank. Captain VD just wouldn't do.

Three minutes, fifteen seconds after landing and debrief, the calamitous flyer was hauled into the old man's office. Goodge, as the pilot's only ally, was sent for and the storm clouds built. The major's clerk shut down and went to the pool at the NCO club—though at dark hours, even that sumptuous facility was closed—indicating his perception that Captain VD was in for a world of shit. The clerk, a cleverly rehabilitated anti-war college student who'd enlisted under the twin influences of a loss of faith in academia and a hit of LSD, was infallible in predicting feces festivals.

The second following day's manifest had Van der Decken flying an offshore system test in his bird, orbiting in long racetracks ninety miles off the coast of Nha Trang, ordered not to return until he got it right. He had with him the castoff flight engineer, Goodge, and a new crew of five linguist-ops who'd lately reported in-country and were just finishing mission flight training. Finding no volunteer takers, and the CO refusing to order an officer to accompany him, Van der Decken flew without a copilot or number two.

Two civilian ocean-going vessels and a Thai Royal Airlines pilot, en route from Seattle to Bangkok, reported seeing the bird at low altitude, flying a box from Okinawa to Disappointment Island south of the Marquesas, to Hawaii, and over to the Solomon Islands. Captain VD's instincts were a bit far afield that day, and it was the last day he was a confirmed visual. Van der Decken, Goodge, five FNGs and the aircraft were written off: combat loss! An end as real as the man's intransigence.

The captain was missed; so, too, the popular Goodge—missed like the heartbreak of psoriasis, the pair of them. The mission crew were all new. No one could relate to them, so, not a factor. The First was thus effectively short an entire crew, but since they were also short two-seven-two—the mission bird Captain VD flew into oblivion—regular manifests couldn't be expected anyhow and everyone just flew more often.

Then it was March. On the fourth, the aft station watch on Junior Birdman's mission flight spotted a P-2 six thousand feet-or-so below them, along the coast off Eye Corps. There was nothing else from First RR up that early in the day, and when the cockpit was alerted, both pilots could make out the Neptune below on a parallel course. They tried to make radio contact but could raise no one. The plane appeared discolored, bleached . . .

somehow not quite right, but with the light playing tricks off the surface of the sea below, observers assumed visual default.

When they reported the sighting back at Ops, it was a mystery; nothing else from the First was out there. And the First Rah Rah had, by then, the only P-2s in southeast Asia. The Navy pled ignorance. Calls to the downtown spooks resulted in a signally cold shoulder; even so, they conveyed skepticism. For them, that meant "You gotta be shittin' me." It became a non-issue.

For a month. Then, Monteith, tooling about over Quang Tri Province one sad day, watching the grunts turn into bloody spray beneath some truly impressive enemy mortar fire, spotted another bird on a collision course with a C-130 going in for a lo-lex, down at treetop level. Monteith tried to warn off the bird but could not make contact. As it bore in on the wavering Hercules, the pilot saw it was a P-2. He dumped the coffee and partially emptied the gravity toilet when he cranked it over and dove toward the field below, ignoring the incoming on the field and the Marines' own mortars and high-angling arty. Even then, he knew he couldn't stop a mid-air . . . and he didn't. The P-2, a ragged, scarred veteran with scabs for emblems but bearing familiar numbers, two-seven-two, flew straight through the C-130 and simply dissolved into grey mist, according to Monteith's copilot.

After that, the phantom ship was seen every so often, at no particular time or place. It seemed to average about once every six or seven days. It got so, depending on their mood, the day of the month, and the phase of the moon, mission crews either wanted desperately to fly everyday, or they didn't want to fly for long periods at a time. Straphangers from battalion headquarters or Group, seeking air time for the orange and blue medal, lined up for observer openings on the manifest amidst rumors of strange doings.

This went on through the spring. In early June, an operator on Bravo crew was standing at the relief tube aft, taking a leak on Laos, and he looked to the side as guys will do, not wanting to amuse themselves by watching themselves. He spotted what he quickly recognized as the Flying Dutchman's ship. The mystery

P-2 had acquired this hinky sobriquet in deference to the literarily elite on the crews remaining. The Neptune was close enough to count rivets, flying parallel to Bravo flight, and even though Bravo was barely pushing 210 knots, the scarred bird adjacent appeared to be at max thrust, straining every cylinder, yet just keeping pace. The op could look right through the port of the phantom ship at the Communicator's station.

Skeletons manned that station and the Controller's station across from it. The operator, spastically spraying the metal decking, ran forward, whisked himself across the wing beam, got on the intercom and called the flight deck. The pilot keyed his mike switch twice but did not answer.

Back in the real world of the Kansas suburbs, the Security Officer, the shrink, Air Force Security, CID—everybody said it was mass delusion. The flight crews would have agreed; they needed to agree; but it was common knowledge that no two individuals in the First Rah Rah could be induced, even by threat of involuntary reenlistment, to act in concert on anything. After that, in debriefs following missions, no one would discuss anything that occurred beyond the skin of the aircraft.

The replacement for Captain Van der Decken was a Major Diaz, an overweight aesthete with swarthy but sensitive skin who always wore flight gloves, even on the ground, and bored the company with tales of his lineage which he said he could trace back to the famous Portuguese explorer of the same name who'd discovered the Cape of Good Hope.

chapter five

Straphangers and Near-naked Sheilahs

Cam Ranh Bay, Viet Nam: January-February 1969

With four 12-hour-plus missions over nine days, Winter finally had reached an accommodation with sleep. This morning's touchdown at 0210 was an hour earlier than usual, thanks to a cranky stabilizer control. Debrief offered the usual menu of equipment malfunction, mission satisfaction-dissatisfaction, relief to be back on the mud ball, and a sphincter spent from half-day unbroken spasms of contracting and release under stress. Inventory of the mission bag revealed a missing page with commo skeds info, but an anxious call to Phu Bai located the scribbled sheet, mistakenly included in the courier drop. Now, winding down, he would sleep.

Would have slept.

Would have liked to sleep—to have slept. The dogmatic iterations were endless.

In the gulf between sleep and awareness, though, Bracken's chainsaw snores from across their space overrode his efforts.

It was not merely Bracken's snoring. Through the wall at the head of his bed came the abrasive thump-scream-shock of rock and roll music pulsing with a seven-eight beat; it was felt more than heard. Winter and the Sandbag shared a wall, one to either side, and for the bar to be open and going strong in the wee hours was not unusual. Officers and regulars of the 1st RR, enlisted Crazy Cats, visiting firemen, Navy SeaBees—anyone could open the bar, even if only for himself. It was a rare individual in Southeast Asia who had enjoyed a drink there who did not know where the key hung from a nail on the wall inside Bimbo Billingsgate's unlocked room. Bimbo was *chargé d'affaires* for the Sandbag.

Winter pressed the wind stem on his Timex; in the ghostly blue glow he read, whispering aloud, "Oh-three-oh-seven. Jee-zus!"

He left the room to Bracken and the chain saw and stumbled through the center passageway, arriving at the Sandbag in GI-issue skivvies: white boxer shorts and tee-shirt. Ho Chi Minh sandals, transformed from their earlier incarnation as a Peugeot truck tire served for footwear. The color and resilience had been leached out of them by the climate and bad roads..

Weak amber light and rock music spilled out the Sandbag's doorway. Three people were at the bar. A mound of residue, suspiciously officer-like, was crumpled in the corner on the concrete floor, head hidden under a conical Vietnamese peasant hat. Major Nichols, the Executive Officer, leaned on the bar, khaki shorts and tie-dyed tee shirt uniform of the day. He was arm-wrestling Chief Warrant Officer Corbin, another non-flying officer whom Winter had not met. He *had* been told about the Assistant Avionics Officer.

He had no wish to meet him; but everybody gotta be somewhere.

Beyond the XO, Winter imagined he saw a long-legged, long-bosomed, long-blonde-haired nymph in powder blue panties and bra. She watched the arm-wrestling, frozen on point as if she'd just wound down a *pas de deux*. Her eyes in the uneven, weak light of the Sandbag were Little Orphan Annie-open-to-the-max, blue to match the underwear. She was barefoot.

She was not an illusion. Winter felt the cold draft of his own near-nakedness, but before he could retreat, Major Nichols spotted him.

"Dave. Dave, c'mon in. Got shombod—*some*body wancha meet." Nichols was flying, and he wasn't even on the manifest.

The nymph demonstrated unusual poise. Stepping close to Winter, she leaned even closer and, *somehow*, murmured softly over the rock music, "Hi, there. I'm Wendy. I'm a showgirl."

Winter, struck with unaccountable panache, said, "Indeed you are."

"A real, really, reely real . . . showgirl," Nichols managed. His hand and forearm, under Corbin's casual pressure, were crushed almost to the fibreboard that served as bar. From the look on the major's face, it was obvious he had not envisioned this turn of events. Especially in front of the reely real nymph.

"You sound . . . British. Sorta," Winter stumbled. He almost said "foreign," but caught himself before such a *faux pas*.

"Well, I'm *sort* of Australian," she laughed. There went first impressions. Despite a chest any showgirl might comfortably be proud of, the hint of irony and roll of eyes that went with her response was Winter's first clue. While Nichols and Corbin arm wrestled, engaging in one repeat performance after another, both caught up in a desperate, unbreakable conflict to transform macho into an art form, Wendy related her story. For a dental assistant-from-Darwin-turned-vocalist, she kept it amazingly low-key.

"I'm with The Trip, a troupe of singers and dancers contracted to USO. We've been making the rounds for weeks in One and Two Corps, playing airbases, fire bases, fire support bases, little, tiny, hacked-out jungle camps. Terrible bloody places. But today, Margery, a friend from Christ Church, one of our troupe, came off sick and I flew back with her on a Garry Owen helicopter to see a doctor at the Sixth Evac here. I met the major, who is just the most thoughtful person ever, at the PX at South Beach. End of story. Ta-da!" Lovely hands, too.

Winter thought her phrase "South Beach" a misnomer; there was little to merit the title at that end of the peninsula. It was relatively south, but there was no beach. And the entire peninsula was in imminent danger of sinking into the sea under the weight of the goods of war marshaled at the First Logistics Command there. A sort of military-industrial Atlantis-waiting-to-happen. Seeking distraction, he thought he should avoid gaping too longingly at the inviting chasm between her mostly exposed breasts if he could, though why he should, he could not explain. He was currently in a suspension of marital vows. And they were a fine, matched pair.

"Is The Trip the Spanish dance company?" Winter managed.

"Not a flamenco in our repertoire," she said cautiously. "Why?"

"We'd heard about a group of Spanish dancers supposed to be coming."

When Winter heard her response—"Sorry. You'll have to make do with us, mate."—it was obvious Wendy was not the come-to-life manifestation of every dumb-blonde joke he'd ever heard. Outsized, outspoken, sexy, she was a gorgeous woman who tripped to a different piper. And tough as hell, he realized, watching her fend off Corbin. First impressions were kick-ass!

She laughingly explained that her state of undress was a result of her truthful answer to Nichols when he'd earlier looked at her skirt and blouse and asked, "Aren't you hot in that outfit?" She had looked over the men's common dress of shorts and tee-shirts and said yes. Nichols, good-hearted man that he was, had offered a solution: "Well, you're among friends here. Take off what you can't stand." And she had, shedding everything except the powder-blue bra and panties, both of material offering little concealment, though somewhat fulfilling the other half of that military dictum—cover. She was a sight to behold.

And she knew it, Winter could tell; she just was not promoting it.

Shortly after oh-four-thirty, seeing no possible benefit in remaining with this strange *ménage à trois*, Winter, wiggling his fingers in a minute goodbye, took his tired body away. Corbin had slid to the floor, silent, leaving shorthanded the *Ship, Captain, Crew* dice game that Wendy proposed to follow arm wrestling. Major Nichols labored on at the bar, unable to win a wrestling match even without an opponent. The silent, unidentified figure on the floor had yet to declare himself. And Winter was flying a back-to-back today, second straight day. All reasons for him to go. Albeit with unaccustomed and unwelcome sensations in his groin.

But he dare not return to his bunk; if he *could* sleep, he'd never rise in time for launch. Nearly five, the sun was already lightening the seaward side of the peninsula. Only wimps needed sleep, as Ratty Mac would have it. Winter showered and made for the chow hall. Today's mission was launching early; he chose to beat the crowd merely as something to do. And he could smell sausage on the outside entryway grill from two hundred feet away.

When he returned from the mess, shortly after seven, the Sandbag was padlocked, quiet inside. He thought of the lovely Wendy, and smiled all the way to Flight Ops.

* * *

When the aircraft had broken ground and was halfway through climb-out, Winter fought gravity, rising from his ditching station on the deck by the Controller position, the position that was his on this, his first flight as *the* controller. He checked: all ops were still hunkered down in their take-off ditching stations. OK! He glanced again at the figure seated on the deck aft, the Major from Group who had endeared himself to no one three nights before on the patio of the Sandbag. The major seeking an Air Medal.

The major, whose name was Nieder, should have made his second flight yesterday, Winter was thinking. As he had learned at briefing, Nieder, who had made a sizable dent in the Sandman's Johnnie Walker stock two nights before after late return from his first flight, had not awakened in time to make yesterday's launch. Careless. No one had awakened him. But it had not driven him away; he'd stayed over. And here he was now, logging his second flight.

Winter was less than enthused.

Four-niner-six flew up the coast, past the diversion point at Da Nang, on past Phu Bai, and settled into a series of protracted figure eights, racetrack ovals, and boxes over, about, and along the DMZ. In theory, CRAZY CAT aircraft never crossed the 17th parallel into No-No Land. When asked if that was true, the pilot smiled at the naïvete of the new Controller.

"Ground fire north of the parallel's a serious given, Chief. That's absolute Indian Country, and the bad guys have no inclination, indeed, no *need* to hide anything," Captain Trunick, the pilot, had told Winter. "And they don't. So in our old low and slow, the usual mission altitude of eighty-five hundred-to-ninety-five hundred feet's out the window. Course, twelve-five's not beyond the range of missiles or larger caliber guns, but at least every asshole in Southeast Asia doesn't feel obligated to fire their personal weapon at us. Lower altitude's an open invitation. And you never know when one of the little fuckers'll get lucky."

After a long, intense period of intercept activity on-station when Winter was busy with Controller duties, they encountered a slack period. He spun the dial, seeking targets for himself. He had his head buried in the anonymous void of intra-spatial communications for more than two hours, when a cramp in his neck forced a break. He took off the headset and stood to stretch, twisting his head on a column of tortured muscles. Glancing aft, he saw the Group straphanger, Major Nieder, sacked out in the top relief bunk. He regretted the view; it added tension in his neck. Winter had not seen Nieder since take-off and assumed—rightly, he later confirmed—that the major had climbed into the bunk after launch and had not left it since.

Winning an Air Medal was a challenging enterprise.

Standing in the aisle, Winter swore. He turned at a raucous cackle behind him. His roommate, Bracken, relief pilot on the mission, sat at one of the aft watch stations. "Something got your knickers in a knot, Davie lad?" Bracken could get by with the "lad" label; he was older than God, though still younger than Surtain. "Not our Group Rep's devotion to duty, is it?" He grinned, but Winter, staring at him, was relieved to see the grin metastasize into sour grimace.

"Burns my ass, Art. Pilots, crew chiefs, ops—all of us, for chrissake, hang our butts out to dry on these missions, and one small item of reward is an Air Medal . . . after requisite time and missions. Now, comes this asshole who sleeps away a full twenty-five hours' air time, and he'll get the same Air Medal. Something ain't quite kosher here, my friend." He felt the inadequacy of his bitching; Bracken could do nothing about the slipshod practice.

"Happening since Christ was a corporal . . . or ever since that dark light colonel assumed command, anyhow." Hearing the pronounced southern drawl in Bracken's voice, Winter cringed.

He, himself, came from that heritage and thought he knew a racial slur when voiced.

The warrant officer had not disparaged their battalion CO as black, Winter understood, but rather spoke to his political opportunism which took advantage of every rule and regulation in the military which would give him, a minority, a step up. Over the backs of inoffensive fellow soldiers—officers and flyers. Even other blacks.

Bracken amplified his ire: "The colonel earns himself brownie points with Group weenies, inviting them up here, authorizing them to log mission hours for the medal. They can't fly missions with the other companies—no room in the small birds. But, hell, the First Rah Rah's got beaucoup space on board these big ancient muthas . . . no reason Teddy Tiptoes shouldn't climb aboard and game himself a medal."

The look on Bracken's face was intense.

He added, "You wanna do something about it? You wanna rock the boat? We got the A-and-D officer up front right now, on the yoke."

Winter hadn't known who the Awards and Decorations Officer was; a secondary duty, in most outfits it was usually assigned to junior officers. It demanded a degree of competence in writing simply to generate all the verbiage justifying one's actions— whatever they were—for an award—whatever it was. If it was not competence that served, then dogged perseverance. In writing recommendations for awards, a melodramatic, overblown body of language was employed which Brenner called "multiplying words." Winter knew it often as fiction.

"Who? Captain Trunick?"

"Cap'n Trunick, the very one. Why'n't you take your complaint to him. He'll ignore you, but what the hell; you'll feel better for gettin' it off your chest." Bracken looked back out the aft station port and raised the binoculars to his eyes, his point made.

Winter could not leave his position to go forward while his ops were active; he might have to commit a Controller act. Too, the Controller's and Communicator's positions were awkwardly separated from the linguist-operators' space forward, just behind the pilots' and crew chief's compartment. It would mean inching his way forward, on his back, over the mid-wing beam, a cumbersome steel structure, part of the mainframe that transfixed the fuselage of the aircraft. The back-crawl exercise would be followed by the stumbling-gauntlet exercise through the tangle of Ops' space, tripping over feet, field jackets, canteens, weapons, parachutes, equipment belts, box lunch containers, cast-off magazines and books—all the impedimenta that defined linguists in their lair. No, he'd wait, catch Trunick later, maybe when they went into Da Nang. They would refuel twice today: once because of the extra-long mission, and again when they dropped the pouch, and took on fuel for their return down the coast to Cam Ranh.

A short while later, spinning the radio dial seeking a viable enemy target, Winter watched Bracken claw his way forward over the wing beam, and a few moments later Captain Trunick appeared in the opening. He grasped the bracket above the tunnel, hauled himself out, stamped on the deck to get his flight suit and various body parts relocated to their proper positions, and headed for the relief tube aft. When he'd had sufficient time to take care of business, Winter got up and went aft. He found the officer seated in the same seat Bracken had vacated, staring blindly out through the port on a world obscured in cloud.

"Captain," Winter shouted above engine noise.

"Yes?" the officer answered without turning around.

"Got a minute? Sir?" Winter made it obvious.

Trunick looked back at the warrant officer. "Yes?"

Winter moved closer to avoid shouting. He hunkered down by the single seat and spoke in as low a voice as would do the job. The subject of his discussion was asleep ten feet away. Now he had the opportunity, Winter didn't know quite how to frame his complaint.

The hell! he thought: in for a penny, in for a groat.

"Cap'n, what's your attitude on the policy allowing people to visit the First, sleep through a couple of missions, and get themselves awarded an Air Medal?" He didn't say *earn* an Air

Medal, for the process certainly wasn't that. Ball in the captain's court, he let it lie.

"Have you some complaint about the colonel's policy? His very-clearly-spelled-out, worked-over, and reinvigorated-weekly policy? That the crux of your query, Chief?"

Winter, mentally inhaling deeply, jumped in. "More or less, sir."

"Hmmph! Yes, you may join the club. There're more'n a few of us with the red ass about that particular policy of our good colonel. Cheapens the whole concept, doesn't it? Makes what we all do something of a joke."

"Precisely my point. But why? *Why's* the colonel insist? Crediting them for a medal, I mean. I remember, my first tour in Third RRU Air, it took a fair amount of paperwork to get someone a medal. Not to mention the bookkeeping for Air Medals." Winter had often thought the process demeaning.

"Still does. Essentially, when one of these clowns—" Trunick nodded at the recumbent figure in the bunk "—flies two or more missions and accrues twenty-five hours, *combat time*," his eyebrows rose, "we're expected to pull data from the flight logs, where he's listed as a temporary crew member, and put him in for the medal. Paperwork, citation, approvals, submission. The whole ball of ugly."

"That's total bullshit. He's no way crew. He's not authorized—"

"Hey, Chief," Trunick held up his hand with traffic cop authority. "Been through all that. I've cited Army Regs to the C.O. here, the battalion X.O. Battalion S-one. Nobody wants to hear." He looked disgusted . . . and acquiescent.

"That is such bullshit. You should make someone—the I.G., for instance—order someone to read the regs. This is ludicrous. Criminal." But then, so was his meanly-mouthed "someone."

The captain stared at him so long Winter suspected he had overstepped. But Trunick surprised him, saying, "Tell you what, Chief. You want to fix the problem, I'll let Jernigan know you want the A-and-D job. God knows, with Safety Officer, Pay Officer,

Casualties and Medical Losses Accountability, in addition to flying missions, I can do without the added allure of Awards and Decorations. If you're seriously pissed, you might be interested in making the change. You got any qualifications? Any experience? Can you, for instance, spell 'award'?"

It took Winter a moment; the significance of the offer, the unaccustomed fulfilment of *Ask and ye shall receive*, startled him. He was already Ops Training Officer, Controller and Communicator Training Officer, and Operations Flight Safety Officer. But, what the hell, those were mostly hollow titles. Besides flying missions, he was not overloaded. He wanted it done; it was time to fish or cut bait.

"I was A-and-D . . . rather, I *acted* as A-and-D for the officer who had the job at Field Station Bad Aibling. Additional duty, twice removed, so to speak. In USAREUR, it had to be a commissioned officer in the slot. But I did the work. The writing, the research, running the paperwork around for signatures. Walking it through Frankfurt. I was just getting into the job when I was curtailed for this outing."

"So you know the job. And Army regs?"

"A.R. six seventy-two dash five dash one, and associated. Yes, sir." Winter knew the job. The added burden of a constant demand for Air Medal proposals for the ops, pilots, and crew chiefs who flew so many long hours was something he would have to adjust to. That was, as he'd called it, just bookkeeping. "Does a clerk come with the job?" he wanted to know.

"Hell yes," the captain quipped. "No way my mama's baby boy is going to type all those goddamned multi-copy forms, citations, and eyewash. My clerk's short, but he'll be replaced."

"Then, if you're serious, let's see the major about making the change," Winter said.

"You being straight with me?" the captain squinted at him.

"Bet your ass, Captain. Straight as a string. I'd like to see the system operate somewhere near what the Army intended."

"As if anyone could effect that, my young Galahad. As if anyone ever could."

Winter ruffled at the paternalism. *Young*, my ass. Galahad or no, he was older than the captain, and the captain was not entitled, unlike his roommate's casual reference to Winter's relative youth. Besides, as Brenner might have put it, Galahad was a subjective denigration.

* * *

Through the balance of a featureless mission, Winter controlled, Sergeant Betts communicated when not performing a crew-chief action, and the five ops operated. The pilots, however reluctantly, obviously piloted, but Winter never saw the co-pilot. He never took a break from the controls, didn't try to grab a few winks in the bunk. The medal-hungry major still lay there. The co-pilot also never went aft to take a leak on the grunts below. Twelve-and-a-half hours! Winter thought; man must have the bladder of a sloth.

Late in the mission, and late in the evening, when their flight orbit took them into safer skies, away from the DMZ and the Laos border, and they had descended to their most productive altitude of 9,500 feet, turbulence began hammering the aircraft in fiercely increasing waves.

The bouncing, jouncing, lumbering big bird stood up well to turbulence, insofar as sustaining itself through the trial, but did nothing to glamorize the experience. Such was the concern of the uninitiated. The old craft creaked at every juncture, and the varicam slammed in and out, seeking its most productive, automated control level. Each shock sent a tremor through the aircraft, together with a loud, crashing thump.

Heat risers from the baked land cooling below kept the plane in constant, uneasy vertical oscillation. Wind shear occasionally brought on heart-in-throat frights as the aircraft precipitately dropped a thousand feet with no warning, then bottomed out with a loud, smacking slap as if it had struck something solid. Like the earth.

Even for experienced flyers, it was queasy time. For a short period, Winter felt uneasy; perspiration broke out along his hairline. He was an experienced flyer, but when he thought of the age and condition of the P-2, he could imagine rivets popping, hoses crumbling under torque, sheet aluminum peeling back like white birch bark. For those less familiar with stressed flight, explanations for the convincingly threatening sounds and vibrations served no purpose. During periods of concern, no crewman would listen to arguments that the P-2 was probably the most stable airframe in the skies, demonstrating this resilience regularly in hurricane hunter squadrons.

Ultimately, for Winter, accustomed to much more severe battering in smaller aircraft, this discomfort never reached the level of serious turbulence. Not even worth noting in the flight log. But he was gratified to see the major in the aft bunk had turned a ghastly shade of greenish-gray.

Later, on the ground at Da Nang at the end of the second mission segment, just before he dropped through the bomb bay doors to the apron, he heard loud words in anger coming from the aft compartment. Sergeant Betts, crew chief, was refusing a directive to do something, Winter quickly identified the conflict, and stepped to the rear to inform Major Nieder, "Sir, we all carry our own weight on the birds. There's an F.O.D. barrel at the edge of the apron."

In a few minutes, standing on the strip, Winter watched Nieder carry his bulging barf bag off the plane, looking for one of the repositories placed about aircraft operations to encourage pick-up and disposal of anything that could cause Foreign Object Damage if sucked into a jet engine intake. The major looked neither left nor right.

Following those minor satisfactions, the home leg of the flight was unusually smooth, the gods of flight offering amends. Winter's crew flitted through debrief, for nothing notable had occurred on the extended, three-landing mission. He didn't feel like eating, and went on to the Orderly Room.

He checked his mail box and removed a large, square, red envelope, post-marked Long Beach, MS. The writing was Nickie's. Seasonal stickers were plastered over the entire back. In a quiet corner of the Orderly Room he leaned against a wall, slit the flap, and pulled out a garishly colored Christmas card with Jeremy's name, scratchy in red ink, surrounded by Adam's exuberant slashes with a green felt-tip marker partly obscuring the comic Santa and reindeer. The snowy North Pole looked like the AB-105 tower at Gartow. He chuckled over it. It had arrived a full two months after the fat man flew his ragged reindeer complement home.

A letter was folded inside the card. The long-awaited follow-up, perhaps. The *resolution,* had she called it?

chapter six

Fairy Dust: WTF? O . . .

Cam Ranh Bay, Viet Nam: February 1969

It was past 1400 when Winter awoke; the air-conditioner was off, and it was a hot one. He was soaked, his sheets twisted, saturated. He showered and when he returned, the housegirl had changed his linens. Nothing likely this late in the messhall; he went into his backup rations stash.

Later, rejecting the notion of spending another late afternoon and evening at the bar in the Sandbag, and having nothing on the fire, he gave in to his first impulse when he had read *THE LETTER*—he thought of that particular missive in caps and italics—and decided he would try his luck with MARS. The Military Affiliate Radio System, praises sung by soldier, sailor, airman and Marine, offered a chance at telephone contact with The World. Only a chance. Winter had never used the free system, but he needed to know about the letter. . . .

What he *really* needed was sleep. Two days sans beddy-bye, two missions back-to-back, had wrung him out. But thinking on the letter, he hadn't slept well during the day yesterday. Couldn't relax now.

He borrowed the CO's Jeep and drove down the coast road to Logistics Command in the setting sun. MARS, situated in a Quonset hut dug into the side of a sandy hill not far from the Exchange, was surrounded by a baker's dozen varied antennas. He'd have to hurry; there was a curfew in effect on the coast road, and he wanted to be back at NAF before stark dark. Though the whole of the peninsula was considered secure, there had been anxious mutterings.

He signed in at a counter that divided the hut. Along the back wall were racks of radio equipment: transmitters, receivers, modulators, generators for backup power awaiting deployment outside for emergency use, and a host of other arcane devices.

Along a side wall were several small enclosures that resembled phone booths. When he went to take his turn on a phone, he learned they *were* phone booths. He'd almost forgotten; he hadn't been in one in years.

MARS provided vastly reduced-rate telephone calls from overseas locations to anywhere in the US or Puerto Rico. Though new to its use, Winter understood its workings; he'd been filled in by people who made frequent calls. Communication with home was made possible by a link of military radios and civilian HAM operators.

He knew there was a downside to the MARS calls, but it seemed to him more on the order of hiccups, not heartburn. The receiving telephone number was assessed the long-distance charges from the HAM station to the terminal phone. When it was determined which responding HAM in the US was closest to the number called, and could convey the call,, the caller was given the option to complete the call, usually making this decision based on distance and charges. A bigger issue was dialogue; only one person could speak at a time. It was not an open line. The first person to speak did so. At the conclusion of that fragment of speech, however long, the first speaker had to use the military communications term, "Over," to indicate to the MARS op and relaying HAM op to switch from Transmit to Receive, and vice-versa. This was a major cause of frustration with wives, girlfriends and parents who, unfamiliar with commo practice, would finish speaking and forget to say "Over," leaving both parties sitting in silence, running up charges.

Then, too, the MARS and HAM ops were always privy to the conversations. It had been known to reduce the ardor of intimate conversations.

Winter was pleased to find few callers ahead of him in the queue. He sat in a chair along one wall, pulled out *THE LETTER*, and reluctantly unfolded it. Short. Not sweet still, upon this —what?—fifth reading? Sixth?

"Dear David:"

How the hell could she even have written that? It began like a real letter.

"This is the hardest letter I ever tried to write. I've written it thirty times over the past months since you left but I couldn't send it and always tore it up.

I won't drag this out needlessly. I'm beginning the paperwork for divorce. It's obvious to me we cannot live together; I will not live apart and maintain a false marriage. We both should be free to find a life.

I won't comment on how we came to this state, but I suspect it cannot have been <u>entirely</u> your fault. Count me guilty, if for nothing else than not finding my way sooner. I know the Army prevents me doing anything while you're "there", but when you come home I intend to have everything ready to finalize ~~matters~~ the legal ends. My lawyer may get in touch with you over some preliminary matters. If you get an attorney, they can communicate directly. Let me know when you do have someone to represent you.

The boys send their love and wish you were here with them.

Nicole

He stared at the letter as if for the first time. Nicole? David? *Divorce?*

Winter was as stunned still, hours later, as upon first reading. Despite a host of indicators, he'd never really thought she would take it this far. Was this just part of her campaign to bring him to heel? Or was it sincere? Did she really want to "be free to find a life"? He knew he did not. For the investment of years, the sharing of good times and bad, the children, this newly presented overture, jacked up to crisis proportions, seemed terribly disproportionate. And in a complete departure from the common cause of such strife in the military—an adulterous relationship with another partner—he could recognize no substantive rationale for divorce.

* * *

David Winter, though far from a prude, had never been sexually aggressive. In his youth, through high school and the most active period of maturation, he had few girlfriends, and then, in that prosaic time of less sensual infatuations, those usually tended to be relationships which never raised the issue of SEX. In those times, copulation was considered to be spelled in capital letters, and treated that way, though hidden from sight. Kisses, minor gropings, the sweet pleasure of the softness of a budding breast: Well and good. But you didn't have SEX with a nice girl. And if the girl *wasn't nice*, but had a tawdry reputation, the butt of locker room jokes and smirks, then a guy didn't want his name connected to hers. Loss of peer esteem carried a severe penalty.

In the years after Korea, in those still-youthful days in the Marine Corps, he'd been in no position to take up alliances with attractive females. Most Marine assignments left one out of touch with humanity, not to mention *nice* girls. In San Diego, there'd been the trips to Tijuana, the unbridled licentiousness of Mexico. Great Lakes, weekend liberty in Chicago or Milwaukee, short train rides away from base. Both towns offered limited opportunities, and of those, even fewer that went beyond a dance at the USO or at The Eagles Club on Wisconsin Avenue.

Suddenly, in a quick blossoming of buried past events, he recalled one fond memory, now quiescent for years. A major exception to this litany of excuses. After Korea as a Marine reservist, he had followed that combat experience with the intention of going "hard-Corps." Back just weeks from Korea, he took a discharge from the 2nd 105 Howitzer Battery reserve unit in Jackson for the express purpose of enlisting in the regular Marine Corps. When processing his paperwork, the battery gunney told him that because he had served on active duty, and in combat, he could be exempted from attending recruit training. It was a rite-of-passage he'd missed when his reserve unit had been called to active duty and, with minimal training at Camp Pendleton, set sail for Sasebo, Japan, with connections to Korea.

"But," the NCO reminded him, "if you have any intention of making The Corps a serious life's work, boot camp is a necessary experience. A must in your record jacket. You are always going to be asked where you went through boot camp," he said. "At P.I.? Or were you a 'Hollywood Marine,' a graduate of the west coast recruit training depot at San Diego."

He was mindful of the fact that recruits for Marine service from states east of the Mississippi River took their basic training at Parris Island, a grim and storied venue in the swamps of South Carolina. There, one was cut off from all vestiges of humanity and society. At PI, one was at the evil will of drill instructors whose unobserved harsh, even mal-treatment, of recruits was never challenged. That prescriptive threat had held for years afterward.

Enlistees from states west of the Mississippi reported to Marine Corps Recruit Depot, practically downtown San Diego, California. MCRD San Diego was set down on the Pacific Coast highway, next door to a Navy Recruit Training Base, adjacent to Convair Aircraft Corporation, and subject to all manner of visitors and public scrutiny. Boots *had it made* in Dago. Beatings were minimal, maltreatment incidental. Thus the scoffing denigration by PI graduates labeling their distaff brothers "Hollywood Marines."

Accepting Gunney's admonition that he should "exempt himself" from the offer of eluding boot camp, he signed on the line. In Jackson, 42 miles east of the big river, that meant a midnight rail ticket to South Carolina. De-train at Yamassee, race onto the bus and cross the causeway to the island. And so, 15 weeks of harrassment, fear, sleep deprivation, and exhaustion; but also bouts of irreversible learning: the many ways a well-trained Marine can kill and reap havoc and in general carry out his mission, were satisfying. PI, too, had been a mixed blessing.

He had arrived at PI in early September. Consequently, his

platoon graduated and outposted in late December. There was just enough time to get back to Jackson for Christmas on a ten-day leave. It had proven to be a surprisingly dismal holiday.

When he reported back at PI on January 2, he reported directly to Casual Company, 3rd Battalion, awaiting orders for assignment. As all Marines are basically riflemen—infantrymen—his next assignment would be 2nd Marine Division's Advanced Infantry Training Regiment at (Camp Geiger) Camp Lejeune, North Carolina, a relatively short bus ride away.

He knew where he was going; he could only settle back and await orders. His days were spent in supervising recruit "roundups," when new, unshaven boots were herded from their barracks into a semblance of a formation and sent scurrying along crushed-oyster paths and across the crushed stone parade ground, asphalt company streets, and interim grassy areas on "police call," the policing-up—as a civilian he would have called it picking up—the most microscopically insignificant pieces of litter on whatever surface he was bidden to trod. But even in this demeaning task, Winter was better off than almost all his associate graduates.

Upon graduation, he had risen magically from lowly serfdom, promoted back to the grade he held in the reserves and when he enlisted into the regulars: Corporal. A junior NCO.

The rank, only an E-3 in the enlisted structure which encompassed seven grades to master sergeant, E-7, was still two grades above almost everyone about him. It gave him carte blanche for access to restricted areas and freed him from many petty burdens. Submitting to one bold urge, on an evening when he wasn't doing anything, he strolled over to third battalion's recruit companies' area and looked up his previous senior drill instructor, a staff sergeant who had assumed responsibility for a new platoon of recruits the day after Winter's platoon had graduated. He sat in the sergeant's Quonset hut "Staff Room" and drank a Coke topped with a shot of DI vodka. The head henchman of recruit training and he had a lot of laughs over incidents during his training. They had all been down the same road at differing times. And they had the cachet of Korean service in common, a history that had garnered Winter many benefits during training.

As a corporal, he was entitled to admission to the Junior NCO Club, a social facility for corporals and buck sergeants, dedicated to weak beer and tall and salty tales. Setting out on a visit to the club for the first time, he grabbed his overcoat. In mid-January, even South Carolina succumbs occasionally to a spate of frigid weather. Today, stiff, icy breezes off the Atlantic left ice on asphalt roads and outdoor washracks. As a "casual" he was allowed no civilian clothes on base and, as he was not allowed in the clubs in utilities unless on duty as Duty NCO or Firewatch, he was in dress greens. He stepped aboard one of the infrequenet buses passing 3rd Battalion and rode out to the Junior NCO club at the rifle range, a separate entity at PI.

He saw only one other NCO he knew across the smokey spaces. The junior drill instructor sergeant gave no indication of recognizing Winter. Good. Besides, he was moderately intrigued by a table seating seven Women Marines—commonly but unkindly called BAMs: broad-assed Marines—and he stared openly at them, savoring the softer sound of their voices, the softer look of their curves as opposed to the male-dominated world he regularly inhabited. He had turned away, making small talk with the bartender, when he heard rising voices. Drawn back to the women's table, he saw a woman—a girl, really; she looked to be about 19—leaning into the face of one of the seated females, and though Winter couldn't hear their voices, it seemed the standing girl was putting the bad mouth on the seated WM. The seated WM being addressed stood up and followed the girl; they disappeared back into a small hallway that led to the latrines.

When he'd finished his one beer and, bored with the lack of activity, Winter pulled on his overcoat and headed for the door. Just as he tugged open the inner door, the girl in civilian clothes appeared at his left and pushed through the opened door. Her heels clacked loudly on the short stretch of sidewalk leading out to the sand-surfaced parking lot. She didn't look back.

"Well, 'scuse me!" Winter said.

The woman stopped and turned about. "Yes, Marine. What did you say?"

Startled that his voice had carried, Winter said, "Nothing much. Just wondered why you couldn't have said 'Thank you!' for opening the door for you."

"You opened it for *you*; you were going out anyhow; I just made use of it." Her voice was crisp, penetrating.

"Yes! Well, sure. Forget it, huh?" He pulled his collar higher against the freshening breeze and stepped around her. She didn't move, but stared at him as he walked past.

A few seconds later, he heard the clackety-clack begin again, and then, "Marine. Wait up." He looked back. She was hurrying toward him. For some reason, it confused him.

She walked up to him, stood close as she adjusted a lightweight jacket about her shoulders. She said, "I'm sorry. I'm usually not rude that way. Fit of temper, I guess. Sorry." She looked down. Winter noticed her shivering, though otherwise she gave no sign of discomfort.

Now he felt awkward. He hadn't meant to turn her indiscretion into an incident; the "'scuse me" was an involuntary comment. "That's all right. My fault. Shouldn't have said anything. I—"

"No! You were right to . . . to call me on my rudeness. I do apologize." She gazed into his eyes for a moment, and in the soft fading light of an early winter evening, he could see her eyes were green. She was attractive; not beautiful, but her even features and lovely skin made up for a lack of classic beauty, whatever the hell that was presumed to be. Her hair, somewhere between light brown and blonde, something his family had called "dishwater blonde," was perfect for her coloring. And leant feature to the green eyes.

"Accepted . . . Miss . . . or is it Marine? Whatever . . ."

She said nothing. He waited. Just as the stand-off was beginning to feel strained, she offered, "It is Marine. Naturally." As if no other explanation was allowed on this desolate stretch of inhospitable ground on this, a Marine sanctuary. "My name is Gin-Barry Lucas."

"Jennifer Barry?"

"Gin. Gee-eye-in. Like the drink." She spoke as if it was a common mistake.

"Be damned. You're the second lady I've met named Gin-Barry. I knew a girl from New Orleans once, name of Gin Barry . . . hmmmm . . . can't remember her last name. It's beautiful. I always liked her name. And here I find it again. How nice." He held out his hand. "Dave. Dave Winter. Corporal, U.S.M.C."

She stared at him without replying. Her gaze, he found, was powerful. Focused and intense. She shivered, breaking the spell, and he said, "You're not dressed for the cold night. C'mon. Where're you headed? To the bus stop? Where's your barracks? Mainside?" He knew it had to be. Except for women recruits, who were on the central part of the base too—mainside —the few WMs he had seen about the PX and at the movie theater were all billeted somewhere in the headquarters area. Though, languishing in third battalion obscurity, he'd seen few WMs.

She hesitated, then acknowledged, "Yes, mainside." She said nothing about the bus.

They walked on up the sandy track leading to the asphalt beach road. The road ran along the curve of the bay-like inlet, fronted the rifle firing ranges, and a couple of miles away made its way past 3rd Battalion and on to the main base area, circling the parade ground. Now, in the cold and dark, conversation came slowly, but was friendly enough. He offered her his overcoat, but she shook her short-cut locks and declined. "No, I'm all right. Thanks, though."

A car parked at the back of the club parking lot started up, pulled onto the sandy drive and passed them, then turned onto the beach road and accelerated rapidly away toward mainside. The thought went through David's mind: The bastard didn't even ask if we needed a lift.

Something similar must have flashed through her mind, for Gin-Barry said, "That's thoughtless."

"Yeah," David replied. That's what it was: thoughtless. Maybe the driver wasn't a bastard. Just thoughtless. He gave her credit for the distinction. But then, she didn't have the hard edge in her voice prevalent among most Women Marines he'd observed, few as they were.

When she shivered again, David, in a move he could never after reconcile, reached and took her gloved hand, pulling her closer to him for warmth. In the breeze, there was little to be gained, but it made for a smooth move, he thought. She accepted his intent; she didn't move her hand. They walked on, closer now. When she shivered yet again, he didn't ask. He unbuttoned and swept off the overcoat, draping it in the same smooth movement around her shoulders. This time she did not protest. David felt a warmth rise about him, as if a southern warming trend worked its way north along the coast. He trusted his greens, and her presence, to keep him warm.

A couple hundred yards up from the club road, on the far side of the beach road, lay the nearest of the rifle ranges. Instead of stopping at the bus stop at the junction, she had stayed with Winter when he walked aimlessly toward the range. Their talk was about family. Gin-Barry was from Jackson, Tennessee, and it brought ironic smiles, him being from Jackson, Mississippi. His father was long deceased; her mother had died the previous summer, struck by lighting while pushing a grocery cart across the Piggly-Wiggly parking lot two blocks from her home. In the short while it took to reach the fringe of the range, their close mutual presence had taken on the feel of normality..

Winter crossed the road and she went along without comment or query. He struck the dirt lane that formed the main line of march along the rifle range. They walked along the length of it toward the sea. He'd not fired this particular range, but he had spent four full weeks out here at the rifle range. The range was a temporary displacement for recruits who, after week five in their basic training, packed up, bag and baggage, and moved on cattle cars and trucks from their assigned billets wherever they lived within the three battalions, to the multi-story barracks buildings located immediately before the firing ranges, a few miles from mainside.

His time at the rifle range had been prime time. Because of Marines' denotation as infantry and riflemen, it behooved them to be the best riflemen they could be. For the four weeks of specialized marksmanship training, drill instructors took a back seat. They were around, but they only held reveille, supervised their charges mostly after-hours, marched them to chow and back, and conveyed them to and from the ranges on which they trained. During rifle training, the DIs stepped back, their harassment subdued, their usually screaming voices muted. Recruit shooters were the province of rifle instructors. And the rifle experts did not want scared, nervous, hostile kids with loaded rifles in their hands, seeking outlets for repressed angst.

It was generally four weeks of down time, though as the four weeks passed and it came time to qualify for record, a separate caste of urgency and pressure manifested itself. Rifle instructors, and even more so, drill instructors, were rated and promoted on the percentage of young Marines "qualifying" with their basic infantry weapon, the caliber .30, M-1 Garand rifle.

Now, strolling along the march line the length of the range, Winter noted there was no 1000-yard firing line on this range. The remaining rifle ranges, scattered up the coast road, all extended to 1,000-yard lengths, a hangover from pre-World War II training when the weapon of choice was the '03-Springfield, a bolt-action rifle of consummate accuracy. It was then common to fire the 1,000-yard course for record. Now, with the semi-automatic M-1, less was expected of that dimension of marksmanship. Only individuals selected for sniper training, the cream of the crop of shooters, fired the extended ranges.

This first range was shorter, the coast road running closer to the sea. The first firing line they passed was marked "500 yds." The berm here, like all firing lines where shooters lay, sat, knelt, and stood for the four primary firing stances, was marked by numbered stakes, indicating shooters' positions. The stakes, numbered from 1 to 50, spread the shooting range to more than a hundred yards in width. This was where each Marine would pursue the marksmanship badge that denoted him as a trained rifleman. Each Marine must earn one of three categories of shooter, thus qualifying him as Marksman, Sharpshooter, or Expert.

Gin-Barry made no comment when David motioned with his chin at the 500 yds. marker. "My favorite distance. Maybe it's just that I'm lazy. I like to shoot lying down." The 500-yeard range was for the prone firing stance—lying on one's belly, legs spread, body propped on elbows, strapped into the rifle by a sling so tight musical chords might be strummed on it..

At 300 yards, he gestured and said, "Kneeling and sitting at this range."

"I know. We W.M.s fire the range too, you know." He did know. Why didn't that bother him as it seemed to bother many fellow recruits who scoffed? He felt no contest.

At the 200-yard line he didn't mention that here was where they fired only "Off-hand," shooting from a standing position with nowhere to rest the rifle barrel. Only that tight sling for support. But it was enough, even with rapid fire.

When they reached the butts, they climbed up on the mound and looked out to sea. The butts occupied an embanked, target-surmounted berm where metal frames were prominent across the full width of the range. Each numbered stake back up on the firing lines corresponded to a numbered stake—alternating white-on-black and black-on-white lettering—in the butts. During actual firing, half the platoon assigned to that range for that day found their places on the firing line; the other half of the platoon "worked the butts." Later in the firing day, their roles were reversed and the butts workers got their chance with the rifle.

Butts workers went down into the trench behind the metal frames, which held wooden target frames with stretched canvas on which the targets were mounted. As each shooter fired at his target, the man working the corresponding target in the butts listened for the snap of the bullet through the target-canvas, occasionally the wooden frame, sometimes nothing, the round passing out to sea, a complete miss.

With that indicator, the butts workers pulled the target down on the mechanical track, marked the hole in the target with a spot: a round, 3-inch disk, black for use on most of the buff-colored target; white if the shot had penetrated the bullseye, the black 5-ring in the center of the target. The target was cranked back up, a larger disk of white or black on a six-foot pole was held in the air, over the site of the shot, thus giving an indication back to the shooter as to where his shot went. The shooter used that visual confirmation to adjust windage, elevation, stance, or maybe just his attitude before firing again. And thus onward—day after day, ministered to by patient instructors, honing skills that would save their own lives and those of their comrades when they made it to the real firing ranges of disputed territories—Marine recruits fired the range..

David Winter had grown up with a rifle, a Mississippi country boy whose father taught him when he was six to shoot the heads off cotton-mouth moccasins on lily pads in the pond. But during those war years, in 1943, Dad was taken when David was only eight and he'd learned the rest of the hunting, shooting, gun craftsmanship, rules, policies, and disciplines from cousins and his grandfather. Being back here now, on this shooting ground, he felt a surge of pride in having fired expert. Low expert, but still 224 out of 250. It was useful accreditation in The Corps.

All that culture of guns and discipline swept over David, surrounded by the very training grounds where he'd honed those skills. He felt no corresponding emotion from the girl beside him . . . nor should he, he thought. Equals or not, wearing the same uniform, it was still the male that carried the rifle, humped the pack, and made his life in the boonies of a myriad contested lands. He turned to her, smiling, and saw her gaze on him, serious. Before he could frame a comment, she tugged his hand, pulling him back off the crest of the butts, away from the almost-featureless expanse of softly rolling, susurrating ocean. At level ground, she led him quickly around the end of the berm and into the trench behind the target frames.

She tugged him toward her, turning into his arms and freeing her one hand, reached up, pulled his head down and kissed him. Despite the hand-holding on the walk, a thing more likely attributed to the weather than any amorous intent, Winter was motionless with surprise. As if caught suddenly in a violent firefight, flares and explosions and the nasty rip of automatic fire surrounding him, his world burst into color. He quickly disposed of surprise, holding Gin-Barry tightly to him, kissing her passionately. The taste of 3.2 beer was strong in their melding mouths.

In moments, she was fumbling beneath his Ike jacket blouse, fumbling with the web belt buckle. There was no time, no place for surprise. She shucked the overcoat; he spread it quickly on the floor of the trench and accompanied her in her slide to the ground. Inside her light jacket, his hand felt her heat through a flannel shirt, and he was rewarded with the wonder of her breasts as she shrugged quickly out of the brassiere, leaving it hanging loose within the unbuttoned flannel shirt left on her shoulders in deference to the frigid air. His mouth was back on her; his hands flicked a button loose, ran a zipper down, and pulled her skirt away, tossing it onto a bench along the butts wall. She wore no slip. The panties were some pale color, indistinguishable in the fading light. Color didn't matter; they came off as she raised her hips in a quick motion, and she was open to him.

He felt her hand guiding him, and though his trousers were not pulled down, there was no impediment. They were joined before he realized he was positioned, she doing evcrything possible to assist. They moved smoothly into a sustained, rhythmic motion, their mouths locked in a frenzied drinking of passion. About them, throughout their micro-universe, there was no sense of cold. Without understanding how he'd gotten here, Winter was content in the being.

The frenzied, mutual burst of passion was over much too soon. In short minutes, sated, spent, they both began to feel the effects of the weather and began dressing without conversation. The atmosphere was one of stunned surprise, rendering them both speechless. Winter replaced the overcoat around her shoulders as she slipped into the panties, pulled up and adjusted her skirt, and fumbled with the bra between his ministering hands. He was straightening his gig line—belt buckle, fly edge, jacket seam in uniform alignment—when a small cascade of sand sprinkled on his head and shoulders. In the next instant, a bright light pinned him where he stood.

"Halt! Right there. Where you are." The voice, loud but indecisive, came from above them on the berm of the butts. "Stay there; I'm coming down."

Winter stared at Gin Barry, caught in a snare of guilt and sudden concern. There was within him still a sense that one did not place nice girls in compromising positions. He felt the need to apologize for having done so . . . but first, was this development what it almost had to be?

When the Marine private, wearing a recruit guard armband over his field jacketed arm rounded the end of the berm and advanced on the two randy criminals, he knew it was.

"O.K., people. What's . . . why're you . . . who are you? Show me some I.D." The light from the flashlight was shaking, giving a surrealistic appearance to their frozen stances. "Are you Marines?" he asked, staring directly at Winter's uniform. He shifted his gaze to Gin-Barry.

"Of course we're Marines," Winter said. He'd quickly overcome his nervousness, now he saw the figure before him lacking any authority, other than that he had stumbled upon them while making rounds. Recruit guard duty normally never produced evidence of anything illicit or illegal. Winter opened his wallet, produced his ID card, and waited. The young guard read the information on the card with his lips moving.

He said, "You're Winter, David D.?" and he looked from the card picture, squinting in the light's penumbra at Winter's face.

"Yes, can't you see, Private. It's a relatively new picture, though without my hair." He knew he wouldn't recognize his own dead brother, Larry, in an ID card photo.

"Yeah, all right, Corporal. What're you doing down here in the butts. The ranges are off limits at night."

"There's nothing posted to that effect. Nothing that says we can't be here."

"Yeah, well, it's . . . it's a rule anyhow." He didn't sound convinced.

"Are you in one of the 'cruit platoons out here to fire the range?" Winter asked the shaky guard. He remembered that a few individuals had pulled range guard for short stretches during his own training; but mostly, recruits in the midst of the firing protocols were ensured they got their sleep so as to be fresh and desirous of good marksmanship, rather than strung out for lack of Zs.

"No. I'm in a First Battalion casual platoon, awaiting new orders after I was in the hospital for pharyngitis. After graduation." It was more than Winter wanted to know.

"I see," but Winter didn't. He'd rather the private were a new recruit. More easily cowed.

"You," the private suddenly blurted out, as if embarrassed at his unwarranted divulgence of information. "Are you a woman Marine?" he directed at Gin-Barry.

"Yes. I am," she murmured softly. She stared at the row of ribbons on Winter's jacket.

"Let me see some I.D." There would be no letting her off with a warning summons.

"Uh, well, I'm not sure I have my I.D. with me. I left my purse in the . . . in the barracks."

"Well, you gotta show me some I.D., or I gotta call the Sergeant of the Guard." He was on firmer ground on that point.

After a moment, she turned toward Winter and gave him a strange, melancholy look, and when the guard gave all indications that he had to take a leak—he was fidgeting so—she reached inside the light jacket and brought her hand out with an I.D. card in it. She hesitated, then thrust it at the guard, staring sideways at Winter all the while.

The guard fixed the weakening flashlight beam on the card, huffed with confusion, leaned closer to the card instead of raising it to his eyes, and suddenly snapped the card down, jerked the flashlight quickly to that same left hand, and snapped to attention. In one move his right hand shot to his eyebrow in a salute, and he barked, "Ma'am, yes, ma'am. 'scuse me, ma'am."

Even before the words made sense to him, Winter felt an on-rush of panic. He knew within microseconds. Moments before, he'd just seduced an officer! And in the dirt of the rifle range butts. Portsmouth Naval Prison was already dusting out a cell, pending his arrival.

* * *

Gin-Barry Lucas, the ephemeral WM lieutenant, hadn't lied about her name, but other omissions, sixteen years later, still ranked as a great mystery in Winter's mind. When they'd left the startled recruit guard alone in the butts, he'd walked her silently back to the main road. Without a word, she continued on to the club, where she climbed into a car, started the cold engine, and whisked away past him without looking. He'd never learned why her appearance in that Junior NCO Club, other than his impression of her dressing down a female private—likely one of her own charges gone astray. And it was only later, when the glow had gone, that he questioned a bit of intemperate judgement: who had seduced whom in the PI rifle range butts? The distant memory began fading, but his smile remained.

* * *

Reluctantly switching off the memory stream, Winter was brought into quick focus. Despite a low, featureless hum of electronics background activities, it was quiet in the MARS hut where he waited. When he'd finished reading Nickie's letter, yet again, Winter looked up and saw that only one caller, a Latino SP4 wearing the patch of the 1st Log Command, remained ahead of him, and was entering a booth. The specialist made almost immediate contact, spoke briefly in loud, high-pitched, querulous Spanish that penetrated the walls of the booth. Shortly, he switched to broken English in which every other word was a curseword, a threat, a prediction of doom for some unnamed conversationalist at the far end of the trans-oceanic call, or a plea for understanding, apparently not to be forthcoming.

The specialist slammed the phone down after less than two minutes and hastened out. Winter spoke his name to the clerk behind the counter, and stepped into the vacated booth.

On the sign-in form, he had given the number he was calling, the house in Long Beach. He heard no administrative talk on the line. A series of uniform mechanical sounds, and then white noise. He had not even heard the HAM ops's voice. Winter waited anxiously to speak.

* * *

Driving back up the darkened beach road, Winter forgot about curfew. He wouldn't care if the APs or MPs or the goddamned Korean Military Police stopped him for being in the zone during curfew. What the hell were they going to do? Send him to Viet Nam?

The voice in his ear had said he had a connection and was free to speak. But when he spoke, there was no response. He thought she had been cut off, and was careful to use the proper commo procedure to facilitate the change from SEND to RECEIVE. Still no response. The line had that sound that indicates a connection is open, active, but was not being used on one end. It was the longest two minutes in his life. The *quietest* two minutes.

The hardest part, Winter thought, what really hurt, was when he heard in the background the voices of his two sons, Jeremy and the younger Adam, initially arguing over something. And just before the broken connection, he'd heard Jeremy ask, "Mom. Is that my daddy? Is that my daddy?" Then the line went dead.

"What the hell?" Winter said angrily. All this time to get the call through, and they lost the connection. Or some careless op had cut him off. "What happened to my call?" he grated.

"It was cut off, Chief." The disembodied voice in his ear sounded disinterested.

"Goddamn it, I know it was cut off. Why?" he demanded.

He heard again the disembodied voice of the MARS operator.

"Mister Winter. The person who answered the call at the number in Long Beach, Mississippi, after saying she would accept the charges, has terminated the connection. Sorry."

Brenner's take on inexplicable comms held sway, a caustic play on radio-telephone protocol: WTF? O . . .

What the fuck? Over . . .

chapter seven

Six Merchants of Toledo

Cam Ranh Bay, Viet Nam: February 1969

Standing at the steel sink in the upstairs latrines the next morning, shaving, Winter was alternately indulging a morning fantasy: anticipation of breakfast in the Navy mess. Breakfasts were good; lunch was better; and dinner . . . sometimes exquisitie. He still held in awe his first meal here after transfer, a noon experience on the day he first arrived at Cam Ranh Bay.

He'd grabbed a tray outside the chow hall, stood in a short line at the fuel-drum grill, and selected a steak cooked to his preference and, slightly overwhelmed by this magnanimous service, then migrated into the cool interior where he was astounded. There, in the line of hot foods, was a shallow metal serving pan filled with deep-fried cauliflower. The dish, not unknown even in remote areas of the world, was a down-home favorite. Certainly not something he'd ever encountered or expected in a military serving line.

With the steak occupying most of his plate, he piled on the crisp, brown florettes to fill out his meal. He didn't bother with any other offering, though several appeared appetizing. And to round out the surprise, he found three bowls of dipping sauce to choose from to enhance the flavor of the cauliflower. He had come to know the talents of the Navy mess officer when he discovered Camembert-stuffed mushrooms, chicken livers wrapped with bacon and braised in a Sauterne, and other finger food from higher in the chain. The steaks, at least once a week, were a windfall in their own right. But that was lunch; right now he had to make breakfast.

He tentatively touched the blade of the razor to facial skin that seemed over-sensitized. He was glad it was Bushmills he'd taken on in the *One-on-One, Winner-Take-Nothing* following the letter, and compounded by the MARS do-si-do. At least he wasn't on his knees this morning. He didn't often drink so much that it incapacitated him; and then by design. He'd received a once-in-a-lifetime lesson in Asmara that kept him, if not on the straight and narrow, at least on the same plane. Almost in relief, he let his mind take him toward that further diversion.

* * *

Asmara, Eritrea (Ethiopia): July 1961

When he was promoted to SP5 and made an Assistant Trick Chief during a day shift, he'd returned to the barracks and decided to indulge himself with dinner at the Oasis Club, the enlisted men's club on the far edge of Kagnew Station. He'd walked up by himself, not seeking company. In the dining room, he'd taken a seat with two other men from his trick and ordered the special; the Polish sausage and baked black beans was often featured. He drank iced tea with his meal. But when he'd eaten, and the three had exhausted any conversational possibilities, he'd followed them into the bar, not thinking to drink but curious as to who was there. Maybe someone would buy him a drink on his stripe. More likely, he knew, they'd expect him to buy a round for all present.

Even that might have served him well. Instead, following Harry's lead, he ordered a rum tonic. The drink was his hot weather response to the more common G&T; he had never cared for the taste of gin, but the quinine-flavored tonic water was settling for the stomach. He might need settling after the Polack & Beans. When Harry took a seat at a table with another five or six guys, Winter dropped into a chair beside him, not paying any attention to the activities of the drinkers. Before he knew it—and he could never later figure out just how it had happened—he was caught up in one of the myriad chug-a-lug games. Everyone but him and Harry were drinking beer, and Harry switched to beer when he joined the game. But as the players were already ahead in the game, most showing effects of losing several rounds, Winter reckoned that as he'd just eaten, and had drunk only a little of the rum drink, he'd just stick with it and watch them go down in flames.

Later computation by the barman indicated Winter had downed 15 or 16 rum tonics; the barman settled for payment for 15, though he insisted it was 16. Winter never remembered how the game was concluded, but he was told by various observers that when the club closed at 0200, he'd migrated outside and passed out, leaning against the decorative palm tree by the front door. He could believe that; his shoulder and back bore the indents and scratches for weeks afterward. There were various versions of how he'd been led/carried back to the barracks, but refused to take on the outside steps up to his third floor room, and settled on a bench beneath the steps by the door to the Day Room. There he passed out.

He was fortunate that it was the first day of his two-day break, for he was sick and hungover for the full two-plus days. Friends brought him sodas, iced tea, milk, and beer, but he could drink nothing. And even the smell of food, when a roommate brought a pizza in for his own consumption, sent him to the deep sink. He'd already been to that sink a half-dozen times, following his initial vomitfest on the floor by his bunk.

On the morning of the third day, when he was scheduled to return to work on the Swings trick, he forced himself out of bed at the unreasonable hour of ten-thirty, and walked across the street for his first meal as a member of the NCO club. He sat alone. Sergeant Bollinger came in, late off a Mids trick, and sat across from him, welcoming him to the club. Winter had already ordered a bowl of oatmeal and a cup of weak tea. When Bollinger's order came, Winter looked down into the plate of three eggs, sunny side up and soft, and a small mound of greasy sausage. He barely made the parking lot before he vomited up vestiges of that late binge. His capacity for nausea and retching was endless.

It had been a worthy lesson, and one he tried to keep in the forefront of his mind, whenever he found himself in a situation involving drink. He didn't do that anymore.

* * *

Cam Ranh Bay, Viet Nam: February 1969

The cold blade's stroke was like the brush from some Gothic raptor's wingtip. Why did razor blade makers recommend rinsing the blade in cold water anyhow? That it maintained the edge sharper and longer had to be bullshit! A hot shave is just that: *hot*. His mind, avoiding memories, maintaining a state of semi-disconnect, wandered on, leaving his numb brain to marvel at the fact that his shaking hands had not so far sliced open his sore face. He rinsed the razor again in cold water

The explosion knocked the razor from his hand. It fell clattering on the concrete floor.

Or he had flung the razor down in reaction to the explosion.

He dithered only an instant. His brain was not up to one hundred percent. Though he felt the concussion, he still somehow thought the explosion not very powerful. Rather, the sense of distance. Automatically adopting the best route to safety, he turned and sprinted back the way he'd come in, heading for the nearest bunker. The routes to any bunkers from anywhere was a thing set in place before the need arose; when the need arose, it was too late for planning..

"Holy shit!" The shout outside the latrine door behind him was loud, broadcasting awe. Winter stopped, turned back. Someone, maybe, who knew what the hell was going on.

"What?" he yelled, running back to that side of the building. On the balcony outside, a visiting TDY lieutenant stood frozen, mouth still open, staring across the nearby clutter of structures to the runways and open ground beyond. Winter crowded the rail and followed the lieutenant's gaze behind a pointing, shaky hand.

He immediately spotted the narrow plume of dark smoke, undisturbed by anything resembling a breeze, feeding into the hot morning air from a cloud of dust and heavier-density smoke on the ground, just off the edge of the main runway. "What?" Winter demanded again.

The lieutenant's voice was tight: "Crash."

In seconds, the dust and smoke about the base of the plume began dissipating, and Winter made out the shape of an aircraft. After a few seconds more the indistinct object materialized into an F-4 Phantom. It was not in a prescribed take-off configuration: off the strip, nose buried in sand, it looked as if rejected by the gods of the air. At that instant, he heard the blaring horns and scream of sirens as Crash Crew deployed.

His mind cleared of pettiness, Winter turned back and raced across to the far stairs and down to first floor. In his room, he woke Bracken, told him a strike aircraft had crashed on take-off, grabbed his binoculars from a nail in the wall, and ran back out the door. He could hear Bracken behind him, Ho Chi Minh sandals slapping the concrete walk. He didn't look back to see if Bracken had grabbed his camera; no need. Bracken didn't take a dump without his camera.

Back on the balcony, Winter adjusted the glasses and watched as two large, paneled vehicles and a fire truck screeched to stops at diverse points of the compass about the stricken aircraft. Crash Crew began their hazardous dance. By now, Winter could see through the glasses that the smoke issued from the belly of the aircraft, the fire there spreading. He saw no sign of movement in or around the cockpit. Could the pilot and weapons operator have punched out during take-off? No! He knew they had not. He swept the terrain about the plane, then back down the strip from where the F-4 would have started its roll. There was no silk. Both canopies were still closed.

Bracken caught his attention, cursing, whimpering. Winter turned, watched him struggle to couple a telephoto lens onto the SLR with hands that were quaking in a spastic helplessness.

No silk, but Winter saw several dark objects scattered along the edge of the strip and, re-focusing the glasses, spotted ordnance—500-lb. bombs, air-to-ground missiles, cluster bombs and gravel bomblets—the aircraft had been trucking to Uncle Ho. Not the time to ponder that. He watched one of the paneled crash trucks backing toward the aircraft. As the Crash Crew apparatus went into full deterrent mode—crewmen responding to various assigned efforts: grunge work, pilot and guy-in-the-back rescue, fire suppression, and what all Crash Crewmen did—the entire crash site erupted in a ball of flame. The fireball quickly rose several hundred feet to become a greasy, black mushroom, then continued in a slower rise over the field as the fire continued boiling up. Beneath the cloud appeared nothing live.

"God! Fuck! Shades of Hiroshima," he heard a winded newcomer mutter.

No other sound was heard on the balcony. Hearing nothing, Winter suddenly feared he was deaf! Instantly deaf! But the visiting lieutenant put the lie to that; Winter clearly heard him praying. Until drowned out by additional Crash Crew vehicles and sirens and claxons at peak.

The fire raged, enveloping the Phantom, and billows of black, oily smoke from the ruptured-exploded JP-4 tanks obscured the view. After minutes, when some of the ground smoke cleared, Winter could make out several ambulances at the outer perimeter of the crash scene. There were small knots of men scattered about, and it took him several moments of manipulative glass work to locate the bodies flung in disarray, mostly on the concrete strip, one on the sand. He realized he was seeing medical personnel administering to the Crash Crew members caught in the blast. There was still no sign of the pilot and Weapons Operator.

The aircraft itself appeared unattended, out of the interest loop. Not of further concern. If the pilot and GIB—who it might be argued *could* have popped their chutes on takeoff, making them no longer a factor with regard to the fire—had not done so, then they were no longer a factor anyhow. Anything inside that cockpit would be beyond Crash Crew's benevolent efforts..

After watching with creeping despair for almost an hour, Winter heard a shout from someone on the ground floor, instructing him to report to the Orderly Room, ASAP. Just before lowering the glasses to respond, he watched a crash crewman, awkward in his heavy protective suit, clamber into the driver's seat and begin attempts to move one of the crash vehicles, the one which had arrived first. The front of the vehicle faced the balcony where Winter stood. A number of crash personnel interrupted various efforts, staring at the back of the vehicle, one pointing with agitation. Some bystanders were medical personnel; others firemen—all common gawkers. As the vehicle began its slow, measured turn and crept away from the still-smoldering wreckage, a number of crash crewmen on foot followed along. When the turning truck's rear faced toward the balcony where Winter, and now a small crowd stood, and when the truck had cleared the smoke, Winter's heart slammed in his chest.

Through the glasses, the body of an airman in crash gear was visible, embedded in the flat steel plating of the truck's rear deck. His back pressed deep into the metal, the man hung with arms spread, sightless eyes staring through the protective faceplate. A model of industrial-age crucifixion. Indeed, laboring in aid of his fellow man, the crash crewman had given his life—Winter had no doubt the crewman was dead—in the pursuit of those hallowed ideals.

So, see what that'll get you! Winter murmured sadly to no one.

When he had dressed and reached the Orderly Room, he was nodded into the CO's office. The major, dressed for flying, said something inaudible, meaningless, relevant to the runway tragedy . . . then, business as usual. "Hear you want to handle our A-and-D, Dave."

"Sir, I told . . . Yes, sir. I'll take the job, if that's all right . . . with you."

"Well, shit, son. If it wasn't all right with me, we wouldn't be having this grabass session. Right?" He broke the awkward silence immediately by smiling; he was just a good ole boy.

Winter brimmed with asperity: What was this maternal downsizing senior officers subscribed to? "Son?" Major Nichols was maybe two, three years his senior.

Still, with approval, CW2 David D. Winter accepted another set of orders from Headquarters, 224th Aviation Battalion, subdirected by 1RRC, assigning him the role of Awards and Decorations Officer for the 1st Radio Research Company (Aviation).

He borrowed a copy of Army Regulation AR 672-5-1 from the Morning Report clerk, and returned to his room. He'd missed morning chow, but the image of the black greasy column and the metallic crucifixion left him without appetite.

* * *

The day's mission had to be scrubbed.

Both runways, twin ten-thousand-foot exclamations of dazzling white concrete, were closed to operations. Crash ordnance was still unaccounted for—rockets and five-hundred-pound bombs buried in the sand; cluster bombs and broken "gravel" bombs had scattered their deadly contents like chicken feed—and an Air Force Red Horse team was at work on the runway. Scavengers had come with a massive crane, lifted and bore away the tangled remains of the Phantom F-4D. It had held together through the crash, the explosion and fire, and then the strain of all that MacDonald-Douglas residue being lifted. The integrity of the airframe was far superior to that of the frail humans sent to service it.

The CRAZY CAT mission was scrubbed without takeoff, so the scheduled crew automatically moved forward and were manifested for the following day's mission. With stand-down, there were ample hands for all petty details. A minor fugue of lassitude enveloped the area, though a black mood of benign neglect did not seem to fit against the bright sky. The smoke and other environmental hazards slowly dissipated from above the strip.

* * *

Lieutenant Billingsgate stuck his head into the room where Winter was reading Army regs and making notes. "Wanna take a ride?"

"Where?"

"Dong Ba Thin." He pronounced the last syllable like Tyin or Tien. Sounded right!

"Why?" Winter had not visited the nearby village across the

bay from NAF. There was no reason. Not even to verify or deny Ito's presumptive pursuit of poontang. Especially not that.

"For shits and giggles! *I* gotta go. Thought you might want to ride along. I presume you know that the five-oh-ninth has another 'No See Me' outfit there," he said, invoking the colloquial term for a Spook or covert activity. "I'm to pick up some gear we're to drag along on the mission tomorrow and drop off in Da Nang."

Winter had not known of other ASA operations nearby. But then, what the hell? When did they start telling him everything? "Sure. Gimme a minute."

"I'll be in front of the Orderly Room." The chubby lieutenant scurried away, seemingly enthused with the notion of a late afternoon drive to a nearby vacation paradise.

Absent any events along the road up the peninsula, they rounded the north end of the bay bored to tears, neither willing to acknowledge it. They came upon the first huts of struggling Dong Ba Thin village where Bimbo's first response was to annihilate a chicken. The scrawny bird, squawking, seemed suddenly propelled under the front passenger-side wheel and disappeared with a slight thump, a cessation of squawking, and a flurry of dirty white feathers. Immediately—suspiciously so, Winter thought, as if tied to the fowl—several ragged children, followed by a harridan of the streets, poured into the dusty path leading into the village. Bimbo stopped the Jeep; the two officers were suddenly besieged by a clamoring crowd demanding restitution, some making threats, others laughing, nudging the mangled chicken with bare, dirty toes. Bimbo said later he'd stopped merely to check for damage to his government vehicle, but the rotund officer was wise to the ways of the Orient.

Dong Ba Thin was OFF LIMITS, though little effort was made to enforce the restriction. First RR troops almost never went there; the only attraction was a plentiful supply of marijuana. For connoisseurs of that outlawed substance, however, Dong Ba Thin weed was rated up there on a scale of zip to hi. Common rumor had it that even the worst DBT Mary Jane was an eight or better; there were no low estimates. The illicit substance had found a popular market in 1st Log Command where soldiers, laboring in the hot sun as disenfranchised stevedores, already at the bottom of everybody's pecking order, had nothing to lose. Some Zoomie losers hedged a bet too. An ASA soldier, on the other hand, caught with weed in the glare of NCO, officer, or MP headlights, could anticipate the loss of security clearance. That meant an automatic fast shuffle down the road to an infantry company. Not the stuff of which ASA dreams are made.

Though there on legitimate business, Bimbo appeared nervous. He glanced over at a pair of civilian policemen who seemed uninterested in the chicken drama. He would keep it that way. "Keep that weapon in sight, but for Chrissake, don't chamber a round, Chief. We're going to leave the bargaining to the Casualty Comp people. And beware the White Mice," he nodded at the police. With those admonitions, he yanked the Jeep into gear and jammed on the gas pedal.

Kids, mama-sans, ancient venerables, more chickens, and one dog, barking without sound, scattered before the rattling vehicle. They had progressed a good hundred yards before the lieutenant slowed down. He did so only to avoid a gaggle of people alongside the road who suddenly spilled into the traffic lane. The Jeep continued at a crawl. "I'm gonna edge by this clusterfuck, so watch it," Bimbo said with inference. He fed the Jeep gas in tiny spurts and it sped-slowed sped-slowed sped-slowed ahead.

Winter was watching closely when the melee, involving only GIs as far as he could tell, burst suddenly into the middle of the road. The Jeep crawled to a halt. There were a dozen-or-so milling participants, all intent on the focus of disturbance. The two officers sat silently, willing themselves invisible, hoping not to draw attention. Most of the soldiers, Winter saw, were without either shirt or jacket; if they wore one, it bore no rank, insignia, unit patches or badges, and no nametag. The confusing muddle was such the two officers could not tell what they were witnessing.

Then, seemingly thrust from the dust cloud in a flash of silver light, Winter saw a familiar figure.

A tall, emaciated officer—the only one wearing rank, incongruous with a single bar of silver—was followed immediately, besieged by at least six soldiers, while another three danced about, their body language advertising menace. Beyond these central players, another six or seven were grouped close. To Winter it appeared the few soldiers at the heart of the action were competing to see which one could pummel the officer with the greatest enthusiasm. There were no weapons evident, but the lieutenant was suffering a beating. Winter didn't stop to consider what he was getting into; the thing looked obvious to him. The soldiers had knocked the officer's headgear off and were enthusiastically beating him with their fists, from all sides.

Winter leapt from the Jeep clutching the M-1 carbine and waded into the crowd action. Bimbo leaned on the horn. The outburst of noise and sudden introduction of a new, armed element caused the six attackers to scatter briefly. But they saw it was only one man—Winter was sure they recognized him as an officer—and, enlisting the aid of several companion standbys, the crowd charged back at the skinny lieutenant in renewed fury.

With that, Billingsgate jumped from the Jeep and yanked a LRRP 12-gauge riot gun from beneath the driver's seat. He jacked a shell into the chamber and blew off a corner of the roof of a nearby hooch. With the boom of the Winchester, there came a shrill scream from beyond the crowd. Winter butt-stroked a muscular black soldier with the carbine, swung about and spotted a short, round soldier in full fatigue uniform, strongly agitated, dancing about on the edge of the road. The soldier raised an old M-1 Garand, but while he fumbled to insert a clip of eight rounds, the crowd disappeared among the hooches, laundries, massage parlors, and bars.

The lieutenant, now on his back, endeavoring to raise himself from the muddy road where he was tangled in pack straps, headgear, rifle sling and a full cartridge belt, pointed his finger into the lowering sky and shouted, "Flee not, you cowardly carrion; tarry a bit, base caitiffs. Not through any fault of my own, but of my horse, am I thus discomfited."

Edging cautiously forward, Winter scouted the immediate area while digesting the lieutenant's speech: antiquarian, he noted, but was surprised he understood him fine. A horse? There was no such animal evident. Edging cautiously forward, he stepped on a piece of paper that stuck to his boot. He reached to pull it free, and was looking down at the bountiful charms of a *Playboy* centerfold. He recognized her supra-endowments from barracks walls elsewhere.

When he helped to his feet the tall lieutenant who had lost his helmet liner, Winter saw he was white-haired. Helmet *liner*? He stared at the shattered fiber headgear in the mud. Was he seeing right? The tall lieutenant's face was set in deep lines that looked like relief map contours.

He wore Army fatigues at least five years out of date: old-style fatigues, worn by no one anymore, particularly in hot, damp climates. They required starch and ironing. Not jungle fatigues. The creases were gone from these togs. The officer was splattered with mud and filth from the street. He wore a nametag, Winter noticed, and checked it out. He suffered a brief frisson that it would be some Spanish surname.

He read "Dewey."

"Lieutenant, you all right?"

"If you mean am I grievously wounded, my response must, in truth, be negative. Though I find it troubling that my . . . situation . . . required your intervention." Nevertheless, he made a small obeisance toward Winter while slapping ineffectually at his uniform, dusting himself, smearing the mud..

"What was that all about? Were they into something illegal?" Winter asked.

"Quite likely. However, I stopped—*we* stopped—" he nodded briefly toward the short private who was still trying to subdue the M-1 "—when that crowd of cutpurses blocked our passage on the path," he nodded at the sorry excuse for a walkway. "They appeared to be in a state of drink. One of the men thrust that . . . that vile picture—" here he nodded at, without looking at, the trampled Bunnie which Winter had tossed back in the muddy street "—right into my face and demanded that I acknowledge that she . . . *she* . . . was the most beautiful woman in the world." The elderly lieutenant was working himself toward a state.

"Aren't there any MPs here? Didn't anyone take your part?" Winter said.

"There were a number of other Armed Forces personnel here—no *guardía*—but when the group approached me, became obstreperous, those others vanished as the wind. They divined what was to come, and likely wished no part of it.."

"You could have just told them, 'Sure. You're right. Right on!' or something. It's likely they *were* drunk. You should know, you can't reason—"

"Too much wine taken, perhaps. But they appeared set on threatening me for no reason. Creating an excuse. Perhaps because of my rank. They were extremely bold."

"But still, why didn't you just ease your way out of it?" Winter argued, while Billingsgate, ignoring everyone, climbed back into the driver's seat and waited silently with the Winchester propped on the windshield lying folded forward on the hood.

"Forgive me. Did I fail to convey that? Not only were they rude and abusive, the men were egregiously *wrong*. I could not agree to their proposition. That . . . that *young cow-like woman* cannot even be thought of in the same breath with someone truly beautiful. I told them briefly of my Dulcia to provide them some measure of true beauty."

"And? . . ." Winter, following the language, struggling to grasp the essence of this bizarre message, this encounter, looked around. Lieutenant Billingsgate was focused elsewhere.

"They said . . . they *demanded* that I produce this person of whom I spoke. My Dulcia. I reminded them that I had *told* them; as an officer my word is sacrosanct. They must believe me, trust my judgment. If that were not so, then what is to be served by my lady's appearance. Then, they would see for themselves, blinded by her beauty. But her beauty is so incorruptible that it must be a matter of my word alone. I believe it was at that point when the first one struck me. And it was not merely those whom you accosted. There were others, young ones on bicycles, and three of them riding a . . . what is that? a *caribao*, a huge domesticated creature."

"Water buffalo, but—"

"I regret I was caught off guard and could not effect the measure of punishment they deserved. However, I digress afar." He suddenly turned. "We must go. Sam—" he called to the round private, "we must be along. Duty awaits." With a wave of his hand he gathered up his gear and, escort tagging behind, marched off the road and disappeared between hooches.

Winter walked back to the Jeep. "Man, that was some strange shit," he marveled. "Did you hear that guy? That officer? Sounded like something out of the Middle Ages."

"I couldn't hear anything with all this street noise. And I never got a good look at the guy. An officer? . . . a lieutenant, you said? Well . . ."

"Funny thing is, I've seen him before. Them. But for the life of me, I can't remember where."

"Yeah. I know . . ."

"Thanks for the hired-gun action, Bimbo."

"My pleasure. Told you, be careful over here. Dong Ba Thin! Bad shit goes on as a matter of course." His head swivelled, alert to threats. "Those guys pounding on the soldier you said was a lieutenant are a gang of hoods from Toledo. At least the six main ones. I don't know how word got out, but half the guys in the army, serving in Viet Nam who come from Toledo, Ohio, went AWOL or deserted and wound up here, just across the peninsula from the largest military compound in Southeast Asia. They mostly run drugs, but some're into hijacking, theft, black market, prostitution, every other scam you can name."

Winter climbed into the Jeep. "Why doesn't the Army clean them out?" Only in Viet Nam! he thought. In any other venue, they wouldn't be having this conversation..

"Nobody'll go in there," Billingsgate responded, driving off. "Into the ville. Those hoods won't surrender peaceably. Can you imagine the headlines if we sent a battalion of MPs in there. No, better be a brigade! Of the Eighty-Second. The *New York* fuckin'

Times would eat our lunch. Considering their commie bias, all those assholes need is some in-house bullshit from the Army. And these Toledo bums don't shy at murder. That's when they're merely protecting their product. Whaddaya think they'd be like, fighting to stay alive?"

The strange interlude stayed with Winter the remainder of that day. Later, he didn't even remember arriving at the compound where Bimbo had business; couldn't recall how or when they had returned to NAF. Something . . . *massive* . . . seemed to lie across his shoulders. A heavy, depressing weight.

He jumped out of the Jeep in front of the Orderly Room. The screen door slammed open and SP4 Gremling, a clerk, called out, "Mister Winter. On the horn.. Right now. He called earlier but we didn't know when you'd be back. He's called back."

"Who?" Winter strode to the door and followed Gremling inside.

"Don't know. Wouldn't say. Use the phone on my desk, sir."

"What's this exchange again?"

"Albatross."

Winter depressed the Talk button on the phone. "Albatross working. Go ahead."

Where there was no static, there was silence. There was not much silence.

He spoke again.

A tinny voice came back at him through loud crackling: "A-bah-truss, you wuh-kin?"

"No, operator. I'm not working. I have no connection. Did you place a call?"

There was the loud, crackling break of signal, harsh in his ears, "Albatross? That you, Dave?" The voice struck a chord, like the half-full, half-empty philosophical paradigm: was it half-buried in interference from a world of electromagnetic emissions, or half-emerging as an ecstatic reaction to familiarity?.

"Who is that?" Winter blurted, incredulous. He *knew* who it was.

"Hel------tross, is that you ----?"

"This is Winter. Who's speaking?"

"A-bah-truss, you wuh-kin?"

"I'm trying, you silly bitch. Get off the line."

"—Luth-- I'm in —Gon I----my---up again. --th Mar---"

Winter stood, handpiece crushed into the side of his head, listening to the Vietnamese female operator imploring A-bah-truss to confirm he remained in contact with the other end of the link. With the twilight zone.

Luther? Luther Brenner?

In Sai Gon?

* * *

His mind, a muddle of contradictions, could not avoid the major question: Why?

Luther, a fairly senior non-commissioned officer, having pulled one tour in 'Nam—"back then," as Winter thought of his first tour—and unlike junior officers and warrants who were on a quick roll-over sked, shouldn't have come up with his turn in the barrel yet. Not for a good while. That simple bastard, he thought, knowing there was nothing simple about Luther Emanuel Brenner. He must have volunteered!

Unlikely as logic would have it, volunteering was the only thing he could imagine that put Brenner back in harm's way. As he thought it, the speciousness of his rationale struck him: Hell, Brenner was in harm's way every instant he was awake. And likely, as he slept.

His iconoclastic friend, skeptic to the world's offerings, far too educated for the role he served, went through life in the Army as he'd no doubt gone through his civilian trevail, primed for confrontation. The education, for instance; Winter remembered the few times he'd gotten Luther to talk about his "tour in academic hell," as he put it.

After early Army service, Brenner had availed himself of the GI Bill and enrolled in college. Brown University, he thought he remembered. Must have been; Luther railed on about the quality of Italian restaurants in Providence.

Always a reader, Luther had leaned naturally into the humanities, finishing a degree in English in two-and-a-half years. Straight into graduate school, he whisked through that as he said like "grits through a redneck's alimentary canal." Having found his calling, he went directly into a Ph.D. program leading to a Doctorate in English. He was taken with the genre and thought he wanted to teach.

But there, his first impediment raised its ugly head. Winter remembered the night in the *dzong* cart, heading for the bars in Gia Dinh, when the conversation segued into a revelation of ugliness: Brenner's thesis adviser, arrogance, a series of unlikely confrontations with university hierarchy, and Luther's eventual bailout.

Dropped the program like a bad habit and, adding fuel to the fire of self-destruction, reenlisted in the Army. Came right back to ASA. And here he stayed . . . and here, apparently, he was. In country—

"Oh, Lord," he groaned, invoking a Brenner lament, "grant me solace, and the devotion of spectral battalions."

chapter eight

Mayday

II Corps, Viet Nam: February 1969

Dragonflies buzzed along the skyline: alien creatures, mythic overtones in their mechanical sweep. Heat hung over the soldier on the hillside, a presence—cloying, sticky to the touch—the tropical world around him soft, indolent. The river below was brown and silent, smooth like polished hickory. Mister Alverson and Piltdown Pilot were dead at the foot of the slope.

* * *

Through child's eyes he saw the river as a monstrous, sluggish flood. At that age he couldn't know that what he saw—the feature that left sediment in the bait bucket, the spice that flavored the catch with its rich, brown tang—was good bottomland, topsoil from corn and cotton and soybean farms, the slim wealth of a poor land, the Yazoo rushing south joining the Sunflower, flowing into the Mississippi, all adding their alluvial ransom to the delta beyond New Orleans.

Upstream was Belzoni and Marksville; downstream, Silver City; and away from the river Midnight and Louise. But young Billy Ray Damson was familiar only with Goat Hill and the few tenant shacks and scratch farms comprising it. His five-year-old world lay, bounded by the limits of his exploration: the river in his front yard, turgid, restless movement in the eddies; a soybean field, flat and shimmering in the sun, stretching away to the horizon behind the house; the tall, blackened stumps of a burnt-over sweetgum swamp to the north; and to the south, a long, snaking dirt road along marshy backwaters and inlets, paralleling the river's parambulations until ending in a muddy clearing where the cable ferry put out to Silver City across the river.

He knew Silver City, where ice cream was a rare Saturday treat in small green and white Dixie cups, flat wooden spoons for quick eating before the Delta summer turned it into sweet, frothy soup. Where Momma worked in the mattress factory. The hulking old brick building that housed the factory had once been a Confederate grain depot, but he knew only that it was there Momma had driven the long ticking needle through her hand and, thinking of the penetrating steel, he felt it. What he remembered most was Daddy cursing because there was no money, reminding Billy Ray's mother, "'pression hard times ain't over," and she needed to get back to work if they were going to eat. There were things a man just didn't do for work, even if he was desperate. But she hadn't the option of pride.

And always, there was the river.

* * *

This river had that slow, southern crawl, and where he lay, huddled up under the vines, he could hear things moving in the brush along the water's edge. On that other river there were long, sleek snakes called blue racers, flashing sinuously through the tangled growth, so black they shone with an azure brilliance in the sun. They were startled out of their inactivity along the path by his tiny bare feet pat-patting down to the boat dock on the river before the house.

Private First Class Damson would have given over to those memories—half exotica, half terror—if he could. But he was feverish and without water. There were sounds in the jungle, below him along the river, and above him in the short grass and scrub bushes along the crest of the hill. He was mired in an illogical dichotomy: part wonder, part fear.

It had been a day and a half now and he was alone. In the first few minutes after he had crawled free of the downed and burning aircraft, he heard the pilot—he *thought* it was Mister Alvorsen—crying for help. Damson tried to go to him, but the crash and the long struggle had exhausted him as he inched his way on his side, pushing, scrabbling with one leg and his hands, dragging the other leg up the slope, away from the flaming fuel.

Every movement was a new kind of agony. He thought his back might be broken, and feared movement, remembering first aid training. But the fear of fire was greater than that of paralysis, and he'd dragged himself up the rise, away. Having used up everything he had fighting his way to safety, he had nothing to take him back. After a while, it grew silent down the slope.

Night had come. The blackness was complete, but the night was thunderous with movement. He heard every insect sound, every tiny jungle creature in magnified suspense: bamboo rats assumed tiger guises; monkeys were North Vietnamese regulars; palm beetles grew outsize, stalking their domain with crashing abandon. Somewhere in the long hours of darkness, the fear and pain and fatigue had overcome him, and when he opened his eyes, it was day again.

His body raged with thirst. He lay in the rising heat for more than an hour before his fevered mind cleared enough to realize that somehow, even through the pain and desperate confusion of escaping the burning aircraft, he had grabbed his web belt. Some quirk of training or instinct for survival. Then he had the canteen—he had water—and a first aid pouch, and the emergency Mayday kit, stuck on like an afterthought by thousands of tiny Velcro hooks. He held the belted kit close to his face and stared at the life-promising package, the plastic fibers like stiff cilia, microscopically obscene. He pushed the kit away and scrutinized it through blurred eyes. He acknowledged the Velcro as merely a device to hold it to the belt. The .38 was muddy, but it too was intact. It wasn't *all* bad, he thought. But then that grace was gone in pain.

And now the found water was gone. The thirst of fever had overcome the training of water discipline, and though he could not remember how or when, he had drunk it all. He listened to the subtle, teasing gurgle of the river and for a while could think only of the water. There had always been the water.

* * *

Living along the Yazoo was both a joy and a burden to a boy. He was allowed to play only as far as the dirt road that separated the house from the riverbank, and he could go to the dock only when Momma or Daddy or Grandpa was along. He went first to listen and watch for the blue racers, and later to fish from the dock for the muddy catfish or to pull up crawdads from the mounded chimney holes along the riverbank with a piece of bacon rind on a string. But Momma had his baby brother to care for when she was not at work at the factory, and Daddy was almost always gone, looking for work or just gone a long time, coming home walking funny and talking loud, his face red, going to sleep without supper, sometimes in the porch swing.

Grandpa would take him to the river when he came. But there were long stretches between his visits, and the old man never stayed long, but stamped away down the dirt road with his battered tin suitcase tied with fishing line, and Billy Ray couldn't go to the river then.

And he could never get into the boat, even tied to the dock, except when Daddy was there. Only when Daddy was there. He'd been on the river twice.

He was scared of the river, too. It had bad memories, things he didn't understand fully but which left him uneasy over time. It was down by the river where Daddy, home late one afternoon from one of his trips looking for work, that sharp, sour smell about him and his eyes wide and staring—Daddy had whipped him. Took a willow switch to him because the day before, they'd put the new kittens into a gunny sack and rowed them across the river and left them in a cane break above the town. In the morning the kittens were huddled in a mewling mass in the cool dirt under the back porch.

"You, Billy Ray. I told you 'bout them cats, boy. C'mere!"

"Daddy, I didn't do nothin'," he pleaded. He stared at his father's flushed face, watched him pull the limber branch from the tree and begin peeling away the leaves and bark. But even without guilt of the charge, he knew better than to run.

"You c'mere, boy, an' don't you sass me."

Billy Ray didn't know how he had done whatever it was he'd done, but he knew he'd done something terrible because he'd wished so hard to get the kittens back. The guilt was still with him, even after Momma came down the path, yelling at Daddy something awful. The mother cat had swum across the river, she told him, and brought the kittens back in her mouth, one by one. Momma had seen her at it, during the night. The whipping stopped and the kittens stayed. Mamma had grit.

And it was on the river where they found the body of a man washed up, wedged into the timbers of the dock. Daddy said he'd been in the water a long time. He was all swollen and black . Billy Ray thought he was one of the field hands from up at Tollivers', but Daddy said it was a white man turned dark from a long time in the water and swelling, and said he'd been cut. Cut bad.

The boy stared wide-eyed as his father took a paddle from the boat and dislodged the carcass. They stood and watched it bob away on the slow current, smelling only faintly of decay.

"That's best," said the dark-faced farmer. "Don't need the law in here, pokin' 'round. Let somebody downstream call 'em." Billy Ray felt as if he'd done something bad then, too, as if he was somehow to be blamed for the body in the river.

* * *

Damson lay in the damp, moldy tangle of growth and watched the ants crawl over his forearm. The flesh was red and angry, shiny where the fire had reached him in the plane. He couldn't feel the ants. In delirium, something in the perverted insistence of this illogical process stirred in him a bit of his own bizarre, indomitable trek down the ranks of enlisted service. He thought the ants would understand. They, too, were near the bottom of the chain. Prospering.

He lay quietly, not moving. He could hear sing-song voices below him, down the river, away from the wreckage. The smoke was all gone now, the fire out. Maybe they wouldn't find it. Maybe he'd just shoot his way out of here. Then, maybe not. Maybe he'd . . . Maybe. . . .

He heard aircraft sounds in the distance, slow and measured; his head throbbed in time with the pulsing beat. Flying a search pattern. He moved his head carefully, looking down the jungled slope, and confirmed again to his satisfaction that he could barely see the crash site, and then only because he knew where to look. From the air it would be invisible.

He tightened his hand around the tiny box and, moving his head, brought his eyes back to focus on the beeper. The rest of the emergency kit was scattered in a tight circle within easy reach: the signal mirror, silk signal panels, fish hooks and line, tetracycline pills, salt tablets, water purification tablets, waterproof matches, and the rest of the items that could not be used. But the beeper, the tiny signal generator, held his hope. All he had to do to make it come alive was flick the switch with his thumb. *Click!* He knew the sound; it would be slight; it couldn't be heard even a few yards away.

They'd all handled the signal sets in the secure world of white concrete runways and air-conditioned briefing room, checking them, double-checking procedures, grab-assing . . . Nobody recognized their potential. No one ever thought *he* would be the one.

He listened again for the big choppers, but they were on another leg of the pattern, out of earshot. The beeper radio signal, though, would carry for miles. All the way, if need be, to that different world of cold sodas, beer, Conexes, and grey-skirted Doughnut Dollies. On a fixed frequency, all he had to do was activate it and the searchers' direction finder would locate him. Ten minutes from a flick of the thumb, he could be in the rescue copter, a Navy Sea King—they'd crashed close enough to the coast, it might be the Navy—or one of the Air Force Jolly Green Giants out of Da Nang or farther south.

The Jolly Greens! The name brought images of a can of peas. But the first time he'd seen the huge footprints on the sidewalk of the Gunfighter Club there in Da Nang, tracks three feet long if an inch, and the caption "Home of the Jolly Green Giants," he'd smiled at the subtle bravado that had formulated the monster prints. Later, when he knew their record, knew their losses in devotion to his kind, he never smiled again at the sidewalk, and was careful always not to step in the sacred path.

Ten, fifteen minutes at most. Possibly less. And he played a quick game then, weighing the odds in his head. What counted was what he struggled to ignore. After complex calculations that were meaningless, he knew he dare not take the bet.

They knew! The sneaky little bastards, they couldn't have missed the plunging aircraft, the explosion, the persistent curl of smoke from the burning fuel, the thin plume constant through the afternoon of the previous day and into this morning. They knew. And they waited.

The bushes were full of them, and the beeper was the bait. They knew, all right, as he knew—the game would come if called. It was what they did.

Damson lay with his thumb on the switch. Several times he felt his hand tensing, trembling, and he put the tiny box on the ground next to his face, out of his hand lest an involuntary movement on his part set it off.

With the switch off, there was no sound. He couldn't remember if there was any local noise produced by the device when it was switched on or not, but there was nothing now, no radio waves high up in the UHF spectrum. He worried about rolling onto the set in his feverish sleep. As he closed his eyes, he moved the box farther away and brought his hand back. He listened.

There was the distant thrumming *Plop! Plop! Plop!* of the big ships and he wondered if there was a radio frequency for prayers. There was a time when that might have counted for something.

* * *

"Let's go, boy. We gotta see Uncle George 'bout the dogs," his daddy had said. "Billy Ray, you come 'long with me, now." Momma was at work and the colored lady down the road had already left for her house with his baby brother.

He was excited when he knew where they were going. He loved Uncle George. He felt at home and safe with the black man who was too old now for field work, could only care for the dogs, his dad's and other hunters', and do odd jobs. He could not have spoken of it, but somehow sensed that Uncle George lived mostly on handouts from his children and what Billy Ray's daddy could give him out of an almost equally destitute household.

Aunty Philoma was dead now and there was an emptiness about the place without her. But Uncle George knew everything there was to know about fishing and where to find the cane that made good poles, and about stringing trot lines and making soup from the river turtles they caught on big treble hooks.

Uncle George knew about dogs, which ones were best on fox, coon, or rabbit, and he told Billy Ray stories about the Morgan he'd once owned, the best bear dog in Humphreys County. The Morgan was an aristocrat who wouldn't work under a shotgun, and he thought squirrels and rabbits beneath his station. But there wasn't hardly anymore bear around the county and the dog got old and lazy and was finally run over, lying in the road, by a truck hauling turpentine from the plant in Midnight.

And whittle! Could Uncle George ever whittle! Whenever Billy Ray went to his place in the edge of the swamp, the old man slipped him the Weatherby three-blader in a quick, furtive move. It was his to use, to experiment with until they got ready to go. Then, he'd have to find a way to slip it back to Uncle George without Daddy seeing. He loved Uncle George, and never saw the wink between the two men.

But this time Daddy left him in the car at the end of the field road, just at the edge of the cotton. "You wait here, Billy Ray. Don't get outta the car. I'll be back purty soon."

Billy Ray slumped down in the seat, staring at the floor. He didn't understand why he couldn't go see Uncle George. He looked out over the dashboard and watched his father disappear into the edge of the swamp, following the path that would take him to the old man's place. It wasn't far, the boy knew, but the swamp was deep and dark, and he couldn't hear the dogs through the thicket. He knew they'd be putting up a racket about now as his father approached the shack, but he couldn't hear a sound.

The fields were empty. Plowing was done and the short cotton grew silent and green in the chalky ground under late sun. He played with a screwdriver for a while, but even that exotica soon lost its appeal. He crawled over into the front seat and stared out across the flat, square, rusty hood, across the cotton, watching the dark wall of swamp for the figure of his father. Off to one side where the windshield was cracked, the pattern of starred glass framed a buzzard spiraling around and around, dropping slowly down until it dipped out of sight by a tall, sparse pine. Billy Ray knew about buzzards; he watched the scavenger and shivered.

He felt cool. His bare legs were warm on the fuzzy nap of the seat, but he wore no shirt, and as the sun dropped lower and the shadows lengthened, he felt the land change, the warmth recede. He burrowed into the seat, whimpering, and wished harder for his father's return.

He knew, too, about praying. Grandmomma Rose made them all do it at the table when they were at her house, and when she came for a visit. He'd heard Daddy tell Momma he wasn't going to put up with that stuff while she was there, and then there was an argument and Billy Ray was sent to bed where he could still hear the loud voices through the board walls; but as long as Grandmomma Rose was there, the prayers continued. When he was sent to bed, he went without prayers, though there were times when he felt he'd like to be able to get down on his knees by the bed, just before climbing in under the quilts, and ask for things which Grandmomma Rose had assured him would be answered. He never remembered from one time to the next how the time stretched out, longer and longer, and answers never materialized. Needs never came.

Daddy had caught him at it once when Billy Ray had just returned from a visit to Grandmomma's house and was used to making his prayers just before bed. The boy got a kick in the rear as he scrambled from the pine flooring into the bed, trying to avoid the big foot, only after feeling the sting and trickle of blood where pine board splinters tore his knee.

But now, all alone by the empty cotton field, since there was nobody here to tell Daddy, and Daddy was the reason for the prayers anyhow, he felt it was all right to try it. Daddy said it was a waste of time and he wouldn't stand still for it, but maybe . . . Billy Ray had visions of all the things that could have happened to his father in the darkness of the swamp.

"Dear Jesus, make Daddy come back. Jesus, I'm cold. I want him. I want to go home. I want . . ."

The boy didn't know how to begin, and he realized his attempts were not adequate to that formal rite practiced by his grandmother. He was also dimly aware that he called on one whom he somehow understood to be number two. As lonely and fearful as he was, he hadn't reached the point of going to the top. Grandmomma Rose said it was a sin for people to go to the Almighty with the wrong things, little things, and though he tentatively attempted contact with the earthly manifestation, the son, he had never gone to Him. Never abused His benevolence.

Through building anxiety, he heard evening doves calling low across the fields, and he felt a thrill of warmth when he heard whistling in the distance; but when he raised up in the seat and searched for the carefree *soul who could be happy all alone way out here, all he saw were tiny swirls of dust along the far edge of the cotton patch, next to the soybeans. Some fieldhand had led a mule along there just moments before, so close, but they were well on their way to the shed by now, and he instinctively knew the whistling had been of the kind to ward off haints. Grandpa told how darkies always whistled in the late evenings and night, and the realization deepened the boy's sense of loneliness and despair.*

"Dear Jesus dear Jesus, please make my daddy come please, Jesus, now," he cried.

He saw nothing significant happening; there was no response from Jesus. Grandmomma said you had to be prepared to wait, but he couldn't wait.

The doves were quiet, the mule dust settled, the whistling faded. There was no sign of a man on the trail leading out of the swamp. Billy Ray expanded his plea, calling upon everyone good, everything that represented hope. "Santa Claus, bring my daddy. Santa Claus, Jesus, please . . ." and he began to cry harder, his small, slim brown body shaking with convulsions. "Dear Jesus, Sheriff Slocum, Santa Claus, find my daddy. Please, everybody at the store. Momma! Momma, where's Daddy? I didn't want to come. I hate Uncle George. Please, Momma, come get me!" He buried his head in the seat, unable to look any longer at the empty path. He felt the tears splash hot on his chest and turn cold as they tracked down his pebbled flesh.

"Uncle George, tell my daddy come on. Make him come back. To the car. Please, Uncle George, he forgot me. Santa Claus. . . ."

* * *

Damson reached for the beeper and pulled it to his chest. He felt the cool moisture beaded on the metal. His body was wet, how much the night air, how much breaking fever, he could not tell.

The dream was clear in his mind. He didn't remember now what had happened. His father had come back eventually, but the details were lost to him. He had the vague notion he'd been punished for crying out, though; punished when his father did finally return. His father was a proud man who disdained charity and could not forgive weakness.

He thought of his father, his strength, his dark face and long arms, and he looked at the beeper in his hand with the moonlight through the brush dappling his swollen, burned arm. He pulled the tiny antenna up from the metal box and put his thumb once again on the switch.

He couldn't hear them anymore—the quartering aircraft. Only the night sounds, jungle sounds, but he knew the Jolly Greens would come with a flip of the switch. Not as quick now as earlier when they were already near, but they would come. If he called . . .

He felt the ribbed plastic trip lever beneath his thumb. Sweat ran down from his armpits, cold in the night air. He listened for the waiting ones around the hill—he knew they were there and he pondered the odds again—and thought he could distinguish the sudden, distinct dry clatter of operating rods jacked back, the clack-clink of brass rounds rammed home by bolts, the snap of safeties. He worried about hallucinating. They wouldn't be that careless. Charlie was too good to be that sloppy.

Damson inventoried his wounds and then dismissed them, as if they were of no consequence, the sum total insufficient to some definition, some threshold. He laughed, almost aloud, thinking of Dick Tracy: Fearless Fosdick, it was, used to say, with the saucer-size hole through his head, "Merely superficial wounds, Chief!" That's me, Damson nodded, Fearless Fosdick. A comic character. Dumbo Damson. He shrugged off a tendency toward self-pity. He thought again of his father, an automatic arming against the collapse of control. He checked his wounds again. He was burning up and the pain in his back had returned; he could barely move. None of that counted, he remembered. Perspective!

He had a flash of memory, a scolding or a whipping for calling out. And once he'd run from Daddy; he never did it again, though his father never chased him. There were things you learned, important things, Daddy said. Rules of life.

The Jolly Greens couldn't help him anyhow, he thought. They would only lead the little people to his secret hiding place. He couldn't share that with them; he dare not. It was his place. King of the Mountain. His by right of occupancy.

Goddamn! He blinked. Off in never-never land again. The choppers! That was what was important—them and the men in them, the Sea and Air Rescue ships, the Marines. Whoever. They came in unprotected, open-assed to the sky and ground whenever a beeper actuated, whenever a flyer was down in the hostile land. And the land was hostile. He had proof of that.

It occurred to him that he had not heard cries from the burned aircraft for what seemed like days, now, and he was ashamed of the relief that gave him. He tried to sort through the right and wrong of it, all the things Momma had told him, prayers from Grandmomma, Uncle George's soft honeyed words like another language . . . and Daddy.

Daddy was right! It was a simple thing to implement; he had only *not* to react. He put the beeper away for the final time. And when he did, as if he'd crossed some line of demarcation, on a new course and resigned to it, he expected to feel the difference. But in that moment, he knew that being right was not enough.

There was no pretense of revelation; he did not turn his face to the void. "God . . ." he began, speaking into the ground.

* * *

A ragged column of small men moved quickly on a red clay dike through the high country paddies. All wore dark peasant shirts and shorts, and conical straw hats with red stars. They carried Kalashnikov assault rifles and three days' rations slung round their shoulders, cloth tubes filled with rice and tea. Two of them carried pistols of American make in leather holsters of the U.S. Army, first aid kits of like origin, and canteens of water filled in Sai Gon. One soldier lugged a ball of camouflaged silk that had been a parachute; a sapper wore steel-colored sunglasses that made his tiny frame appear more than ever that of a child.

They came from the site of an American plane, crashed two days before. They'd found two dead white enemy soldiers and took from them what was not burned. The squad leader carried the plastic-faced packet of flight maps. In his pocket were all the cigarettes.

They'd searched the crash site, but the squad leader was anxious; newly arrived from the north, he pushed his comrades toward their greater mission. They moved quickly and were now six kilometers away, the crashed plane and dead men a fading memory.

* * *

Damson thought he was conscious again, maybe for the first time. The dark of night was shot through with rays of the morning sun, starting its cycle. Dawning bird sounds built to a rattling crescendo; the jungle breathed in a vast, moving wakefulness.

Damson saw himself rising up from the chilly, clammy ground, his limbs straight on a soft bed of green, the pain gone. He heard voices from an echoing chamber, calling to him. They beckoned him upward, toward the clouds, smiling; it was all understanding and forgiving up there. The timbre of helicopter music was loud and spectral. There was the beating of air about him as a whirlwind urged him upward.

chapter nine

Reinforcements

Cam Ranh Bay, Viet Nam: February 1969

Less than one hundred kilometers away from Damson's travail, the muddle of infinite perseverance amid daily routine proceeded apace at NAF-Cam Ranh.

"Dave, you busy?" Billingsgate called across the road. He was togged out in flight gear.

Lord, not Dong Ba Thin again! "Not especially. What do you need?" Ito was flying the Controller slot today; Winter, standing down, had been working on a training lesson plan.

"I got tagged at the last minute for Ito's mission; he's got some kinda medical thing. And we got incoming personnel due in over at the Air Weenies Flight Ops in about twenty minutes. Can you take my Jeep and go pick them up?" Billingsgate commonly referred to the XO's Jeep as his own. He could have made a good case in court, based on precedent; he had the vehicle far more than Major Nichols.

"Sure. I guess. Who is it? I mean what . . . officers? E.M.? ops? mechs? . . . what?"

"Don't know. The Air Force called. They don't release that kinda private info. And Group's mum on the subject." Giggling, the lieutenant turned and rumbled off, the untailored shapeless legs of the flight suit flapping like loose skin on a short, dumpy puppy.

Winter went for the Jeep and drove around the field to the Quonset that served for incoming passenger operations. He sought a spot of shade to park in, looking about ruefully. The nearest shade was somewhere kilos inland, in III or IV Corps, God forbid.

A gaggle of Vietnamese civilians—military dependents: women, children, pigs, ducks—were being herded into one corner of the building, exuding a foul miasma. The Viets tended to throw up in aircraft, and the group now off-loading a C-123 appeared to have acted in concert, complying with habit. Winter never doubted the efficacy of cultural affectations.

The airman told him the C-130 was about ten minutes out, and any passengers would be bused over. Winter fled the fragrance of vomit and duck shit and soiled baby clothes to sit in the sun. In the open, it only smelled of Viet Nam; admittedly a curse of its own . . . but a lesser one.

A squeal of brakes woke him, destroying a luscious dream. He was out at Raymond Lake near the town where he was born, but gone from for years, lying on a muddy so-called "beach." It resembled a beach only in that it bordered water, but it served for swimmers who would get away from city pools and chlorine and watchful lifeguards. He was on the verge of drifting off, his head cushioned on Helen's flat belly. The sun had had its effect on her, too, and soft, burbling sounds—not quite snores—came from her partly, deliciously, open mouth. She smelled . . . *fantastic*: suntan cream and girlish perspiration, the perfume of sun-warmed, soft flesh, and a slight muskiness that stirred him. And then, a squeal of brakes!

Seated in the Jeep in a lazy, after-lunch state, he'd drifted off. His mood, disrupted, quickly shattered when he remembered Helen had gone off to Ole Miss, married some jock in NROTC who went on to a career in Subs, while she sequed into an alcoholic punch board for non-deployed sailors. Winter stirred, straightened his cap, and waited for the U/I passengers to alight from the blue Air Force bus. He thought again, as he had before when he saw Bimbo Billingsgate acting as chauffeur: what the hell was an officer doing handling transport duties? Just lucky, I guess, he thought, but he didn't care. Better that than sitting on his ass reading regs.

The first three off the bus were airmen. Then an Army Spec-5 who reminded him of Magic Marvin. No, it was an Army Spec-5 who *was* MM. *Nevva hachi, GI.* Seeking a connect, he thought it had to be someone else; that couldn't be SP5 Marvin O. Marsh stepping off the bus. But then, the specialist looked up, saw

Winter, dropped the B-4 bag he was carrying, and popped a salute. The mesmerized warrant officer didn't return the honor. The proprieties were out the window; he was out of his element, couldn't comprehend. The last time—

And behind Winter's former clerk, Luther Brenner stepped off the bottom step onto the tarmac, grimacing in the sun. *Warrant Officer* Luther Brenner, by God! WO-1 bar and all.

Enduring the double mirage while just emerging from the sun-suffused nap, Winter suffered a rush of disorientation. His mind refused to even try to find logic in the presence of these two familiar figures. He sat, gaping, and later could not refute Brenner's assurance that his mouth had hung open.

He sat. He could do nothing else.

"Mister Winter . . ." Marsh said, still holding his salute.

"Salute the man, Dave, goddammit, or he'll stand there on point until we all turn into Vietnamese quail." No doubt about it: *that* was Brenner.

"Well . . . shit. I guess . . . what . . . *How the hell . . . What the hell's all this?*" He touched the steering wheel and burned his hand; he wasn't hallucinating.

He jumped from the Jeep, gave Magic Marvin the honor and held it long. He cut away the salute, stepped forward and grabbed the young soldier by the arm. "Jeez-us, it is *not* good to see you here, Marve . . . but I'm so glad to see you," Winter said with fervor. Logic could wait.

"Yes, sir. I've been excited since I first started paperwork. Didn't know I would wind up in the same outfit with you, but, you know . . . my network. Billy Tuckwell—Sergeant Tuckwell—from ASA Europe, now in the personnel shop at Group. He told me where you'd wound up, made it work for me. Glad to be here, sir." Though he couldn't have been in country many days, Winter knew, he saw the mousey eyebrows were already bleached from their field gray color to white in the Southeast Asian sun.

Turning to Brenner, Winter said, "I suppose you can explain all this. The bar. Your presence. So forth."

"Bet your ass, Chief. Just so happy to be back in the land of lackeys, laggards, dullards and louts." Brenner's face did not light up with a smile; that would not be Brenner. But Winter could detect a sense of excitement in subtle body language, and tics across his ex-sergeant's face. "Parroting Balzac, 'Nothing about me surprises me, and nothing should surprise you.'"

"Well, don't let's forget the good stuff," Winter said.

"Yeah. Uhh, good stuff. What's that?"

"Those are double-u-one bars, right."

"Right again. Boy, nobody can fool you, Chief."

"My point exactly. 'Chief.' And you're not. Not a chief. You're *still* junior, and I'm waiting for my salute. Didn't you learn anything from Marvin here?" He waited, watching the surprise leach color from Brenner's cheeks.

When he'd given it sufficient time, and just as Brenner popped his hand up to the brim of his cap, Winter laughed and threw his arms around his best friend. "Got you!"

* * *

The new men's arrival coincided with a beach party, GI talk for a drunken *fête* planned wa-a-ay back, early that morning, before the arrivals. When a beach party was committed on the patio of the Sandbag, anyone was welcome, though the food was set aside for 1st RR people, their specific guests: donut dollies, nurses, or visiting firemen. Pay-as-you-go bar. Wholesale.

The three of them, Winter, Brenner, and Marsh sat on broken lawn chairs on the SeeBee Memorial patio and went through the catechism of catching up. When Winter pointed out how fortunate they were to have arrived just in time for a party, Brenner labeled it serendipity. Marsh stared at the new warrant, awaiting further explanation. He didn't wait long.

The CO was out on a mission, along with Bimbo Billingsgate, CW4 Surtain, two other pilots, and the ops and crewchief; but Winter had introduced the two new assignees to most of the rest of the company who felt an obligation to attend all beach rites.

"Right after you left, sir. Put my request in—had to extend a year—and made a few phone calls. It all moved rather smoothly," Marsh explained in response to Winter's query.

"How'd your family take it? I guess they're blaming me. Your mom already thought I'd corrupted you." Winter had spoken with Marsh's mother on one occasion on the phone, and she seemed very nice. Marsh later told him his mother had been quite taken with her son's boss.

"Well, they're pretty much used to me going my own way. Didn't have to explain to Dad. Hell, he loved World War Two, to hear him tell it."

"Still—"

"Can't you tell, Dave. This was in the works all along," Brenner said easily.

"You, too? Did you plan this little reunion all along?" Winter asked. "And the bar . . . I never thought you'd get the one oh-five-one slot they opened this year. You said yourself, when you went before the board, that the word was it was surely going to go to Sergeant Marshall at Rothwesten. And they only made one appointment, right?"

"Wrong. After the board, they upped it to four. Not many took a shot at it because they thought they were only making one, and the odds were long. But when it increased to four, it put me in a good position. Marshall was only third. I was actually the second one notified. Appointed on Christmas Day. Unusual, but that's the day the orders came through to the field station, and I talked to the XO and told him I wanted it as soon as possible. Biggest problem was finding enough sober officers, besides the colonel, to hold the commissioning ceremony. And nobody, not a single warrant officer in the station, had an extra brown scarf. After the ceremony, I had to give back the one I borrowed. Cheap shits." Brenner laughed.

"The rest is history," he added. "Like you, background in ARDF, so when I had to take a command transfer, I asked for the two two four. No problem. Once there—now that took a bit of doing, to get to the First. We really must upgrade the quality of personnel people at battalion. Amazingly dull, unimaginative people." He threw wide his arms, "And here we are."

Reminiscing over fellow soldiers, outrageous events, and vital memoirs, they talked their way through an injudicious number of San Miguels as the evening wore on. The three of them paid no attention to the ongoing activities about them on the patio; they'd spent their time in similar pursuits and there was nothing of note. The few females who had chosen to attend, and managed to find rides to NAF, were not of interest. Except for one new Air Force nurse, whom Brenner kept his sights on, the motley collection were, as he put it, "without merit." Not dogs, exactly, he agreed; merely unaccustomed to admiration for beauteous assets.

Running the gamut of subjects, the three had advanced to the point of gentle reviews of common pasts and conjectural futures, until a few minutes after 2300 when the alert siren went off. At that stage of the beach party, it had a surreal quality.

All movement stopped. As a sign of the seriousness, drinkers stopped drinking. Those seated jumped to their feet, some glancing around in panic; others, older hands, without panic but with questioning concern. One of the MARKET TIME Navy pilots took the opportunity to cut two of the not-so-pursued heifers out of the herd and push them toward the nearest bunker. As they moved, some of the pilots of a new Navy patrol squadron who had not been in country long enough to become accustomed to alerts, preceded the women into the nearest bunker.

* * *

Only minutes later, a runner from the Orderly Room approached a different bunker, one set of billets over, where he presumed some First RRC people might have gone to ground. He called into the black space, "Any Crazy Cats in there?"

"Yo."

"Here. A bunch."

"Yeah, here. What's the alert. We heard no incoming."

There was no answer; the runner had run on, elsewhere. ¿Que pasta?

When the panic and noise of the initial Alert response—assuming an attack—had settled into a heightened but extended state of anxiety, a voice cut through the fug of body odors and dank, moldy air in the bunker. "That Mister Winter up there?" came from deep in the murky bunker interior.

"Yeah, who's that?" Winter didn't recognize the voice.

"Sergeant Alvarez, sir. From Group. We were in the Third together, back in 'sixty-four."

"Well, hell, good Sarge. How's it I find you hiding in here with Squids and things?"

A chorus of groans, chuckles and threats arose about the sandbagged walls.

"Up here T.D.Y. Personnel things," Alvarez replied, maneuvering his way forward to the bunker entrance, ignoring muttered imprecations. "How long you been here, sir? You assigned to the First?"

Winter had a flash of recall. It was Alvarez who'd crashed through the Orderly Room screen door at Davis Station and subdued the mad DEROS-ing Specialist Miller in the famous (Acting) First Sergeant Pepperdine confrontation in 1964. Hell, he thought, that was in the fall, right after he moved into the Air Section. Comes now under the heading of *history*.

"Yeah, controller on CRAZY CAT. Been here 'bout two months. I was at the two-twenty-fourth, S-three for about four months before that. How come I didn't run across you at Tan Son Nhut?" Winter responded.

"I've only been back in country about three weeks. Came from Shemya." Another, smaller but vigorous ripple of groans went up; there *were* ASA types in the bunker. Shemya, in the Aleutians! Where there was a girl behind every tree. And there wasn't a goddamned bit of greenery taller than lichen in the whole chain of islands.

"When the alert's over," Winter spoke loudly to overcome the babble of voices now rising about the bunker, "let's stop over at the Sandbag and catch up."

"Sandbag? I thought we were *in* the sandbag." Alvarez's voice, questioning, held an element of humor. Winter presumed he'd got the word on the Sandbag before he left Sai Gon.

"Sandbag, singular. We're in sandbags, plural. Sandbag's the downhill version of the Sandman Lounge, of questionable fame and absent virtue." He leaned out and searched the sky. Nothing of an alien nature falling yet.

"The bar. Yeah, I heard. But that's only officers, right?" Alvarez knew his place in the scheme of military things.

"It's for anyone who can crawl on their scuffed knees into the space and reach the bar. O.K.? Follow me over there; I'll meet you outside when the All-Clear sounds." Winter had the whimsical thought that the last interface they'd had, Winter had followed Alvarez through the smashed OR door. It was he who took the rifle from Miller while Alvarez wrestled him to the floor. Or was it the table? Good man!

* * *

After a period of dead time, the runner reappeared, asking again, "Any Crazy Cats in there?"

"Hey, asshole. We already provided that info," a voice called. "Get your shit together. You came and asked and left and haven't told us dick. We've heard no ordnance. What's the alert?"

"Sappers. Coming ashore just across the highway from N.A.F. gate."

"Swimming?"

"Boats. Sampans, fishing boats." The runner fled, staying in his pattern. Why had he come? Winter wondered.

"Ahh, shit. Now I gotta go draw my weapon," one malcontent griped to another.

"Better that than *not* draw your weapon." Crazy Cats began exiting the bunker.

Just as Winter, Brenner, and Alvarez emerged, a loud explosion filled the humid night air. They ran to the space between barracks and peeked around the corner, looking toward the sound which had come from the beach area. A column of smoke hung in the moonlit night air, just above the gate guard shack at the end of the NAF street where it met the coast road. But the guard shack still stood.

"Christ, a goddamned satchel charge. They really are in our face," Winter shouted.

"Hell, Dave, I don't even have a weapon issued."

"C'mon, we'll find you something." He led Brenner toward the Arms Room. He felt sudden panic, looked around, but could not see Magic Marvin anywhere. He didn't remember if he made it into the bunker with them or not.

They heard rifle fire from an M-16 coming from the direction of the gate. Magic Marvin would have to wait. Red tracers arced out over the sea. Green tracers returned.

At the arms room, with .45s issued, chagrined they hadn't been issued rifles, the two warrants and one sergeant headed back toward the BOQ, intent upon ensuring everyone was alert, outside, and armed. Passing the Orderly Room, Winter heard the First Sergeant yell, "Tscheib. Specialist Tscheib."

"Here, First Sergeant," came from the dark toward the hangers.

"Get the duty six-by and load all those ladies and get them the hell off this compound. We're under attack."

"But—"

"But's ass, Tscheib. Get it in gear. Get these gals outta here. We'll be in all kinds of shit if one of them gets blown up over here." The First Shirt turned away, barking orders at another hapless soul. Winter heard the response of Sergeant Boch, telling Top he was without weapon.

"Sammy, here. Take my forty-five. I've still got my own in my room?" Winter offered.

"Boch! Stay where you are. I'm gonna need you. Soon as we figure out just how serious this is. We're likely gonna be busy," the First Sergeant growled. "Tscheib, get moving!"

Winter and Brenner dashed across open space and crouched behind sandbags of another bunker several buildings closer to the gate. From there they could see a gate guard returning fire at bursts of AK-47 fire from the beach area. "They gotta know they're in a world of shit," Winter said, nodding toward the firefight. "The Zips. With the alarm sounded, this compound'll be swarming with APs, MPs, and Koreans in about two minutes. They'll pull out," Winter prophesied.

"Don't bet your ass on it, Dave. Keep your head down." Brenner was doing his Combat Kelly thing, on his belly, low, looking around the edge of the sandbags at ground level.

The firing died down: first the green tracers ceased, the red trails dwindled, stopped. Good! Winter thought, noting the gate guard's fire discipline. Or else, he's dead.

They hadn't heard the truck, its start-up lost in the exchange of gunfire, until it roared past them, horn blowing, lights flashing. The lights went back off as it passed the three, but they could see the hurricane fencing gate swinging open. Someone had done their job and called Security at the gate. So the guard probably was not dead. Tscheib and his cargo of assorted femininity thundered through the gate, squealed into a tight left turn, and roared off up the coast road. No green tracers pursued it.

Two Jeeps loaded with Air Police carrying riot guns and M-16s skidded to a stop just inside the gate. The cops deployed in and around the gate shack, and there was still no firing. Winter and Brenner held their position, waiting for developments. They could see an occasional figure dash across the faintly lighted area around the gate, then disappear into the murk. They wondered if the NVA had been subdued, had gone away, or better yet, were killed. No one offered answers. They burrowed down to wait.

After some fifteen minutes of little action—an occasional M-16 round from a nervous Air Policeman—they heard the high-pitched whine of a straining motor, overlaying the growl of gears, and they watched as the two-and-a-half-ton truck raced back down the coast road and tried to make the turn into NAF without slowing, a feat that would have challenged a sports car. Too much speed for poor road conditions; the surface was silted with loose, dry sand. And the gate was again shut.

As the guard ran for the gate, an explosion just outside the fence lit up the sky. The truck ploughed across the narrow entrance and, just before hitting the fence, flipped in a constrained half-gainer and smashed down onto the road. It skidded several yards and came up abruptly against the low berm along the base of the fence. Instant silence. Then, as quickly, a chorus of shouts, warnings, imprecations arose from the MPs, unseen in the murk of the night against the sea. These were answered by a medley of confused orders and counter-orders from strangers.

When Winter, Brenner, and Alvarez reached the guard shack, the gate was open. They could see across the coast road a squad of armed men, advancing in line, moving away, toward the water. A brief flurry of firing broke out. The two relaxed: red tracers. The Security Police were clearing the beach. But that explosion . . . ?

An Air Force Air Police sergeant was assessing the scene, warning his people to keep their eyes open, pointing toward the sea, and at the same time trying to pry open the passenger door of the truck which faced the sky. The truck lay on the driver's side. The cop, standing on the up-ended running board, wrenched the door open, leaned and reached a hand down inside.

As the Crazy Cats approached the truck, the AP stepped back down off the upended step and said to no one, "He's dead." The ones who heard turned away, uneasily.

"Shit," Winter said.

"One of ours?" Brenner asked.

"Yeah, a linguist. I think. Spec-four Scheib left out of here, driving a six-by. I presume that's his truck. And him. Like we can spare a linguist."

"Jesus, Dave. You're getting into the swing of this thing, aren't you?"

"No!" he said quickly. "I just meant . . . this was so useless. I didn't know the guy well; flown a couple of missions with him. He was okay. Now, this. And for what?"

Brenner's expression was closed, his eyes exhibiting a hooded aspect. "So what's new?" he asked "It's not like he was a battle casualty."

"My very thesis, to use a phrase of yours. I just mean . . . this thing just goes on, and we're losing almost as many through non-hostile-fire incidents as we are in combat. I'm beginning to wonder . . . ." Winter stared blankly into Alvarez's face.

"The truck accident reminds me. Remember Mouton?" Brenner said.

"Mouton. Mou—Oh, yeah! Bad Aibling. Oh-five-aich. Troublesome lad. Had trouble with Magic Marvin in the club. Yeah, I remember him, all right."

"Driving one of the Ops trucks with a hut on the back, coming back from maneuvers, he jammed the whole kit-and-caboodle up under that arching overpass on the *Autobahn* near Ingolstadt."

"Ran off the road? Drinking? What?" Although not exhibiting great surprise, Winter showed interest in past associations.

"No, apparently not. Just driving in the far right lane and jammed that sucker right up into the span of the bridge. Most guys assigned to drive would have known about that hazard, stayed in the left lane. USASAEUR puts out a hazard warning every year before maneuvers. Of course, Mouton probably would've ignored any such official documentation. Maybe now, though, the Germans will take our complaints to heart. We've been bitching about that delicate sweeping arch as a driving hazard for years."

"Yeah," Winter agreed. "What do you think the odds are? Mouton injured?"

"No. Started a campaign to get the U.S. government to sue the krauts for the cost of repairs to the van." Brenner chuckled and shook his head.

"Anyhow, thanks. I realize you organized this jiffy little welcoming party, and with no notice at that, and it's not that I don't appreciate the gesture, but can we forget about the proprieties. We've got a war to win!" Brenner said.

"First thing tomorrow, Tiger," Winter promised him.

* * *

Ambling through the humid night breeze off the South China Sea that hovered some two hundred meters away, the two men reminisced: Pepperdine, Miller, SFC Peebo, other commonly serving soldiers they both remembered.

"Oh!" Alvarez came to an abrupt halt. He said, "You were in

Asmara, as I remember. Did you ever know a sergeant major by name of Torrence? Jeremiah Torrence?"

"Sure, knew him when he was First Sergeant of Ops Company in Asmara. Musta' been 'sixty-two when he came in there. Old soldier, even then." Winter looked off with a distracted air toward the surf he heard beyond the coast road. "I'd have thought he'd've retired by now. I knew him, as I said, because he was First Sergeant before I left Kagnew. But he was also one of the few guys I knew there who was from Mississippi. My home," he added with inference.

"Then you'll want to know: Torrence was Battalion Sar'nt Major of the Three-oh-third. Long Binh. I knew him, too, from Herzo Base, 'sixty-six. Thing is, he was wounded last week in a mortar attack on the compound..

"How bad?"

"Don't know. Head wound. They med-evac-ed him to the P.I. Haven't heard anything."

Winter stood, mesmerized now by the surf. "First time I've heard Torrence's name or thought of him in years." They walked on a few meters, when Winter stopped again. "Tell you a funny story. That is, if you can stand the long drawn-out version." When Alvarez laid a curious gaze on him, Winter was forced to explain. "My mentor, Brenner, says I can't tell anything in less than installments." He chuckled. "'bout right.

"Anyhow," he began as they moved on toward the Sandbag, "Jerry was First Sergeant in Ops Company there at Kagnew Station. Crazy Bruce Phillipson—you know Bruce, don't you? He was in the Third with us in 'sixty-four, 'sixty-five."

"Sure. Big mutha . . ."

"Yeah," Winter agreed wryly. "Anyhow, Crazy Bruce and Hatin' Harry Spruance, Leeks, and Darmanian, and some others were down-country somewhere . . . likely on the way to or from Massawa—" he stopped and reflected. "Musta been on the way back from the CIAAO Hotel and driving that damned old three-quarter ton that always vapor-locked on the mountain road. They rounded a blind curve and came upon a dead baboon, crushed on the edge of the road. Not unusual; probably targeted by one of the Italian truck drivers who drove that road regularly. But when they pulled up, just to look, I guess, a baby ran out from the rocks. Turned out, it must've been the baby's mother that was dead. And the baby—a little shit, all eyes and screech—was jumping up and down, screaming the way they do, and alternately trying to shield the mother from these big savage human things."

"Well, upshot was, Bruce insisted on getting the baby away from that already-moldering corpse. And when he went to try to shoo it away, the creature leapt at him and clamped onto his leg. Didn't bite him or anything; just held onto his leg for dear life. Must have transferred his maternal instincts to Bruce.

"Bruce said he didn't know what else to do. Thing was too young to survive on his own, and Bruce, for all his 'don't-give-a-shit-about-much' attitude, took to that baby baboon. Immediately bonded with him. Put him in the truck and held him all the way back up the mountain. By the time they got to Kagnew, the baby was asleep, still wrapped about his leg. Bruce put a shelter half over him and carried him into the barracks."

"No shit! What was he going to do with him?" Alvarez was always one step ahead.

"I don't think Bruce ever even thought about that. He just . . . well, he let instinct take over and he cared for that baby like he would a human child. Bruce was in a room down the hall from me, then, and Ratty Mac and Godolphin and . . . can't remember who else, but of like mind, all lived in that room. And it became home for the baboon.

"Bruce and his roommates fed the thing from a bottle at first, bringing milk from the messhall. After a few days, when someone with a farm background told him the 'boon needed more substantive food, they began bringing other stuff from the chow hall." Winter smiled, and raised his gaze to a cloudless sky—nothing falling: neither snow nor rain nor rockets nor mortar rounds—noting the clearance. "Went on, say-y-y, five or six weeks. All Bravo Trick knew about the 'boon, and some others who had contacts there. Nobody believed they could keep it a secret very long. The houseboy who worked Bruce's room took exceptional exception to the beast. Eritreans don't cotton much to baboons. Lots-a bad folk lore and such.

"And they *couldn't* keep it a secret. One afternoon, while we were working a set of swings and nobody was in the bay or the Bravo rooms, First Shirt—Torrence, at the time—did a walk-through. I don't think he ever knew or even suspected anything was going on. Just a casual walk-through, at random. But when he went into Bruce's room, first thing he did was step in baboon shit.

"Well, the C.O. was adamant about keeping pets. Wouldn't allow dogs. Made Grogan get rid of his cat, some kind of Manx or something. Fine cat. Hell, the captain even argued with the major who was Ops Officer, trying to convince him to get rid of the two gazelle that ran free in between the two security fences. That got him nowhere," he said, suddenly remembering with a slight pang. "Then the damned sentry dogs killed the gazelle when some dumb shit let them get into the run without putting the Tommies in their hutch.

"But, no go on pets. Torrence didn't much give a rat's ass one way or the other, I think, but . . . good soldier, good First Sergeant, he had to do something. 'course, didn't take him long to work out who the monkey belonged to. The baboon. Called Bruce on the carpet, read him the riot act, and threatened to take a stripe if the 'boon was there even one more hour. And Bruce, bless his cantankerous big heart, gave in to the order.

"If you remember Bruce—'Crazy' Bruce, appropriately named—then you'll remember he didn't sweat the small shit very much. But I think he knew the gig was folding. Didn't want the baby taken and put down by the post vet. So he borrowed Marangia's old Fiat, and him and Mac took the 'boon back down on the mountain, somewhere near Nefasit, to turn him loose. Got out of the car and walked, carrying the baboon, well off the road into the mountain scrub. Put it down with some stuff from the mess hall, which the 'boon immediately chowed down on. Tried to walk quietly away. But the damned thing set up a screeching fit, took after Bruce. Chased him back to the car. When they got it started and took off, it followed the car a good half mile back up the mountain. Bruce said he could hear it screaming until they were well out of sight, around a bend. Bruce said, even miles away." Winter concluded the disjointed tale with a poignant sniff. "I think he still hears that baby baboon screaming, sometimes."

Alvarez scratched his ear and looked sideways at Winter. "Well, Top was just doing his job, I guess. But he's fucked up now, for sure. Bad head wound. Haven't heard anymore on him." As some kind of excuse for his lack of knowledge, he added, "I didn't know him well."

"I'd kinda like to find out what happens to him. He was from down close to my home, in Jackson. Some one of those little country towns, down route forty-nine, south of the capital . . . or one thirty-seven. Nice guy, I always thought. And I remember, too, he'd been in Korea. Early on in 'fifty-one, with the Seventh Infantry Division. Before I ever got in country." He said, turning in the door to the crowded Sandbag, "One of your better Lifers I ever knew."

chapter ten

Baldur's Bale Fires

Cam Ranh Bay, Viet Nam: March 1969

Specialist Five Marvin O. Marsh basked in a state approaching grace. He had found, as had his mentor Chief Warrant Officer Winter before him, that the Sandman Lounge stocked his first choice of the world's fine whiskies: Bushmills. Maybe the only thing the north of Ireland did better than the Republic. Jameson, a southern affectation, was the champagne of whiskies; Bushmills, nectar of the gods. Winter had introduced Marsh to the Irish nectar, and he partook to keep the faith.

When Marsh asked for another drink, acting-bartender Bimbo Billingsgate, as well as Marsh's two other drinking companions, Warrants Winter and Brenner, reacted in unison with elevated eyebrows. No one was counting, but this was the specialist's fifth. Billingsgate looked questioningly at Winter, then Brenner.

"I didn't take him to raise," Brenner said, palms out in denial.

"Nor I." All three looked curiously at Winter when he spoke.

"Well, all right. That's not exactly true. I did take him in charge," Winter fatuously acknowledged. "But he's raised. He's a growed-up little soldier and he can damned well drink what he chooses. Pour, Bimbo!" he commanded.

"A post-pubescent, grown-up, little soldier-toddler," was Brenner's rejoinder.

"Well, screw him if he can't hold his liquor," Winter came back.

Billingsgate poured another double Irish. "Didn't take you two long to pick up on the Sandbag rules of engagement."

"Done this shit. Winter and I, together. Asmara. Tan Son Nhut. Rothwesten. Gartow. Bad Aibling.," Brenner commented, pushing forward his goblet for another ration of Chianti. Winter recognized the drinking vessel Brenner had brought with him. It was a parting gift years before from a bar slut in Taipei who professed to Luther, "Rosie love you too much."

Lieutenant Billingsgate, delegated Club Officer, had found for the new warrant a quantity of jug Chianti. Cheap, but of inestimable bouquet. Characterizing the wine as swill, Billingsgate argued to Brenner that he wouldn't know the difference: warrant officers did not possess the social graces to distinguish among vintages.

"... and considering that's the only Chianti this side of Hong Kong, it must taste pretty fair. Right, Luther?" Billingsgate dogged him.

"*Damn* fine, my cherubic *sommelier.* Relatively light . . . a charming little beverage. Barely tart, a bit fruity, but gracious—"

"F'r God's sake, Mister Winter. I forgot to tell you," Magic Marvin blurted out.

The trio looked at him with surprise. He had been sitting quietly, drinking . . . and still pronouncing his sibilants. They waited.

"I was on the horn to Group this A-em, and who do you think I found out's coming here? For assignment."

For once, Brenner did not attack the clerk's fractured syntax.

When no one played the game, Marvin dropped his bomb: "The Wine Troll."

There was immediate, enthusiastic silence.

After long seconds, Billingsgate, rinsing a glass, said, "What's a Wine Troll?"

"Exactly," Brenner replied. "Not who. What."

Winter exploded. "What the hell is this? A B.A. homecoming? Jeez-us!" He turned toward the bartender. "Wine Troll: an anomaly in our time. In our world. In our army," he intoned ponderously. "But, fair question. What *is* a Wine Troll? To start, he's a P.F.C. Or he was when I left Bad Aibling last September.

"An oh-five-eight—oh-five-aich—in Collection Branch at B.A. Name's Darmanian. Luther and I knew him in Asmara in 'sixty-one or two. One of the few draftees to wind up in A.S.A," Winter said, convinced the Army had erred in so doing. "Came from a wealthy family. Had a degree from some Pennsylvania school—Lehigh, maybe. Hated everything about the military, but did his job well. Then got himself so enraptured with Moselle and Rhine wines that he . . . ceased to function. Outside his job, that is. Reenlisted in the midst of a raging drunk. Still a good op; but with no initiative. Alcoholic burnout." Winter's voice tailed off in melancholy.

"Well, there is a bit more to Troll's story, Dave. Don't forget Tiger Lady," said Brenner.

"Jeez-us, did you have to remind me?"

When no one elaborated, Bimbo said, "Hey, you can't leave us on a 'Tiger Lady' note."

Brenner signed up for the revelation. "Let's see, guess that would have been early in nineteen sixty-two," he looked at Winter, "sometime before you DEROS-ed."

Winter nodded; he remembered it all; he just didn't want to talk about it.

"Darmanian, a bright kid from a good home, had a college degree, and was your average all-around American lad. For more than a year at Kagnew, I don't think he ever went into a bar downtown Asmara. He'd drink a beer occasionally in the Oasis, and at either of the R-and-R centers, Massawa or Keren, he'd have a drink at the bar. But not downtown. He didn't take any chances with the bar girls and whores, that way, I guess."

"Yeah, until . . ." Winter offered.

"Yes, until Tiger Lady." Brenner smiled smugly. "You know, Dave, I was the one who actually discovered Tiger Lady. Though not by that name. I followed Harry on one of his forays into the Bausgh one night, and waited while he got his ashes hauled. We always tried to go in pairs for such activities," he said pointedly to Bimbo and Magic Marvin, "to keep down guys getting rolled or worse. Especially in the Bausgh; that was a rough side of town.

"Anyhow, sitting in Tina's waiting room while she did the honors with Harry, I was looking through an Italian magazine and I looked up to find this very dark girl—woman— staring at me through the drawn curtains. Must have been a hallway there I didn't know about. Anyhow, she swished the curtains aside, and I was suitably impressed. She was young, and a large-size girl. She had more tits than any three Ethiopian bargirls, and a sexy body everywhere else. She looked well-fed, not always the case with the Ethis. Well, naturally, things developed. She was inviting me into her space—not exactly a room, but curtained off well enough.

"She spoke zero English, whereas most of the bar girls and whores had some English. I later learned she was Sudanese, new in-country and a relative of Tina's, and it didn't surprise me. She was that much bigger. But I have to tell you, when she dropped her housedress, she had a knockout body. She was a black Gina Lollobrigida. She was good in bed, too. But unlike Cathy, she didn't go for anything but straight-up, Missionary sex. Nothing hinky. And when she came out after Harry's finished with Tina, he got a look at her and wanted to go for seconds. But, as usual, Harry had no money left, and she was new, and she didn't grant good times on credit." Brenner had the attention of everyone on the patio at this point.

"But Harry spread the word, and pretty soon, she's got more customers than any other gal on the circuit. Never did know her name, and I don't know who labeled her Tiger Lady, but there was no denying her attractions. Mostly those monumental tits and lush hips. And Troll, not then known as Troll—Darmanian— heard about her and for the first time, he went downtown on a lancing trip. Set out, determined, just from what he'd heard, to take Tiger Lady to transports of delight she'd never known. I have no idea where he got the notion he might be able to do that."

"He told me," Winter said, "that the picture he'd formed in his mind, after hearing you guys talk about her, was so appealing that it convinced him to forsake his vows and have a go. I don't know if he really had vows, or was just . . . well, then he was a bit shy."

"I know. That's the impression I got. That he just sort of fell into a good thing. So, anyhow, when he set out to subdue the Tiger Lady—" and here Brenner looked about, saw that he'd drawn a crowd, and was in his element "—he made a job of it. Apparently, he had something going for him. I heard he was getting her regularly at reduced rates, and he even took her down to the Italian restaurant a couple of times. Only case I ever heard of a G.I. squiring a whore into the better class of town. If there was a better. Well, except for Harry of course, who took Big Mary Wassaf to Keren and tried to get her in the R-and-R center hotel."

"So, just another jump-job, right?" Bimbo Billingsgate said.

"Well, so it might have been. At first. But I think Darmanian, for whatever reason— and there were other hints of some dark side to his upbringing, wealthy family or not—he said he was in love with Tiger Lady. Not just lust; he insisted it was love. It got so bad, his infatuation, that he began overstaying breaks at her place in the Bausgh, and during sets, he'd take off downtown and not get back for the next trick. Watch NCO put him on details a couple of times, then just gave up and turned it over to the first shirt. Torrence came down hard on him. Well, you'd expect him to, wouldn't you. Mississippi background, Torrence could abide Darmanian's screwing around with a black woman, but when he started that shit about being in love, things got sticky. There were commiserative nods about the circle of drinkers.

"When Top's tricks did no good with Darmanian," Brenner soldiered on, "he upped the ante and turned him in, to the Old Man. Captain Isaacs called him in, read him the riot act, and confined him to the post. Yeah, like that's going to work! He should have handcuffed his ass to his bed frame. Not a full day until the kid's back downtown, shagging Tiger Lady.

"In the meanwhile, Darmanian must have written to his sister, who was in grad school then, telling her about this inspiring love miracle that's occurred, and how he's determined to save this gal from a life of sin, or some such shit. Thought his sister was his soulmate. But the sister got on the phone to mama, who wrote a letter to the C.O., demanding that he do something to wreck this relationship. Captain tried again. Short of putting a prisoner chaser on him, there was no way to keep the kid on post. Darmanian, not knowing his sister's blown the whistle on him, writes her again, telling her how the First Sergeant and the Commander can't do anything to put a crimp in his activities.

There were chuckles about the table. Everyone thought they knew where this was going.

"The next missive that rockets across the Atlantic came from the office of Mrs. D's congressman, and he's not asking; he's *demanding* a stop be put to Darmanian's exotic doltage, or the C.O. will be in some deep doo-doo with D.A. Captain slaps Darmanian with an Article 15, busts him to P.F.C. for disobeying an order, and gives him two week's confinement in the lockup. Yeah, you know what's coming, right. The day he's released, he doesn't even get back to the barracks. He heads straight for Tiger Lady's." Brenner sighed; he'd known all along where this was going.

"This might still be going on, playing out in a hundred different ploys, but I guess the constant appearance of M.P.s, driving up with siren going, brakes squealing, was putting the crimp into Tiger Lady's business. *She* gets one of the English-speaking *gharry* drivers to bring her to the post, where she entrances the gate guard and gets a phone call to the C.O., who allows her on post. He interviews her, through the driver, and gets the message. Chances are, looking at her—and she always dressed to show off her assets—he might have understood Darmanian's fascination. But he had all he needed, with her making a complaint.

"Can't have local nationals creating a rift with resident American forces. C.O. zipped a FLASH message back to the Hall, got Darmanian transferred out of country. Sent him up to Germany to finish out his four-year enlistment, of which he had some two years left. And that's where, in his broken love despair, he discovered the attractions of Moselle wines, and *Voila!* Thus was created the Wine Troll.

When his two years were up, and drunk at the time, he reenlisted, took his reenlistment leave and flew to Asmara. But Tiger Lady had moved on, some said to Cairo. I think it's more likely she went home, set up shop in Khartoum. She certainly had the financial wherewithall, after a couple of years in Erritrea. With all those empty G.I. wallets left in Asmara."

There was a silent sense of contentment over the group. Wine Troll was now explained. No longer a mystery, though in Winter's, Brenner's, and Marsh's minds, still a threat.

* * *

"I hold no wake for Troll, but I see no reason he should be foisted off on the First," Brenner said after a long, reflective pause, leaving behind any hint of mythology. "Troll won't answer the criticality of this mission. Maybe we can broker a reassignment." He spoke with the assurance of a fait accompli. "Hell, he's an oh-five-aich."

"I was told it was a done deal," Marsh contributed. They knew immediately he'd already made efforts toward revision. No one could figure the 05H assigned to a linguist job slot.

"Well, into each life a little shit must dribble, true. But nothing's a done deal, Marvin, until we're all dead. You should know that, slickie boy," Brenner explained. Without prior exposure to the common Viet Nam expression, Marsh yet understood the pejorative nature of it.

"What do you think, Luther? We maybe better take every warm body we can get, and worry later about fitting him in?" Winter proposed, making a declaration into a question.

"You're thinking, exalted leader, but you're thinking wrong. Especially regarding Troll. Don't even entertain the thought," Brenner said..

"That's right. We take him, he'd fill a slot," Magic Marvin, the eternal administrative guru, pointed out. "As far as Personnel is concerned, that cuts down on our needs by one."

"Likely. Now there's in-depth perspective," Bimbo chimed in.

"Bells," Brenner said in an aside.

"What?" Magic Marvin said. "D'jou say 'bells'?"

As Winter looked on, silent, pondering the tone of Brenner's voice, and expecting deviation from reality, Brenner expanded.

"Church bells. Our solution," he assured them. "The sound of church bells reduces a troll to a pile of rubble." Simple as that, his tone implied.

"Luther—" Winter began warningly.

Billingsgate let out a sharp bark. "Right. Gotcha! Turn the fucker into pebbles."

"I thought I was the one getting drunk," Marsh muttered.

The new warrant lectured on pedantically: "Trolls are primarily builders of giant structures. Dark figures in mythology, they contract with humans to construct towers, walls, buildings, even dams. And bridges. Especially bridges. Trolls live under bridges, you know. Their price for their labor is taken in human souls, and they command payment, not only for the labor but for the soil upon which the structure is built. Trolls own the earth, of course."

After a pause of embarrassing silence, then an unsourced "I see-e-e," a babble of the other three voices drowned out Brenner's litany. A joke, pointed disdain, re-hashed scuttlebutt. Anything to avoid a Brenneristic departure. But, having found a niche, he was not to be denied.

"Trolls have historically been cheated of their wages—souls—and that's why they have a perpetual hard-on for the world. They're negative figures in myth and literature. Stiffing them on their wages, though, is why they steal babies, seduce wives, and otherwise fuck up the farm."

Assessing his friend's degree of drunk, Winter felt duty bound to cover for his serial lunacy. "So, that's it, then. Church bells," he said mock-seriously. In an assault of conscience, he asked, "Luther, where do you *get* this shit? I know the education thing, but for Christ's sake, half the crap you dump into the ordinary, run-of-the-mill conversation can't be part of the curriculum. You been my friend and co-hort for a few years now, and I always just let that shit slide. But I gotta tell you, sometimes . . . sometimes. . . ."

Disregarding Winter's appeal, Brenner, begrudging them a smile, a small faux assurance, said, "Another way, probably the easiest if you know the troll's name—and we do in this case—King Olaf's legend says you speak his name aloud and keep on repeating it until he vanishes."

"You mean, like 'Wine Troll. Wine Troll. Wine Troll. Wine . . .' ahh, shit," Billingsgate said, unable to stay the course.

"No, his *name*. The Wine Troll is what he *is*; his name is Darmanian. And when you pronounce it, keep on and on . . . 'Darmanian Darmanian Darmanian Darmanian Darmanian Darmanian,' et cetera, like that." Ignoring their bemused expressions, somewhere between humor and incredulity, he paused.

No one offered a mediating distraction. "Well, sounds good to me. Nothing else to be done, it seems," Billingsgate said, intent on popping another Black Label. He took a deep swallow, then murmured, "God will punish the Carling people, one day."

Into the protracted silence, Brenner injected, "Fires."

"Fires? What?" Marsh said forcefully.

"The most reliable method for ridding oneself of trolls is by lighting bonfires at crossroads, using nine kinds of wood, and hurling toadstools into the flames." Brenner had advanced to poking the air with a finger. Chianti was an equal-opportunity dram.

"I don't see why we don't just do that," Winter offered. He had a momentary flash of a non-mythical bonfire at a crossroads. Nui Ba Dinh. The sacred 105mm round, fire mission called by God. 1965. "I mean, hell. No problem finding a crossroads, and building a fire . . .? We can haul out one of the shit-burner barrels for a start. And with all those dopers across the bay, we should be able to find toadstools. Or is that mushrooms. I guess that's mushrooms," he sighed.

"We have plenty of time," Brenner responded seriously. "To use the fire device, we must wait until Saint John's Eve. June twenty-third."

A brief litany of early church teachings flittered through Winter's mind, though he could remember few specifics. Six months before Christmas. Summer solstice.

"The fires of Saint John's Eve are called Baldur's Bale Fires.

Nordic myth. Baldur, ruler of a kingdom somewhere in a cold land, struck on a way to rid his realm of trolls. Easy."

The proposed solutions, stuck in a twilight zone, were anchored solidly between madness and the desperate delusions of ancient peoples.

"Oh . . . and you can make yourself invisible to trolls by wearing a hat. No sweat."

* * *

The day Brenner finished the last of his aircraft training, Winter was on the manifest for a mission. Ito was on the same flight. The last time Ito had flown on his flight, Winter recalled, the mission had been aborted due to electrical problems on the bird. Before he met Ito for briefing and gear issue for today's scheduled flight, Winter stopped by the Orderly Room and checked his box. Several pieces of paper, all official. Nothing from Long Beach.

From deep in the stack, beneath a host of bureaucratic communications, Winter pulled out an award recommendation. He looked at the recipient's name: Tscheib, Wallace W. Startled, he realized he was looking at a recommendation for award of the Purple Heart for Wally Tscheib, the linguist killed in the truck crash during the recent sapper attack. Which made no sense. His wasn't a Purple Heart scenario; Tscheib wasn't killed in combat action against an armed enemy. He'd flipped a two-and-a-half-ton truck onto his head. Winter checked the signatures. Recommended by Captain Warren. Approved by Major Jernigan.

"What the hell does Warren have to do with Tscheib's death?" Winter asked of no one. "Tscheib was a linguist; he worked, when he worked, for Chief Ito. Or on flights, for whoever was Controller. Me, usually. Or the Ops Officer. Never Warren." Winter didn't even know what Warren's non-flying job was.

When he found him at the hangar and asked, the captain calmly replied that he was back-up for several jobs and named off a shopping list of questionable secondary functions.

Winter protested Scheib's Heart recommendation, citing AR 672-5-1, chapter-verse.

"How can you say he wasn't killed by enemy action. What about that mortar or rocket explosion that flipped his truck?" Warren argued.

"That was a satchel charge, and it was nowhere near his truck. The APs and the gate guard concurred; it had nothing to do with the wreck. Tscheib was drunk, he was speeding, he tried to take the turn too fast. He had an accident. End of story!" Winter said.

"I don't agree, Chief. Doesn't matter," the captain said commandingly. "The C.O.'s already signed off on it."

"He'll goddamned well un-sign it, then. This's not a legal recommendation. There's no point in putting this in. For one thing; I have to reference the A.P. report, and when U-SAR-Vee sees 'accident' on the form, they'll kick it back and ream our ass. And it's just flat-ass wrong. It demeans the whole system of awards. We can't give a Purple Heart to someone who doesn't warrant it, however dead he might be. Too many troops suffer and die to justify one, and it's often the only non-service award they get. Nossir, this is a no-go."

"Just put the papers through, Mister Winter. If headquarters balks, I'll take the heat."

"You won't have to take heat, Captain. This's not going forward."

Winter walked away and filed the recommendation in the back of his lower desk drawer. Though he shared the desk with other officers performing assorted other functions, no one ever opened that drawer.

Captain Warren stormed into the CO's office, bitching about the insolent warrant officer. The major called Winter in. When his A&D officer had dissected the travesty, Major Jernigan instructed Winter to bring the recommendation to him, where he promptly tore it in tiny pieces.

Winter was relieved. He had wondered what would happen when his reliance on the regs conflicted with the old boy network. Now he knew. That makes one in a row, he thought. But why the hell hadn't Jernigan deep-sixed it to start with? Why sign off on it?

* * *

The mission launched that day in aircraft, tail number '496, the bird that often displayed a nasty tendency toward electrical failure. It was the aircraft he and Ito were on previously when the mission experienced an abort for electrical instabilities.

And it was the aircraft today which aborted due to electrical problems, long before it reached operational orbit . There were no backup craft airworthy. Nothing to launch. After their short return flight, the crew stood down. But they had launched. It counted for a mission.

Checking back by the Orderly Room, just hours after he'd encountered the Purple Heart malfeasance, Winter found more paperwork. Another recommendation for award. The Army Commendation Medal this time, an ARCOM. Recipient: Tscheib, Wallace W. Recommending officer, Captain Warren. Signed off again by Major Jernigan.

After turning in his gear and allotting some thirty seconds to debrief for a mission that didn't happen, Winter went seeking answers, starting with the Captain again. He hadn't a hope of resolution. Warren, whom he found at the Sandbag, saw him coming, lowered his head toward the bar, and growled at Winter, "Now what? Misspell a word? This one's by the book, Chief. And the C.O.'s signed off." He smiled smugly.

"No, spelling's fine. Congratulations, Captain. You got something right . . . even if the entire award is bogus. Why the hell's he being recommended for an AR-COM? He didn't earn it with his suicide-by-truck. And from my observation, he didn't earn it by mission work. Barely adequate. Nice enough guy. Did his job. But not worthy of an award. For that matter . . . for any award for performance, someone in his chain-of-command has to be the recommending officer. That's Ito or me or the Ops Officer. Wanta guess what those chances are."

"Boy, you're a tight-ass, Chief. You going to cut off Air Medals to the troops, too?"

"No, hadn't thought about that. They *earn* it; they get it. Tscheib didn't earn any AR-COM. And you sure as hell didn't justify one, not with this shoddy, sophomoric scribbling. Even if you had been in his chain." Winter was trying, without a lot of luck, to control a rapidly developing case of red ass.

"You'd best remember who you're talking to, Chief. Note the bars?" he said, nodding toward the place where his railroad tracks would normally be. But as he was standing at the bar wearing an olive drab tee-shirt; the question was academic.

"Oh, I didn't forget you're a captain. *Sir.* And as a captain, I can't believe you didn't know better. Where do you come off writing recommendations of any kind for Specialist Tscheib? You weren't in his chain-of-command; you weren't his rating or review officer. What's with the unwarranted accolades?" He could thank Brenner for those words, he thought.

The captain turned away, refusing further comment.

Winter went by the CO's office; he was out; Winter wrote him a note: "This is the same kind of crap as earlier. Request you deep-six it, Sir." He signed it, "CW2 Winter, A&D" and stapled it to the recommendation. The Awards and Decoration function was under control.

It was the last time he had to deal with the captain about Tscheib . . . though not the last time the dead linguist's name came up.

Following the failed flight of -496, Winter returned to his desk and began the boring accounting task of compiling numbers of flight hours to validate Air Medal awards. He worked at the flight logs until halfway through the evening meal and broke to grab chow.

He sat with Ito and Brenner, who lingered over coffee and a second helping of chocolate pie. The decibel level rose in the messhall as one of the First's aircraft mechanics on the line ran up the recip engines of a mission bird to a high intensity.

"When you left Asmara, had they instituted flight on jets?" Brenner shouted to Winter, changing the subject from something equally banal. "Commercial jet service had come in by about then, but I don't remember what month you left in 'sixty-two."

"July."

"So you did go by jet. From Cairo."

"Yeah. Matter of fact, I was one of the two first to fly jet. Ethi Air Lines DC-6 from Asmara to Cairo; over-nighted; caught my first commercial 707 the next day. T.W.A. to Athens, Rome, Paris, Newfoundland, New York. Hell of a jaunt." Winter was fondly reminded of those heady days, going home to mama. "Day-and-a-half to CONUS when it took four days to get there in a Connie." Those fond memories *were* in the distant past.

Unexpectedly thrown into the ring with memories of Nickie, he started, shivered, swept his thoughts away. He had to be careful where his traitorous mind took him.

"Overnight in Cairo?"

Winter, recalled into the conversation, nodded. "One night. Nassar the big cheese then. Didn't have anything good for the U.S., being we were allies of Israel, of course. But we didn't have any problems. Being on civilian flights, we traveled in civvies. I still have a picture of me and . . . damn, I can't remember the guy's name . . . worked in the Comm Center. A corporal. We flew to the states together. I have a picture of the two of us under the palm trees—remember those goddamned scruffy, old, dried-out palms at the airport in Asmara?—both of us in suits, for Christ's sake. Hadn't worn a suit during my whole two years there."

"I can see it now," Brenner said seriously, "Sartorial elegance. Wearing that blue Hong Kong special, weren't you?"

"Hell, it was the only suit I owned, but it wasn't from the B.C.C. Still the best one I own. Though, as you might remember, I had a couple more made up when I *did* go to Hong Kong in 'sixty-five."

"Get to do anything the one night there? In Cairo."

"Once we realized we weren't being dogged by Nassar's agents, we went out, walked along the river. Saw the queue of small craft along the Nile, the same lateen-rigged *dhows* we saw in Massawa. We stayed in the Semiramis Hotel, pretty nice digs for a G.I. Right across the street from the Sheppard. I knew about the Sheppard from something I read. Probably *Exodus*." He stopped, looked down. He smiled, a gentle, reflective nod to a pleasant memory.

"My brother, Larry, gave me a copy of that. Had it with him on his ship." He stopped, shook his head as if dispelling gnats, and said enigmatically, confusing the listeners, "Or was *Exodus* even published then? The Sheppard was the old British bastion of good taste and the good life in the Days of the Raj. I got to eat breakfast there the morning I left Cairo."

He remembered threading his way through the lobby of the Semiramis that was tangled with building materials and white plaster dust tracked across princely carpeting. "The Semiramis was re-doing their kitchen-dining room, and it was closed. We'd eaten out the night before, and that morning the hotel issued us chits and sent us out the back door, across the street to the Sheppard.

"By the time we finished eating, though, uhh, what's his name and me, we barely made the bus to the airport. There was a glitch at the front desk, and they didn't tell the driver we were over at the Sheppard. No one told us when the bus was coming. We almost missed our flight." He smiled in memory. "I wouldn't have minded. Could've handled a couple days in The Land of the Pharoahs. Pyramids and bad traffic."

"Fuckin' A!" Ito muttered.

"Hell, Fred, you were never in Cairo," Brenner pointed out.

"Oh, wasn't I? You're right. But you make it sound nice."

Ignoring Ito's non-sequitur, Brenner focused on Winter's previous musing. "Dave, how come you never talk about your brother? I know you had a brother, and he died. But you never go there." He spoke casually, as if the knowledge was of minimal interest. But his eyes were fixed with intensity on Winter's evasive face.

After a few moments, closely approaching awkwardness, Winter looked at him and said, "No particular reason, Luther. Larry was a dear soul, my younger brother. My . . . charge, if you will, as we had no father then. And I let him down." He sniffed.

"How's that? Let him down?" His tone implied Brenner thought that unlikely.

"I was the one, the male, that Larry looked up to. I needed to provide guidance. And I didn't do a good-enough job."

"I can't imagine that to be true. What happened?" Like the Brenner of old, he was a dogged raconteur, and demanded equal response.

Like dredging something up from the depths, the onlookers felt the resistance of whatever Winter was to say, but following Brenner's lead, they waited. And fulfillment was their's.

"I'd been in Korea. In the Marines. Larry was ten, I think, when I returned from that mess. Like kid brothers everywhere, he idolized his big, bad-ass, Marine brother." He smiled deprecatingly to soften the self-criticism. "Tagged after me everywhere. Hell, I was only seventeen, but there was a world between us. And with dad gone, I was it.

"After I'd changed services, and while I was gone—married, wife, kid, career, the whole cucamonga—he wrote me regularly. The two years in Ethiopia, at least every week. And his theme was he wanted to follow in my footsteps. Join the service; likely Marines, I thought, as he expressed great things about the Corps. Then I pulled my first tour here. In 'Nam. And shortly after, public opinion started to go south. Larry was in college by then. He fell in with . . . " he hesitated, looked at Brenner, and said, ". . . you'd say he fell among thieves. And I guess he did.

"He was sweating the Draft; he had a high number. And by then, he'd been influenced to believe he wanted nothing to do with this promissory land. So he dropped out of college, went down, signed up for the Coast Guard. You know how hard that must have been. Hell, Coast Guard and Air Force quotas were filled for years in advance, guys so eager to avoid the Army or the Marines and a straight shot to 'Nam. But he'd had good college grades, and fell into something that gave him a boot up.

"Larry'd spent a lot of time on the coast—the Gulf Coast; not far from Jackson—he even worked on a shrimp boat out of Gulfport one summer. He was familiar with the Coast Guard, knew their mission. Something he could believe in. I guess." His face had taken on an ashen hue, and the words came harder.

"After training, he was posted to a team, or crew, whatever they call it, working out of Mobile. I got letters. I'd even gotten letters while he was in training. And he loved it. Thought it might even hold career possibilities for him. He'd been looking into the Coast Guard Academy, and with his college, he had a good shot at it.

"Then, in the spring of 'sixty-seven, in a hurricane that rounded the coast coming up from Florida, his cutter was lost. Most of the crew survived. Not Larry. No one ever saw him . . . go down. Didn't see what happened to him." Winter looked now only into his own inner spaces.

"They salvaged the boat, but there was no sign of his body. Just . . . lost at sea."

"Well, shit, Dave. That's not fair," Ito advanced.

"Nothing's ever fair, Fred," Winter replied, gently, knowing the dark well from which his friend's words sprang.

"Hell, Fred. Get a grip. How long you been in the Army? And you still believe in the Easter Bunny, virgin birth, and . . . *fair!*" Brenner would not offer Ito the same space that Winter had.

"Give our small Oriental friend a break, Luther. If you can bedazzle us with trolls, Fred can surely imagine a camel ride in Cairo," Winter lectured, turning the conversation back to the interrupted digression on days and nights along the Nile..

"Listen, Mister Do-Right," Brenner said to Winter, forcefully, semi-seriously. "I've told you before. If we're going on together, through this war and through this life, you have to accept the premise that there are no absolutes. Simply no black and white. Everything, in Viet Nam, and in real life, is some shade of gray. Myth stands as good a chance of having the answers as all this so-called reality. Whatever we might wish about that, for whatever and every reason, from making life easier to understanding such stories to seeking an end to this little Viet Nam tête-à-tête, is just that—an unfulfilled wish." It should have been clear to him, following the circuitous route of the conversation, that he was losing his audience, but Brenner soldiered on. "So, let's on with it."

"Kill a commie for Christ," Ito declared.

"Something like that."

"Fuckin' A!"

chapter eleven

Seeking Cinderella

Cam Ranh Bay, Viet Nam: March 1969

Concluding his assigned tour in Viet Nam a few days later, Captain Warren rotated stateside where he was appointed to instructor duties at Fort Rucker, Alabama, Instrument Training Division. Informed at his departure farewell by the commander what every operator, co-pilot, flight engineer, and house girl already knew—that he was deemed incapable of adequate performance as a Command Pilot in combat—Warren became history. For those who missed the ass-chewing, Warren passed it on, in modified caste, to his only friend in the 1st RRU, CW3 Mischoff, in an angst-ridden bitching session in a letter back from The World.

Warren would benefit by the assignment to Alabama, as would those consigned to duty under his tutelage; and untold multitudes of future aviators would learn proper instrumentation, safe pre-flight and post-flight checks, and circumspect radio procedure from that anomalous pilot. But all new aviators whom he trained would thereafter always approach their flight tasks with a certain acquired trepidation. The latter was confirmed by the hesitant flight dynamics of a new CW2 aviator in the 146th who had trained under Warren's ambiguous authority.

* * *

The bleachers were crowded with movie goers. An evening breeze wafting over the berm behind the screen was refreshing, bringing the smell of the salt sea surf across NAF compound. The evening movie, *The Thomas Crown Affair*, had progressed to the erotic scene where Faye Dunaway sat, caressing a priapic chess piece, offering Steve McQueen blatant invitation. Among the audience of soldiers and sailors, there was loud argument as to whether that select piece was a knight, a bishop, or just a lucky pawn swollen with desire. When the first rocket hit the runway three hundred yards away, Faye Dunnaway's success or failure became obscured in darkness.

The screen's immediate blankness indicated a trained combat projectionist.

All personnel in chorus expressed dismay at a growing phenomenon of inconvenience. The audience in the bleachers split to the winds toward a best-known or favorite bunker. There was no time for drawing a weapon, and no need for one; rockets did not presage a ground attack.

Normally.

Winter headed for the bunker between his billet and that of the TDY Navy crew, who were relatively new. Though Winter was unaware of it at the time, few of the this particular Navy rotating flight crew had ever experienced enemy fire.

This crew, as did all new Navy crews, flew the P-3 Orion. Flying plush. They had arrived in February, replacing VP-1, who flew the last Navy P-2 Neptunes in country. The P-3 squadrons, who rotated in and out of country on an uneven schedule, from Cubi Point or Sangley Point in the Phillipines, or from Okinawa or Japan, were deployed in country to fly MARKET TIME, coastal interdiction missions.

When the games began, Winter was at the movie with Brenner and Ito. Ito was asleep, but the rocket put an end to that. The three made the bunker at the same time. A second rocket hit somewhere on the far, Air Force side of the field. There was no secondary explosion; the second munition also had missed its aircraft target. Then mortar rounds began dropping on the Air Force side, seeking out the fast movers. A second coordinated attack within days!

Since Winter had been at Cam Ranh, no incoming fire—mortars or rockets—had struck aircraft. The best way to get the aircraft, as agreed by the Viet Cong of old, the NVA of current trend, Americans, Aussies, and Thais, was by satchel charge delivered via hand by a sapper. But the viciously competent Koreans, tasked with security of the peninsula, minimized that threat.

Once inside the bunker, the three Army men of the 1st RR tried to stay close, near the front entrance. No one wanted to go deep inside. Rumors of snakes and other undesirables languishing in the always-damp, always-dark interior of the shoddy, sandbagged bunkers were convincing . The onrushing troops who arrived after the trio pushed and shoved their way into preferential positions, and Winter, Brenner, and Ito found themselves driven farther underground.

Two more rockets in rapid succession came to earth somewhere beyond the NAF ramp. The question in everyone's mind was the same: how long could they continue to miss? Forever was a good choice, but knew that to be mind sop. When the mortars stopped falling, someone near the entrance called out, "How many here from V.P.?" referring to the Navy squadron.

There was no answer.

"Anyone here from V.P. Forty-seven?" he called again, louder.

No reply.

"Oh, shit, nobody alerted our pilots."

Winter couldn't make out who spoke.

"Can't they tell incoming, when it's apt to be bouncing their asses out of the rack?" Brenner called.

"Maybe not. Most of them, it's their first deployment. We got training sched—"

Ignoring the speaker, Brenner thrashed his way back toward the entryway. Bodies made room for him to pass. Out of the bunker, he ran to the edge of the sidewalk skirting the Navy billet and began shouting: *"Outside. Outside, you Deck Apes. This is not a practice. Alert! Alert! Incoming! Get outside . . . into the bunker,"* running as he yelled. The sirens had not yet gone off, but doors began popping open, upstairs and down. Men in various degrees of dress appeared. Those from the landing above leaning over the rails, questioned this obvious joke.

"Get in the bunker," Brenner shouted. *"Right below you, right there. Get out. Now!"*

By this time other voices from the bunker were shouting similar directions. Bodies began to stir; lights went out; a thunder of feet came down the center well stairs. Brenner rounded the corner at the end of the building and raced down the far side of the billets, pounding doors, exhorting indolent Navy officers to save themselves. Most, initially, either did not understand, or thought it was harrassment: "Welcome to Viet Nam!" While Brenner pursued the emergency exercise, four more rockets fell in no discernible pattern across the open spaces of the airfield.

One young officer strolled casually from his room onto the sidewalk on the ground level, berating Brenner for his antics. Brenner brushed him off and ran on, spreading the word. A Navy chief moving toward cover, one of the SeaBees from the billets nearby, took up the slack.

"Mister," he addressed the young officer, "get your ass in that bunker around the corner. *Now! Move it, move it, move it, you swab.*" The chief, like others in the late movie audience, wore only shorts and a T-shirt. The young pilot had no idea whom he was dealing with. And the bellow of "Move it!" brought back all the boot camp angst and hysteria inculcated into his being, from day one in the Navy. He moved. Shorts, no shirt, no shoes. But he moved.

When Brenner had made a circuit of the MARKET TIME billets, and then circled 1st RR billets, opening every door, checking for holdouts, he sprinted upstairs to do the same. On the second level he encountered Bimbo coming from the opposite direction, performing the same mission. Together they clattered back down the stairs and to the bunker, by this time Standing Room Only. Except that one could not stand; the maximum height beneath the cover of wooden beams and partially filled sandbags was less than five feet. Bodies, Army and Navy, jammed the space. Ito and Winter had worked their way back near the opening, and sat together against the side wall of sandbags. Brenner and Bimbo joined them to a chorus of groans and complaints.

"That's all right, gentlemen. You don't have to thank me now; just ensure the donations reach my accountant," Brenner chided the Navy.

A round of laughter, followed by a smattering of applause,

answered him as they gave in to the situation. Nothing to do but wait it out, and pray that one of the random rockets did not end its earthward plummet atop their bunker. The bunker was only marginally useful as a shield against low impact ordnance: small arms fire, shrapnel on a level plane. Above them, a single layer of sandbags paid only lip service to secure shelter. That realization must have occurred to the occupants, for there was a rapid damping of the laughter.

"Hey, you guys," a voice called from the rear of the bunker, "any of you from that Army outfit? The ones flying P-2s. Anybody here from that unit?"

"Yeah, several," Winter answered. "Why?"

"Is it true you guys have a dog flying missions? We heard about some Zip dog on flight status. Got a bunch of Air Medals."

Winter couldn't answer. The only dog he'd ever known in Vietnam—and that one *did* fly with the old 3rd RRU Air—was Oink. Four years before.

"Yeah, that's right," Billingsgate called out. "Twenty-seven."

"Twenty-seven?"

"Air Medals. He's been doing this a long time."

There was a flurry of chuckles and comments, questions. Billingsgate, the only one of the four gathered together who could speak with any authority, waited until the hubbub died down, and responded.

"Say, I guess you're not Army, then."

"Right. Goddamned right. Navy, mate."

"Well, then you don't know from shit about our canine's qualifications. Our airborne pooch earns his keep."

The discussion turned into a general services rivalry argument, while in the background the air was suspiciously devoid of explosions and sounds of impacting ordnance.

* * *

"You're a dipshit, Luther. Taking that chance for a bunch of squids," Winter said quietly.

Brenner took it as a gibe, as it was meant; Winter, had he

gotten out through the huddled masses first, would have done the same. "If you think that was foolhardy, then I guess you haven't recognized in all these years that my entire existence has been a non-sequitur. Thank you, Jesus."

He immediately followed this blasphemy with another non-sequitur.

"Perhaps I'll write a novel about this war," Brenner said abruptly. "But the war's so discontinuous it cannot hold the cohesion of a novel. Still . . . perhaps I'll call it *Stories From the Lives of My Friends*. That will reduce it to no more than a novella. But then, no doubt, like Chekhov, I would fritter away the impulse until I had lost my vision completely."

"This war will be the same as all others: a lot of young men will be writing novels when this is over. If it's ever over," Winter speculated.

"Ah, but the writing of novels is held to be the province of the cultivated. Those, like officers, with a consciousness of personal freedom. Enlisted pukes never had personal freedom." When Brenner quit speaking, there was quiet all about. Every crouching GI in the bunker, from pilot to aircraft engine mechanic, was listening. What most heard was a new notion.

"But the art . . . the art is totally beyond me," Brenner concluded. "All rather Chekhovian, *Nyet*?"

Shortly the waver of the siren—the first time they'd heard it tonight—cut through the night air, releasing the kneeling, sitting men to evacuate their shelters. Winter followed the other three onto the street. The lights were coming on again in latrines and Orderly Rooms, firewatch stations and billets; through open doors lamps could be seen flashing on. World come alive!

CW2 DeMartino crossed the street toward their group, coming from the bunker nearest the hangar. "Bimbo, d'ja hear. One of the mortars hit a nurses' quarters on the Air Force side."

"Anybody hurt?"

"Don't know. We're grabbing whatever wheels we can find, going to see."

All five redirected their steps toward the Orderly Room.

* * *

Benford *was* strange. I don't mean his mammary fixation; nothing strange about that. But I flew with him, worked with him on the ground, and he was strange with a capital *Weird!*

His diversity likely had its genesis in nurturing by a family of devout southern Batiste extremists who, after the shock of Benford's unheralded birth, relocated in the early 'fifties from the Georgia highlands to L.A. Adopting a reactionary Beat life force in the transition, adhering religiously to drug devotions, they sought the Haight-Ashbury motherland for three years before learning they were four hundred miles too far south, in the wrong city. Directionally challenged, incensed at the lack of civility among their co-devotionists who had left them in ignorance, they became overnight converts to Hollywood Buddhism, rebelled at its banality, tried a fling at Santería, and ultimately became Democrats.

But what happened after the mortar attack, though also strange, was somehow . . . beautiful. A love story, of sorts.

The day before the attack that night, I'd been on the manifest to fly, but when I showed up for briefing there was a note on the bulletin board: "WO1 Brenner. Stand down. Wallings will take Controller today, 3/22. See Major Fitz at 1300. CW2 Winter." A matter of little concern, it eventuated, but curious at the time. One was almost never scrubbed from a flight that late. But Winter was running on fumes even then. I don't remember what happened in the meeting with Fitz, but I was watching a flick later, with Winter and others, when we got incoming. Must have been about 2130.

Rockets. Mostly beyond NAF. And mortars. Heavy mortars, probably 82mm, impacting across the strip in the Air Force compound. Lousy mortarmen: they obviously were targeting aircraft, but were off by a good two hundred meters. After some time, when the mortars had ceased and the rockets stopped and the All-Clear sounded, after the goddamned Koreans had opened fire with the 155s, whoever was available from CRAZY CAT commandeered vehicles and headed across the strip to lend a hand in the Air Force area. Might as well; counter-fire would go on the rest of the night. Thanks to our Allies, the gunners of the Korean White Horse Division, even one round of incoming meant the end of sleep as we knew it.

Benford was along with us. First thing I ever saw him step up for.

When we got there, the in-country Flight Ops building was nothing but smoking splinters. There had been an airman clerk on duty, but no sign of him; only some bloody rags. The latrine next door was gone too, leaving behind only the stench. One round had impacted on the Air Force nurses' quarters, beyond a taxiway. Air Police were all over the place, a number of Air Force and Army officers, and for some reason assorted Navy EM. Probably from the SeaBees billeted next to us. The standard Mongolian Maypole Cluster Fuck!

The Jeep I was in with Benford stopped at the nurses' hooch. Just the one round had found a target here, and though many of the girls were off duty and might have been here and conceivably hit, most of them were at the O Club at a whing-ding for a visiting fireman. Only one nurse was slightly wounded. The medics were working on her, giving more hands-on care than appeared necessary. There wasn't even much structural damage to her hootch, but furnishings and personal gear were blown everywhere. I was reconnoitering some dark corners and beneath residue with a flashlight when I heard Benford exclaim: "Whoa!"

We all gathered on him, expecting more casualties. There was no one. Benford, resplendent in fuchsia-colored swim trunks, a Hawaiian shirt, and Ho Chi Minh sandals, was holding before him in awe a woman's brassiere. A large, woman's bra. A large woman's bra. Or, as Benford read it, a woman's large bra. He was mesmerized. Turning it over in his hand, carefully, as if gently manipulating the bounty for which it was designed, he hesitated, then read out in hushed tones: "Forty-four dee." There was stunned silence.

Then a reverent, hushed murmur from 360 degrees: "Jeez-us! Forty-four DELTAS."

It was only a moment before critical intelligence technique kicked in.

"Whose?" Tantos, despite his vow of warp zone abstinence to his Montana Blackfoot Indian wife, was not unaffected to the point of not asking; but Benford led the pack. At that moment was initiated for him an inexorable pursuit of his personal Holy Grail.

In the midst of panic in the night, even as the rubble was searched for bodies, Benford began his inspirationally engendered program, critically examining nurses as they streamed back from the club. After a while, having spied no likely match, he subsided into dour disquietetude; but finding no further signs of human carnage, he could also allay his fears that the owner of the bra might have been blown into another dimension.

The nurses were lucky, except for the one lightly wounded. And she was reputed to be lesbian, and thus of no interest to Benford. And ugly besides, he said. Way too small up front, everyone agreed after careful assessment.

The following day, mulling over options, Benford reduced his search to just the residents of that hooch. It was unlikely someone had been visiting and had shed her support garment while there. Benford, being enlisted, thus poorly paid and therefore of little interest to any of the nurses who might otherwise choose to be benevolent, had little success in approaching them directly. For one thing, he was unknown to them. And, as I said—and even nurses can be reasonably perceptive—Benford was strange.

Several days went by; stares and curt replies constituted the limits of information he was able to gather about the Quonset hut's residents. Over the next few weeks, Benford spent all his free time hanging about the Air Force compound, spying on the nurses as they came and went. He was run off a couple of times by the A.P.s, and told to bugger-off once by a nurse major with a large pistol which, though not issue, Benford was convinced would surely do him irreparable damage. He even enlisted the help of other similarly fascinated, but less vigorously addicted, fetishists, until he was put on official notice by the commander of the Air Force medical facility.

But he couldn't stay away. The fascination was too much. The bra, and its presumptive cargo, had reached the point of idolatry for him, icon for a soft, creamy, bouncy heaven of quasi-religious significance. He'd been drawn to expansive bosoms since puberty, and hadn't the maturity or mental capacity to overcome this shallow compulsion—along with millions of other GIs, of course. But Benford was committed! His ardor made the rest of us seem unappreciative.

The bra was stapled to the wall locker by his bunk with a large, neat, hand-lettered sign stapled above which read "Who's Tits Fits?"

It was useless for me to point out to him the grammatically incorrect pronoun usage. And lack of subject and verb agreement. The meaning was clear. And like the Prince's minions, fanning out over the countryside, looking for the foot that fit the crystal slipper, every breast-bedazzled clown in CRAZY CAT was on high alert to solve the mystery.

Cathy The Captain, tight-mouthed as she is, let me in on the joke after more than a week had gone by. And it was a joke by this time. Every time Benford showed up on the Air Force side of Cam Ranh Bay, there were ill-concealed snickers and cruel teasing. But Benford had prey in his sights—at least in his imaginings—and he was not to be dissuaded.

"Brenner, you know Barbara? The little brunette surgery assistant?" Cathy asked.

"Sure." Not one of us it was who didn't know every nurse's name on the Air Force side, as well as at the Army's South Beach recovery hospital on the ass-end of the peninsula.

She sniggered. "The *Bra* is hers." By this time, the entire population spoke of the bra in italics and capitalized. There was no other bra. Anywhere. It had gained fame across the warp zone. "It was hanging on her bunk when the mortars came."

"Can't be. It just cannot be! Barbara's a little skinny shit. Only about five-one. She can't weigh more than a hundred pounds. A chest flat as Kansas," I protested reasonably.

Cathy sniggered again. "Exactly. The *Bra* was a joke gift to her from the girls. When under the influence of evil drink, she's always spouting off about how she's going home through San Fran and getting herself some implants. Says she's going to 'beef up' like that Carol whoever who works in the Go Go Club on North Beach. The one in *Playboy*."

"*That* one," I acknowledged.

Whatever Barbara's intent, whatever the attitude of all those involved, the secret was kept. Nobody ever told Benford. Last I heard was that he extended his tour at Cam Ranh. I was down in the Delta when he came up for rotation. Far as I know, he's still there, seeking the breasts that can fill out that magnificent piece of lingerie. The North Vietnamese Army's best efforts in Re-education Camp would not be able to deny Benford his vision.

* * *

A week later, compounding the *felonious interruptus,* atoning for the truncation by the recent rocket attack, and for the one interrupted by the sapper attack when Tscheib died, the First Radio Research Company (Aviation) scheduled a "rain check" beach party. They invited the standard guests, a select few good contacts among SeaBees, Navy storekeepers, Army supply people, and any female who could get transportation to NAF. For a special few, they would send the Old Man's Jeep, provided it did not involve crossing a minefield. Beach doings was scheduled for a Saturday night. Without exception, one day was pretty much the same as the last, just as the next promised; but having a Par-tee, making it Satur-day provided a certain cachet.

He wasn't flying that day, so Winter showed up on the leading edge of festivities. He'd agreed to split a rare windfall of Guinness Stout with Brenner, and was balancing on the edge of one of the hazardous patio chairs, working on his share. He spotted her when she came around the corner with Bimbo and three other girls in civvies. She just had to be a nurse, he thought; she was in that age group, about twenty-four or -five, had auburn hair, and took his breath away. Had to be a nurse. Bimbo had said he was going to the Sixth Convalescent Hospital at South Beach to chum for "wimmin." And she had that antiseptic look.

Winter and Brenner were the first ones Bimbo's little group encountered entering the zone of festivity, and the chief merrymaker stopped to introduce everyone. He got the girls' names wrong, mostly; it had not been a long acquaintance. But he got *her* name right: Moira.

Oh, Jesus, Winter murmured to himself, she's Irish, too. Moira. Beautiful.

Brenner acted as if he'd been introduced to the North Calgary Bird Watching and Small Engine Repair Society. Winter knew him too well, though, to assume that meant disinterest. It was all a devious part of Luther's master plan. If Luther had a master plan. If the guy beside him was, indeed, Luther E. Brenner; in the hot, humid, windless night, the guy might be anyone.

That evening, the new interest, Moira, never experienced extensive visitation rights into the Sandbag. Winter feared once there, she might be so taken with the decor she would not wish to leave. Much more likely, one of the drunks would start groping her and drive her in a screaming fit back to South Beach. He moved to forestall such calamity.

He asked her to sit. Wait! He fetched her a drink. She asked for Jameson's, as if the possessive was the name of that fairly decent Irish whiskey, or that the liquor belonged to Mr. Jameson. Winter, himself, had switched from the stout to Bushmills. He clinked glasses, murmured "Sláinte!" and followed it up, in case she missed the allusion: "Up the Republic!"

Moira gave a slight, wan smile; it was clear she hadn't a clue what he was on about. Winter took a moment to re-group: So much for heritage. She did have a fine, declarative body, though, he shrewdly observed. And in tight peddle-pushers, a resoundingly firm after-effect. The liquid Irish enhanced the view from all angles. It was about then, in the midst of becoming stricken, that he experienced a slight, quick-passing spasm of recall—a girl named Nickie. But he'd had just enough Guinness-evolving-into-Bushmills to blur the sailing of that ship.

Moira was, indeed, a nurse. A second lieutenant from the 6th Evac, and she'd been in country "all week long." My, my. And was full of useful information, such as the fact that she was the middle one of nine children in a ranch family from Cody, Wyoming. And she regaled Winter with tales of horses, cows, pigs, life on a ranch, aspirations for life *off* a ranch, highschool sweethearts, though she'd been gangly and dull and wore braces most of her high school years and didn't have ". . . hardly any beaux at all" in that fallow season, she declared. She'd almost married in Nursing School, a fellow student, but he turned out to be diversely oriented, vis-á-vis sex, what some insensitive souls would have labeled AC-DC, and she'd found she didn't really believe she wanted to deal with that and all its potential hazards.

Not only had the ship Nicole sailed, word had funneled back that it had been lost at sea. There was no immediate sense of disaster. The mixing of mataphors and Bushmills left him oblivious to wavering fidelity. In one brief flash of awareness, he had the temerity to think, ". . . fidelity's not just *not* sleeping around." The fragment of thought could have framed a philosophy in a more sober mind , he thought. Or maybe not. He was now over-supplied with philosophies.

Fidelity held no brief as he watched Moira closely, his gaze rapt on her face and inevitably, caressing her body. She was not a sex goddess, Winter admitted, and was grateful. She was too lovely for that distinction. Her body, her curves, were sculpted in beauty for the beholder, not in grotesquerie for competitive ogling. And those shadow-grey eyes—he couldn't explain why he thought in terms of the distaff spelling, with an "e" and not the more common "a" but the affectation made sense on some subliminal, non-conscious level—those eyes were not the windows to her soul. They were twin wells of solace, paired invitations to sincerity and contentment and . . . dare he think . . ?

Ludicrous! 'tis the drink. A shudder, not of disdain or disgust; merely of disbelief, brought him from his reverie. All the dis-es in the world might assail him at a moment like this, but he realized the improbability of stumbling on someone here, in this unlikely

Nirvana, someone ten years his junior who might look upon him with fixation, with fascination, with . . . real attraction. But the possibility thrilled him as nothing he could remember for a long time.

The hazy night raced by, and even as he gauged its passage with the implication that soon she would be gone, he was powerless to slow its fleeting. By the time she whispered to him that she had to use the "little girls' room," Winter had reached the point where he did not even point out to her the unlikelihood of finding such a thing within mortar range. Brenner might have done so. Brenner was a grump. Winter merely nodded her toward the center stairs. "We go up."

She looked up, as if seeking a john in the humid air, but followed him quietly, tiptoeing so as not to wake the dead about the periphery of the patio. And well so. It was two hours before they returned to the beach party.

* * *

She was a fake, Winter thought. Probably something she'd adopted in college or nursing school as a play on her Irish name, Moira Burke. Whatever, Irish was not her drink. It was not so much that it was unkind to her; it tended to avoid her. No matter how much she drank, she made no concessions to inebriation. No concession, but Winter would learn, by the time he had led her to a borrowed room, coaxed her out of the tank-top and vest, that she was more affected than she let on. But she was cute about it. She attempted no ploy, nothing devious or deceptive; she just held her liquor as well as she was able, and when she couldn't, she didn't..

Commendable, though not quite as unaffected as outward appearances suggested.

Winter, too, was well into drink taken when he realized that both she and he were casually be-sotted with each other. It made it much easier to get the peddle pushers out of play. Following that strategic revelation, there seemed no impediments for either of them.

* * *

Winter and Burke, Moira and Dave. It was a catechism learned quickly by friends. And it happened with the speed and authority of summer lightning. As the weeks slipped by, no one in the First RR tried to cut her out of the herd when Winter was not around; and no one at the Sixth Evac ever suggested she go out with someone else. "Once the bans were posted, so to speak," she jokingly said to Winter one night after two weeks of almost nightly visitations, back and forth. Regular as dysentery, except for the nights he graced the belly of a Neptune in some far, northern land's airspace.

He had become almost as well known in South Beach as she on the patio. And there had been no further communications from the home front to raise specters of extant ghosts.

If there was a beach party, or a more casual visitation by nurses from the Sixth, and Winter was away on a flight, she either did not come to NAF, or if she did, was squired by Brenner or Ito and effectively denied to prowling sharks.

One quiet evening when only three other officers were present on the patio, Captain Wolfe, the "Lone Wolf," by nature and by choice, sat with Winter, Moira, and Brenner. Moira sipped at a poor excuse for a martini while the First's officers attacked the liquor stocks with relish. "Why do you guys all drink so much?" the nurse asked, seemingly genuinely puzzled.

Wolfe got it in one. "Well, when you live in a state of constant terror. . . ." He didn't elaborate, but images of derelict aircraft filled the minds of all at the table. No one even considered that she might think Wolfe casting macho images into the conversational winds. The fear was too well internalized.

* * *

After several weeks, one early morning in the mess hall after a flight debrief, Brackett said to Winter, "Dave. You seem to be pretty much at ease in this . . . this new relationship. With the nurse. Moira."

Winter, waiting for the conversational ploy to play out, after a few moments said, "Yeah, I guess that's a fair assessment."

"Don't bother you none you got a wife and two kids back in CONUS?" It was unusual for Brackett to impose his obvious views into someone else's space.

"I guess if it was going to bother me, in the sense of really *bother* me, I wouldn't be doing it, now would I" He knew Brackett meant well . . . but damn! And he knew he'd spoken truth.

This arrangement, this unlikely pairing of the nurse and the Controller, continued through the last of winter, though no one could tell the season by the weather. But for Winter, and it seemed obvious, for Lieutenant Burke, there were worse ways to experience a war.

chapter twelve

Rumor

Cam Ranh Bay, Viet Nam: March 1969

Winter sat facing Brenner on bunks in the Navy's MARKET TIME billet. There were no quarters available for Brenner in the Army BOQ. There would be none until the officer shuffle was finished: CO departing, XO replacing him, new officers incoming, and two officers finishing their tour within the week. Brenner made do with temporary quarters with the Navy. It beat sleeping in a bunker or the bomb bay of a P-2.

Barely.

They had been sitting quietly, neither feeling the need for speech since leaving the flight line. "Any news from home? Nickie? The boys?" Brenner posed carefully, risking an outburst..

"Let's not go there," Winter said evenly, and introduced other issues, "Did you ever get the rest of your baggage?" Neither dare he risk broaching the subject of Moira.

"Not yet, and I give them only another week."

Brenner had landed in country at Bien Hoa a few weeks before, was transported to Long Binh for overnight billeting, then to the 509th transient billets in Cho Lon; from there to 509th Group Headquarters at Tan Son Nhut, to BOQ Number 1 which had no space, to the Newport BOQ, hot-bedding in the room of a Special Forces captain TDY up country; then to Cam Ranh Bay—all within a period of four days. Somewhere en route, his personal footlocker had disappeared. "Army de-materialization," Brenner called it. And when Winter told him the story of the Million Dollar Conex, the new warrant let drop a hint that he would work his claim in that fashion if his box didn't turn up. It was a subtle threat to the command to prompt aid in, and speed up of, return of his property.

It had not the slightest affect. Brenner never thought it would.

Brenner lowered his head and peered menacingly from beneath a furrowed brow, effecting his own direction change, saying, "You know what I'm thinking?"

After a pointed lack of response, Brenner answered himself. "I'm thinking this outfit is dead on its ass. Dandy operation and all, fine life here, but no spirit. No *joie de vivre*. Because they're not challenged enough. He took another pull on the Black Label beer, grimacing.

"You been here—what? All day, now?—and you're going to make that right? How?" Winter braced himself. His good friend, Luther E. Brenner, was an original; known worldwide across the Army Security Agency as iconoclastic, curmudgeonly, and original. No one would say original *what*? But when Luther took the Army—or any part of it: any person, unit, function —to task, Winter recommended battening down hatches.

"We gonna employ . . . *rumor ratiocination!*" he said enthusiastically.

"Ahh, Jeez-us, Luther. Spare me."

"Hell, David, my man, Viet Nam's the very ground zero of Rumorville. A breeding-ground-zero, you might say. If you were inclined to puns."

"So, for openers, what . . . ?" Winter looked askance at the "mood enhancement fixes," as Brenner termed his playful strategies.

"I think . . . maybe . . . Yes! I think that's it. The *Chinese are entering the war on Hanoi's side* ploy is about due, wouldn't you say? Again. Haven't heard that one since 'sixty- five. How can G.I.s serve in a war without a sense of overwhelming threat? And how long do you estimate it will take to spread that one across the four corps?"

"Why insist on stepping on your crank, Luther? You just got here. Just got your bar. They ever pin down your little game, you'll be watching sunsets through striped windows."

"Hah! Never to fear, *meine kleine heimatlos Freund*. Old Luther Emanuel leaves no spoor when the game's afoot."

For chrissake, Winter thought, he's in a mood this evening. He thought of ways to divert Brenner; all possibilities were drastic, none promising.

"Yessir. Think I'll kick it off tonight, maybe at chow. See how long it takes it to make the rounds. After all, paraphrasing Napoleon, 'An army travels on its rumors.'" He stood and pulled on a fatigue jacket against the mildest of evening breezes. "Ready for din-din?"

Walking to the mess hall, Brenner was silent. No doubt getting his ducks in a row to explode his rumor bomb in the mess, Winter thought. He remembered one of Brenner's earliest, and likely his most successful, exploitation of the rumor mill. A self-fulfilling pronouncement.

There had come a time in early 1965 when it became apparent, even down to the level of enlisted men in Viet Nam, that the fractiousness of local foreign nationals, in and around Sai Gon, did not marry well with objectives of the U.S. government. Marvin the ARVN was not getting it done. Everyone expected some escalation, likely a ramping up of Army troop levels. No one considered the government might go with a more radical approach . . . no one but Brenner with quirky intuition. And whether that was sincere or not really, in the end, didn't matter.

Brenner crafted a substantive rumor, buttressed with a couple of fake teletype messages alluding to something more in a supporting vein, that the First Marine Division was being sent from Okinawa and would soon take charge in I Corps. Eye Corps was the biggest threat, being, as it was, so near North Viet Nam, though perhaps not as crucial to the country's welfare as the rice bowl of IV Corps. And Brenner was right, in most things, surprising even himself. No one, not even Brenner, had *really* thought Johnson would go with the first team to adjust a little contretemps in what the president referred to as "this little pissant country."

But the Marines poured ashore at a Da Nang beach, hazarded only by the large number of soft-drink peddlers and bikini-clad Lolitas—peddlers of another kind—lolling about and conducting business on the steamy beachhead. This landing bore no resemblance to Tarawa, even discounting the lack of fire. Two battalions of the 9th Marine Expeditionary Brigade became the first American units to prosecute the unpleasantness building in the former Indo China. The reality of this premiere support resulted from complicity between the Marine publicity machine, and a small coterie of spook-minded wizards in the Pentagon.

And when they'd landed, nine days after Brenner first floated his rumor, no one remembered that he'd prophesied the First MarDiv, but got the Ninth Brigade. There were Marines on the ground in Viet Nam, and Brenner's stock floated at a gracious high for the remainder of his time in 'Nam, giving credence to the many rumors he subsequently hatched. The Army's 173rd Airborne just behind. Thinking on those dicey times, Winter never doubted Brenner's success upcoming, though he didn't give his friend even that much encouragement.

Brenner remained silent.

* * *

The mess contained only one small group of Army enlisted men among a sea of sailors and Navy officers. The two warrants filled trays and joined the EM. Winter knew SP5 Hannah, one of Bravo Crew's senior linguists, at the table. He nodded, "Hannah."

"Evening, sir." The soldier took a bite of something and chewed for a moment. "You're a reader, I know, Mister Winter. I was just telling the guys about my trip."

"You just got back from R and R, right?" Winter remembered.

"Yessir, Taiwan. Spent every penny I had. Had a couple of beers but not a single whore. No steam and cream jobs, no shack-ups." A recent convert, from the little Winter knew of Hannah. Brenner, reading the tea leaves, had he not had his mind set on the upcoming rumor hatching, might have said Hannah was constructing a *curriculum vitae* for canonization.

"How'd you manage such unlikely abstention?" Brenner marveled.

"Books."

The two warrants stared.

"Books! I bought books. You know . . . don't you know about the Chinese publishing industry in Taiwan?" At the officers' blank looks, Hannah continued. "You can get practically any book ever published. Might be some things they've missed, but not much. In English, or any other language, newly printed, well bound, right from sidewalk stalls and warehouses. The Nationalist Chinese don't honor copyright law for any nation. And they're cheap." Hannah seemed to have signed on as a roving ambassador for the Taiwan thievery.

"What's cheap?" Brenner wanted to know.

"I paid four bucks, American, for a brand new, single volume, complete works of Shakespeare, suspiciously like the Oxford single-volume edition. Bound in real leather. And Churchill's six-volume set of the Second World War in buckram, eleven bucks."

"Holy Jesus!" Brenner said. "Do you have to have a contact? Make prior arrangements or anything?"

"No. There's a section of the market that's nothing but book sellers," Hannah said, shaking his head, spraying food. "You just look until you find something you want. Buy it right off the tables. And I was told if you have any special wants, there are facilitators who can find anything for you. A lot of the traffic's in classical pornographic works, *Kama Sutra* and such. But, anything . . ."

"That all you got, The Bard and Churchill?" Winter asked.

"No. I read a lot of First World War, and Second. I bought thirty-two volumes. And I only spent a hundred seventy-five bucks."

"But you could have bought more? There's no limit on how many you can bring back? What I mean, won't there be a problem with customs going back to the states, since these books are extra-legal, so to speak?" Brenner asked.

"Hell, I don't know. I hope not. I know other guys bought books and they never had to pay customs. Never had 'em refused. John Bowers left here for the states, gettin' out. Going to med school. He bought textbooks in Taiwan for med school for about one-fifteenth of bookshop prices. Customs never touched him. Unless you're departing from one of several certain outfits, nobody checks your baggage or personal property shipments," Hannah added optimistically.

"Yet," Winter added.

"Yet. Right."

Brenner looked over Winter's shoulder as two Army aviators came in the door and headed for their table. He recognized Winter's roommate as one.

"Dave, d'ja hear?" CW3 Bracken said. "One forty-sixth lost a bird a few days ago . . ."

Glancing at Brenner, Winter said, "Yeah. We heard. Still don't know who or how. Anything new?"

"They got the operator back. Guy named Damson. Am I right in thinking I heard you mention a Damson."

"Shit! Yeah, I know Billy Ray. Didn't know he was flying. He swore—" He saw the futility, changed direction. "Was he . . . what about the others? The two pilots? They OK?"

"No. CW2 named Alverson, new to the one forty-sixth, and a Lieutenant Mabry were killed in the crash. And—"

"Aww, Jeez-us Christ. Piltdown Pilot's dead?"

"Alverson and Mabry. Don't know . . . whatever Pilot you said."

"It's his war name: Piltdown Pilot. First Lieutenant Mabry. I knew him at Tan Sanh Nhut. Flew with him in the one forty-sixth. William Mabry. I didn't know Alverson."

"Yeah, tough," Bracken added.

"Oh, man, that is grim. They tell us what happened?"

"Nobody's sure yet. Damson apparently was in bad shape when the Jolly Greens found him, three days after-the-fact. Out of his head, dehydrated, feverish. His back's broken. He hasn't been conscious to tell them anything.

"All we know's the Beaver crashed into the base slope of a mountain in Two Corps, near the coast. The crash site was partly covered in jungle, hard to spot from the air. Search patterns been flown all over where they were found. Took a while." Bracken seemed to go introspective. "And strange thing . . . when Damson was recovered, the rescue crewman who rappeled down to get him into the lift found the beeper in his hand. Working, but turned off. Damson never used it. They might have gotten him out days earlier if he'd activated it."

Even Damson's bizarre behavior of the last few months he had been around him didn't account for that, Winter thought. And the man's personality had never promised altruism.

Different strokes!

Captain Trunick, the officer with Bracken, spoke up, "The pilots were still in the aircraft. Crispy Critters. Fuel fire. We have to hope they were already dead or unconscious when the flames got to them. The operator—Damson—he was burned too, not so bad. He managed to crawl from the bird." He shook his head. "Screw that; Nomex flight suits don't help with that shit."

"But you're not going to quit wearing yours, are you, Captain?" Bracken said.

"Don't be silly."

* * *

The following day a weather front moved in off the bay just before mission launch, delaying take-off. The crew, waiting to board, were soaked through, and when they did launch, in takeoff were chilled to the bone as they climbed to altitude.

Winter listened as Sergeant Tompkins, Communicator, made radio check passing Nha Trang. "OUTHOUSE Two Two, this's CAT'S PAW Four Two Niner. Radio check. How do you copy? Over."

Distinct lack of response. Weather noise; no voice.

Tompkins repeated the call twice, then moved to the next station. "SPRING HOUSE Four Four, this's CAT'S PAW Four Two Niner. Radio check. How copy? Over."

Same one-way communication. Move down the chart.

"GRAINHOUSE Five Five, CAT'S PAW Four Two Niner. Radio check. How do you hear me? Over."

Still no response.

Winter reminded Tompkins of SMOKEHOUSE Three Three, the

first alternate on the daily comms rota, which should have been the second station called .

"You musta' missed the first part of the briefing, Mister Winter. They advised that SMOKEHOUSE site was hit last night. Got the receivers. Transmitter's okay, but they couldn't hear us if we called. I'll go to control."

He dialed the transmitter to a different frequency and called, "BIG HOUSE One One, this is CAT'S PAW Four Two Niner. Radio check. How do you read me? Over."

The station, control for the net operating out of Nha Trang, responded immediately.

"Uhh, CAT'S PAW, this is BIG HOUSE. I copy you . . . a-a-hh, about three by two slash three. Weather's breaking you up. You're in and out, but readable. Do you have traffic?"

"Negative, BIG HOUSE. CAT'S PAW, over."

"CAT'S PAW, BIG HOUSE. Did you call my primary? Over."

"Roger that, BIG HOUSE. The entire net. No answer. Must be the weather. Over." Tompkins seemed anxious to get off the air with BIG HOUSE.

"Uhh, roger, CAT'S PAW. Nothing further. Over."

"CAT'S PAW, out."

Well past Nha Trang, Tompkins did not dwell on the communications inconsistencies. Control, on its different frequency, was likely a more powerful radio set, or the freq happened to be clearer, or there was less cloud cover between the bird and that particular station in downtown Nha Trang. Or the gods of talky-talky were pissed off. He would never know the reason, but lacking traffic either way, it was a moot point.

After another seventy minutes with a tail wind -429 took up a racetrack-shaped orbit over the South Viet Nam-Laos border to work the Ho Chi Minh Trail. Launching late, the mission was timed to keep the interceptors over the target unusually late to seek out new targets, and attempt recovery of some old friends they'd lost track of.

After two hours on target, night overcame them. Six hours left to fly the dark skies.

Ericson, one of the linguists, doing his thing past what would have been normal time on station, picked up a voice target and quickly identified it as prime, nominated a control station for Bad Guy comms along the trail, likely a headquarters, unit association unknown. They were disciplined communicators and had not given away that knowledge.

The enemy station transmitter was operated by a woman—not unusual. Her voice, almost sultry in an "enemy sort of way," Ito had once said, was easily recognizable, and Ericson smiled and said it was like old home week. In slack periods during the evening, several linguists, without an active target, rolled their receivers to that frequency just to refresh themselves with the voice of the NVA *co*. Only Ericson was copying her.

Four Two Niner was on the northern leg of its track late in the mission, almost midnight, when Winter left his Controller position for a relief break. When he'd finished at the relief tube aft, with success, he went forward, sliding on his back over the mid-wing beam and thrashing his way through the linguists' compartment, speaking to various ops as he went. It was a slack period and no one was copying a target. Several ops dozed. The crew chief, in his space behind the cockpit, was tilted back in his seat, asleep. Winter leaned past him, between CW4 Surtain and CW3 Babcock and greeted them loudly enough to be heard over airplane noise.

Surtain lifted a hand; Babcock turned and spoke. "Dave. Getting cabin fever?"

"It's not been bad, once we got out of that goddamned rain."

"We'll hit it again going back. Weather says it's intensified."

"Oh, good. Now if only Ito could have flown this one. Any turbulence or disturbance—*any*thing—and Fred's convinced we're going down."

"And well we might be."

Winter, leaning to the twelve o'clock between the pilots' seats, faced forward along the aircraft's track. Both pilots were looking where they were going. Before Winter could fashion a rejoinder to Babcock's chilling truism, the sky directly in their flight path lit up in an intense, white-yellow-red eruption. Instinctively, from his artillery days, Winter counted the seconds, timing from the eruption to the reception of sound to estimate distance. He never heard the report, but thought he felt a concussive wriggle. The explosion could not have been more than a few miles away, he thought. Five or six, maybe. And from where they were in their orbit, it appeared to be on or near the DMZ.

Afterglow lingered for an instant following the flash-flame. Beyond the center of the eruption, the three warrants watched as flaming shards of light scattered, falling in feathered irregularity, diminishing in brightness as they descended. In a few seconds the retinal impressions faded and they were staring into a black void, their night vision temporarily destroyed. No one spoke. After a silent minute or so, with night vision returning, they could make out only scattered flickers of lamp light from mountain villages.

Winter felt the pressure of the silence. "What? ARC LIGHT, you think?" Certainly a B-52 strike could account for the explosion, but he knew he was off base. This eruption did not appear ground-based. And ARC LIGHT would have provided more than one explosion.

"Mid-air," Surtain answered quietly.

"Collision? Ours, you reckon?" Winter asked.

"Charlie don't fly," Babcock said, his voice strained.

"Oh, shit. Can we do anything? Make a call?" Winter felt an anxiety to do *something*.

"I'll check around, report it," Babcock said.

Surtain said, "There's nothing on guard channel; not had time. Call CRICKET and CROWN. I'll alert WATERBOY. Give them as good a fix as you can. Tell them we can see nothing on the ground. No fires. No chutes. Nothing," he murmured as he was looking out the cockpit to port. "Probably have to wait for the flights to come up missing." His voice was a deep hollow.

Winter slid back aft, claimed his seat, and spun the dial, looking for chatter that might give them a clue. The linguists, informed of the mid-air by the plane captain, could find no enemy targets and followed Winter's lead, looking for friendlies with information.

"This is a happening," one of the linguists kept repeating.

Another linguist, anxious and irritable, queried, "Aww, fuck, Mitcoff. Is that 'a-happenin,' per your Red Neck syntax? Or are you saying, 'This is *a* happening.'? As in, an event. A thing occurring. 'splain me that, Jo Jo."

The babble of excited operators' voices continued, but could not be heard beyond their upper flight deck positions. Winter suspected everyone's minds were filled with friendly loss.

* * *

In the wee hours, the aft station watch spotted Air America bound for Vientiane. The sleek, civilized business jet with innocuous markings slipped by to starboard a good fifteen hundred feet above them, clear in cloudless skies. When the watch keyed the intercom and reported the jet, Winter leaned over, looked out the port hole by the Controller's station, seeking the courier flight. He could not find the aircraft, but he realized the weather had blown on through the region. The sky was clear with a three-quarter moon.

There was no excitement over the sighting; often, on late night missions, some crewman spotted one or another of the CIA-associated aircraft. They flew regular courier routes encompassing Tan Son Nhut, Nha Trang, Da Nang; Vientiane, Nakhon Phenom, Ubon, Udorn, or Bangkok; and sometimes to Malaysia, the Phillipines, or Cambodia. They were rumored to be hauling weapons and supplies to questionably loyal hill tribes, native insurgents, bandits, and war lords, in any of the countries visited. Another persistent tale was their activity in the Golden Triangle heroin trade along the Burma Shan State-China-north Thai borders. That rumor was so persistent it had taken on a truth of its own, regardless of verifying evidence or no.

Four Two Niner made the Da Nang fuel stop, dropped the pouch, and bumbled its way down the coast to Cam Ranh. The entire crew was somber over the mid-air. Nearly 0300 when they were able to get to bed, all mission crew were awakened early for interview by Air Force intelligence. The light colonel and captain who came with questions seemed grateful that the collision was witnessed and the bare fact of it reported, though there was nothing anyone from the crew could add to flesh-out the basic report.

The Air Force officers acknowledged that two aircraft were missing, both flying missions the night before in the Eye Corps-North Vietnam border netherland. One was an Air Force MISTY F-105 flying out of Thailand; the other, a Navy F-8 Crusader from a carrier on Yankee Station. They operated under two separate controls, a commonly hazardous enterprise. Each control focused on its own charges, and often maintained, against the dictates of good sense and regulations, a *laissez faire* attitude toward anyone else, though the areas of operations might overlap.

Too bad. So sad. The two Air Force intel officers, both pilots, treated the incident with dignity and a sense of grief. But Winter could detect the readily accustomed attitude of, Thank God, wasn't me! He couldn't fault them for that.

* * *

"Yo, Winter Man," Ito called. "Over here." He motioned Winter to his table where he sat alone in the mess.

"Frederick," Winter said somberly.

"You look like shit, excuse me for saying so."

"Well, you're a particularly toothsome little item today yourself, Inscrutable One."

"Heard about the mid-air. Man, some mean shit, huh?" Ito shook his head, his worst suspicions confirmed. His eyes were slitted to no visible eyeball.

"No kidding. Don't guess we'll ever know exactly what—"

"Drivin' in heavy traffic's a bitch. You know that could happen to us. Anytime. And we'd have split seconds to realize we were toast. Downed like that Greek guy. Aviator with feathers.." Ito seemed to glory in the fears he bore about him like a robe. "Oh, and if that's not enough, China's joining the war."

"Oh, really," Winter managed with a straight face. "On whose side?"

"Give you one guess . . . and it ain't us."

Winter leaned over the table and asked, "Where'd you hear this? Nothing official, I presume."

"Better'n official. Straight from the comm center."

"Oh, yeah. That's a solid source."

"They got it off line. From ASA-Pac." Ito had the upper hand now.

Winter decided to ease him off that particular pointy stick. He looked cautiously about. "Fred, don't worry 'bout the Chinese. The whole thing's a Brenner creation."

"The fuck you say. This came from the comm center, not Brenner."

"Exactly. He's pulled that shit before. He started this rumor a couple of days ago. Just talked some jive here in the mess in a mixed crowd. It's pure fiction. Brenner can sell shit to a hog. He knows the word'll spread like wildfire. Fascinates him to see how far and how fast the rumor spreads. And he's not wrong. See, in just a couple of days, it's already made it to Pac headquarters and back. Not bad for a country rumor." Winter chuckled. "Goddamned Luther."

"Well that's just hunky-dory. Had me scared shitless. Everybody believes the rumor. Don't believe it *is* a rumor."

"Because it came in over the wire, right?" Winter insisted. "All it takes is one little trick like that to give substance to anything he conjures up."

"Why? I mean, what good's that kinda' shit gonna do Brenner? Just makes people nervous, scared. He can't make money off it, can't even enjoy telling anyone it's a joke without spoiling it."

"That's just Brenner. He's got more angles than an Escher painting.." Winter grinned. "You should hear some of the doozies he circulated in Europe when we had the Russkies on our doorstep."

"I just bet. Well, shit. I won't know what to believe, with him around," Ito worried.

"Just don't believe anything. That's what Brenner advises. That way you're never disappointed."

"Don't tell me *you* subscribe to that theory. Shit, you got terminal empathy about the world, about people and things. That attitude would stress you dead," the little warrant officer protested.

"Yeah, but see, I know it's Brenner. I can always tell when Brenner's on a fling."

"Well, shit."

Winter left the mess, walked to the Orderly Room and checked his box. He had a couple of official papers, one of them an *Info Copy* for A&D. He read the set of orders from USARV for award of the Soldier's Medal to one SP5 Wallace Tscheib. Winter exploded.

Demanding to see the CO, he was invited in. Major Nichols, new to command of the First by two days, waved him in, said, "Dave. What you got? I'm about to make a check flight. Will this take long?"

"No, sir. Just a question about this Soldier's Medal for Tscheib. Have you seen this?" He proffered the order copy.

Looking over the form, Nichols's mouth drew down. "No, I had not seen this. Fucking Jernigan musta' signed off on that, just before he rotated out. Son of a bitch!"

"Yessir." Winter looked blankly at him, shook his head knowing there was nothing to be done by either of them, and reached for the paper. "For the Awards and Decorations files," he growled. He saluted and went out of the new CO's office.

He heard behind him, "Sorry 'bout that, Chief. That shit won't fly with me."

He almost believed Nichols.

* * *

That evening, in a poker game in Jernigan's still-vacant room, Captain Trunick looked up from his hand of assorted colors and numbers and said, "Have any of you heard . . . there's a stag movie floating around the Navy billets starring Raquel Welch. Stark-ass naked, doing evil things. Anybody seen it?"

There was a chorus of enthusiastic response, but no positive answer. So far, the fair Raquel had eluded First RR. A thing that seemed unlikely; Bimbo at least would have known.

Goddamned Brenner, Winter grinned, and asked for two cards.

* * *

On the next mission he flew, Winter left the crew at the Da Nang fuel stop, meeting a driver at the strip who waited with the courier. The driver, a PFC from the 138th RR Co., almost hidden under a coat of grease and smelling of oil changes and brake fluid, drove him to an Orderly Room. It was hidden in a corner of the clutch of unpainted buildings on the back side of the airfield, where he was given a bunk among the few pilots of the 138th who flew regularly out of Da Nang. Most of the company operated out of the airfield at Phu Bai, prior Trai Bac Station, now coexistent with the 8th RR Field Station located near Hue, old imperial capital of Vietnam.

Someone had left a Jeep at the Orderly Room for Winter to use, and had informed the supply sergeant, who woke him at 1100 for chow. He had a quick shower, put on fresh fatigues he'd brought with him on the mission, stuffed his still damp flight suit in his bag, ate in the mess, and headed for III MAF, headquarters for Third Marine Amphibious Force. Third MAF was a customer, a regular and devout user of the intelligence produced by CRAZY CAT, and Winter had come to liaise with them on matters of mutual interest.

At III MAF, Winter encountered First Lieutenant Lonegren, a Marine mustang officer— directly commissioned from enlisted grade—who had worked a NATO mission for a time out of Operations in Bad Aibling. When he finished his business with III MAF tasking authorities, Lonegren directed him—Winter driving his highly prized vehicle—to the Gunfighter Club, the Air Force Officers' Mess at Da Nang Air Base. En route, on the perimeter road around the twin strips which were continuously launching and recovering strike aircraft, they drove past a tent separated from all other structures in the area. A sign in the sand designated the temporary site of the Da Nang morgue. Winter shivered, remembering his unfortunate blunder at Tan Son Nhut when he stumbled into the Vietnamese morgue tent and found himself amidst the carnage of three nations' leavings. The memory cast a pall over his thus-far not-disastrous visit.

He parked the Jeep in a zone marked "For Commanding General Only," a spot pointed out to him by Lonegren as especially useful.

"C.G. never drives himself, of course. When he comes here, his driver pulls up, disembarks the man, and usually goes to fill the tank, get his own meal at the N.C.O. Club, or other triviality. C.G. don't use the parking space," Lonegren assured him.

Winter, having visions of his borrowed Jeep with a Denver Boot on it, rationalized that it wasn't his Jeep, and if someone booted it or otherwise nominated it for grief, should he care? Heading up the walk he was surprised to find himself threatened by this newly emerging "don't give a shit" attitude.

The sidewalk that led into the Gunfighter Club was a serious concrete affair, poured by one who knew his business, likely a tenant Air Force Red Horse squadron. It bore huge, green footprints, irregularly three-to-four feet in length. Welcoming phrases and claims to ownership by the Jolly Green Giants led the walker directly into the lobby.

Da Nang was home ground for a number of Air Force squadrons, mostly fighter or fighter-bomber; there were also recon and Forward Air Controllers, and others. But the Jolly Greens had the most glamorous appeal.

Winter had not seen an officer's club on a par with this one since Frankfurt. Air Weenies did themselves proud, he thought wryly, remembering Brenner's litany about Air Force priorities. But he was made welcome by Lonegren and his comrades, and when the others learned he was a prior Marine, he could not buy his own drinks.

Hard-pressed to break away long enough to eat a meal in the evening, he fled the scene as soon as he could. He napped a few hours and when the duty NCO woke him per instructions late in the evening, he leisurely made his way across the field and waited a short while in the ramp area where he met the CRAZY CAT mission bird and flew home to Cam Ranh Bay.

chapter thirteen

The Upas Tree

Cam Ranh Bay, Viet Nam: March 1969

Winter showed up in the Ops building just after lunch, fresh from the big city. He looked like hell. I couldn't get a rise out of him, though not for lack of trying.

"Dave, you heard the rumor?" I thrust my face at him, projecting a shameless leer. He stared at me for maybe a full minute, then shook his head. He wasn't interested.

I persisted.

"Yes, my warrior brother. Soon will come the *Chinois* hordes— and be careful of your pronunciation if you pass this on . . . *hord-d-des*; we don't want a stampede—for I hear tell they're coming into the war." To maintain the integrity of any charade, the premier requirement is not to spread around the giveaway. I knew Winter had let Ito into the scam, but there were all the other ops and pilots and people still out there, uninformed. At risk. And no feedback about Raquel.

"Your ass, Luther." He shook his head and wandered on through the building.

"There'll be news at tonight's banquet," I taunted after. No response. I saw Sergeant Boch staring quizzically across a file cabinet. "What do you think, Sarge? About the Chinese?" I didn't listen for his answer, but followed Winter on through the length of the Quonset hut and out the far door. He had disappeared.

That evening, when I reached the Sandbag patio and had initiated my first San Miguel— grateful the supply lines were open to the Philippines, thereby avoiding the Carling Black Label threat—I saw Winter seated by himself on a picnic table bench, near the flimsy wall that aspired to a shield for the senior officer quarters beyond. Majors and above lived on the near side of that next building, and as we had only three such staff grade officers, there were empty rooms. I might have been happy, I thought, might have prospered in one of those empty spaces; then, perhaps not. I felt no bitterness. The Army game was my playing field.

The far side of that building was used by Naval Air Facility for billeting, but none of us knew who slept there. Probably North Vietnamese submariners.

Not wanting to pry into Dave's earlier distancing, I merely nodded to him. It seemed likely that he was in a Nickie funk, either because he'd received no mail . . . or he *had* received mail. Or even more likely, a Nicole-Moira funk. Neither a profitable venue for my curiosity.

Bimbo had the grill going and some contraband pork chops were smoking over the coals. Dave, finishing one, licked grease from his fingers, turned to me, and said, "Watch."

He tossed the bone toward a small eruption in the wire covering the inside of the wooden slat fence. Immediately, a grizzled muzzle probed the opening and snatched the bone. Gone in a second. Dave turned to me.

"Know what I think?" he said.

"Of course," I replied.

"What?" He didn't even sound skeptical; it was a question.

"You think Major Nichols is penned up beyond that fence, and you're being Mister Nice Guy, feeding him scraps."

"Oink!"

"Oink? *Oink!*" He'd gone me one better. "What the hell you mean? Oink, of one-forty-sixth nee Third R.R.U. fame? That Oink?"

"I been watching that snout through the hole in the fence.. Dog has that same scar on his nose, the one he got attacking that Zip corporal on the flight line in 'sixty-five. Remember, fucking Zip slashed him with a bayonet and we had a fight with the First Shirt because he wouldn't put Oink in for a Purple Heart." Winter was on a roll. When things are slack, it's fun to watch him go into incensed mode.

"Yeah," I lied. I vaguely remembered the dog had a scar, but I didn't remember how he'd come by it. I wasn't sure Winter did.

"So, one dog's nose is pretty much like another, I would imagine. Even down to a scar, in this country."

"That same shit-brindle brown color, crooked fuzzy jaw. About the same size, best I can tell through the fence. Gotta be Oink." He was adamant, but curiously didn't seem excited about his find. I must have Inadvertently shown interest. He stood up, said, "Come on," and we set off toward the end of the fence line. Winter said, "I heard tales about an Oink here at the First. But I thought it was just a name that had caught on, sort of a generic G.I. mutt, from the time of the original Oink at Tan Son Nhut." He grabbed a scrap of charred pork as we passed the grill and tossed the blistering meat back and forth between his hands as we walked.

Hell, three, four years before? I'd not wasted any time thinking on it, but had I done so, I would have assumed the Third RRU's mascot to be long dead. If not the local foreign nationals, the Koreans had been in-country a while, and half their cookbooks featured bow-wow as the *pièce de résistance*.

Beyond the fence, we looked toward the backside of the hole. There sat a large, scruffy-looking creature of the canine species. He didn't run from us; he glanced curiously once, then turned back to his food source. As we walked up to him, I had visions of a reunion. That we would all go out for drinks together, talk over old times. Treat the war as non-news.

Winter knelt down by the creature, spoke his name once, and waited for the dog to acknowledge him. In 1964-65 for a while, Winter was in almost sole possession of the dog's affections. They were inseparable for a period, and it was Winter who first sneaked him aboard a U-6 on a mission.

"I do remember Oink's first mission,' I said. "Stoetzel, jokingly I think, agreed you could bring him on the bird, and then had a shit fit once you'd launched and he found he was carrying not only an operator, but the op's best friend." I didn't say it, but Stoetzel, for all the crazy shit he pulled and all the good times he promoted, came within a whisker of running Sergeant Winter's young ass up a flagpole. But then he later signed off on the spurious recommendation for Oink's Air Medal.

As if resenting my comments, the dog turned to face Winter. He made low, burbling noises deep in his chest. His ratty, grease-clotted tail set up a minute vibration that could not be construed as wagging, but seemed to convey awareness. Suddenly he barked; one sharp, throaty eruption and he leapt forward, right into Winter's face. He was too quick, belying his seedy, indolent appearance; and I could do nothing to save Winter from a savage mauling.

And mauled he was . . . with a wood rasp tongue. I hoped it was Oink. I didn't like to think there were two dogs in the world so slavishly devoted to this one man.

After the ice was broken, after the licking assault, and after Winter had fed the quarter-pound slice of blackened pork to the beast, they went off somewhere together. Having a brew and carrying on a conversation with the two of them one minute, I looked up and they were gone.

Moira showed up that evening, making a quick stop to introduce a new nurse to the Sandbag, and she to see Dave. He was nowhere to be found. I told her he had met an old friend he'd not seen since 'sixty-five and they were gone somewhere. She took it in stride. Uncommonly fine looking women. I watched the two nurses all the way back to their borrowed Jeep, then looked elsewhere, guiltily wondering if Dave had seen me scoping out his squeeze.

I still harbored concern about the Winter-Burke coalition. Following their serendipitous meeting and subsequent seeming-dedication to each other, I feared it to be a relationship that had no future. Something temporary, though intense. The Dave Winter I knew was still a married father of two, in all respects. If that circumstance was in abeyance for now, it was not a thing discarded. I felt a sense of unease for the future. And I wanted to see neither of them hurt.

So that my time was not entirely wasted as I waited for the two uncommon companions to reappear, I gave some thought to my next project. I thought it time to let the rest of MAC-V know that Uncle Ho had a nuclear capability.

* * *

March was crumbling, the days tripping by. On the 31st, Winter was on the manifest with a mixed bag of linguists, including the one Laotian speaker. CW4 Surtain was aircraft commander. MAJ Koenigseder, the new XO, flew co-pilot. Koenigseder was National Guard; how he managed an active duty slot in the First was anybody's guess. Besides an unwarranted arrogance, and lacking the foundation of trust accorded most of the First's pilots, there was little to distinguish him.

Briefing was brief. More of the same! The crew straggled across blistering concrete to board -531. The plane was not a happy ship, but it had survived almost two years in country, and had just come from engine change. Chances were better than even that the flight would make it through an entire mission without bowel-emptying trauma, so thought the majority of the crew. The bird was ready; the crew was sweating under the wings. The crew chief—known variously under that title, or as aircraft captain, flight engineer, or most often, Shit Bird, came running across the apron waving the ARC LIGHT frag/warning report. The full complement of flying soldiers mounted up and were rapidly away, only some forty minutes late.

Two hours later, ploughing through cloudy but relatively calm skies, -531 was nearing the target area at 9,500 feet. The crew had settled in, already sweeping the bands, looking for targets of opportunity; there was nothing on their schedules for this hour.

Winter sat at the Controller's position, paralleling the ops' efforts, but listening for the sharp, brittle rhythm of a manual Morse signal instead of ding-dong voices, awaiting the bank to port which would take them into the heart of target country. He had the volume cranked up, trying to pull a faint Morse signal out of a blizzard of weather-induced interference. The humid atmosphere and the edge of fronts along the coast produced a cacophony that tended to drown out weak signals, so when the explosion came, he barely heard it.

The sound was only slight accompaniment to a severe jolt of the airframe. Winter jerked the earphones off his head, peered out the starboard window, port-hole size and shape. He saw nothing to fear.

The five operators, as a body, ripped the cans from their heads and stared about wildly. The aft-station watch, seated on the port side of the bird let out a cry: "We're hit!"

Only Winter heard the cry over the aircraft noises; the watch had not used his intercom. The ops, unhearing, continued their panicky, searching scans. Where they operated on the forward upper deck, there were no windows; they could see nothing beyond the skin of the aircraft. This only acted to increase anxiety as they suspected the worst.

Winter stood, leaned across and looked out the port window and saw smoke pouring from the port-side recip engine. He heard aft-station watch reporting the smoke in a squeaky voice. Good news: the prop was still spinning; bad news: smoke mostly obscured it. Trying to determine how soon the aircraft would crash, the ops, donning headsets, began pressing the intercom key, jabbering. Questions, shouts, curses, prayers—the intercom was overwhelmed. Winter, on his Controller's panel, shut off intercom to the ops' lines. As he remained on that line, he heard Surtain speak in a comforting baritone.

"Well, troops. Looks like we blew a cylinder on the port recip. I'm gonna shut her down."

Good news: Surtain gave no evidence of anti-aircraft fire, great evidence of suave control of whatever situation they'd been plunged into.

Still, not good news: the bird was only two hours into a thirteen-hour flight. Consequently, it retained roughly eighty-five percent of its initial fuel load. A lot of weight. Without the power and stabilizing effect of the huge R-3350 powerplant on the port side, the aircraft would transition quickly into a hazardously unstable configuration. Too unstable, perhaps, to allow banking the aircraft without risk of losing control.

Imagining quickly the worst-case scenario, Winter envisioned the aircraft having to continue flying straight and level until sufficient fuel was exhausted to enable control. But they were flying a zero-degree heading now, due north. The bad guys were due north. North Vietnam was due north. It was not wise to go much farther due north . . . but with the threat of loss of control, it was equally unwise to try to turn and head south. They would fall from the sky, realizing Chicken Little's worst fears.

"Pilot to crew." Winter saw on the panel that Surtain had overridden his shutdown of the intercom and now held everyone's attention. "This one's aborted. We're headed home. I'm bringing up the port J. thirty-four . . . take up the slack. No sweat. We're squawking MAYDAY now, just in case, and considering possible landing sites, but we should be able to make Cam Ranh.. Hang tight. Controller, take care of your people."

"Aye, Chief," Winter responded without thinking. The pilot's intercom clicked off. "Crew, shut down positions. Deadline the sets. Get any classified materials in one batch and get it back to me. Take up ditching stations. Chop-chop."

What melodramatic crap! He didn't need to remind any of them to get the lead out. Some ops were already ahead of him, and a brown burn bag with about an inch of stacked paper folded inside came back hand-to-hand and was slid over the wing beam to him. He stashed the classified papers in the Mission Bag.

Winter looked back toward the rear of the bird. The aft station watch, SP4 Keys, stood behind him, rubbing his hands, his grin a corpse-like rictus. Winter saw his lips moving, but the pilot calling WATERBOY, radar control in the northern sector, blocked Keys' voice. When Surtain had given his status, Winter said, "Sorry, Keys. Couldn't hear you. Go ahead."

"Shit, Mr. Winter. I thought that was triple-A," he said, talking rapidly. "Thought we caught some thirty-seven or fifty-seven millimeter, for sure. Just a malfunction. Just a cylinder, huh? It's OK, then. Right? It's OK? Mister Surtain's a cool head. We're going home." Despite his rationalizing, Keys continued moving in a nervous, tight circle, his eyes fixed brightly on Winter.

"Don't know yet, Keys. Get back on station watch." He pointed, and the soldier darted back to his post as if he'd just been awaiting direction. He settled in, buckled in, and his eyes froze on the slowly wind-milling prop of the dead engine. Occasional wisps of smoke still eddied out around the cowling.

Winter, confirming that the starboard engine was doing its job taking up slack from the dead port engine, was fixated on the starboard wing. The prop was faithfully spinning, its dull black surface creating black-and-silver-and-red arcs through occasional cloud. There was no sensation of the aircraft moving into an unstable mode, no sense of slipping out of control. The roar of the engine was comfortingly loud. And he'd clearly felt the surge when the port jet came up on line. All was still good with the world.

Another few tense minutes went by. No more than a year. All hands were getting antsy in ditching stations, which meant for the operator-linguists up on the ops' deck crowding onto the floor, seated, facing aft.

Surtain announced he was experiencing erratic operation of the starboard recip now, and Winter glanced out his port hole window, only marginally alarmed . . . until he saw the tight streamer of smoke peeling back from the right engine. He stared, thinking, I'm looking at this all wrong. Surtain's already shut the other bugger down. We *couldn't* be having trouble with our only other recip.

What am I imagining? He shook his head to dispel the bizarre. Wiped his eyes, to clear his vision. Pressed the mike button. "Pilot, Controller. We've got smoke coming from the starboard engine."

No reply.

"Pilot, Cont—"

"Got it, Dave." CW4 Surtain overrode all systems. As he spoke, things went down hill.

Winter, frozen in place, couldn't take his eyes from the remaining, now untrustworthy starboard engine. His vigilance was rewarded. He called forward. "Uhh, Chief, there's oil streaming back over the wing now, just started, from the top side of the right engine. Nope," he amended, "top *and* bottom. Just a small stream—spaghetti thick, at first—it's getting bigger."

Winter was confident he could control his voice and not embarrass himself though he felt threatened by everything about him. He felt a surge of empathy for Ito.

"Crew, Controller, this's pilot. Hang tight. The major's raised an emergency alternative for us at Thuy Hoa. Fighter strip, but they've got enough concrete to take us . . . if my brakes hold out. And I don't lose hydraulics." Winter tried desperately to remember back to his flight training: what was the relationship of the hydraulics to active power?

There was a loud click, a confusion of overlapping voices, and Winter could hear the co-pilot, Major Koenigseder, babbling in an excited voice, "We gotta ditch, Chief. We can't keep it in the air without recips. I'll alert them—"

The intercom clicked back off; the voices went away. Winter felt the aircraft start to bank gently to port. He was sure he could feel it sliding out from under them. At the same time, the noise level decreased sharply, then rose again in a different pitch, as Surtain shut down the right recip and brought that starboard jet on line.

Intercom on: "Pilot to crew. We're cleared into Thuy Hoa. We only have to negotiate about thirty degrees of heading change . . . we're halfway there. Controller, ensure all hands secure in ditching stations."

In the background to Surtain's measured comments, Winter could hear another voice in the background, in the cockpit: Koenigseder. Had to be. Not over the intercom; but yelling in the space of the cockpit: "Let me have the controls, chief. I'm the senior officer here. It's my—"

"Get your hand off the controls, Major. Altogether off. As Aircraft Commander, *I'll* have us on the ground in ten minutes. Get a grip." Surtain's intercom clicked off.

The crew—five operators, flight engineer, two aft-station watches, the spare pilot, CW3 Estes who was sleeping in the aft bunk until wakened by Keys, and the Communicator, Sergeant Gibson—all were in their ditching stations without excess dither. One new linguist yelled out, "What if we have to jump?"

"Mister Surtain's got it covered, kid. We ain't gonna hafta jump. We're almost into Thuy Hoa. Bear with it." Gibson, who had flown with the old warrant officer almost a full year now, knew where to put his trust.

Seated at Winter's feet, Gibson looked up at him and mouthed, "We're fucked if we have to jump. We're already too low for a safe jump. And if she falls off level flight, none of us'll get out of this mutha." He blinked and looked away.

Winter felt and heard the varicam's wracking movement; the flaps were crawling out but could not be taken to max because the weight of the plane dictated a higher speed to maintain flight; the spoilers were flexing. The aircraft was making every sound it was capable of . . . except that of two powerful Wright piston radial engines firing on all 18 cylinders. A distinct absence of that comforting drone dominated the audio range.

"Pilot to crew. We're cleared, straight in. Emergency landing. Button up." The pilot added no peripheral information. Winter was the only one, besides the pilot, co-pilot, communicator and aft watch who had a view outside. He saw they were down to 900-or-so feet, and saw parked fighter jets, fuel bunkers . . . 700 feet . . . a couple of small, white buildings flitting by . . . no strip yet. He felt the pit of his stomach descending with the aircraft. Six hundred!

A fire engine flashed by, caught in a turn. Then down, five, four, three hundred.

The short, sandbagged control tower flew past. One hundred fifty. One hundred. Sixty. Then bottoming out.

The two main tires struck lightly, settled onto the strip, and the aircraft was still moving too fast. The flaps, cranked quickly to FULL put as much drag on the slipstream as possible. The nose of the bird dropped slowly, smoothly. When it touched, there was a slight shudder throughout the aircraft, and immediately Winter could feel the effects of the brakes as the pilot tried to push the pedals through the frame of the aircraft. He heard the tower informing the pilot that the right engine was on fire. He looked out.

They weren't wrong!

Winter checked the port engine—the original problem child, the one Surtain had feathered first—and saw it still windmilling. He remembered—you had to have at least one recip turning, to keep the generators cranking enough electrical power to handle electronics, communications, and some necessary navigation aids. That passive windmill mode would not serve the entire aircraft, but enough to handle emergency duties, if well managed. But -531 still thundered down the strip, faster than was comfortable. Winter feared they would run out of Thuy Hoa landfill.

A line of trees that Winter could see out the window, curving around in front of the long length of the airstrip, grew rapidly higher. The bird was past any airfield structures now, so there was little to fear from that sort of collision. But they were running out of airstrip.

He felt a sharp juddering through the airframe as the brakes ground and shredded and burned away. One wheel—Winter couldn't tell which—locked up; the momentary jolt lurched the aircraft left, then right. He heard the jets laboring under acceleration and deceleration—alternate impulses, and then they were gone. A short skid, straight ahead. A jolt, an absence of sensation . . . and they were stopped. With concrete left.

Welcome home.

Signed, Mother Earth.

Winter was desperate to know the condition of the brakes and tires. To no purposeful end; they were home free. But a murky memory of a tale heard, not experienced, took root in his consciousness, and nothing he focused on could dispel the uneasiness of fearful replication.

* * *

Viet Nam: February 1965

Old Man Self, his body twisted in an unnatural attitude, stamped on the left rudder pedal, cranked the yoke hard to port and forward toward the panel. The RU-6 rolled ponderously onto her left side and plunged toward the mottled green carpet below. He held the banking dive for what, in Reese's judgement, was a dangerously long time, given that time equated to lost altitude. From where he sat behind the pilot, the operator could not read the stamped warning notice on the control panel, but he knew that DeHavilland, beloved of their creation in this high-wing, single-engine utility aircraft, nevertheless felt obliged to post the notice which he recalled said something to the effect of "This aircraft not designed for acrobatics, flat turns, and other aerial maneuvers that overstress the structure." Covering their ass, Reese knew. And his, he hoped.

Reese urged into the intercom, "Uhh, Chief, the trees and ground and shit are coming up fast." He was looking over the pilot's shoulder at the altimeter, watching it spin down from mission altitude of 2,500 feet, passing now through 1,500. Not much to spare.

The intercom clicked. "Son, how long you been flying? Trees and ground don't come up. We're going down," Self said, imparting newly uncovered truths.

"Roger that, Chief. And goddamned fast, too. Uhh . . ." Reese tried to keep the nervousness out of his voice while imploring rational action.

"'s okay. I know it's down there. Somewhere." The pilot chuckled and pulled the yoke into his belly. He held it cranked left and the small unarmed reconnaissance aircraft continued in a spiral, shallowing out in its loss of altitude.

"I can't get good readings this low; the angle's too shallow and I'll never be able to get an aural null," Reese urged, leaning forward as far as his harness would allow, noting the altimeter fluttering around the eight on the hundreds scale; the thousands were past and no longer pertinent to his concerns. "What're we doing down here?"

There was no answer. The pilot continued to work the pattern and leveled out near 500 feet. But operators—non-pilots—liked distance between them and the planet. Mister Orozco had put it succinctly, advising those who flew with him not to worry about how much clearance there was; just so there was clearance. "It's only when you're out of clearance that you're torn to shreds."

"Chief—"

"Thought I spotted a stand of upas."

"What? Stand of who?" Dialogue became stilted, open-ended.

"Upas. Stand of upas trees."

Reese looked out the window to his left. He could see pines, some bamboo along a stream, and some tall deciduous trees that from his perspective had crowns that exceeded the aircraft's present altitude. He knew the treetops really were safely below them, but they were honking big suckers. Probably mangroves. Mangroves only grew where there was plenty of water, and if there was such a place, it was here in IV Corps.

"Where?" The operator swept his eyes over the landscape visible to him.

"Musta' been a trick of the light. Don't see them now. They're big tall muthas, light- colored bark."

"What about 'em? Why you want to find them?"

"I want to know where they are so we can stay away—"

The familiar *Clink!* like a crumpled Budweiser can announced an alien object passing through the aircraft's thin aluminum skin. Reese knew it was a bullet, imagined he heard the report, but couldn't be sure; hell, they were low enough. At the instant of impact the Old Man reacted, jamming the throttle to the firewall. The roar of the engine made everything after a guess.

"I see the sonuvabitch," Self said as he worked the controls, not to gain maximum distance from the threat as Reese would have preferred, but to get a sighting of their assailant. Reese was busy, sniffing for the smell of fuel. If the round had ruptured a fuel line, or worse a tank, it could bleed out, leaving them in a glider. Or worse, catch fire and explode. Lots of terrifying scenarios, but the operator could smell no fuel. Self's words came through to him.

When he followed the pilot's gaze, Reese spotted the sniper. He pushed his sliding glasses up into place. The spectacles were smeared with oil-grease-sweat; he jerked them from his head and reached for his handkerchief. At that moment, Self banked sharply left to come around on the sniper, a move Reese was not anticipating.

With the sudden maneuver, the glasses flew from his hand and disappeared on the flooring, bouncing behind the equipment rack. He couldn't take the time to crawl around on the G-forced, imbalanced deck.

He wrested the M-14 clumsily from behind the seat, fought the length of it to get it to the window. He reached up, jerked the sliding Plexiglas panel down. Yanking the operating rod, he chambered a round and flipped the selector to automatic. Twisting the strap about his arm, he aimed the rifle at the dark blotch of vegetation where he had last seen the shooter. With the plane bouncing in the updrafts off the hot, humid land, he loosed off a long burst.

Everything beyond the front sight was a mirage, a pointillist landscape. What he thought was the enemy could well be a shrub or a water buffalo, but he held his finger down, feeling the comforting buck and bounce, the reports loud even over engine noise as the rounds cranked off. The aircraft passed over the figure on the ground, and following his hazy target over the sight blade, Reese released his safety belt, stood, knelt on the seat and still firing, tracked the shadowy figure as it passed below the plane. He leaned farther out the open port and held the target as best he could as it disappeared beneath the Beaver, keeping his finger on the trigger, savoring the recoil, until the bolt locked open. Empty! Twenty rounds, gone in a flash.

The yelling penetrated the fog of excitement, fear and adrenalin surge that wrapped him.

"YOUGODDAMNEDSTUPIDFOUR-EYEDMOTHER FUCKERYOUBLEWUPMY TIRE!" the pilot screamed.

That was silly shit, Reese decided, still caught up in the action high. He released the empty onto the deck and jammed a full magazine of 7.62 mm into the rifle. Hell, why would he shoot the tire? He ignored the pilot's screams, wondering if he'd hit the source of all this bother.

* * *

For four years before the Marines landed in 1965, there had already been another military organization doing their job in country, sub-rosa. Ground operations of these "radio researchers," their covert title, eventually were deemed insufficient to US policy needs, and a tandem air operation was conceived, enthusiastically designed, and amateurishly implemented. When the new pilots and manual Morse intercept operators of the 3rd RRU Air Section began their exacting new pursuits, it was with abysmal ignorance of this magical Land of Oddz.

Every kingdom cherishes its store of tales and legends, the fiber of myth binding intact the functioning of that society. But ignorance of the upas tree account in Asia was surely the fault of spotty, inadequate intelligence. Strangely, it was not some trouble-making enlisted man who revealed this oversight to the Third Air, but a pilot, WO-1 Moreland. A former ASA traffic analyst, thinking to better himself through the Army's Warrant Officer Flight Program, Moreland was subsequently rewarded for his enthusiastic adventurousness by assignment back to Viet Nam upon graduation from a series of pilot-training programs. A reader by default, he stumbled upon the legend of the upas tree in-country. It would be his repayment for Viet Nam times two.

Following initial discovery, Moreland quickly accumulated, organized, archived, and printed up for presentation a body of knowledge regarding the upas tree, advocating the info be relayed to all new, in-coming personnel.

The upas tree was known to grow only in the deepest jungle. It resembled a beech tree. A tall, graceful tree—its first branches often beginning only after sixty-to-eighty feet of trunk—with smooth, pale gray or dirty-white bark, the upas (*Antiaris toxicaria*) became the subject of many and varied legends.

The tree was intensely poisonous, without question, both bark and juice from any part of the tree. A scratch by its bark, branch, or twig on one's body resulted immediately in deadly infection. The sap from a newly severed branch or twig initiated severe rash. Any person or animal unfortunate enough to ingest the juice shortly passed from this iniquitous vale in agony.

Fumes caused by abrasions on the tree's trunk, limbs or even leaves, carried a poisonous message upon the wind. No animal could live within fifteen miles of this arboreal plague. So enervating was its presence, birds, whose mere shadows touched the tree while flying above a forest harboring the upas, fell lifeless from flight.

Natives used the milky sap of the tree to prepare a venomous unguent for their arrows, though no one bothered to explain how the juice could be safely gathered and converted to a usable form without transporting its user to heavenly bliss.

Condemned criminals were tied to the tree to die in unmentionable agony. Sceptics questioned how the executioner could get close enough. . . . But legends don't concern themselves with details.

The literature on this phenomenal tree had been enlivened in the late eighteenth century by an expatriate French surgeon, one M. Foersch. References to the deadly growth were manifold and ubiquitous. When Brenner had first heard the legend, he scoffed at the notion of "the spurious tale of fearsome fauna" and sought to educate worried Gis against the myth.

But it was years before 3rd RRU flyers discovered that the fearful *Bohun Upas*, "the tree of poisons," was a Javanese phrase, not Vietnamese. This led to further research, further revelations: the legend was a folklore standard of the island nation of Java. Upas, it was eventually revealed, was a Javanese word for a poison derived from the gum of the anchar tree, a member of the fig family (*Moraceae*), and a native of the Sunda Islands, many leagues from Viet Nam.

But pilot Moreland's invidious payback lingered, long after that discontent airplane driver flew away from Asian shores. Even after exposure of the frenetic scare. Despite the unveiling of its purely fabled roots, stories of the upas tree continued to hold new operators and pilots in thrall until other fears overtook them. Fears that grew as they developed a proper respect for a low political form of peasant life called charlie.

* * *

"No use heading for the barn," Self said in a tight voice, glancing down at the mass of debris that had formerly constituted one of the two useful front tires on his bird. "We'll finish the mission. Blown tire don't bother me, long as we're airborne. We're only gonna have a problem when we go to land . . . and I ain't in a hurry to do that. Let's burn some av-gas."

Reese chased dits and dahs for another hour and ten minutes, all the while sweating mission end. When he finally and reluctantly told the pilot his skeds were finished, the Old Man turned the Beaver away from the mouths of the Mekong, toward the fearsome concrete of Tan Son Nhut.

They came in over Cholon, crossing the Song Sai Gon, and entered the pattern, Self squawking emergency, taking up a position in the stack of landing aircraft. He followed a Mohawk, behind a C-130, behind a tactical fighter, A1E. CW3 Self had explained the nature of the emergency to the tower, but declined to break the queue when offered.

Through the downwind leg and onto base, he held it slow and steady. Just before turning final, he heard on the same frequency another aircraft, an inbound jet, declare a fuel emergency. The tower instructed Army -274 to orbit and hold . . . unless he chose to implement his own emergency override . . . in which case, he still must orbit and hold: the jet took precedence. You could buy two dozen RU-6s from the Canadians for the price of one jet.

When he was given clearance for final leg and landing, Chief Self was careful to stay well behind the jet in the pattern. Ambient turbulence—hot, whirling, kerosene-smelling roils of stressed air—trailed the jet for a mile or so and would have made, even with two wheels, an even more challenging adventure of the dreaded landing.

He had performed one-wheel landings occasionally at Vung

Tau. The runway there lay athwart a narrow spit of peninsula—
the only land available —and pilots contended commonly with
fierce cross winds. But at Vung Tau, once he had dropped the
wing into the prevailing wind and got a wheel down, affording
less chance of getting wind under the wing to flip the plane, he
had clear sailing. And, he had the other wheel to fall back on, so
to speak. To set down on. That was not the case now at Tan Son
Nhut.

The Beaver drifted toward the concrete, well clear of the
ARVN motor pool, over the browsing buffalo, a cluster of skimpy
and unproductive rice paddies, the grass, the endline of the strip,
and across the marking stripes. He eased power, leveled flaps,
and the plane settled gently toward the blazing white surface.
He held the RU-6 in an awkward attitude, left wing high, playing
a dicey game of interpolation between stall speed and hoarding
air as long as possible.

The right wheel touched, bounced, touched again—still the
left wheel was held aloft. He let the craft settle onto the right
wheel, adjusted prop pitch, and pushed the throttle to three-
quarters while juggling the one-legged bird.

Self hadn't time for sightseeing, but Reese watched a lone
army-green pickup truck pacing them, racing along the grass
verge of the strip. The op kept his eyes on the truck and recognized
one of the Third Air's mechanics driving. He didn't want to look
down at his folly.

The left wheel settled, made contact and was set spinning
by the initial friction between the exploded rubber and the
concrete. The Old Man fought the controls and held it aloft as
long as possible—longer than possible, Reese conceded. When
the aircraft leveled out and weight pressed the left wheel onto
the surface equally with the right, the square-wheel syndrome
took over. Violent jerking and shaking engulfed the aircraft. The
wheel struts threatened to rip from the fuselage. Reese, an ostrich
in the back seat, saw pieces of shredded rubber flying past the
window.

A quarter mile down the strip, Self stamped on the brakes

and chopped the power, at which point the left strut bore fully into the strip surface. Two-seven-four whipped raggedly about, counter-clockwise, and came to a juddering, grating halt. The pilot jerked his door open, looked down at the stub of the landing gear: no sign of tire or wheel. His eyes tracked back along a savage scar in the surface of the runway, and saw bits and slivers of macerated rubber, broken metal fittings, pieces of wheel—the spoor of a wounded Beaver. There was no smoke— nothing left to burn—and no fire. Self slumped in the seat, harness intact.

The pickup truck wheeled up beside the pilot's door and Specialist Nicholas, a mechanic on fire watch, called out, "You okay in there?"

Self looked around. "Where's the goddamned crash crew? I declared an emergency."

Nicholas shrugged. "Guess they're all across at the far end of two-five left. A Continental bird came in squawking emergency. They got stews on board," Nicholas said in explanation. "Everybody's over there. I got a fire extinguisher."

chapter fourteen

This Will Win the War

Viet Nam: April-May 1969

Brenner met the flight crew from -531 on the Air Force ramp as they deplaned at Cam Ranh Bay. Driving a two-and-a-half-ton truck, he waited quietly while everyone clambered aboard; the major insisted on the right front seat. Surtain nodded to Brenner; no one else seemed to notice their driver was an officer. The close call had settled uniformly on them like a film of dirt. Fear left a gritty residue.

Avoiding any mention of the absent mission bird, Brenner said to Winter, "You guys been flying, it appears. Probably haven't heard."

No one asked.

"Yeah, American troops are being pulled out of Viet Nam and sent to the Philippines and Thailand."

"This is no time for your bullshit, Mister Brenner," Winter growled.

"Hush, Dave. You're such a grouch. This's no shit," he said excitedly, talking back over his shoulder. "This is the move that's going to win the war. First, we draw down all our troops, send them to the P.I. or Thailand. Some to CONUS. After we get our boys out, we round up all the other good guys: the Aussies, South Viets, Koreans, Thais, Flips, and civilians, put them all on boats and sail them into safe waters out in the South China Sea. Then we bring in every aircraft we have around the world, mount a massive bombing campaign, kill and obliterate everything alive on the landmass of Southeast Asia."

"Brenner—"

"No, wait. Just a sec'. This operation will win the war, I tell you." He displayed no hint of humor. "When there's nothing left after ARC LIGHT and TAC strikes but gray ash, we run Rome plows from the Ca Mau Peninsula, north to the DMZ. Turn Viet Nam into a parking lot for the Air Force BX-es in Thailand."

Even coming from Brenner, Winter thought the proposal piqued a sense of purpose in the addled minds of the shaken airmen. He waited . . .

"Then, we sink the ships."

"Aww, jeez," Winter moaned. It looked to be a long summer.

* * *

Each time, at the nadir of consciousness, poised to slide into black, blissful sleep, the exploding engine jerked him back to confront his fears at 9,500 feet.

Winter had no clear memory of events; he could not recall what he had done, what steps he had taken, whether or not he had performed up-to-snuff. He presumed he "done good," as Surtain had told him; the CW4 was no bullshit artist. And, they *were* all safely on the ground. But his actions be-damned. He knew who the hero of downtown Thuy Hoa was.

Avoiding visions from that dicey period, he tried compiling in his head the words to use in an award recommendation for Surtain's magnificent bit of flying, but he couldn't remain focused. Repeatedly he found himself at the moment when all three wheels of -531 were solidly down on the tarmac. And immediately after. Nothing before. He recalled every nuance of those few post-recovery minutes. . . .

* * *

The jets whispered down to STOP, the whine melding into the sound of sirens on crash trucks, crash crew ambulances, Air Police Jeeps. Ordinary shutdown sounds were absent, as if the plane had died somewhere up there, in mid-flight. Which, in a sense, it had. Despite the comforting whisper of the jets cycling down to stop, the normal sound of the fluttering props when they cut power was missing. The creaking, rocking motions of the aircraft at stop while the recip engines still rotated—missing. The intercom was dead, even white noise—missing. The lights on the galley panel were dark, the coffee pot off.

Coffee's off, mission's over.

Winter slid over the wing beam to the forward deck and pushed his way through the operators. Some remained seated as if exhausted; others, wired, were on their feet and pacing, talking, babbling, laughing. He checked the intercept positions, verifying receivers zeroed out so no surreptitious spy—neither NVA nor US Air Force—could read frequency and determine the aircraft's targets.

Over the growing quiet, as the sirens wound down, Winter heard the choppy flutter of a helicopter. He watched a small, stubby, unfamiliar twin-rotor chopper slip by his window, circling the earth-bound Neptune.

Chief Warrant Officer Surtain shouted back down the fuselage, "Un-ass this thing, troops. More ricky-tick!. Still a threat of fire." As if to emphasize the pilot's concern, the first of the de-planing operators opened the bomb bay, and a cloud of dull red dust whirling about the aircraft suddenly billowed in through the open hatch in the rotor wash of the chopper. Experiencing his first "red out" under the benevolent cloud of fire retardant, Winter gagged. He recalled: the fire retardant powder was made from dried cow's blood, and reeked of fire and fear and burned flesh.

Winter slipped through the hatch onto the strip, weapon and helmet grasped in one hand, the mission bag securely under that arm. Holding the other hand over his nose and mouth, he looked quickly about. Through the red-out, he saw Air Police busy pushing back gawking mechanics and service personnel.

Turning back toward the dispirited P-2, checking that all his ops were clear, he saw Pursell clumpf down out of the bomb bay doors, his field jacket in a bundle under his arm, struggling with rifle and a brown paper bag. Winter chose to look away as Oink's ugly head popped out of the jacket roll.

He knew -531 and crew must present an odd picture to bystanders on the ground: classic Navy airplane; "US Army" painted on the nose; a group of unidentified, similarly dressed military people in gray flight jammies spilling onto the strip, none of whom wore nametags or service affiliation, no badges or indicators of rank. And none anxious to talk.

At the nose of the aircraft by the tricycle landing gear, Surtain followed the major down the short ladder from the cockpit. The atmosphere outside the plane had all the signs of bi-polar disorder: excited babble alternated with sullen silence.

Winter walked around the vertical stabilizer to stand and stare at the port engine. The damage from the blown piston could easily have passed for that of ground fire. The skin about the cowling was burst open, metal peeled back. A titanium banana. Streaks of burned oil and charred fibrous material plastered the cowling. The hole where the cylinder had exited the engine on the in-board side was the size of a basketball. The damaged aircraft presented a sad picture . . . but now on the ground, a safe one. The threat of fire never materialized.

As he stood surveying the damage to -531, Winter spotted an Air Force two-striper in an AP helmet taking a picture with a Polaroid camera. He stopped before the airman, held out his hand, and demanded, "Give me that photo. Classified mission bird." The airman sheepishly deposited the photo into the warrant's hand, even as the latent image grew visible. As they were forbidden cameras on mission, the stolen picture was the only color shot the 1RRC ever acquired.

* * *

Mission aircraft -531 was dead on the strip, and had to be towed off the runway like a *caribao* carcass while aircraft waiting to land orbited above. Some who could not wait—anxious at the delay like a cross-country motorist queued up outside a Sinclair station restroom—drifted away to other venues. Once -531 was off the active strip, there it sat; there would be no flying that wreck back to Cam Ranh Bay.

Surtain exited Operations, leaving the co-pilot major spreading disdain and aggravation among the Air Force people, describing how he, as senior, had commandeered the aircraft and brought it in, saving the crew and the plane. Surtain walked away without comment. Everyone on the plane knew who to thank for their intact body. Air Force gawkers, recalling overheard communications that got the bird here, knew whom to credit with a superb bit of flying.

"Let's go hop a ride," Surtain ordered. "Flight Ops says there's a C-one-twenty-three taking off in fifteen minutes, direct to Cam Ranh. Dave, you got the bag? Everyone got all their gear? Weapon? 'chute? Everything cool? " he asked.

At Winter's nod, Surtain motioned toward an approaching Air-Force-blue crew-ferry bus. The men filed on board. The major ran from Flight Ops and clambered aboard. At the end of a 30-second ride, the crew straggled off the bus and walked up the open ramp of a C-123 with both engines already turning.

The shabby aircraft reeked of vomit and chicken shit. Like any experienced in-country traveler who managed hops on semi-scheduled aircraft, Winter recognized a convoy bird. They hauled anyone seeking a ride, along with crated artillery shells, boxed ammo, C-rats, medical supplies, and domestic animals from here to there and back anywhere south of the DMZ. Vietnamese, to whom airsickness was a religion, dragged along their wives, kids, and fowl hanging head-down from field packs. Chickens and ducks—their GI rations, kept alive until a cooking fire was built—were as much a part of the Vietnamese Army's quarters-and-rations benefits as a rifle and helmet.

But all in all, the ride home was payment enough after the trauma of the emergency.

* * *

Brenner drove away to return the truck to the motor pool after he had deposited the flight crew by the Operations hut. They filed inside, reluctantly, like schoolboys caught in a prank, being marched to face their maker. Reluctance was due more to the broken air conditioner that awaited them rather than the abort. Afternoon heat at peak temps and humidity beyond saturation hung over the peninsula. The briefing room was insult on top of near-injury.

Debrief was an exercise in pointlessness, though no fault was presumed on the part of any crew member. Someone *would be* checking maintenance logs to determine who had performed the engine change, tracking back through the shop, the logistics chain, probably even Avionics. Blame *would be assessed . . .* though perhaps unjustifiably. For now, just get it over with.

When the last crewman exited the steambath debrief, he patted the doorframe in passing, consigning to the building his belated but heartfelt appreciation for having made it full circle.

Winter headed for the Orderly Room. He removed a sheaf of papers from his box, glanced through them, and re-deposited all official communiques. At the bottom of the stack was an envelope, return address, Long Beach, MS. Not the scribble of a small boy, so . . . Nickie? He slid it, unopened, into his flight suit pocket and headed to his room.

Peeling off the dank flight suit, he spread it over the back of a chair in the space between his and Bracken's room. Pulling a can of Barq's Root Beer from the small fridge, he popped it open and settled onto his bunk, skivvies cold against his thighs, drying slowly in the chilled air. He slit the envelope slowly and deliberately with his Kabar.

A letter. From Nickie. In her own words, to him. Typed! *She never typed her letters . . .*

He came slowly to the realization that here, in his hand, after some seven-plus months in country, was a second letter from his wife. He hesitated, almost fearing to read it. But, faint heart . . .

Late April (?), 1969
Dear Dave:

This may come as a shock to you after such a long time. I do apologize. Despite our problems, as an Army wife I know how important mail should have been— to you and to me. You have not been gracious in the letter department either, at least to me. But then I've not provided you much incentive have I? It's good that you have written the boys regularly.

I'll just get on with this. Please understand this is not anger and denunciation from an ill-used wife. If anything it's you who've suffered mistreatment. But for what it tells you about those you're serving with, I think you need to know what I'm about to tell you.

I received a letter two days ago postmarked Fort Rucker. A snide and hateful act. Some sort of revenge (I suspect) against you. The writer, under the guise of "doing me a good deed" but who did not reveal himself, took great pains to assure me of his best intentions. (I assume it was a man.)

He told me of your involvement with a woman, apparently an Army nurse you met there. He did not give me a name but told me much about your liaisons. Where they took place, the frequency of them, and the attractions of this nurse. He seems to think you are <u>smitten</u> (he actually used that word and <u>liaisons</u>) with her, and to all outward appearances are happy in this relationship.

<u>I hope that's not absolutely true.</u> <u>I'm not convinced our life together is finished.</u> For the boys sakes and admittedly for my own I hope it is not.

I'm aware it was my panic and angry reaction to the assignment, that and our subsequent drifting apart, that drove you to this turn of events. You are simply not a man who would normally cheat on his wife. I've always been gratefully aware of that. In our case <u>you didn't cheat on a wife</u>, for I recognize you in truth did not have a wife since Italy.

I cannot do in this letter what needs to be done . . . to be said. I'm sorry, for my own actions, and that you've been forced to go to someone else for warmth and understanding. But, looking upward —

I've read that the Rest & Relaxation program now permits you to choose to take your R&R in Hawaii. Airlines are offering service wives reduced fares there, and we could get reduced rates at Honolulu hotels. Is this something you would consider doing? Can you? Or is it too late?

Are you entitled to R&R, and when? I guess bottom line I want to know: could you? would you? will you? If so, find out when you could go and I'll make arrangements this end. I understand the R&R would be for six days; is that right? I just need to know when and how long so I can make return plans.

Please answer soon so that I can make arrangements for the boys <u>if you agree to meet</u>.

Nicole

Reaching for the Bushmills, Winter poured a stiff measure. He moved his eyes slowly up, then down the page. He glanced again at the signature. "Nicole." Not "Love, Nickie." Not "Fond Regards," nor for that matter, "Fond Regrets." The salutation: "Dear" before his name was an incongruous note. Mixed signals. And "Army wife"? She had previously clearly indicated she was through with that. Where was this coming from? His mind wandered.

He sipped at the glass, sucked in air. Dry? Had he drunk all that Irish? That quickly?

He poured again, began reading again and suddenly realized what had left a sizeable hole in her message: there was no mention of *The Divorce!* He read it once again.

Same words. Nothing disingenuous he could discern, nothing with an obvious agenda, other than what she wrote. But, then, there was that she had not written . . .

Return to the Bushmills. More reading, over again . . . and again.

Could it be what it seemed? Could that previous letter, with all the impact of the threat of divorce, simply be disregarded now? As if never written? Of course, he thought wickedly, aping a Brenner sentiment, the Divorce Letter was seasonal, enclosed in a Christmas card from his sons. How graphic was that?

* * *

The glass was dry again. He looked at his watch and realized he'd been immobilized here, drinking, re-reading the letter, for more than two hours. He poured another shot, this time circumspect with measurement. The fine whisky settled on him like flannel.

Then he knew he'd stalled long enough. Christmas present or not, that threat had been sincere. He'd never considered it a tactic. But this—

No! he answered his own earlier question forcefully. *No!*. It could *not* be what it seemed. The Nicole he knew, mother of his children, long-time lover and friend, would not have accepted a *home-wrecking bitch*—likely how she'd describe Moira. His Nicole, learning of his infidelity, would never respond with the other cheek. Never would she have assumed the blame, even had she truly been the only one at fault. Nicole was incapable of savoring a meal of crow.

So, what's the deal here?

Angry, suddenly, with himself . . . with her . . . he looked at the letter again to confirm a silly truth: Nickie could not punctuate worth a damn. But judging her with Brenner's eye was unworthy. He looked at the envelope and read the same lack of message there.

When the bottle was empty, his vision was clear enough that he could still read the label. He scrutinized a blank space where a message might have appeared, emblazoned in fire, unaware his mind was grasping for something he could take as found.

Wasn't there!

Nicole's presence, her . . . *intention* with the letter. He was so focused on that ambiguity, he only felt a tingle at the edge of awareness about—*Someone had written her a poison pen letter!*

Later, reflecting on this squalid sequence, Winter sought to determine just how much the events chronicled in the letter, and the results of it, had to do with his deepening distrust of the ever on-going war. It seemed an unlikely pairing; but, he argued counter-intuitively, that was only because he didn't know anyone's hidden agenda.

* * *

Winter walked from the midday glare into Supply and stood silently, watching Ito's doomed argument with the Supply Sergeant over issue of another, preferably new sidearm. The .45 he carried hung on him like a cannon on Jimminy Cricket. The pistol was simply too big for his grip. But the sergeant, falling back on bureaucratic standards practiced by all supply sergeants when it suited them, gave him chapter and verse why he could not get a different weapon. Ito didn't want to hear it, turned away and saw Winter standing inside the door, watching.

"Hear that shit, Mister Winter? You have here the very essence of *haole* mentality. Can't give me a thirty-eight because they don't stock enough ammo. Only enough for pilots. Fuck me! Are pilots burning up ammo shooting V.C.? You tell me. Hell, I'll buy my own ammo. If not in the P.X., I'll get it down on Tu Do." His reference to the black market that flourished on the main street, downtown Sai Gon, was an indication of his anger and pure bluff. Ito did his black market trade in Dong Ba Thin.

Winter walked out with the diminutive warrant officer, forgetting why he had come there himself. To counter Ito's mood, he steered the conversation into other quadrants. He didn't intend to mention the letter, but it slipped out.

He wouldn't talk with just anyone about the letter; not, for instance, Bimbo Billingsgate. Or the CO, or even Bracken, his roommate. But Ito, yeah; Brenner, for sure; and Magic Marvin. Enlisted man be damned; he was a friend. And Nickie's friend, too.

"So, are you going to Hawaii? Please say yes," Ito pled after hearing the gist of Winter's unease. "Take me as hold baggage. Man, you're talking home." Ito had forgotten the Supply Sergeant, and fairly skipped alongside Winter, half turned toward him as they walked.

"Hell, I don't know, Fred. The letter's left me . . . I'm confused. I'm not sure what her game is, but sure as shit, she's playing one."

"Why? Why would she do that? You got two crumb-snatchers. You think she really don't wanta get back together with their father?" he said chidingly, disbelieving of such duplicity from his friend's wife. From what he knew of her. Which was little enough.

"Well, I did see the C.O. Asked if I *could* go. He didn't know I'd not even put in for R-and-R, back when they came around soliciting sign-up." Winter didn't say it, but he had not planned to even take the six-day break. Out of country for such a period was desirable, but to take an R&R anywhere, even Bangkok—probably the best bargain, along with Kuala Lumpur—was a significant expense. Flight there and back was free, courtesy US Air Force; but hotel rooms, sightseeing, meals, drinks, other enticements, added up quickly when he lived on a $100 a month. Practically everything he drew on payday went home for the family. How could they afford a trip to Hawaii?

"What'd he say?" Ito pursued.

"The C.O.? He's got the First Shirt working on it. Thinks it won't be a problem, and if they can't find me a slot on a near-time flight, he'll find someone who's already booked and get them to switch with me."

"Decent of him. Better watch out for Nichols; apt to turn out to be human." Even as he said it, Ito was shaking his head in disbelief. "Well, if that don't work, we always have the standby slots with the R-and-R Center folks."

"Yeah, but that won't help. If I took one of those, it would be spur-of-the-moment when someone doesn't show up. *I'd* make it to Hawaii, but Nickie wouldn't. She has to have time to schedule a flight, to farm out the boys. And for me to make hotel reservations. It's probably different in Hawaii than the other R-and-R sites."

"No. You don't make prior reservations. Once you arrive Honolulu, when you get your in-processing brief, they offer you a selection of hotels. Take your pick. They're just about all on Waikiki. *Anything* on the water, or with a view of Diamondhead, will cost you your first-born male child, normally. On R-and-R, you get it for half or less. Meals at break price, too."

"Sounds like the thing to do," Winter acknowledged. "I'll have to wait and see what Top comes up with."

"Screw that, I wouldn't hold for Top. If Nickie's waiting for an answer, go talk to Bimbo. He'll put you on a flight tomorrow, and in the Hilton. And they'll probably pay you."

"Ri-i-i-ght," Winter said, rolling his eyes. "Want to go to early chow? I'm flying. Got a thirteen hundred launch."

"Not this early. The rice balls won't be done yet." Ito waved and peeled off on the sidewalk leading to the hangar. He continued walking but turned back and called to Winter walking away, "Have you worked out who the asshole is that sent her the letter?" He did not wait for an answer.

* * *

Unable to find a vehicle to transport him to the Air Force side of the field, Winter was walking along the edge of a taxi strip, the long way round the airfield, when a three-quarter ton truck pulled up and screeched at him. He was astounded to see a face he knew: SP5 Mladcik Vlad Woijczek. Good Soldier Woijczek, an odd memory from Bad Aibling, had later been encountered again at Tan Son Nhut when Winter was with the S-3. And now here he was.

As uneasy as the soldier had always made him feel, with his strange facility of perfect memory but no practical logic, Winter was glad to see him now. He was melting under the ceaseless sun, and though the truck had no top for cover, at least it would get him to his destination faster and get him out of this broiler. He might even inveigle Woijczek to wait for him while he conducted his little business, and bring him back around the strip, both relieving him of the long, sun-burnt walk, and reduce the risk involved in walking across the airstrips. Dashing sixty yards between aircraft launches was not his favorite pasttime, albeit exciting.

But he'd forgotten just how damaging the specialist's diatribes could be.

"Thanks for stopping, Woijczek! What are you doing up here at Cam Ranh?"

The soldier stopped his preparations for driving, and turned to stare at Winter. "Where, sir?"

"Cam Ranh. Where we are. Cam Ranh Bay Air Force Base. Two Corps."

"Oh, I had no idea, sir." He put the vehicle in gear and started slowly down the length of white concrete. "It is a good thing I came when I did, then, sir?"

"Oh, yes," Winter assured him. And then to preclude what he presumed might become one of Woijczek's infamous lectures, said facetiously, "I was in danger of landmines." He instantly knew when he said it, he'd chosen the wrong diversion.

"Yessir. That would be covered by Department of the Army Field Manual comma F period M period numbers twenty dash thirty-two colon letters Landmine Warfare period chapter numbers one colon letters Introduction period para numbers one dash two period letters application period letter a period Landmine warfare is applicable to strategic and tactical military—"

Winter had no hope of interrupting Woijczek's eloquent delivery, and the pace of it and insistent pertinacity to what he had mischievously said that prompted this delivery, made it doubly damning. Winter stared across the shimmering concrete runways, regretting the necessity for this ride. But he considered the time it would require for him to walk the distance, and settled in for the full treatment.

chapter fifteen

ARC LIGHT

Cam Ranh Bay, Viet Nam: May 1969

Standing under the wing in the shade, Winter checked his watch: thirteen-forty hours. More than a half-hour behind schedule. Looking across the ramp to the Ops building, he saw no winged Mercury hastening to them with the release to fly.

"Where the hell is Boch? I thought he went to get the ARC LIGHT frag report."

"Just so," CW3 Bracken confirmed. "May not be in yet."

"It's always on time. Usually early. Comes in about ten, ten-thirty. Maybe the teletype's backed up with traffic."

"Unlikely," Major Nichols chimed in. The Commander was flying left seat today. "ARC LIGHT frag's got a priority that doesn't permit hold-up. McFadden," he turned to one of the ops, "go check on Sergeant Boch, will you. Tell 'im, get the friggin' ARC LIGHT report and get here."

"Right, sir." The soldier, in the ubiquitous unadorned flight suit, rose from the shaded aluminum slab where he was dozing against his parachute, and moved off at a snail's pace under the white-hot sky.

He was back within minutes.

"No ARC LIGHT report, sir. Teletype's down. Not our end. Circuit."

"Can we get the report from the Air Force?"

"Here, you mean?"

"Yeah, of course here. Here's where we are. With the teletype down, we know we can't get it from Seventh Air Force in Sai Gon."

"No, sir. We could maybe . . . *you* could maybe go over there, talk to them, if you can find someone who knows you, can confirm your clearance status and need-to-know. Maybe. No guarantees." McFadden had no great faith in any inter-service system; he did have a realistic view about Nichols' chances. He added, "But likely, Air Force here has no back-channel."

Without further hesitation, the major said, "Go tell Boch to get his ass on board. We're going."

"Sir?"

"Get the friggin' crew chief and let's get in the air. Now."

McFadden turned in appeal to Winter, who shook his head, denying any part of this circus. *Nobody* flew without warning fragmentary orders—ARC LIGHT frag. It was gospel! You had to know where the BUFs would be dropping tonnage—the sole *raison d'être* for the Big Ugly Fuckers—so as to stay at the other end of the playground. If you didn't know, all bets were off. It was presumptively a flip of the deadliest coin they knew.

No one else seemed disturbed by the major's decision, however. Ops mounted, chattering, grab-assing. Bracken and new pilot CW4 Perko took their places. Perko was new to the First RR, new to the P-2V aircraft, but he had a thick packet in his flight log. Probably good stuff, Winter thought at the time; he had seen Perko when he checked in wearing a First Aviation Brigade patch on his right sleeve,. No telling what he'd done with that outfit on an earlier tour. Ash and trash, executive flights, DUST OFF, gunships—First Av did it all.

Winter saw MacFadden and Boch jogging across the apron.

* * *

It was after 1600 hours before the mission aircraft reported on station. Winter heard Bracken ask Major Nichols over the intercom if they weren't running an undue risk without the frag report. Nichols reminded him that today's mission was nowhere near any of the recent B-52 target areas. Sometimes, CRAZY CAT had to work their skeds and flight path around the ARC LIGHT target impact boxes. They knew well the location of the most frequently targeted ones.

Flying the fully loaded bombers all the way from Anderson Air Force Base on Wake, and considering their inherent mission, gave ARC LIGHT—the B-52s' strategic bombing missions—priority.

And on mission, they had all watched the strikes turning the world into chaff, fusing earth, mountains, rivers, trees, jungle, monkeys, coconuts, maybe even a few enemy troops.

Marine Lieutenant Lonegren had told Winter that troops on the ground a half mile away from a B-52 strike zone could suffer bleeding from the ears and "ARC LIGHT eyes," a condition where the eyes turned red from ruptured blood vessels in the eyeball. He could not imagine what it would be like to be the subject of such directed activity. He didn't want to think about it.

The new pilot, Perko, listened to the intercom exchange and chewed his lip, sitting in the aft station watch seat. He was not unfamiliar with BUF effectiveness. The heavy bombers lived in a world of their own, leaving it to others to stay out of their path. And until they began flying too-oft-repeated missions on targets with increasingly improved missile defense, at their 35,000- foot altitude they had been more or less impervious to ground fire. It had left them arrogant.

"The Man said not to worry! So, let's not worry." Winter's commitment to the sanctity of command, however, felt a strain during the first few hours of the mission.

* * *

McFadden had acquired a target early in the mission, an enemy voice radio operator who sent sked info in the clear indicating more than 100 messages waiting to be sent. Mac had already asked for help, Anderson relieving him after three hours. McFadden stood at the coffee urn, wringing his hands, massaging his wrist.

"Got a hot one, Mac?" Bracken asked, on his way to the rear when relieved by Perko as co-pilot. Word was filtering about that McFadden had got onto a "good 'un" and it would likely involve all ops before mission end. For a change, the Communicator worked steadily, relaying the copy to ground and ultimately to the Eighth RR Field Station at Phu Bai. And there seemed no end to the four-digit groups spoken by the enemy operator, broadcast into the ether.

The Communicator broke transmission to call for a replacement so he could make a relief call in the rear of the bird. When he stopped sending, ground came back with a priority message, reporting that the radio traffic CRAZY CAT was intercepting and passing to the ground was in fact one long, related message reporting the total logistics activity at a major border-river crossing between North Vietnam and Laos over the period of the last three months. Hidden in the body of ambiguous four-digit code were numbers of trucks, cars, pedicabs, bicycles, ox carts; soldiers and agents, oxen, domesticated water-boo, perhaps Arabian stallions; and men, women and children who slaved on the road complexes that made up the Ho Chi Minh Trail. And because no one came down the Trail empty-handed, there was also a summary of all the supplies they carried: AK-47 and pistol ammunition, RPGs, 37- and 57-mm ammo for antiaircraft guns, grenades, the Russian answer to the Bangalore Torpedo, uniforms, food, medical supplies including entire operating room sets, fuel, spare parts, pay for the troops, mail—pretty much subsistence for an army. Everything that had made that river crossing was being revealed.

The ground's message indicated McFadden's copy warranted a priority high enough to override anything else. The message further directed the Controller to ensure that the copy be treated as the most important thing that might ever have been encountered on the air waves.

The essence of the ground station's message was: Keep copying; keep sending.

Out.

When the Communicator returned to his position from toilet break, and read the ground's message copied by his relief Communicator, he related its contents to the Controller. Winter acknowledged with a nod, surprising the sergeant by not showing greater interest.

Winter, when he heard the Communicator's intercom comments to one of the ops asking for information, snapped out of a reverie that was a world removed from a Mekong crossing on the border. He was still pondering Ito's parting question about the hate-mail originator. And yes, he had thought about it—he *was* thinking about it—and was sure he had the answer.

The anonymous letter had to be the product of Captain Warren. Warren was the only one he knew, male or female, who bore lasting enmity for him, so far as he knew. Recently.

Some might—no doubt did—envy him his relationship with Lieutenant Burke. But when he had met Moira, she was new in country, had no other suitors; and if someone was trying to break them up now, squealing on him to Nickie wouldn't do the trick. He had a momentary surge of guilt when he thought of the letter from Nickie. The Blame Game quickly subsided.

Warren had been left nursing a grudge against him, Winter knew, for the running shootout over unwarranted award recommendations for SP5 Tscheib. Even though the captain had eventually gotten the dead soldier a medal, his ire at initial defeat by a lowly warrant officer no doubt rankled.

And Warren was assigned to Fort Rucker, Alabama, where the letter originated!

* * *

The upper deck's collection operators stayed busy through the late afternoon and into the dusk as the Neptune droned across, in, up and down, around, and through a boredom-breaking selection of flight patterns: circles, race-track ovals, boxes, Xs, and long-line passages in and about the primary target area. After locking on the priority target that McFadden was once again working, the aircraft commander knew he must remain in collection range until, if need be, departure was forced by fuel depletion. There was no in-flight refueling for P-2s. Even so, Nichols would push the safety margin to minimums.

Under the gray cover of early darkness, those with access to a window or port saw occasional flashes of light along the Trail. Most activity—the movement of men and supplies— occurred in the hours of darkness, the columns of worker ants less visible then to the tactical fighter-bombers that incessantly roamed the skies above the Trail, seeking targets of opportunity. The presence of lights indicated high priority movement, or the presence of undisciplined movers, the latter a thing not likely.

On the far northern leg of a northwest-southeast oval encompassing the three contiguous countries' common borders, the aircraft droned through the dusk seemingly without enemies. No ground fire had been detected during the long hours of pattern flying; no one "down there" had treated them as a threat or indeed, as an enemy. Assuredly, they must be considered such, but perhaps not on a scale warranting expenditure of hard-won ordnance. Winter, only occasionally distracted now in considering ways to mete out justice to the distant Captain Warren, sat and watched the Communicator continue his interminable message to the ground, passed to him as interminable copy by McFadden and alternates. Winter assumed the Communicator, who had not said so, was assimilating the heavy work load as part of the rich panoply of Army life. He snorted.

Seeking distraction again, Winter pondered the curious letter from Nickie.

Musing, glancing out the window-porthole, Winter watched a VW Bug-sized, long, quasi-cylindrical object fall through the dusk in the gap between the fuselage and the trailing edge of the starboard wing. Outboard, farther away, he saw another, smaller only through perspective. He experienced a frisson, a slight shift in the space-time continuum, during which the descending black containers seemed no more than a curiously awkward phenomenon . . . given that they seemed to be falling through his aircraft's personal space.

Immediately following a jolt of recognition, he screamed into the intercom, into the pilot's ear, *"Break left! Break left! Port break! Falling ordnance to starboard. Break left. Break to port."*

He could hear nothing; there was no verbal response from the pilot, but the aircraft lurched violently to port, standing on that wingtip. He realized he still held down his mike button; his thumb would not respond to a mental order to release. Trapped in a scarifying vacuum where his thumb led him into the dark labyrinths of hell—through a now distorted view of the sky in which he thought he might follow the tumbling objects back to their source, but could see no source, though he could look straight up, flying as they were on the left wingtip—he noted more of the 750-pound bombs forming a column from far above to whatever space remained below. Winter held his breath; at 9,000 feet, it would be only seconds before ground impact of the bombs.

Would CRAZY CAT clear the impact zone?

The other threat—the continuing stream of ordnance from B-52s flying twenty-five to thirty thousand feet above them, unseen, bombing blindly through the Neptune's flight path—could not compete. It was not likely his flight would be taken out by an iron bomb . . . but they might easily be removed from contention if too near ground zero when the bombs exploded. This fearful dichotomy found no room for expression in Winter. His focus was fixed on moving his thumb off the intercom switch.

When that was managed after exaggerated struggle, he was swamped with a babble of loud voices: orders, screams, curses. Everyone who could wedge his way into the intercom net was full of advice, all having to do with (1) directing the flight of the aircraft to the port side, (2) doing it *Now!* (3) suggestions to hang onto one's ass, and (4) advising the BUF pilots to commit unspeakable acts with close kin. This overwhelmed him in just seconds, just years . . .

The blasts, felt with a wrenching torque as a giant hand reached down and grabbed the aircraft, shook it violently, and tossed it away in fierce disdain, caught him before he might be tempted to contribute anything to the intercom community-speak. With the aircraft now in a tight turn to port but in level flight, Winter marked the first concussion by leaning across the intervening space between his position and the Communicator's port window. Why wasn't the pilot making greater speed away by diving the bird while banking?

Through the muddle of flashing insights, questions and fear, he felt helpless. With that first hammering detonation effect, he realized that, had they dived, the maneuver would have put them nearer ground. Nearer impact. Nearer the environment-changing explosions.

Winter's breath was gone. His eyes wouldn't focus, caught in the Mix Master effect of concussion, disorientation, and forced vertigo; but he felt his stomach and surrounding organs attempting to push out through his anus to balance pressure. The immediate second concussion was more of the same, only slightly less impact. The succeeding ripple of detonations kept up the same game, until by the time the hidden bombers—normally a cell of three; Winter prayed it was no more—had expended their ordnance, the Neptune was only popping a few rivets with each further explosion. The impact area was directly to their rear.

The relative stability and silence following the ARC LIGHT seemed to offer only a brief respite for the flyers. The cell which had played through over seconds, had taken hours from the evening . . . from their lives. Three BUFs, each carrying 24 iron 750-pound bombs on external pylons and 42 internally, would have rearranged several hundred acres. To a man, the CRAZY CAT crew could not believe the bombing was spent and their plane remained airborne. The pilot asked for visual checks: "Report any damage. Any smell of fuel or hydraulics? Anyone hurt?"

Bracken's dry voice came through from the co-pilot's right seat, "Who's footin' the bill for my goddamned laundry?"

Obligatory laughter was minimal, subdued.

Someone—one of the linguist-operators Winter was sure—without identifying himself, said sententiously, "ARC LIGHT report: Don't leave home without it."

There was no scolding admonition from the pilot.

* * *

The remaining hour and a half on target was unproductive. Not a man could focus on the mission. Ops found their white fingers gripping a frequency knob that would not turn, and they were convinced some enormous force, having to do with the emergency bank-and-turn, had frozen the dials. But as the trauma abated and fear drained away, the hands found function with the knobs. Still, no further targets were acquired. Maybe the ARC LIGHT got them all. Right!

The endless message initiated by McFadden was not really that; it had ended, sometime during the interval of chaos and frantic damage-avoidance. Every man on the mission had the same thought and wish: did the ARC LIGHT erase the enemy communications center? If he missed anything on the tail-end of the message, the operator concluded, it was only a few groups, likely boilerplate, admin trash. He didn't worry about the loss. If the analysts couldn't make money off what they'd been provided, they'd better shut down the field station and go home.

On the ground at Da Nang, there was no horseplay. No one on the crew mentioned the fun and games to the courier pilot or escort. Nor to the Air Force ground and fuel crews.

Winter never left the aircraft. Crew could smoke on the aircraft during flight, but here on the ground, with fueling in progress, the smoking lamp was out. He didn't feel he could walk far enough to find a safe place to fire up his briar. He wasn't interested in going through the ritual; and the thought of tobacco left him cold anyhow.

He sat at his Controller position, staring blindly across to the scattered lights on Monkey Mountain, bemused. He had not known a 750-lb. bomb was as big as a locomotive. The longer his stunned mind lingered, the larger the deadly munitions grew until they merged with the limits of his universe.

* * *

However bad he felt after the bout with sudden fear, and despite the void in his life occasioned by non-correspondence from the mother of his children, Winter's newfound interest could bring him up into the world of the living. More, the zone of celebration.

His almost nightly trysts—a word he'd always despised in literature, but one which he now felt a kinship for as it bore the nature of his desperate, longing-inspired time spent with the nurse, Moira—was a guarantee.. But even as he felt himself giving in more and more easily, more and more often when their respective schedules could be merged, Winter found an overbearing sense of concern, if not guilt, he still felt no free rein to an un-entangled relationship.

Somewhere back there, back in the world, there lurked a woman, a onetime love of his, the mother of his sons. His companion; his other half. Still, lurk she did.

* * *

The new Executive Officer stood before the entire roster of pilots, operators, plane captains, and anyone else likely to find themselves on a mission flight. He waited. The noise continued, unchecked. He cleared his throat twice, but could not be heard over the babble. Five days after the near-miss on the Lao border, the tales only grew more graphic, louder. Brenner, the junior officer in the briefing room, eventually shouted, *"At-ten-tion!"*

The command effected instant silence, but within seconds, men began turning, looking, seeking out the high-ranking officer who must have entered the room to warrant such an order. Major Grange at the lectern was gratified and quickly grabbed the vocal initiative. "Crazy Cats, especially you guys from yesterday's crew, sorry to use your sleep time, but we're here this morning for only one reason: we must address ways to better ensure maximum security on our flights. Especially, in light of the two recent . . . uhh, mishaps—the blown engine and the no-frag, near miss up north. Indications are that there were some actions, or lack thereof, that could have jeopardized security . . . on both those missions."

Winter jumped to his feet; Brenner jerked him back into his seat by the arm.

"What the hell's Grange babbling about?" Winter asked in a loud, harsh whisper. "There was no security risk, not on either flight. I know; I was Controller on both. And both times, the ops kept their cool, controlled classified documents, and when I got my hands on the classified stuff, I did likewise, inventorying, bagging, and securing the material. Until I got the signed chit from the courier on the ground at Da Nang." Brenner looked at him speculatively, as Grange continued speaking.

"We need to find ways to enhance our procedures, especially on board the aircraft," the Major continued unctuously. "Can we have some suggestions as to ways we might improve? Oh, I can tell you . . . we will be getting water-soluble paper for mission use only. At the first hint of a . . . No! Perhaps not that early, but if sincerely threatened, a hit by groundfire, an emergency landing, bailout—anything crucial, the paper, which can be written on with pen or pencil or typewriter, can be placed in a container and liquid poured over it. Within seconds, it turns to jelly. Un-*readable* jelly."

"Water?" came from one side.

The major nodded the affirmative.

"Coffee, tea?" from the back.

While the XO tried to keep up with the taunting list of every liquid known to God and Ghandi, Ito asked, "Can I tinkle on it?" His enigmatic, inscrutable face betrayed no humor amidst the raucous laughter..

"Yes, yes. Piss on it, if you have to. *Any* liquid. Though I would not suggest gasoline, lighter fluid, or such." Now he had his audience in a responsive, light mood, the major was content to await other suggestions. His brief burst of comedianship needed help.

The Navy lieutenant who was on loan as an Instructor Pilot on the P-2s, who flew as seldom as he could manage, said, "Don't carry the shit on board. Anything classified, written down."

"Right, Ivory," Winter snapped. "We're just flying around up there in charlie land for shits and giggles, for you to log an occasional hour of flight time. Or, on the night before a mission, all my ops get together, hoist a few Heinekens, and memorize the full mission particulars. Including backup data for you pilots."

"Mister Winter, I don't think that's called for," Grange said in a syrupy voice.

"Nor do I. Let him keep his silly squid shit to himself."

"Mist—"

"We could burn it," plane captain PFC Gregory reminded them. Gregory had recently caught burn-bag detail three days in a row and was qualified to attest to the effectiveness of conflagration. "Put it in a can, in the sink in the galley . . . in the toilet—"

"Listen up," said a voice using the full range of acoustics, "all you people here who might one day wind up on an aircraft which I am flying, or flying on," Captain DeGrandcourt said evenly. "If anyone . . . *any*one sets fire to anything, tobacco excepted, on my bird, I will personally shoot the sonuvabitch dead. Are we clear on this point?" There was no verbal assent; the answer seemed obvious.

DeGrandcourt and Captain Lamb were two of the most popular pilots in the company. On active duty from an Army Reserve Aviation unit in Los Angeles, they had chosen to serve their one-year activation in Viet Nam, leaving their civilian employer, United Air Lines, with open slots. The captains were popular because they were accustomed to keeping their passengers/customers mollified by safe and comfortable flights. In Viet Nam, they continued that practice by routinely avoiding thermal updrafts, storms, turbulence of any kind, as well as the more pronounced enemy ground fire.

And DeGrandcourt was the only officer in the 1st RR who always wore his sidearm.

* * *

Caught in his dilemma, threatened by the dichotomy of his fractured relationship with Nickie and his unbridled passion for the young nurse, Moira, Winter tended to let his mind savor, more and more, the events of the past. "I tend to live in the past," he recalled reading a comment by the *Boston Globe* journalist, Herb Caen, "as most of my life has been there."

But the diametrically opposed loves in his life so dominated his mind, and infused the element of romance into all other emotions, that he could not avoid lingering on the scant smattering of even moderately serious relationships he'd known. He'd not been a jock in high school, and he wasn't possessed of great confidence in dealing with the softer sex, raised as he was in a household of two women: one, his mother, shy and easily dominated; another, his grandmother, who was anything but shy and easily did the dominating. Without the influence of a father who'd made the bad move of being stricken down in David's youth, she dominated his life too. The present state of uneasy contretemps left him anxious and often with the feeling that he had not two mistresses . . . but none.

chapter sixteen

Winter in the Tropics

Cam Ranh Bay, Viet Nam: May-June 1969

Oink was the first crew member off the mission flight, hitting the paneled aluminum in streak mode. Winter could not keep up with him, didn't try. He futilely held his pounding head with one hand, while he off-loaded his gear, mission bag, and helmet, along with a sealed box he'd been given in Da Nang for Major Grange. In his misery, he was further assaulted by the aggregation of smells from the aged aircraft, none pleasant: burned oil, kerosene jet exhaust; melted electrical insulation; the stench from the toilet trap that had shaken loose on the Da Nang landing; burned galley grease; and the usual rank body odors and stale beer farts.

Trudging across the apron, watching Air Dog disappear in the direction of the Navy mess, Winter called out to one of the linguist operators, inducing the surrogate to turn in his gear and chute for him. He managed suspended awareness during debrief before heading for his bunk.

No doubt when and how he'd gotten sick. Last mission, three days before, the return flight was hung up at Da Nang, waiting to re-fuel without fuel trucks, stuck on the ground for over four hours. They hadn't touched down at Cam Ranh Bay until the sun was coming up: an 18-hour workday. Exhausted, abandoning judgement, he headed directly to the Sandbag to recoup some sense of worth through the medium of San Miguel Export. One became two, became many.

Heat and humidity had peaked by the time he'd hoisted his last one, mid-morning, and when he stripped off the flight suit and lay down on his bunk, the air conditioner was on high and a desk fan blew the deliciously cold draft directly over his sweating body. He slept through to evening and knew he was in trouble when he awoke to a splitting head and could barely move out of the rack. A head cold of immense proportions, chest tight as a kettle drum. He shambled to the mess hall, drank soup, orange juice, and grape Kool-Aid, took a handful of APCs, and returned to his bunk to sleep, hoping to throw it off.

The catarrh demons were in full arousal the following morning, leaving him in worse shape. He could have excused himself from the manifest, found a substitute. But, what the hell— Y.A. Tittle played hurt.

Two days later he remained on everyone's sick list, but he was still on the schedule. When the aircraft climbed to altitude on takeoff, he accepted that he was in for a bad time. Barometric pressure changes are not kind to congested heads and chests. The fantasy of begging the pilots to keep the aircraft low enough to avoid decompression embarrassed him. But he found no way to relieve the piercing pain of popping ears. Repeated stabbings, like sharp, rusty bolts through his head, created tension throughout his body until he realized he was dysfunctional, and finally asked the senior linguist to relieve him.

Still, the mission flew on, full sked. It was hours before touchdown.

After debrief, Major Nichols, aircraft commander on the mission, ordered him to sick call. He loaned Winter his Jeep and driver to get him across to the Air Force Dispensary, closest medical support. And well so, Winter thought, avoiding the chance of Moira seeing him in this condition if he went to the medics at 6th Convalescent.

He was back at NAF in short order with a brown bag full of liquids, capsules, and pills, a sore ass from the penicillin shot— surely with a corkscrew needle, he thought—and a buck slip restricting him from flight duties until completion of a regimen of antibiotics and a return trip to the flight surgeon. It made for shortage on the manifest.

Winter spent the next two days in bed. He despaired of enforced bed rest, but there was nothing else for it. His fevered mind harkened back to 1964 and the bout with dengué fever in the 3rd RRU. Now, as then, friends came with cups of soup from the messhall, juice, cold water, cold tea, cold sodas, cold beer.

Brenner, *true* friend, brought a half-liter of Courvoisier. The third day, totally slept-out, the antibiotics depleted, he forced himself from the rack, showered, and stumbled over to the Operations hut, electing to get some ground work done.

With Magic Marvin typing, Winter caught up with the outstanding Awards and Decorations backlog. He was exempted from teaching in-flight safety classes; his voice was gone. He spent two more days chewing a new batch of antibiotics, APCs, and some cold capsules Ito picked up for him at the South Beach PX. He kept up the only known treatment—soaking up fluids as the Sahara soaks up afternoon squalls. The last of the hoarded Courvoisier. His appetite was gone; the positive result was loss of weight, affordable as he had put on extra with the topnotch Navy chow. He had not seen Moira for a week.

On the fifth day, Major Nichols called him in and tasked him to go TDY to Commo Mountain, the ground relay site perched on a mountaintop not far from Phu Bai. For an instant he considered reminding the CO that he was on a no-fly restriction, but knew the argument would be that he could fly, he just could not fly and work. He let it go, for he had turned the corner with his affliction and felt better. He'd had no alcohol for two of the last five days, and when he left Nichols' office, he felt the first pangs of hunger and detoured to the mess hall.

* * *

Commo Mountain—location of the communications relay which allowed CRAZY CAT's intercepts to be passed to the 8th Field Station via UHF radio—was so named by default. A visiting general officer had objected to the title of "Tit Top," painted in two-foot high da-glo orange letters on a black background posted at the entrance to the site. The change of name was deflating to the personnel assigned. The firmly conical mountain was, after all, classically proportioned, a "luscious reproduction of softer breastworks," Brenner commented.

Commo Mountain, from Cam Ranh Bay, was an 80-minute flight north to Da Nang; another 20-minute air hop northwest to

Phu Bai; and an unnerving forty-five-minute drive northwest-west-northwest again across open country and up a sixteen-percent-grade dirt road in a Jeep, swooping up and down in sickening undulations as the road crested two subordinate hills before tackling the mountain.

Winter's semi-terminal head and chest cold was in remission. Still, on the C-130, and the U-8, he used earplugs, though Bare Ass Barrister kept his flight below five-thousand feet for the short hop. When Sergeant Girault met him on the apron, saluting and mouthing something, Winter became alarmed—he could not hear or understand what the NCO said. Then he realized he still had the plugs in his ears, popped them out smiling ruefully at Girault, and returned the salute while his head still roared like a wind tunnel. "George," he said, shaking hands with this old Asmara hand, "long time, no drink." Georges Pierre Girault, from Thibodaux, Louisiana, was a famous tippler, a recidivist from the brown boot army.

"We'll get a beer on top." Girault assured him. He glanced at his watch and squinted west where the sun was lowering beyond rising land. "Better get with it. Be dark in a little over an hour. We wanta be on the mountain, in the compound, 'fore we lose light" he said, turning to the nearby Jeep almost obscured by mud and dust and vestiges of what might once have been camouflage. Winter was struck once more, as he'd noted years before in East Africa, how Girault's diction and use of the English vernacular was a considerable remove from common Cajun-speak.

The drive west was uninterrupted, though just before dusk they watched a VNAF fighter-bomber unloading napalm on a series of low hills to the south, ill-defined prominences that disappeared in a sheet of flame. What vegetation there was ignited, and as long as the two men watched, the fire grew, smoke rising straight in the absence of wind. Shortly after, the road took a 40-degree turn back toward the north and began ascending the first of the three features they must surmount. They left the fires to do the worst they could on their own.

The road ran straight up one hill, down into a shallow swale, then up the next, higher hill, descended into a second depression for a quarter mile, then up the long incline to the crest. Winter had seen a photograph taken by one of the previous communicators who had served his time on the mountain and returned to Cam Ranh. The photo was taken from a distance with a long lens and perspective that blended the three segments of road into one single, climbing trail, straight as a string. It was not evident in the photo that there were depressions between the hills. It was not even evident that there *were* three hills. The lush green of early summer melded the upthrusts into a smooth verdant mat and the road appeared to climb from the plain to the crest without deviation.

Driving up the third tier, Winter had the bunker in sight for a long stretch. He could make out the aperture in the PSP sheets and sandbags that constituted a bunker/gatehouse as they got closer; then the unmistakable silhouette of the .50 caliber machine gun; and finally the gunner. As they approached, a second figure came from the bunker and swung wide the timber-and-barbed-wire gate. Passing through, Winter glanced up and saw binoculars hanging about the neck of the gunner at his post some nine or ten feet above the ground. Having identified them from afar, the gunner now ignored them, his eyes busy scanning the terrain below. Both soldiers wore the Screaming Eagle patch of the 101st Airborne Division. Real *troops* assigned to baby-sit the ASA troops, Winter noted with chagrin . . . and with rueful gratitude.

Clambering from the Jeep, Winter watched an extremely tall, thin man in fatigue trousers, jungle green T-shirt, jungle boots, and sun glasses ambling toward them. No one he saw, except the two airborne troops at the gate, had on a shirt or hat. Field conditions! The troops here were far from the flagpole, relatively free from visitors, and the weather was cooperative: hot, low humidity with occasional slight breezes. He waited as the tall soldier—at least six-five, Winter thought— walked up and held out his hand.

"You must be Dave. Tally Hewitt. Welcome to Fort Savage."

Tally!—First Lieutenant Talbot Hewitt. Mountaintop Officer-in-Charge. Winter had heard much of him, had talked with him over the air many times during missions, but they had never met.

At *least* six-five. Maybe more.

"Lieutenant." Winter shook his hand and looked about. He saw two more sand-bagged bunkers strategically placed. The site, on the crown of a very small mountain/big hill, had little space to work with so that the three bunkers provided adequate overlapping fields of fire down the slopes on all sides. The trio of defenses were manned, even now in full daylight, though Mister Charles and the Sapper Chorus could be seen easily three miles away. But dusk closed in from the east.

"I just got word about thirty minutes ago you were coming. I requested someone more than a week ago," Hewitt commented. But if Winter expected a bitch session about bureaucracy, he was to be disappointed. "How long you plan to stay?" Hewitt had a quirky smile hinting that the answer was of little import.

"Just long enough to discuss whatever it is you requested a visit from the First R. R. for." Winter blanched at his own convoluted syntax. "About commo problems, I understood. 'course, it would be," he added, taking any edge off his snitty response.

"Well, yeah. I guess you know, we're assigned to the First," Hewitt said, waving his hand to encompass other soldiers. At Winter's surprise he added, "That's right. Me and the other communicators and the generator mech. It's our asset; First R. R.'s, and we man it."

"I assumed it was Eighth Field Station's."

"Phu Bai might argue the mountain is theirs, but the site is ours. Our security force is from the One-Oh-One. They rotate more often than our people. Their command doesn't want them living the easy life for too long; have to take their turn in the barrel. We get relatively few serious threats here, due to our location. The mountain slope's our best defense. 'course, having the eleven Bravoes doesn't hurt," he added, acknowledging an obvious truth.

Hewitt swept his arm in a semi-circle, raised one eyebrow and said, "Having said that, about few threats, c'mon over here," and walked away toward the nearby edge of the tiny plateau. Just below the crest, steel angle-iron stakes were driven into the rock and soil of the slope; multiple strands of barbed wire were laced through the stakes and tumbled in ugly, rusty coils above. Two GIs of the screaming eagle, wearing heavy gloves, were busy stringing shiny, new razor wire, interlacing it among the older barbed variety. Laboring on the steep slope, they displayed the agility of mountain goats, and the wire spooled out lithely as Winter watched.

Several hundred feet farther downslope, he saw several more airborne soldiers spread in a nominal skirmish line, working their way up the slope. They carried in their hands only sidearms for weapons. In between the two groups, Winter could make out several unmoving figures— small "blots" was the word that came to mind—clad in black cloth, where clothed. One of the climbing figures halted, waved his hand above his head in a warning motion, raised his sidearm, and Winter heard the flat crack of the .45. The blot nearest the trooper spasmed and lay still. Winter recalled the dead sapper on Nui Ba Dinh in 'sixty-five who turned out to be a bundle of unfilled sandbags. These modest clumps were not sandbags.

"Little skirmish last night," Hewitt murmured, staring down at the rag dolls. "Unusual. They know the One-Oh-One's up here; they usually don't fool with us. And the climb's a bitch even in daylight against no defenses. What could they have hoped for? Silly buggers . . . didn't even have mortar support."

"Some gung-ho squad leader, looking to make his bones," Winter said. A guilty ripple pulsed through the back edge of his mind at those caustic words, when he—Lord help me, he thought—might have done the same in his younger, Captain America days.

Christ! Nickie had called him that. In Italy. On that terrible mountain road, that night.

* * *

While Girault went to check on the outpost's beer supply, Lieutenant Hewitt gave Winter the visiting fireman's tour. After five-minutes' walk around, they sat in the shade of a camouflage fly tent drinking Tuborg—a luxury Winter marveled at, but went unremarked—and talked over ways to improve communications between the mission birds and the Field Station. They agreed the obvious major problem was lack of an auto-repeater system for relaying radio transmissions, to and from the aircraft. The antiquated process—not a system—in place was that the linguist ops aboard the plane intercepted, copied enemy coded transmissions, passed the copy to the Communicator, who then, by voice, broadcast the same four-digit groups to the mountain by secure voice.. The relay ops on the mountain copied the traffic by hand, re-broadcast it by voice to the Field Station. Hewitt was right to put that concern at the top of his gripe list. It meant double work and potential loss of message integrity. But it was not the only discrepancy.

The 8th Field Station at Phu Bai was not so far as to make distance or signal strength a problem on that, the latter leg of the two-step commo link; and because of the altitude of the relay site, standing tall above a flat plain, the mission aircraft almost always had a clear communications line-of-sight path on the first leg. Only occasionally, if the aircraft moved too far south or too far west along the Laos or Cambodia border, would their signal be impeded by upthrust peaks, intervening weather, or fall-off in signal strength. And in an emergency, needing to pass something really hot even under trying conditions, the bird could fly back toward the mountaintop site and transmit when in range. All in all, conditions, though not optimum, were not impossible.

Subsequent discussion dealt with Hewlitt's problem child, SP4 Draxler, a communicator who suffered from an unknown medical problem, enduring serious pain constantly, but who would not go down to the Field Station for sick call. The OIC had even ordered him down, but he refused, insisting they couldn't afford to be without him.

Arrogant, but not far wrong. Commo Mountain staffing was on the thin side. Hewitt had relented, after threatening to have him courts-martialed, and then struck the disobeyed order from the logbook. He'd tried friendship, coercion, and bribes to get the man to make sick call. No, Hewitt had no idea what his problem was; Draxler would never say. But when the pain struck, he bent over in agony, holding his stomach, until finally straightening with tears in his eyes.

Could Winter do anything? Would he discuss it with the CO and get him to work something out? It was probably an ulcer, but looked serious enough for military Medicare.

They discussed turnover of personnel who were short, and Hewitt asked who Winter had in mind to replace the short-timers. Winter had no one; he hadn't thought about it; he hadn't thought about the relay site being manned by 1st RR people, nor that the responsibility might fall in his baliwick. He now realized he would damned well *have to* think about it and get back to Hewitt, ASAP. He wondered who at Cam Ranh might constitute a manpower pool for such replacement. Or could he get them from the field station? No! Likely, the problem was his.

The two officers exhausted their needs, but the Tuborg held out and they talked well into the evening. Chow was called and, seeing no way to avoid it without pissing off the current "cook by roster," was eaten by all hands. Afterward, Winter could never remember what they'd been served; but even the good-natured Magic Marvin, using a term he'd picked up from Brenner, would have labeled it "swill" of one denomination or another.

A short, but quiet night followed. The slopes below the crown had been, and remained, cleared. At sunup Winter stood on the roof of the bunker facing east-southeast back down the road, drinking breakfast coffee made yesterday, watching the sketchy traffic along a distant road. A multitude of tiny aircraft made war noises off toward the coast.

He and Sergeant Girault made the nerve-grating descent of the hill road in low gear, four-wheel drive, foot on the brake. By the time the road leveled, they could smell burning brake shoes. The pilot, Bare Ass, awaited him at the airfield, and within minutes they were airborne, headed east.

* * *

At Da Nang, there was a delay with the Marine duty flight. Winter caught a ride to III MAF on an ammo truck and found Lieutenant Lonegren at his desk. They went to a corner of a storeroom that served as "the coffee bar," a tongue-in-cheek descriptor for a 30-cup coffee maker that hadn't been cleaned since the Somme; a box of sugar in one dirty, crystalline lump from humidity; and a can of dry creamer which nobody touched, creamer and green being incompatible terms.

Winter negotiated with Lonegren for a visit to a Marine field unit—sometime soon, he urged; he was getting short himself. Supporting III MAF with hard-won, Eye-Corps intelligence, Winter had long felt there was, curiously, too little physical or command contact between them.

The Marine officer agreed to set something up. When could Winter come?

Probably a couple of days next month, late; he'd call. He'd fly a mission, get off the bird at the courier drop-refuel at Da Nang, overnight with Lonegren, and make his way out to whichever outfit he could gain an invitation from. No sweat!

Returning to the airstrip, he wasted a couple more hours waiting for the Marine duty R4D scheduled to land at Nha Trang, Qui Nhon, Cam Ranh Bay, Bien Hoa, and Tan Son Nhut on its regular bus sked south. A loadmaster, without knowing when the bird would fly, told Winter that if he really enjoyed the ride, he could catch the same flight, in reverse, the following morning. It was information; not a joke.

Uneasy, knowing any delay was almost certainly due to maintenance on the ancient cargo plane, he found his mood souring.

Winter thought he might just wait at Da Nang for that night's mission bird and hop home aboard it. But he needed to get back, catch up on a burgeoning backlog of A&D paperwork. Heroes seemed in plentiful supply; he'd compiled an unenviable stack of recommendations for Bronze Stars, two Purple Hearts, a half-dozen Army Commendation Medals, and a ton of Air Medals, due to the heavy flight schedules. And he wondered about the curious R&R that he didn't yet know was to be his or not.

The Marine milk train finally launched, and he got off at his stop.

*　*　*

On the ground at Cam Ranh, no one met him on the ramp, and he walked across the airbase to NAF. Sweating in the afternoon sun, he regretted he'd not called ahead and had someone meet him with a vehicle. It was partly lack of interest but, had he tried to call, the 18th Century phone system likely would have defeated him. He arrived at the Orderly Room cooked only medium rare.

In an unexpected but positive payback, his cold was entirely gone!

Major Nichols was out. The First Sergeant was out. Magic Marvin, double-dipping as Orderly Room clerk, was in. "Mister Winter, you got a confirmed seat on the R-and-R flight to Honolulu a week from today, June eleven." He handed Winter a set of convenience orders, authorized by the 224th Aviation Battalion headquarters at Tan Son Nhut, Sai Gon, who issued an order number to 1st RRC via telephone or teletype. The First cut the orders.

Winter felt no reaction to the news. Realizing that, he wondered if he was disappointed, or if his recent bout with physical degradation left him emotionally under the weather.

He dumped his bag on the floor in his room, grabbed clean skivvies, and headed for the shower. After a long, hard pounding of hot water on his head, neck, and chest, he dried off, returned to his room, downed a handful of APCs followed by a half-pint of orange juice, dressed, and walked outside feeling better. A night's sleep and he'd be right as rain.

When the CO returned and parked before the Orderly Room, Winter borrowed his Jeep, drove across to the Flight Surgeon's office, and badgered the Air Force Major into restoring him to flight status. Driving back around the perimeter, he stopped and picked up a walking soldier he didn't recognize, but who was wearing a CRAZY CAT patch on his fatigue pocket. The hiker proved to be SP4 Jimerson, an oxygen tech, one of a small group of communicators who also worked other jobs: mechanics in some cases, clerks, and one man detailed to maintain the swimming pool, which the First's supply officer had cribbed from some unlikely source in a likely criminal endeavor, and donated to NAF for general use.

After brief discussion along no particular lines, Winter thought Jimerson clearly an organized young fellow, and talked to him about his willingness to "go to the mountain" as a replacement in Tally Hewitt's circus. The specialist indicated he wasn't really taken with the notion, but would not fight such an assignment.

Tantamount to being gone from here, Winter thought.

That night, again using Nichols' Jeep, Winter went, for the second time, to South Beach to try to get a phone call through to Nickie using MARS facilities. Last time was a bust, but then she'd subsequently written *the letter*. He'd reacted, and he now had news for her. Surely she'd take the call. And if not, he had his answer.

After waiting less than an hour, Winter got a free booth and almost immediately had a clear connection to Long Beach, Mississippi. Once given the go-ahead by the MARS op, he knew he was connected. But there was silence on the line.

"Hello. Nickie? Can you hear me? Over."

Silence.

"Nicole, if you're there," he said in sudden exasperation, "please give me some kind of acknowledgment."

Silence.

He was about to replace the receiver when there was a slight click, Nickie responded, and he was speaking to her.

* * *

It was late June, and I felt the insistence of taking myself to task for dithering away the summer in a funk: Brenner, get your ass in gear! I felt like an over-age actor, second lead in a drama playing *Off*-Broadway to the third power: I was employed, but didn't like the part, didn't like the play, and there was nothing on the horizon but bad reviews and dwindling attendance. A worthy but disturbing metaphor.

I'd never felt different about this war, though I didn't feel empowered to lobby against it. I found myself now more often among the majority in attitude, rather than minority . . . or alone. Not a logical position for a disaffected, non-conformist, agnostic, political independent with an iron deficiency.

I'd thought part of the funk was simply missing my compatriot, but Winter was only gone six days. This funk was of long duration. And when he returned, he was no fun to play with. Something had gone out of him, a change I now realized I'd seen coming. He jumped back into the swing of things, making his mission flights, performing the ancillary duties with dispatch, making meals, and shoring up the flimsy bar in the Sandbag. But it wasn't David Winter, posterboy of the Republic.

Some two weeks later, he was obviously drinking heavily, not a thing I'd ever known him to do religiously. As far back as Asmara he was known take a drink. But he hadn't been dependent upon alcohol. Our first tour in this cesspool, he wasn't much of a drinker: he took his commitment to the war far too seriously. In Germany, where the *Bier* was critically fine, he drank . . . but even there, not to excess. Hardly ever saw him with a buzz on, in Rothwesten, on the border, or at Bad Aibling.

He hadn't a reputation for drink down south this tour either, but of course the measurement was subjective, and I wasn't here then, didn't know. But I have observed him here. And now, just returned from Hawaii, every minute he's not flying or doing make-work with his A-and-D comedy routine, he's a major supporter of the Sandbag, where it all starts and ends.

On the patio, I had collected him and Ito, Bimbo, Bracken, and a couple other pilots who weren't on my last mission, thus suffered from ignorance; I had them sufficiently attuned and waiting for the story about the DMZ brush-off.

"C'mon, Brenner, you ass. Stop screwing around!"

I didn't keep them waiting long. I suffered a flash, a warning of getting old.

"Flying Controller on that one, a mission scheduled later in the day than usual, we were flying a racetrack along the DMZ and, as usual at night, flying without belly lights." Nothing new about that; at our altitude if we turned on the lights we'd invite every little commie trap-shooter in Viet Nam to do his thing. *Pull!* Draw groundfire like flies to shit.

"The Thud, that ever-popular Air Farce workhorse, pulling out of an ordnance run in a balls-to-the-wall climb, afterburner cranking—and him with no lights either—came up through our airspace on the port side where I couldn't see him. But I felt the turbulence when his after-shock hit. Couldn't have missed us more than twenty, thirty feet. Aft-station watch pissed himself. Grange, the pilot, with a visiting warrant co-pilot, Johnnie Gressett from Battalion, reacted properly. They did zilch."

"Brenner—"

"Nothing *to* do. By the time anyone realized what the hell had happened, it was over. We were intact, though our collective psyche might have been a bit scuffed. Pilot reported it, but you know how that goes: Army bitching to Air Force about Air Force blunders is like safe crackers complaining to cops about the humidity affecting their fuses. .

"Goddamn F. One-oh-five jockey, intent on finding a diddle in a haystack where he could put his bombs, apparently didn't clear his airspace with his control. Another few yards and he would have cut through that P-2V like a fart through cheap pants. In that case, I would not be regaling you now with this arresting monologue." I thought the emphasis warranted.

So arresting was my tale that no response was immediately effected. Took all of ten seconds for the second-guessers to start.

But after that mission, once word got around, there was wholesale threat of mutiny if we didn't start flying with the belly beacon on. I don't think it ever really got too serious; nobody burned their bra. Can't imagine what, if anything, will happen about it . . . but my point is this: with everyone else at the bar finally reacting to my tale of adventure, asking questions, adding comments, my man, David, said nothing. Gave a wan little smile, like he'd witnessed an act of nature. Maybe after his two missions scouting disaster, that's all it was to him. If so, it was on the order of a frog swallowing a rhino, act of nature or no.

The summer wore on, fierce as ever. I broached the subject of his recent R-and-R once—once only—asked about Nickie. He walked away from me. Didn't say anything; didn't even look at me. Just walked away.

Bad shit, Homer!

A week or so later, when he had gotten back to keeping his seat in the mess hall when I approached, I followed a Spartan meal with a measured pursuit of knowledge. What the hell?

I asked him if he'd seen lately the two apparently Spanish soldiers that he used to mention now and then. The ones nobody else ever really saw. He looked at me as if I'd told an offensive religious joke. Never answered me. I didn't know what the hell to make of that. I sat and let him walk off without a word. I mean, I'm not sensitive about being discounted as a fount of fascination, but . . .

* * *

Dave and Moira were back on. Actually, I don't think they were ever *off*; but I wondered how he'd explained his six-day absence. It never occurred to me he just might blatantly tell her the truth.

She and Grange's main sqeeze, a nurse major from the Sixth, showed up a night or two later. Dave was at the bar, a regular non-flying attraction for him lately. Moira joined him, while Bonnie—the Bonnie Major—headed for Grange's room across the patio. I heard her knock; the door opened, and I didn't see her again that evening.

I brashly and deliberately broke into the conversation between

Dave and Moira, saying to her, "Well, hello, you sprightly young thing. Haven't seen you in a few weeks."

I swear, neither in word nor tone of voice did I imply anything. Question anything. It was as banal a comment as I'm capable of. She smiled at me, batted those huge grey eyes at Winter, and said, "Well I sure didn't want to be caught hanging around over here like a barfly while he's away on Waikiki with his wife. That would be . . . unseemly . . . it seems." And smiled again.

Mother of God, the wench has been reading again.

None of it got a rise out of Dave, though. If I interpreted all this surprising exposé properly, Winter must have told her all about Honolulu. And if it was bad—as I suspected it must have been—and if Lieutenant Moira was serious about Warrant Officer Dave—which I thought she was—I could see where she viewed matters as they stood as nothing to be upset over.

Deliver me.

chapter seventeen

Retrograde

Cam Ranh Bay, Viet Nam: June 1969

"Dave, get up," Ito whispered. Winter growled and thrashed in the damp sheets, flung them aside, and sprang to his feet.

"Right. Where to, inscrutable one?" He stared about blankly for a moment, and began pulling on a jungle fatigue jacket that had dried in the few hours of air conditioning after his flight.

"Le's get a brew. You eat?" It was 1015 hours.

Winter shook his head. "Not hungry. Ate at three, after debrief."

They walked through the mid-billet passageway to the other side and found the Sandbag locked. Ito walked three doors up, opened Lieutenant Bimbo Billingsgate's door, and retrieved the key from a nail. When the Sandbag door was yanked open, it was immediately obvious that the bar had not been cleaned off before whoever closed up last night or this morning; it smelled strongly of stale, spilt beer and sweat. Ito hadn't signed on for demeaning scut work, and he carefully avoided the messy bar. Grabbing two San Miguels from the fridge, he joined Winter at a table on the patio, the only one with a fully ribbed umbrella.

The two warrants were content to sit in the shade and let the mellow brew caress their throats without the need to speak. Both had experienced the local San Miguel in the Phillipines, and it was water boo piss; all the good stuff was labeled Export . . . and exported. No need for speech. Winter could mimic Ito's inscrutability. They had been doing just that for nearly an hour when Brenner sauntered up. He looked them over without greeting, hesitated, went in, got a beer, and joined them, dragging up one of the partially splintered, wooden-slatted, deck chairs.

"Dave," he nodded, "haven't seen you about much." He nodded at Ito. "Fred."

"I been around . . . 'bout as much as I could," Winter remarked, his face a mask of studied indifference.

"Make that two," said Ito. Frederick Ulysses Ito, no fireball instigating repartee, was a functional straight man.

The tone of the conversation remained at that stagnant level until Bimbo came out of his cave, yawning, growling, hibernation interrupted after an early morning debrief. The four of them continued abuse of the San Miguel stock.

"I heard the grossest thing yesterday, talking to some lieutenant from a Fourth Division Lurp team," Bimbo offered, apropos of nothing.

"Where'd you run into him?" Ito pursued his own unrelated curiosity.

Billingsgate needed no urging. "Over at the R-and-R hootch. Waiting for his flight to Australia. He'd been out on long-range patrol, didn't even know he'd come up on the list for R-and-R. He had to scrounge a ride on a chopper to get here from Gia Lai Province. Sucker was in grunge fatigues that couldn't have stood the flight to Sydney—not that they would have let him board like that. Came straight out of the jungle, nine days on a Lurp. Then after all the rush, his flight was cancelled. They scheduled another for a few hours later, and I brought him back here, got him a new set of fatigues, and ran him through the car wash."

"You're a good man, Charley Blue," Ito offered.

"What's the earth-shaking news? The 'grossest thing' you heard about," Winter said in a tone that prompted questions of the other three, unspoken but apparent.

Never deterred from recounting bad news, Billingsgate went on, "Said they have a problem up in the mountains. Two Corps." At the burst of sniggers, Bimbo said, "Yeah, yeah. I hear you, but *besides* charlie—tigers!"

"Oh, shit. Here we go. Do I detect a Brenner echo? A rumor? Gonna wind our clock, Bimbo?" The snide tone remained with Winter. Brenner stared at him as if resenting the slur.

"No, nothing like that. He just said, when there's action, especially a running fight—with him and his Lurps, that's often—tigers are apt to drag off any bodies left behind. Even in daylight." Bimbo's measured delivery imparted sincerity. Or a Brenner rumor. "They found remains, even."

"I heard they sometimes do that to live troops," Ito contributed in a worried drawl.

"That's probably bullshit," Billingsgate said heatedly, as if the harsher reality would diminish his own thesis. "But dead bodies . . . Hell, yes, I believe that. Leave your buddy in the bush, whether he's wearing black jammies or tiger-stripe camo, he might wind up feeding the kitty." He shivered, testament to the fear such possibilities evoked.

Winter thought of the hyenas that night in the Eritrean desert. Nobody ever questioned the hazard of hyenas dragging off dead bodies, *and* live ones. Especially children, babies. Why should he have trouble believing that about tigers taking live GIs? Hell, they had annual statistics in India to account for the harvest of humans by tigers. He wanted off the subject.

"What do you hear about the draw-down, Bimbo?" Winter asked, in a new tone.

"Draw-down? The troop cut?"

"The twenty-five thousand Tricky Dick's calling back from 'Nam, 'bout now, far's I can figure." He'd read the leading edge of speculative articles in the Honolulu paper. Seemed silly, he thought: here we are, dog-paddling to stay afloat in this quirky circle jerk, and the prez cuts five percent of our manpower. Supply-*blind*-sided economics.

"Heard the same as you. Supposed to be done by sometime in July. Ain't gonna be any of us, you can bet your sweet ass." The three warrants looked at Bimbo with contrite disdain; he was doing nothing but shoring up his GI state-of-gripe. Billingsgate had sworn a blood oath: he was staying in Viet Nam until the war was won. He didn't say who must win to satisfy that commitment.

An easy silence settled on the group.

A pair of Phantom F-4s, launching in tandem, screamed down the runway and afterburnered their way aloft, out of sight within moments, though their thunder lingered. Billingsgate, welcoming distraction, said, "I bet you, any-a you, the next aircraft to launch will be a jet." He looked from one to the other. "Five bucks."

"Sh-h-h-h, that's a stacked deck. Eighty-five percent of the aircraft that take off from Cam Ranh are jets. That's no bet," Winter pointed out.

"OK. Then, I'll bet you five bucks . . . the next aircraft to launch will be a recip engine."

The three goggled at him. "You serious?" Ito said, his voice pitched high.

"Serious as chancre sores. Five bucks. A prop job."

Winter knew Bimbo had paid his way through the University of Michigan by gambling. Good poker player. Dangerous as a krait with dice or blackjack. Any game of chance. Bimbo would bet on anything, bet either side of a bet—as he'd just offered—and always paid up on the spot when he lost. Which he didn't make a habit of.

Brenner took the bet. Everyone but Billingsgate got up and walked out from the patio to a point in the scrub sand between buildings where they had a view of the strip between the SeaBee barracks and a hangar. They waited only four minutes, and stood in awe, admiringly, as a pair of A1E "Sandys" fluttered aloft, their powerful engines driving huge four-bladed propellers, roaring like the City of New Orleans in a tunnel. The converts returned to the table where Brenner handed over a five-dollar scrip note, shaking his head. "Remarkable!"

* * *

A few days later Winter took a C-130 taxi and flew to Sai Gon for a mandatory class in Awards and Decorations dictate, a dream scheme by USARV to standardize the writing and awarding of decorations, medals, badges, and other trappings of military glory. Nothing he was exposed to there was new to him, but he did get the chance to spend an evening with Ratty Mac. He was surprised to find Mac wearing staff sergeant stripes. The rocker was the only thing new, though; underneath, he was still

The Terror of the Horn, Ratty Mac's alternate *nom de guerre* he'd approved for his East African persona.

The sergeant and warrant officer walked out the gate of Davis Station and down the dark road through ARVN dependents' quarters to the Howard Johnson's on the nearest corner. This facetious title denoted a noodle-and-vegetable cart, a sort of Vietnamese snack bar, parked at the street intersection. The same old gnarled, dwarfed peasant, both eyes occluded by white clouds, still dished out hot soup, noodles, and *Ba-Mui-Ba* beer as he had when they'd lived on Davis Station in 1964.

They ordered *phô* and *Ba-Mui-Ba* and sat on the rusting frame of a long-dead ARVN Jeep, slurping, gurgling, talking. "Muckin' charlie still makes the best *phô* in town," Winter said appreciatively.

"M-m-m-m-m."

They ate a while in silence.

When his bowl was empty, and he had rinsed it in the roadside ditch and placed it back on the counter, Mac was surprised to see the old man stick it down into a small bucket of soapy water. Then he rinsed it in another bucket of murky liquid, and placed it on the counter to dry. "There's a new policy. He never usta' wash the bowls. Musta' had the county health people on his ass." Mac rubbed his stomach and turned away, belching. "Might have to skip chow here for a while. Wait 'n see if anybody else comes down with amoebic dysentery."

There was no logical response to that. Mac went on, "So, how's life in the northern latitudes, Dave?"

He didn't answer immediately. When Mac had gotten his second beer, he turned to stare challengingly at his unresponsive friend. As if he *knew.*

Winter said, "You won't believe this, I'm sure . . . but it's getting to me, Mac."

"Pshaw! Pshaw! What's this I hear? Combat Kelly on a downer? The man who treats war as faith? Surely not."

"Combat Kelly's furled his colors, I fear. All this time—the Corps, first tour here, the 'heart,' language school, Germany, back here second tour—I had my shit straight. I had a vision . . . thought we were doing the right thing. Americans. Helping the Vietnamese fix their country. Spreading democracy. High-minded ideals." He frowned. "Buying cheap carved elephants from Thailand and shipping them home at taxpayer's expense. All that other good military stuff."

"Listen to you. You sound like me. You enunciate better, use better language, but you sound as confused as me. Fucked up as a soup sandwich." Nothing came in response, as Winter recognized Sergeant Pepperdine's treacly aphorism. "Well, aren't you?" Mac insisted.

"May be. I don't know . . . when I began . . . when I . . ."

"This only since you took that R-and-R? Something happen in Hawaii to cause the change?" Mac looked at Winter, one red eye squinting expectantly. "A change in circum—"

"I don't want to talk about Hawaii, Mac. But, no. I don't think so. And it's not as if it happened overnight; it's been growing on me for . . . ahhh . . . a while now." Winter rinsed his bowl and watched as the old man finished the ceremony. He got a second beer and sought an avenue to a new subject.

When he sat back down, he said, "Johnnie Gressett's been up to Cam Ranh, flying with CRAZY CAT. I knew him before, flew with Johnnie when I was here with the S-three, Two twenty-fourth. Is he back down here now?"

"Warrant-three? I know who he is. Don't know if he's back at Tan Son Nhut or not. If you think about it, you'll realize I don't run in those exalted circles."

"You know *of* him, though?"

"Yeah. He was at the table next to me one night in the club with a buncha' pilots and some weenie lieutenant from S-Four, getting drunk, and telling this long, meandering tale about how the Air Farce screwed over the Army with multi-engine aircraft. Gressett flew Caribous on an earlier tour. Thinks they're the greatest thing since pop-top beer. Told some hairy stories of flying Caribous in and out of tiny fields. He said when the zoomies took over the Caribou, it stopped being the Ol' Reliable it was with Army flyers.

They put the thing on regularly scheduled maintenance, limited hours, limited loads. Typical Air Farce ineptitude."

"That's my man. I heard that song and dance myself. Did he mention the time he wound up flying down a street into the town, lo-lexing ammo pallets out the ramp in the battle for Dai Do because the town was surrounded and going through some severe shit? You hear that one?" Winter showed a streak of his well-known appreciation for anything militarily competent.

Mac had missed that episode, but Winter didn't try telling the tale. Gressett was a qualified raconteur; it was his story. Winter said, "Introduce yourself sometime . . . he's friendly to enlisted pukes. You'll hear the tale before long . . . or you can always ask. Tell him I put you on to it." Winter finished the beer and went back for another. "Johnnie's got perspective on the war. He's on his third tour. He can remember when it was real; has an opinion on when it went bad."

"Yeah, well, it ain't gettin' any better. And if this shit ain't real, then don't hit me with more myths." He took a long pull of the formaldehyde-laden beer, then added quietly, "If something I heard is true, it's gettin' worse. A lot worse."

"What something?"

Mac looked about, and when he'd verified no one was near enough to overhear, he said, "Dave. Mister Winter," he added to show seriousness. "This's not for publication, *Capish?*" At Winter's understanding nod, Mac said, "Downtown one night last week, drinking at the Casino. . ." His face brightened. "Hell, you remember the Casino. Second home. Anyhow, got to talkin' with a guy from the American, down here on in-country R-and-R." Mac scouted his surroundings again with narrowed eyes, as if he feared troops of the 23rd Infantry Division might be skulking nearby.

"He had a few under his belt. Talked about some severely bad shit up-country. Involving American troops. Then it was like he realized he'd said something classified or something."

"Whaddaya mean?"

"He just shut down on me. Moved to another table."

"What was it about? A battle? Heavy losses?"

"No, not really. Other way 'round." He said nothing further for a moment.

Winter puzzled over the obscure answer. What the hell did that mean? Mac let him ponder for several longer moments, and when he saw the dawning of light in Winter's eyes, said, "Shh-sh-sh-sshhh. We best not talk about it. But, yeah, I think you got the notion."

Winter tried to pry it out of him, but with all their history, there was nothing forthcoming. He had a suspicion of the "severely bad shit": an incident; a shooting; deliberate killing of non-combatants, maybe . . . *massacre?* He couldn't abide that thought—and Mac wouldn't spill it.

Walking back to Davis Station, each buried in his own thoughts, they heard from down the darkened road behind them the cry of the Universal FTA Bird, some troop with either too much *Ba-Mui-Ba* taken . . . or not enough: *"I hate this fucking place!"*

"He's still here, then?" Winter said.

Mac stared at him silently.

* * *

Winter showed up at the chopper pad early the next morning, bidding for a seat on a rumored Chinook commute, a CH-47 cargo flight going to Qui Nhon. The pilot had told him the night before in the Davis Station Club he could drop him at Cam Ranh and not even break his flight pattern. Winter had spent the night in the Newport, hot-bunking in Sapperstein's room while that worthy lounged on some Australian beach with a Sheilah of his choosing. This morning he'd walked to Gate Nr. 2 and caught a cyclo across Tan Son Nhut to the pad across the street from the new PX. *BX*, the Air Force called it. In that elite branch, they didn't inhabit posts, as did the Army, but bases; ergo, Base Exchange. And though Army grunge could spend their MPC there, it was Air Force territory: Air Force run, Air Force product preferences. They did, however, even in the absence of any meaningful assignment of female zoomies, continue to stock women's hair spray, a major negotiating tool in bargaining with downtown whores.

The cyclo driver pulled to the side of the road. Despite urging, he refused to move. Ahead of them Winter could see MP lights flashing. He saw a dusty blue ambulance, its doors sprung wide. The vehicles were converged about a UH-1B that sat nearby a CH-47.

The Chinook flight he hoped to take? Now what?

He flipped the driver some scrip and got out, grabbed his bag and walked toward the epicenter of activity. Soldiers stood about in small groups, talking in low tones, almost all of them wearing the red and blue patch, two large A's, back to back: 82nd Airborne. Where the hell did they all spring from? One brigade, he knew—he could never remember which, as they rotated in and out of hot spots, sometimes exchanging roles with a brigade from Fort Bragg—worked the territory northwest of Saigon. Iron Triangle country, the Fishhook. War Zone C.

An MP, not from the 82nd, but serious in his job, stepped forward and raised his hand. Winter stopped, waited.

"Sorry, sir. You can't go over by the choppers."

"I'm supposed to be flying up the coast on that Shit Hook this morning," Winter nodded at the CH-47.

"I don't think the Chinook's going anywhere, sir. We had an incident here this morning. Grenade explosion. The Chinook took some shrapnel. I know they got at least rotor damage and the pilot's windshield, Perspex—whatever—is shattered. You better plan on some other way north." The MP was even-handed in his job; he didn't effect the John Wayne persona common to many. He came ridiculously close to being friendly.

"Grenade? Dinks got in this close? Hell, there's guards—"

"No, sir. Sorry, my mistake." He looked around, gauging the proximity and attentiveness of soldiers scattered about. He said quietly, nodding back over his shoulder toward the Huey. "Paratrooper killed himself with a grenade. Right here on the pad. 'bout half an hour ago."

Winter could see through the milling soldiers occasional

glimpses of a camouflaged poncho liner flapping in the early breeze, covering a mound on the concrete.

"The hell you say!"

"Yessir. The really weird thing is, he was to be on that Huey this morn on a hop over to Bien Hoa today. Tour was finished. He was scheduled on a Freedom Flight to Travis tomorrow. His duffle bag's still on the pad, there by the Huey," he said, pointing. The MP spoke with an attempt to be professional, detached. Winter could see it did not come easily.

"Jeez-us! How do you know it was suicide? Coulda' been an accident or something, couldn't it? Nobody'd kill himself this close to DEROS." There had to be some mistake.

"No, sir. CID's already looked at it. They found most of his right hand, flung into the instrument panel of the Huey. The ring with pin was slipped up over the second joint of his middle finger. And the grenade was tight in his belly. What *was* his belly." The young MP, not someone Winter would have called a kid, looked slightly white, tight around his jaws.

"Nobody knows a reason?" Winter asked.

"Nobody here. They're trying to get hold of someone from his company now." His voice trailed off as he and Winter watched the medics lift the stretcher under the poncho liner. The litter shifted, tilted, awkward in its unusual configuration with the body mounded, obvious under the cover. Something fell off the litter—Winter couldn't tell what, and was grateful for ignorance— another medic scooped it up, raised the green-brown-black cover, tucked the stray part onto the litter, and walked alongside

Nearby, directly across the street, two Vietnamese army privates washed the walls of the new American BX. Dark rivulets ran down the wall beneath the sponges.

* * *

Winter went to the 146th and asked about a ride, wasting a couple of hours chasing rumors. Nothing going his way. But as he was searching for a ride to the Air Force terminal to catch the duty C-130, Sergeant Duncan caught up with him and told him there was a U-8 being ferried to Da Nang, and the pilot was waiting for him. Duncan drove him back, directly to the bird, just as the pilot, despairing of the wait, received taxi permission from Ground Control. He jammed the brakes and waited while Winter lifted the right door and clambered in with his bag.

The pilot then went through the rigamarole with Ground Control, taking a ration for the confusion from some slick-sleeve airman transmitting from his little air-conditioned glass house in the sky. The pilot, whose name Winter never learned, stopped listening to GC and wheeled the Teeny Weeny Airlines bird into the queue for takeoff. Though there was no wind, takeoff was reverse of the normal two-five runway, and it was a long taxi, a long queue for takeoff on runway zero-seven.

The no-name pilot didn't talk. He didn't seem in a bad mood; he just didn't talk. Brenner might have suggested he was struck dumb by the magnificence of his passenger . . . no matter if the passenger was Brenner or some lowlife like Winter. Winter was grateful for the silence, however, and dozed during the flight, bothered by indistinct flashes of something terrible occurring just off the wings of whatever unlighted stage he labored on. He wasn't thinking of Mac's ambiguous, shady warnings, but the quasi-dreams left him feeling uneasy. Drained.

No-name taxied him right into NAF ramp space at Cam Ranh, waited only seconds while Winter got his body and bag out of the U-8, then revved his engines, taxied back to the main, and got airborne before another aircraft could land or take off. It was just dusk.

* * *

When Winter entered the Orderly Room of the 1st RR, the first words out of Magic Marvin's mouth were chilling. "Mister Winter. One of your communicators, up on the mountain . . . he's dead."

"Dead? An attack? Firefight?"

"No, sir. Medical causes."

"Who was it? Anyone I know?" Winter asked.

"Don't think so, sir. Never heard of him, myself. Draxler. SP4 Draxler, Kenneth K. Worked for Lieutenant Hewitt up on Commo Mountain. Inoperable stomach cancer." Marsh continued typing as he talked. The phone buzzed and he picked up the receiver to give short shrift to someone on the other end, never seriously breaking his conversation with Winter.

"Be damned. Hewitt just told me about him when I was up there. The kid had problems but wouldn't go on sickcall. Cancer! He was a young guy, I believe. Didn't look more'n twenty-two, twenty-three—"

"Just twenty."

"—and he died of cancer? Give me a goddamned break?"

Marsh stopped typing, looked up at Winter and with a prim override in his voice, said, "Better yet, give Draxler a break."

"Of course. Sorry, Marve. That wasn't smart-ass. I just meant, it's so freaky for a young, normally healthy soldier to . . . dying in such an unlikely way."

"I know," Marsh said disconsolately, contrite toward his favorite officer for a lapse of taste.

Winter did not pursue the subject, but wondered if Hewitt had managed to get the kid to a doctor. Maybe better he should have tied him, hand and foot, and transported his ass down the mountain to Phu Bai when he first gave him the order to go.

Likely wouldn't have meant anything, though; with cancer, he was probably already doomed. Winter worried that Hewitt, a young, looked-to-be pretty-promising officer, might blame himself for having done nothing.

Nothing *to* do.

He walked over to the Sandbag and heard loud rock and roll coming from the open, lighted door. A bit early for this stage of decay, he thought.

He checked around the edge of the door to avoid being trampled in case of weird doings. Major Nichols was stapled to the back wall of the bar, obscuring view of a half-dozen Playmates and numerous aphorisms of military life. He'd only once before seen this ritual: the staple-ee was helpless, his jungle fatigues appended to the wooden walls with industrial-strength staples through slack parts of the jacket and trousers material, tightly outlining the body of the victim..

A stapling was a test of one's friends, wherein the stapled victim could only get something to drink if someone chose to offer it to him: he was genuinely immobilized. The other instance of his observing this rite had been when a favorite chauffeur, a CW4 flyer was departing for the states. The warrant he'd seen in that predicament had enough friends at the bar to enable his condition: he was plastered to the max. This instance argued for the major's marginal popularity: he was only mildly incoherent.

Winter hadn't realized Nichols was even *that* popular. And was he leaving? He didn't know how long Nichols had been in country, but he'd been CO of the First RR less than two months. Part of Tricky Dick's draw-down? He thought not.

Not really wanting to know, he leaned back from the door, walked away before someone could involve him. Nichols, OK as an officer, not terrible as a CO, was still not his favorite person.

chapter eighteen

Caesura

Cam Ranh Bay, Viet Nam: July, 1969

That was when it had all started. That four-day odyssey in 1960 that took him, new in the new service, on his first Army deployment away from family to Eritrea (Ethiopia).

Well, no, not really! The problem had its real origins a couple of years earlier, with that 1958 alert and deployment for Lebanon, Winter decided. What a circus that was: a broken down aircraft carrier, the USS Antietam (CVA-36), three months before the end of his last enlistment in the Marines. He knew in retrospect that Nickie, married then ten months, had never quite grasped the idea of Fleet Marine Force. Deployments were the name of that game: the clue was in Fleet. There was an infamous apocryphal note that pointed up the underlying problem: "Turd, if the Corps wanted you to have a wife, they would have issued you one." That drill instructor epithet, which had never caused a smile on Nickie's face, was not false. It was still the style in the Corps. And all the new-wives' wailing and weeping in North Carolina piney woods or on sandy Miami beaches, in the desert air at Twenty-nine Palms, or the toney elegance of San Diego's La Jolla, wouldn't change that.

But at least, if he had to be abroad, an assignment to Europe or even a civilized Asian state, with wife and children accompanying, was preferable. The Army offered that, where the Marines never could. The change he'd made in services held that promise.

Until his first assignment out of Intel School put him in Eritrea (Ethiopia) for 18 months without dependents. So much for a better life!

Hard on the heels of that assignment shock, newly arrived at Kagnew Station, he enjoyed the promise of curtailment of three of those months. But then came the Berlin Crisis, overseas extensions-in-place, and he'd wound up absent from family a full 24 months. After the trauma of service change, turning both their worlds upside down, Asmara was even harder to explain to Nicole. Then came the grace of Milwaukee.

After that two-year respite, he was off again, on his way to Viet Nam, and though it meant another year of separation, the conflict in that place at that time, in 1964, did not seem overwhelmingly threatening. At the very end of that involuntary tour, however, with plans already made for his homecoming, the mortar shell on that bloody LZ. That had pushed the envelope a tad too far.

Somehow, finding the strength, confirming her love, Nickie had worked her way through his recovery as the complacent year in Monterey imposed its magic. He knew when she found herself pregnant, it brought new horizons, new hope. On to the assignment at Rothwesten, Germany, where after a year he was commissioned warrant officer and transferred, all in one swift action, to Bad Aibling, garden spot of Europe. There in the beauty and solace of the assignment, David whole again, and the two boys underfoot, Nickie had found her element. She basked in the relative assurance of a stable life. Newly assigned to a three-year post, her husband an officer and enjoying a better life himself, and she with the children, in comfortable quarters with good neighbors and good friends, life took on more appealing coloration.

Then last spring, after only a year of peace—and that more than a year ago now—came the truncated tour at BA, the return to Viet Nam, and her inability to sustain that burden. After the hostility of those few remaining months in Bad Aibling, the turmoil of the move home and settling in the new home in Long Beach, he'd come to 'Nam with failing expectations.

But, surprisingly, after some sparse months, there began to appear signs in the few and far-between letters. The phone calls. The shock of her proposal to meet in Hawaii, and the wrenching dichotomy of his need for her and, by then, his relationship with Moira. Neither alliance, he felt, promised him a bed of roses.

Hawaii, only a month earlier, had promised some ephemeral chance at, if not unbridled delights, then hope, where he sought

. . . what? Among a world of mixed signals, he felt apt the last line of Yeats's *After Long Silence*: ". . . young we loved each other and were ignorant."

Ain't that a bitch! Had his Irish forbears suffered that shortfall also?

* * *

Hawaii: June 1969

Military dependent wife Nicole Winter was among the gaggle who met the Air Force bus transporting R&R personnel from the aircraft to the terminal. Chief Warrant Officer-Two David D. Winter, staring out the folding door, scanning the anxious faces while awaiting his turn to disembark, found her unsmiling face searching the uniforms on the bus. When she spotted him, she gave a quick, shallow smile that did not extend to her eyes.

Winter was quick on the message. There was the impact of that hate mail. But with Moira just hours away; he was in no mood to grovel. He labored with mixed feelings. True, the army nurse had become an encumbrance, of sorts; but only if they were ending their relationship. Neither he nor she willingly sought to end the affair, letting it run its course while confident it had no future. Both were people who needed warmth, liked to share, and were still very much attracted to each other the last time they were together. But that allure might not survive this reconciliation gambit. Did he subconsciously seek that? Winter wondered.

The complication of Moira aside, Winter reviewed the state of *things*, wondered where was this surprise visit with his wife going? He'd been preparing himself to tell all to Nickie when they were together in Hawaii. He owed her that. He would admit to the affair, ending any questions his wife might have stemming from that hateful letter; acknowledge Moira was a mistake, but that it had ended, and besides, he had not deliberately sought a liaison with the lively young nurse. A contrived lie, but it was what he wanted to believe. He was relatively sure that, in some important ways, he still loved his wife. How could he know?

He did know he still loved and wanted his two boys in his life.

Whether Nickie wanted him was her card yet to play.

When he was finally off the bus, trapped in the tangle of wives' and husbands' reunions, and actually could touch the mother of his children, the meeting was awkwardly subdued. He put his arms about her; her immediate response was less than exuberant. She kissed him, tasting of something he could not identify, slightly fruity. Likely a new mouthwash or breath mint. The merging of lips lacked fire. She did not cling to him, seemed rather to slip unobtrusively out of his grasp, light and tentative though it was, and she said nothing until they'd moved far enough from the greeting ground to be heard and understood.

"You look thinner," she said, holding him at arm's length. A moderately evasive opening, he thought, considering she had conceived of this get-together.

"Probably," he admitted, noting she looked good. Wearing even less makeup than he'd been accustomed to over the life of their marriage. But then, she'd never needed it.

They followed the crowd of military and spouses, bustling after the Air Force tech sergeant who had met Winter's bus. After the military briefings, with info for both spouses and instructions, handouts, emergency telephone numbers and the usual admonitions, the crowd split up for transport to their respective hotels. The Winters had chosen the Hanging Curl, some elusive allusion to the fanatical sport of surfing.

When the Air Force van had deposited them along with a Navy couple at the Curl, David, looking about in awe, deemed the hotel sufficiently opulent. It was convenient to Waikiki's full attractions. It served their needs. He didn't notice much about the accommodations.

* * *

Their initial love-making—a benefit of their marriage he'd not been assured was to be his—was perfunctory. There seemed no reluctance on Nickie's part: she undressed before him without hesitation or shyness. She prepared herself in only moments in the bathroom, and she acted and responded to his overtures and preferences much as he was accustomed to in their former life, though with a tangible absence of feeling. The act itself felt uncomfortably self-conscious for his part: over too soon, mutually unsatisfying.

It would continue in that vein throughout five days and nights, and after the first couple of sessions, a hint of—for want of a better word, he thought of it as an *alternative*—mood. The unbidden result of a duality he had consciously sought to avoid.

Inevitably, he found himself thinking more and more of Moira.

Before and after making love to his wife. Then, though he fought it, *during* the act.

He did not consciously compare the two women in his life. Not their bodies, their technique, nor their fervor. He consciously sought to avoid the latter, for that would quickly drop Nickie from contention. He cringed at his own judgement.

His wife's body had always pleased him. Even after the two boys' birthings, she'd regained her prenatal weight and shape. She was modestly built, without pretense or immoderate self-derision. She often volunteered the opinion that she'd not been blessed in the bosom department; but at the same time, was convinced that not having oversize, demonstrative breasts, with all the attendant weight and lactating demands, that she likely bore less chance to have later-life troubles. Her sister had suffered greatly with breast cancer, ultimately taking her own life in despair and depression following a radical mastectomy and continuing cellular explosion.

David considered Nickie's endowments "about what he would choose," he'd told her, given such a choice. She always smiled ruefully, but he'd had a suspicion she never believed him. He had not lied. But exploring the attributes of his later, unexpected young nurse lover, he did revel in the lushness of her endowments. He suddenly blushed, remembering Ratty Mac's description of female breasts as a "rack," as if her prongs were to be counted for the gamebook. But even so, lush breastworks or lesser, the dichotomy was not the physical thing.

From the first night with Moira in Doc Chupak's cramped little room—Doc was off on R&R in Singapore; and they, sweaty and tangled in sodden sheets, fighting for first deshabille, panting and scrabbling, all the while trying to keep their noise below the decibel level of launching aircraft—it had been an epiphany. Giggling like newly exploratory teenagers. From that first encounter, he'd been almost overwhelmed by her sense of— *commitment*. More than that, almost a religious zeal in her total giving. He never found that sexually explosive gift of hers as wanton. He knew Moira had not been a virgin; but he couldn't believe she had ever given herself to someone before on the same scale of passion, so complete he thought of it as *Grande*.

Thinking now on this, as he'd only peripherally passed over the thought before, he felt a sense of humility. Arising from the confusing mish-mash of emotions, he tried to suppress any of those half-assed self-adjudications that he might have made, playing self-psychiatrist, wondering about the wonky tendrils of father-figure inducement.

But even as newly weds, twelve-or-so years earlier, there'd not been that same passion in his and Nickie's love-making. David made a conscious effort to move his mind from those channels. He tried to look upon Nickie only in the most positive light. He took upon himself all the blame for their troubles. If not fully agreeing with her denunciation of his career pattern and his love of the "militant fantasy," he didn't seek to excuse himself from her judgement.

But the physical side of their relationship was obviously lacking from the start, there in that vacation haven. And as the skies over Diamondhead cleared and promised well for beaching and picnicking and making the tours in glorious sunshine, clouds lowered in his mind, darkening any horizon he could envision.

Neither could they talk. On several occasions—the breakfast table of their first morning room service, standing in line for a movie that neither wanted to see, walking the length of Waikiki in isolated unease—he felt compelled to break the awkward silence. But try as he might, he could not manage to articulate the words.

And she, transparently on the verge of speech, remained silent.

Neither would, or could, take the first step back from the abyss. Winter felt the yawning black void opening before him, even as he teetered on its rim, but could do nothing to avoid it.

He wanted to, needed to, but never could bring himself to discuss Moira. He made no allusions to her, no explanation for her. He felt a moral coward, but was content to live with that assessment

Nickie left impressions after each act of quasi-consensual sex that she was purposefully avoiding a comparison performance for him. If she did know of the existence, the reality of Moira— and she had written of that knowledge—she never gave further voice to it in Hawaii. An unnamed and innocuous guest in the bedroom, the ghost of Moira left David with the strange sensation of shielding an unwelcome visiting relative for whom he could offer no explanation.

Their awkward, silent withdrawal from any form of negotiations seemed mutually acceptable; he didn't know how to get around it. And he could not determine if it was better left this way, or if he should just blurt it all out. But Nickie never offered him the excuse to do even that. And the hourglass emptied steadily over the six-day covenant.

Their time together, no matter how carefully both sought to craft an amicable outing, or a domestic staying-in of an evening, it all came down to stand-off. Even the haunting majesty of the harbor tour, Ford's Island, and staring down at the enormous metal tomb of the *Arizona*, could not seem to shake either one out of a state of self-absorption. A kind of egotistical power play to ensure the other did not somehow use the moments of reflection to gain an upper hand.

The lack of empathy, either one for the other in the moment of that visitation, came late in the night to Winter and left him saddened. It seemed to epitomize the entire, disastrous attempt he'd imagined would give them some route to recovery.

When the pointless tours and gig rides, boat excursions, restaurants and long, only partially bearable nights were done; when the sixth day came and he scrambled aboard the bus for the return flight to Cam Ranh Bay—comfortable that she could catch the flight for New Orleans late that evening on her own—nothing had been settled.

And he felt strangely relieved.

R and R: Ravagement and Revenge. Romp and Relaxation. Even rape and randiness.

But Rest and Rehabilitation?

Hardly.

* * *

Cam Ranh Bay, Viet Nam: July 1969

Winter and the other -poker players scrambled into the bunker before the second mortar round impacted on NAF. The attack rescued him from a steady diet of bad cards. The Crazy Cats, along with a smattering of other military cultures, hunkered down and waited.

After the second explosion, there was no further incoming, but the bunker-bound Army and Navy personnel remained in place: there was no protocol for mortars. After five mortar-free minutes had passed, after counter fire had erupted and the Koreans were earning their keep, all hands straggled out and back to beds, to poker tables, to rhe Sandbag.

"I hate this shit," Captain Lamb grumbled, inspecting his San Miguel bottle for telltale signs of pilfering.

"Well, no shit, Captain Marvel. Whereas I truly love having my young ass targeted at oh-dark-twenty-five hours by some fucking rice-paddy ranger," Brenner raged.

"I don't mean incoming. I was referring to the Koreans. I hate it when those kim-chee munching bastards get an excuse to fire up that mercenary ammo. The ammo *we give them*. It takes minimum aggravation—one mortar round, one arty shell, one rocket—and those fuckers open up with one-oh-fives, one-five-fives, M-ones, cap pistols . . . everything in their frigging inventory." Lamb, who lived in Venice, California, when he was not whiling away his time behind the controls of a commercial 707 in alien lands, was not unaccustomed to noise. Still, it formed a viable basis for diatribe.

Brenner knew Lamb was tight-jawed because he'd learned his Army Reserve aviation battalion in Los Angeles, activated for a year, was on maneuvers in Bavaria. Even in CONUS at his regular job of piloting United flights from LA to elsewhere, he never got a flight to Munich. He wasn't senior enough to bid for, and expect to get, that cream of civilian flights. Flying P-2Vs in Vietnam did little to assuage his angst.

"Well, shit, Lamb, they went to great trouble and expense—our expense, admittedly—to have themselves and their guns ferried over here to provide us support. And think about it, my man; just in the White Horse, they have three one-oh-five and one one-five-five battalions, clamoring to fire that back-log ammo," Brenner intoned with seriousness.

The Korean 9th Infantry "White Horse" Division, was headquartered at Ninh Hoa, close neighbors to Cam Ranh Bay, and it was they, with four battalions of guns, and a multitude of infantry troops that made the peninsula the safest zone in Vietnam. Protecting the Air Force Base, its tenant Naval Air Facility, the 6th Convalescent Hospital, and the logistics monster at South Beach was raison d'être for the White Horse. They missed no opportunity to let US troops know they were on the job. Their massed guns, registered on all approaches to all locations on the peninsula, and firing from high ground, were quick to counter any threat.

"And in addition," Winter chimed in from just outside the door, "in addition to the White Horse with three infantry regiments and four arty battalions, we've also got, in Two Corps, the Korean 'Capital' Division, and the spiffy 'Tiger' Division with another two infantry regiments and four battalions of guns. And, not to be outdone, the ROK Marines sent their Second 'Blue Dragon' Brigade north to Eye Corps." He glanced around, seeking well-deserved approbation for his esoteric knowledge.

"Sometimes I'd trade all their well-intentioned bullshit for a platoon of Nungs," Lamb muttered.

"Not me, my man. I can sleep when I get back to the world. Right now, I relish every round the gentlemen from the Land of Morning Calm fire, covering my young ass. I buy drinks whenever I come across a ROK troop in a bar. No, sirree. Keep it up, Venerable Master Lee."

"Roger that, Mister Brenner," Winter said, stepping into the cramped bar space. He had reluctantly returned to the poker game he'd been part of before the attack, but new blood were playing non-poker games. He'd bailed out.

The Korean presence in Viet Nam had long been a sticking point. The US bought their allegiance, furnished their uniforms, paid their troops, provided rations and medical aid, bought their artillery ammunition, small arms ammo, and put gas in their vehicles, which also were gifts from Uncle Sugar.

"All God's chil'ren, get on the band wagon," Magic Marvin had said, reflecting the general attitude of unappreciative Americans.

"I can put up with their boom-boom serenade. I don't even mind that we give them access to our PX and they buy out or steal every piece of camera and electronic gear in Southeast Asia. Just keep those guns limbered up and manned," Winter intoned sincerely. He caught the top of the San Miguel bottle on the counter rim and snapped the cap with his fist. The edge of the pressed-board counter was chewed like a boarding kennel baseboard.

All the manufactured grousing over the Koreans was pointless. They knew it. It was what it was!

chapter nineteen

Allies

Cam Ranh Bay, Viet Nam: July 69

Bimbo Billingsgate, facilitator for beneath-the-radar acquisitions understood as illicit, declared he had to make a run to Ninh Hoa. It would be pointless to say he had something cooking with the Koreans; there was no other reason to go near Ninh Hoa. Winter and roommate Bracken, neither on that day's flight manifest, tired of paperwork, bored with heat, volunteered to ride shotgun. They went for helmets and weapons. After ten wasted minutes looking for the armorer with the key to the arms room, Winter borrowed an M-16 from one of his Ops who'd just come off a courier run. Bracken had held onto his sidearm after the previous night's flight.

The drive inland was featureless, the road almost deserted. They passed one Jeep-load of Air Police on patrol. As they neared the Korean headquarters compound, Winter noted the absence of any vegetation alongside the road. The ground was cleared back a full 300 meters. He nodded out at the sparse, lunar landscape.

"Yeah. Fuckers don't do a half-bad job clearing fields of fire," Bracken agreed.

Winter looked ahead, up the road, and said, "Bimbo, slow down. Checkpoint."

The lieutenant, distracted, gazing across the empty fields, kept driving without acknowledgment. Bracken's head swivelled between the sand-bagged checkpoint they were approaching at high speed and the disengaged driver.

"Bimbo!"

"Yeah, got you." He stamped on the brakes when he turned and saw he had no more than fifty feet to the striped pole across the road. The flimsy pole would not have impeded the Jeep's momentum; the .50 caliber machine gun that protruded from the sand-bagged embrasure might have done.

A teen-aged Korean guard with an old, slung M-1 Garand bigger than himself grinned over yellow teeth and waved them through as he leaned on the barrier, raising it.

"Place looks deserted," Bracken observed as they drove.

"Don't bet on it. Gooks just don't leave anything laying about; some other Gook will steal it." Bimbo was onto something: he knew about theft. "Man, these muthas are the best thieves in the world. Got it all over Raghead 'Slickie Boys' and French 'Apaches.' Zips and Ragheads can't touch 'em for deft hands. They'll steal the watch right off your arm, you leave it hanging out there."

"Well, hell," Bracken protested, "I got a fifteen-year-old hooch maid can do that."

"While you're awake . . . setting the time?"

The Jeep crawled, the lieutenant observing speed limits not posted.

"Yeah," Winter agreed. "They were good. Clean out an entire company area in ten minutes, and you'd never track your gear."

"When? In the war?"

"Oh, yeah. No other reason to go to Korea. Put up with that shit."

They passed a row of pyramidal squad tents, not surprisingly US Quartermaster look-alikes, precise in alignment, flaps folded in the same manner, the same specs on each. What they could see through the open doorways was clean and folded and arranged as if for inspection.

Winter knew that it was—awaiting inspection. Regular as indigestion.

At the end of the row of tents in a small, flat field the size of two tennis courts, they saw their first ROK troops. What looked like a full company of Republic of Korea infantry was drawn up in formation. Along the edge of the small field was a low-rise berm fifteen-inches high. On the berm, three soldiers were standing at attention. They wore no uniform shirt nor tee-shirts, as did the remainder of the formation. They looked hard, their ropy muscles not hidden in any indulgent fat. A Korean master sergeant stood close by, leaning on a pole. The rockers on his US-style stripes reached below his elbows. An officer stood at a brace between the three men and the formation, screaming an unending stream of apparent threats, abuse, profanity, and promise. Possessing Olympian breath control, he screamed without cease.

When he abruptly went silent, the master sergeant took his cue and stepped forward carrying the pole, which looked to be the entire trunk of a moderate-size sapling—smooth, carved and worked to shiny hardness.

Bimbo slowed the Jeep to a crawl, all three Crazy Cats watching the play.

The sergeant said nothing. He made a semblance of quick head-bow to the officer— whom Winter now saw was a captain—and quickly hefted the pole. He spun completely around, swinging the pole flat out, and caught the three soldiers across their backs at the exact same moment with the flail. One of them, shorter than the other two, took the blow across his shoulders while the other two were struck mid-back. All three went headlong off the berm into a ditch on the other side.

Bimbo slowed even more, barely rolling, though not daring to stop and draw attention. But no one could miss this medieval military discipline. The sergeant shouted one word.

The three soldiers scampered back atop the berm and came to attention again.

A second time, the pole whistled in a roundhouse, knocking the three men into the ditch. This time, only two of them climbed out when ordered.

The Korean captain, who had turned to stare at the Jeep, said something to the sergeant in a low voice. The sergeant tossed the pole aside and paced up and down before the two remaining upright soldiers, speaking in a low, controlled fury. From the road, the Crazy Cats could hear nothing.

Bimbo sped up and drove on past the field of punitive awards, and the Koreans' headquarters, the only building on the post. He pulled up at a large tent where boxes, crates, and bundles of materiel and supplies, all with US markings, were stacked outside: the ROK Supply Point. When Bimbo went inside to do business, Winter and Bracken remained in the Jeep, thereby improving their chances of still having a Jeep when business was concluded.

Bimbo came back, started up and drove the Jeep between the main tent and another, smaller canvas shelter. He crunched to a halt. A canvas flap went up and two Korean privates hauled a couple of boxes out and manhandled them into the Jeep, dispossessing Winter of the back seat. The two Koreans met no one's eyes. When they were satisfied with the placement of boxes, dour, unsmiling, silent, they retreated into the dark recesses and pulled the flap into place where it was quickly dogged down. No one appeared to present a bill or collect for the transaction. Winter climbed up and wedged his butt on the edge of the box above the back right wheel.

Billingsgate knew the drill: no further words needed. During the loading, he had remained behind the wheel and kept the motor running. He drove out now from between the tents, found the road again, and passed the area where field discipline had been dispensed. It was empty. There were no troops in sight, and they saw no other soldiers on the post. At the crossroad, Bimbo turned left instead of right. They departed the post from the opposite end from where they'd entered.

"Where're we going?" Bracken asked.

"Just wanta check something. Heard a rumor. Won't take but a coupla' minutes." He drove at top speed, passing through the Koreans' other gate without slowing. The private on the bar barely swung it clear before they dashed through.

The road, a poor grade of asphalt or slurry of some ill mix, turned suddenly to dirt and sand. The verge was no longer cleared; brush and salt grass grew to the road edge. The sudden closing in of the vegetation stirred a feeling of claustrophobia in the three officers, and Bimbo pressed the accelerator to the floor. Bracken caressed the .38 impotently, his head on a swivel.

They hadn't far to go. Around a curve they saw thatch coverings and a few corrugated tin roofs ahead. Drawing closer, a six-strand, five-foot-high barbed wire fence came into view, surrounding a cluster of houses. There was adornment of some kind gracing the tops of the fence posts. Someone, it appeared at a distance, had impaled melons on the poles. Within seventy-five yards even Bimbo with Coke-bottle glasses could begin to make out the tortured, distorted grimaces on the faces of the severed heads impaled on the bamboo stake posts.

Eyes closed. Eyes open. Horrified expressions. Eyes missing.

A cold chill swept over Winter. Bracken said in a whimper, "Great God Almighty! What the—" He never finished the sentence; everyone knew what the . . .

Billingsgate, in an involuntary homage to great evil, slowed the Jeep.

"The fucking Gooks did this," Winter said, confident from having seen it before.

"Which Gooks?" Bracken whispered.

"Koreans. Mister Lee."

"Yeah, I heard," Bimbo confirmed. "A sapper team hit their base back there a few nights ago. They captured one of the sappers and kept him alive long enough for interrogation."

When he didn't go on, Bracken asked, "And he led them here?"

"Here. Somewhere else. What's it matter? The message is out. Word'll get where it needs to get." His dismissive tone implied Bracken should know this.

"Oh, Jeez-us, look. There's a woman . . . two of 'em."

They saw no live Vietnamese.

The Jeep sped up, reached a wide spot where in better times markets might have been held. Bimbo wheeled in a turn and sped back past the sculpture of horrors, back down the road past the Korean stronghold, across the peninsula and directly to the Sandbag.

Bracken, jumped out of the vehicle. As if he could mitigate the horror, he said, "At least I didn't see any sign of kids."

Winter said nothing. One or two of the grisly trophies appeared awfully small.

None of the three men mentioned to anyone else what they'd

seen. To mention it meant a discussion, a reexamination. Looking too closely.

At allies . . . At American culpability, sponsoring the vandals' ingress.

* * *

Winter held her hand crossing the coast road, leading her onto the sand, toward the water. He looked back. In the nimbus of light from the guard shack, he saw the gate sentry staring, shaking his head. The young Navy guard had told them politely they weren't allowed to walk out the gate. In a vehicle—no problem. But on foot was a no-no.

Winter argued they were only going across the road onto the sand, and would remain in sight of the guard shack, if that's what the guard wanted. The Navy seaman, hesitating, thought that what he wanted was to get through his shift without a ration of shit. Which he was sure he would get if he stuck to his special orders with this Army warrant officer. Which he was not going to do.

"Yessir. That'll be just fine, sir. Whatever." And besides, that was one Number One chick the warrant had in tow.

Warrant Officer Two Winter and Second Lieutenant Burke ploughed through the fine sand to the edge of pathetic surf. A tidal swell, possibly some monstrously large surface vessel moving silently in the dark beyond shore vigilance, slopped small wavelets at their feet, creating friendly echoes of past beach frivolities. Out of time for both of them, the effect was comforting. They sank down just out of reach of the highest splash, seated on warm, dry sand that was clean, as far as they could see in the fringe of guard shack security floodlamps.

They sat for several minutes without speaking.

As each second passed, it became harder to break the silence, until he knew the time had come. Winter still held her hand. Covering both her small hands with his, and not looking at her but at the faint horizon, he said, "Burke. We gotta talk."

"We do, Winter." She showed no anxiety, for which he was

grateful. He hadn't known what to expect. He still did not, but her calm response was encouraging.

He didn't speak for several moments, and she turned to him: "Do we talk about Nickie?"

"Don't especially want to," he said with a wry grin. "But I suppose we have to. *I* have to." He leapt in with both feet.

"Moira . . . I can't meet any . . . great expectations." Silence. He was pissed; he'd blown his opening. "That you might have." Silence, and his efforts were not improving. "About us."

"And what expectations would those be?" she murmured, bailing him out while studying the effect of distant flare light on nervous water down the coast.

"Well, for starters, I can't marry you. Not now. Not until . . . not unless—"

"I don't recall you asking." There was an uneasy pause. "Or the subject even coming up." He was discomfited by the calm she exhibited.

"Dave," she said softly, "I don't expect you to marry me; I never expected that. You made me no promises. You were always up front about your situation, about Nickie . . . and the boys." She bit her lip, worked at a tiny, dry flake that likely, he thought, felt the size of a Frisbee. "It is mostly about the boys, isn't it?" It was obvious she wanted it to be.

"Partly. I have to be truthful, though; I honestly don't know where we are—Nickie and I—and I don't know what will happen. In the near future. When I get home. And after." He held her hands with one hand and the other resting on her chin, gently turned her face toward him. "Burke, my head's in such a mess. I don't half know what the hell I'm doing. Or saying."

She disengaged her hands, turned to him and put both arms about his neck, pulling him to her. She kissed him lightly—softly, without the passion that signaled foreplay.

He knew exactly the moment he lost her. He tasted the change in her lips, so subtle, so infinitesimally innocuous. She was here, within his grasp . . . but she had gone. He pulled her to him; she let herself be molded onto his body. Her free hand stroked his arm as if soothing a child's anxieties.

He knew he could have her yet. Now. Here, on the sand in full view of the gate guard. Not exactly Burt and Deb, but it would be worth any risk. She would make it of *Eternity* caliber. So would he, and she knew that. He knew she knew, yet she yielded to him.

But that was not on the agenda.

She pushed upright without pushing him away. "Dave . . . " She breathed faster, a greater depth in her breath intake until she was almost shuddering. He felt the tension through her body.

"This is some kind of . . . serendipity? Is that the word?"

"It's a word. You mean, something's happening here? Something fortunate, for one or both of us?" he said, disbelief in his tone.

"Both. I didn't know how to tell you." She dug her loose hand into the beach, let dry sand trickle through her fingers. "I've known all along there was no future for us. Together. I knew from that first night in that awful, cramped bunk with the soaked sheets."

"Yeah, the age thing's a bitch. No way around—"

"Oh, piddle. Big deal. You're what, eleven, twelve years older?"

"Nearer thirteen. That means I'm forty percent older'n you. True, you'd catch up a bit over the years, but we'd have to live to infinity to make the difference unnoticeable."

"You know it's not age," she said in a tone that would allow no argument. "But you've lived a lifetime ahead of me . . . without me." She sounded as if he'd committed some social faux pas. But he knew what she meant: a wife and kids were an accomplishment out of her league. Even that other war, his but not hers. Leaving her out of contention. "All along, I've known I could never come between you and them. I didn't stop it . . . us . . . because . . ."

She needn't say it; he read her thoughts. "I know. Me, too." They were on the same frequency, speaking the same language, yet marginally out of synch. Each phrase he uttered caused a slight echo in his mind, so that he thought he heard it from her.

She laughed suddenly, causing in Winter a tiny wash of revulsion, quickly gone in curiosity. She covered her mouth in a child-like gesture.

"I'm sorry. It just occurred to me what I've been feeling lately. I've had the most awful case of the guilts."

"Guilt? Because I'm married, because—"

"No, Dave," she insisted gently, a mild rebuke. "I think I assimilated all that, all those relations, after that first night. No, I've been feeling . . . like I'm caught in . . . ohhh, I don't even want to say it. You'll think I'm squirrelly or something."

"Hardly that." He dismissed the possibility with a head shake.

"Winter, I care for you. Very much. I do love you, but it's almost . . . incest! As if I'm in love with my brother, been making love to my older brother. I never had a brother, but if I had, I would have wanted him to be you. You are really a sweet man, Dave. You're a wonderful lover. You're attentive and caring—all that—but you are, above all, a sweet guy. What more can a girl hope for, in this day and age? It's why I could behave as I have done for the past months."

"I never—"

She waved him off with her hands. "I know. I know. It's just . . . a little ranch-farm gal from Montana. I was raised in an environment where my recent behavior wouldn't have been understood. Would not have been tolerated. Not even by me."

He attempted to speak.

"No," she shook her head. "Let me finish. It wasn't deliberate; wasn't because I rationalized about us and our lack of future. It just happened." She stopped.

"What happened?"

She hesitated, searching the dark waters, then turned toward him and said, "I've met someone. Someone I work with. Been around him since I got here and . . . nothing. But recently, he's . . . we've talked about seeing each other. I've not been with him, in that way—" a naïve expression that, in the midst of the two-way street of confusion, made him smile; she could never talk rough "—just had a drink at the club a couple of times."

"A doctor?" Classic!

"No, Hospital Admin. A captain." She had the look of a puppy expecting a rolled newspaper.

"You like him? I mean, do you think . . . do you like him?"

"I could." She took a deep breath, grasping the front of his fatigue jacket. "Winter, this is as good as it's gonna get. Can't you see . . . this, tonight, is tailor-made for us. We've got no future. You're getting short, going back to the world, your wife and boys. It won't be like I'm suddenly all alone. I'll have someone." She let a grating edge enter her voice, "Hell, Chief. I'll forget you before . . ." Her voice softened. "Well, before the end of time, anyhow." He saw moist eyes before she averted her face.

She's made the big move. Give her help, Winter, he admonished himself.

"Yeah," he said, looking out to the horizon at a number of black silhouettes passing silently between the two isolated figures on the beach and the distant, translucent skyline. "You're probably right. Now's as good a time as any, before we do something stupid, or find ourselves arguing. Get angry. Get hurt—"

"That's it. We care for each other. But then, there's life. Something that gets in the way while you're waiting for good stuff to happen."

"Deep, Burke. That's actually pretty good. Brenner might have said that." He chuckled.

"He probably did. Dear Luther. That's another thing good about being with you; I love your friends. Your family, really. Luther and Fred, Bimbo, Magic Marvin. I want to wrap Marve up and take him home with me."

"Marve might take a bit of wrapping." He worked hard to play the misdirection game. "Consider him the surprise package of this unit. There's a lot to Marvin doesn't meet the eye. But he's been a close, loyal friend, enlisted scum that he is."

"Da-ave!" Her reaction to his words was heartfelt; still, her lips quivered on the edge of laughter. She instinctively knew he couldn't be serious.

"Just a little Brenner humor there, Burke."

"Hmmph! You need some humor. Besides this festering triangle, what's bothering you? It doesn't really seem to be *all* about . . . us. Or Nickie. Is it?"

He sat for a while, saying nothing, staring out to sea. Seeking the convoy that had gone. He patted his jacket pocket, but he'd left his pipe and pouch in the billets. He rolled his cuffs down, buttoned them against a non-existent chill, became instantly too warm, rolled them back up precisely two rolls. Like Westy. Had it written into regs: two folds . . .

"A major cause of problems between Nickie and me, according to her, was my so-called 'fascination with war' and my convictions. Doing something about my beliefs; not just mouthing platitudes and sitting home waiting for the Shriners to march by. She claimed I read too much on war. That I idolized war heroes, had a distorted notion of rights and wrongs and what one should be willing to do to fix things."

He felt his language growing clumsy, emotions overwhelming his logical train of thought. This would lead to weak arguments. Anger. Brenner had chided him that if Winter was a character in a Dickensian tale, he'd "sputter." By God! He would not sputter.

"I try to make clear that I'm interested in the history of warfare. I am. I'm a soldier; my life, my career. It's on-the-job training. The more I know, the better I am at my job, and the more ready I am for the next higher job. I think Patton may have been the last general who did that. Knew his history. And Harry Truman, the last president."

"That's not a terrible thing. Do you mean—" She stopped in confusion. "No, none of my business. I'm not going to ask. Go on."

"My first tour—I came over here in 'sixty-four," he pushed on.. "Hot to go. Eleven years after leaving Korea. Was lucky there; never got a scratch. Came to 'Nam ready to kick ass, take no prisoners. 'Kill a commie for Christ,' as Ito says. Thought we were doing the right thing. Never saw an atrocity committed by our side. Ever. *They* were the ones did that. And we made good mileage on their heavy-handedness.

"Got my come-uppence in The Iron Triangle in 'sixty-five. Bad enough for me, it scared the hell out of Nickie. Took us a long while to work out all the kinks caused by that mortar shell."

"I knew you'd been wounded. But . . . badly?" Her lips had parted, poised. He wanted to kiss her; dared not.

"Kept me in hospital two months, then re-hab for three more. All that visiting she did, being around some truly ugly wounds and diseases on the wards, I think that worked on her as much as my actual wounding. After re-hab, months on crutches, than a walker, finally a cane. In Europe, when it got cold . . . even here, up in Eye Corps, when it's chilly and humid, I reach for that cane. Though I don't have it here."

"That's like—"

"I know. Ghost cane." He let out a short bark, nothing like a laugh. "Like ghost pains. Never mind. That's stupid. Not the same thing, by a long shot." Amputees! for God's sake. Not by a lon-n-n-ng shot.

"After language school for Russian, I went to Germany. New career pattern. Being a warrant with two technical specialties, I was sure I'd not go back . . . not *come* back here. I was assured that by Branch. By Arlington Hall. By my CO. But nobody bothered to tell DoD I was untouchable. *Et, voila!*" He would keep it light, but in the back of his mind, he sensed a roiling black anger that seemed to grow and expand, moving to fill his consciousness.

"Lots of guys are pulling second tours, now," she said softly. "It couldn't have really come as a great shock." She wasn't sure if this was one-on-one blasphemy, or something else.

"No. Well, yeah, I guess it was a shock. Getting that message. Lots of oh-five-ones in Europe and Unit Ten and CONUS who hadn't pulled their first tour in 'Nam, yet. But it's my own fault." She looked at him with curiosity. "I applied for special assignment. When DoD saw my paperwork come across, they knew that if I got the assignment they'd never see me again, never get another combat tour out of me. They preempted my special assignment to get one more tour in. Over here." His eyes, diverted, sought to bore holes in the sand.

"But, see, it's not just the second tour. After the initial shock, I didn't try to avoid the assignment. That's what really caused the rupture in our marriage. She thought—Nickie thought—I should have refused the orders, or gone to Canada; something improbable. I would not. Could not. And so . . .

"I came back, second tour, still fired up with righteousness. When I stepped off that bird at Bien Hoa, I knew things had changed. I mean, I'd read every newspaper, every magazine, watched every TV special and news show for those intervening three-and-a-half years, keeping up, trying to really understand. But what opened my eyes was walking across the tarmac at Bien Hoa, seeing that sea of vehicles. A flotilla of airplanes. Modern billet structures, as far as the eye could see. And troops. My God! Over half a million troops over here last September. "Later, on the streets of Sai Gon, I saw it even clearer. Bumper-to-bumper traffic. Everyone who walked when I was first here was now on a bike; everybody who'd had a bike before now had a motorbike, and if he had a motorbike before, he was now driving a Renault. Ones who'd driven Renaults before were driving Mercuries and Chevvies, and those . . . well, you see where I'm going."

"But isn't that common in war? Over time?" She was missing his point.

"Well, yes. But that was just an outward symptom. We've got half a million plus over here, and as far as I know the Vietnamese government still doesn't have a viable Draft. We have Thai and Filipino and Aussie allies. We're paying Korea's bills to help, and there're even German doctors. Probably some others I don't know about. Speaking of Allies," he said cautiously, "I saw some evidence a couple days ago about just what we're paying them to do." His voice had risen.

She was afraid to ask.

"What could be even worse, just a rumor so far, and it might be a Brenner-like kind of rumor, but I heard talk about an atrocity committed by Americal troops. Can't confirm it. Don't want to. But if there's talk, even in a world of rumors, there very well could be a reason for it. And, God, I dread that." He got to his feet, pulled her up, and they walked, skirting the rising tide. She kept silent.

"My best friend, an iconoclast, lapsed atheist, irony-bound pessimist views all this in the light of his disaffection. None of it pierces his armor. I understand that. I deplore it, but I understand it. But the real kicker is, I'm starting to understand, I mean really understand him. And to agree. And when I've reached that point, something has definitely been lost to me."

She remained silent, holding her sandals now in one hand, scuffling the sand before her.

"I've lost friends here. You probably have, too—maybe got friendly with some casualties who didn't make it out of the Sixth. But I'm talking guys I've served with, some for years. Other places, other times. Frank Balence, and a kid named Tscheib, Piltdown Pilot Bill Mabry, two new W-Ones, pilots, up in the One-thirty-eighth, though I didn't know them. Just days ago, a kid paratrooper blew himself up with a grenade on the chopper pad at Tan Son Nhut. He had his boarding pass tied to his jacket; he was flying out, going home that morning. Something he couldn't put behind him. It killed him, as surely as if a one-twenty-two fell on him."

"You haven't lost as many as other units. I've seen—"

"I know, and that's curious. A.S.A. hasn't had high casualties here. Of course," he said mockingly, "A.S.A.'s not even here. But it's not numbers. It's not quantity, it's . . . you know, 'Every man's death diminishes me . . .'"

"This is the kind of pressure R-and-R is designed to ease. That didn't happen, did it? Oh," she said, her eyes growing rounder, larger. "I didn't mean to ask . . . I don't want to know." Her head was moving slowly, side to side, denying him the right to tell her what she needed to know. What he needed to tell her.

"No. You have to know. The R-and-R was a killer from day one. I think Nickie was prepared to make an effort; I know I was; but somehow it just didn't happen. We couldn't . . . find one another. And I don't really know what that does for any future there. I don't know if the boys are enough to pull us back . . . to allow a marriage." He tried to read on her face what she was feeling, subjected to this melange of excuses and confusion.

"But it's not just the war deaths. The horrors, bad as they are. The anti-war rhetoric stateside, overseas, other countries, abusing our returning troops. Like we're the ones instituted this bitch. The hokum. The cheating and stealing and lying, in the news and out. Look at something as small change as my A-and-D duties. Awards and Decorations. That's turned into a cheap race to see who can accumulate the most medals, which consequently don't mean anything.

"I saw an Airman First in Honolulu, at the airport, had three-and-a-half rows of ribbons. He looked about sixteen. I asked him what some of the medals were, never having seen most of them. I assumed they were service awards for some places I'd never heard of. No, Honolulu was his first time out of the forty-eight. He seemed very proud, pointing out to me his ribbon for N.C.O. school, two or three just for being in service. Commendations for his unit, going back to nineteen-forty-seven, before he was born. A sprinkling of assorted colors and stripes, bars, and little thingies that didn't mean anything to me. But he sure as shit looked a fair warrior."

Her lips parted, about to speak.

He gestured aside her intent and said, "I'm putting people in for Air Medals who log their time flying maintenance flights out over the ocean, checking out an engine change. Or a paint job. Almost every N.C.O. and officer gets a Bronze Star when they leave, earned or not. Hell, hundred-and-first airborne have a Xerox-ed form for recommending troops for a Silver Star, minimum verbiage.

"It's just getting . . . I don't know what I'm doing anymore. I don't know what I'm doing *here*. What any of us are doing." After a long silence, while she watched the misting of his eyes, he looked back at her and in a tone devoid of warmth, said, "But we've straddled the tiger now; we can't get off."

"Oh, Winter . . . That's all too far over my head. I'm just a bedpan and APCs nurse, a failed Catholic, afraid of what that means, and not sure where to go from here myself. You have so many friends. You'll be all right. And you can be grateful for one thing . . ."

"Really! What's that?" Had she found a passage through the morass? He waited for warm words of encouragement as they turned toward the lights across the road.

"I'm not suing for custody of Oink. And I won't take the house." Her unsmiling eyes held his for a moment, and her face cracked across with a grin. A yelp. A hug.

Winter felt a painful tug somewhere deep. How could he let this one go?

chapter twenty

Anachronism

Southern Mississippi: Summer, 1969

A small tornado, he thought, staring through the side glass at the town. One decent wind—hell, a ten-boxcar freight running loud in the night could have wiped it out. It had been that way as long as he could remember.

This bus still made the same run out of Jackson as when he was a boy: down Route 137, through French, here to Waterford— the town's unlikely name bestowed by some expatriate Irishman in the misty past—and on to the coast: Gulfport, Long Beach, Pass Christián.

The Coca-Cola sign on the side of Parkins Drugstore, rusted and chipped, spelled old. Fading with the town. The white glass was gone from the globes atop gas pumps at the Conoco station where the 1944 model surplus Jeep still rested on blocks back of the grease rack. Across the street, Roy Bailey's Shell station had been replaced by a spic-and-span, bright, new white Southland center advertising diesel fuel and propane.

Waterford.

Home!

"You still make that fifteen minute stop at the Corner Cafe?" Jeremiah Torrence asked the bus driver. He was standing behind the driver, leaning forward to watch the road, and he read the man's nametag backward in the mirror—S-N-I-B-O-R. He had a quick flash of memory: some Robinses in school . . . had he known the family? No, Robinsons those were. Sharecroppers—

"Naw, ain't no Corner Caf-fay no more," the driver said, stretching his long neck out of the loose collar. He twisted his head around and Jeremiah Torrence thought of shooting turtles on Bottom Crick.

The bus slowed for a log truck making a wide swing into the street. The driver glanced up at the tall figure in his mirror, the wide gold chevrons and star on green, the ladder of small straight gold bars that marched up the right sleeve, the angled gold hashmarks up the left. The bus driver wiped a bony hand across his mouth. His knuckles were large, grotesque on skinny hands. Perspiration stood out on his freckled forehead, and what remained of the straw-colored hair was pasted to his skull. "You been gone from here a spell." It was no question.

"A spell," the Sergeant Major answered slowly. Been a spell since he'd heard that phrase, too. He felt himself smiling.

The driver couldn't see the soldier's face clearly, even in the noon blaze of Mississippi summer. The old bus was built before overhead skylights, and the barracks cap bill threw an angle of shadow from the ambient light inside the coach, down across the forehead and eyes, diagonally across the mouth. He could see only the edge of a terrible scar, but he saw the smile. And misunderstood it.

"Glad to be back, I 'spect. Heh! All you boys 'bout the same; go off over there'n that war, chase them slant-eyed gals, then come back down home to find some peace. No joke intended, you know." He grinned broadly at the lie, showing stained teeth in a broken, checkered pattern.

The bus came to a stop. The driver retrieved the earlier subject. "Naw, ain't no Corner stop no more. I pull up to the old Pure station at the edge of the circle, long enough to let off and let on. You gettin' off there? That's the Water-ford stop."

"I guess not. Where you talking about? What circle?" Jeremiah Torrence watched a large brown dog of questionable lineage, bearing the patched blanket of mange, amble across the asphalt street. He knew the dog's foot pads would have been long since scorched tough, made cartilaginous by contact with the killing-hot road surface. With admiration for his own daring he remembered hopping, skipping, fast-shuffling across that street in the summertime when the dust between your toes could put blisters on watermelons.

"Yep, you have been gone a-while. There's a traffic circle now, out past the livestock pens. On the edge of town. Hell, there's three, four stores out there. Coupla' service stations. This town's the damnedest place I ever did see," he added, shifting conversational gears. "Got six hundred people, come good weather, and got nine service stations. They ain't on no main road. I don't know how nine gas station operators can make a livin' in this piss-ant town. They ain't no too-rists; farmers get that guv'ment gas. What they sellin' here?" He winked at the soldier.

Jeremiah Torrence, startled, thought he'd missed something. Then he realized the driver meant corn whiskey. Moonshine.

Moonshine. Corn. White lightning. Uncle Claude, that time he burned his smokehouse down thinking government agents were closing in, and the two strangers turned out to be Jehovah's Witnesses. Claude chased them with a double-bit axe all the way to the Yalobusha line, cursing them and Jesus, the federal government, God, and Eldridge's Lumberyard for selling him pitch pine boards for that smokehouse against his better judgement.

It was hot that summer, hot all those summers. Hot like only Mississippi could get.

And Korea!

And he was caught.

Again.

Enthralled by the cycle of pig pens and hot summertime blood and snow all alone.

He hadn't wanted to think about Korea, the half memories. Bad memories. He looked away, to the town, struggling against the memories. Anticipating the circle coming up, he tried to pick out the new businesses Robins mentioned.

Gallagher, now, he'd had a new business, back in Omaha. Selling some kind of plastic doo-dads for the kitchen. At least, so Gallagher'd told him. But that had been before the levy, before Korea.

Now Gallagher was dead in a rice paddy and they'd left his body, already bloating, in the cauldron of that hated valley, only an inanimate stench, a presence by the time they'd breached the trap and straggled back with whomever, whatever they could and he felt himself slipping into that hated cycle again . . . and it couldn't be stopped . . . went on . . .

Nobody would have carried Gallagher's body, even had it been possible and the doctors had warned him helped him find ways to move his thoughts to other paths and he just had to do it, just had to . . . sit and wait for the men as they came forward were they a dream? he'd already given up seeing them now they were here.

Jeremiah Torrence reached up and touched the scar. He glanced up at the mirror, bent down until he could see the fresh rawness of it. A perplexed expression flitted across his features. He pulled the cap down farther and straightened.

"What were you saying?" he asked the bus driver.

"I ast, was you one-a them crowd used to raise hell with old Blaylock, the marshall here? When you was a kid." The driver checked the side mirror.

"Blaylock. Be damned! Sure. Old man, white hair. Yeah, old Marshall Blaylock, always wore that Stetson. Yeah, I remember him. Packed the biggest damned six-shooter I ever saw. Used to give all us boys hell for smoking."

Now *that* was a while back. A spell.

"Yeah, that's him. My half-brother. Older'n me," Robins said. It sounded like an excuse for something. "Betcha didn't know, that old Peacemaker wasn't never loaded. Not after 'bout nineteen forty-eight. Town council voted to take his bullets away 'cause he'd shot up a store one night when he got mad 'bout a faulty piece-a merchandise they sold him. I don't think they was any shells anywhere around for that gun." He shook his head in silent awe of some undefined transgression.

"He still around?" the soldier asked. It was a sharp memory. The most vivid memory he recalled. Funny how suddenly the old man stood out so clear. He hadn't thought of him for . . . years.

"Naw, the old fool walked into the bank one day to get a free calendar—right after Christmas, it was, that year—and some nigger with a single-shot Iver-Johnson 16-guage blew him apart at the beltline. Nigger was robbin' the place, naturally thought ol'

Roy'd come for him. Shame, too. Sent the nigger off to Parchman, burned him three months later; planted Roy next to a walnut tree on daddy's place; and the bank didn't have no money anyhow. It was right after payday for the field hands . . . monthly, you know, in the winter. Bank was out of calendars, too."

Jeremiah felt disoriented for a moment. The bus driver had a million of them. This non-sequitur apparently held some thread of meaning for the driver, but the sense of it was beyond him. He'd have to accustom himself to the speech patterns again.

The pneumatic *whooosh-hiss* was followed by a sudden in-rushing of furnace heat. "You gettin' out here? Your ticket's for here." A smell compounding cotton seed meal, diesel smoke, hot tar, and the dry, talcumy aroma of parched dust swept into the bus and created a brassy taste in the back of Jeremiah Torrence's mouth.

A black woman in a flour-sacking dress maneuvered her bulk up the aisle of the bus carrying a cardboard box tied with trot line. The Sergeant Major read Oxydol on the box and watched her as she placed one massive leg down the first step, shifted her grip on the chrome bar, wrenched the other leg beside the first. The bus driver made no move to aid her. She started the two-step cycle again; the soldier moved forward.

A light-chocolate hand reached in through the bus door and gripped the woman's arm.

"Minnie, child! What you doin' downtown, all by yo'self? Lemme alone, now. I can still walk. Leave me be . . ." The voice trailed off and Jeremiah Torrence watched the old black woman place the cardboard box on the ground, reach up, and open a bright yellow parasol bearing the most hideous painted excuses for goldfish he'd ever seen. It might have been pieced together from a cast-off shower curtain; every rib of the umbrella poked through the fabric. The oriental look of the fish bothered him.

"What?"

"I ast wuz you gettin' out here?" Robins stared at him with suspicion.

Jeremiah Torrence weighed the driver's look with his own

movement to help old aunty. He marveled at the tenacity of these people, these ways. How resilient ignorance was.

The barrel he'd seen once, up in Tennessee, came to mind. A droll comment along the side of the highway: a 55-gallon stave barrel, white stripe painted vertically down the side toward the road, a dipper hanging on each side of the demarcation. Hand-lettered labels read "White Only" on one side of the stripe, "Colored Only" on the other. He'd stopped the car to admire the unknown commentator, but knew as he did it was a feeble effort.

Jeremiah Torrence realized he was not following the conversation with the bus driver. Robins had asked him something else, and he heard only the echo of it. He put his hand to the scar and massaged it, rubbing at the dull pain, until he saw Robins staring at him again. He jerked his hand down. "Can you let me off on the road, beyond the town?"

The skinny, freckled arm snaked out, ratcheted the door shut. There were only the two of them now, the driver and the scarred soldier. Jeremiah Torrance estimated the bus would be in Gulfport before it got cool again, after the door standing open for only moments.

"You bought a ticket to Water-ford," the bus driver said. It was a pronouncement to which there was no argument. No appeal. It was a position.

"You're right. I had no call to ask. Here, let me get my bag." The soldier reached back into the seat behind him for the B-4. "Can you get my duffel bag from under—"

"How far you wanna go?" It was a mean gift in the fierce heat.

The streets were empty of human pedestrian traffic. A large mustard-yellow sedan with a tall antenna, its smoky windows sealed, whirred up the street, tires sticking to the soft asphalt, creating a sucking sound as the car cruised forward through the torrid-humid silence.

"To the fork, where the road branches to Magee." Jeremiah Torrence stood poised, the AWOL bag in his hand. He tugged at the uniform blouse. The driver looked in the mirror at the rows of brightly colored ribbon on the man's chest, glanced at the scar again.

Robins put the bus in gear, looked at his watch, shifted gears again, pumped the brakes to fill the passive streets of Waterford with a series of loud, flatulent *whooshes*, checked the wide mirror outside, the mirror inside, moved the shift again . . . and edged out into the street.

"Whatcha want out there? Ain't nothin' around there, 'cept that row of nigger shacks back on the slough." He worked the bus up through the gear chain.

"My folks live there. I grew up there." Jeremiah Torrence smiled, remembering the cool shade of magnolia trees in the front yard, their sickly sweet summer blossoms. Lot of good times in that big house, and fishing on the slough. Frog gigging in that leaky old flat-bottom. "Just going home."

The driver gave him a look then, strange and appraising. "Where 'bouts you mean you growed up? Down the road to Magee? I don't know many folks 'round there, once you git away from the highway."

"No, right there. At the fork. That big white house, two story. Red shutters." There was a nagging ache just behind his eyes. Jeremiah Torrence shifted his gaze and stared out the side window. He watched the scrub pine flash by, alternating with scattered tall, long-needled sugar pines. The red graveled soil poked up through burned pastureland. Even the kudzoo was wilted.

There was silence on the bus. Only the sucking, whirring tire sounds.

The driver spoke, again testing the conversational waters. "There ain't no big white house anywhere 'round that fork, soljer. There ain't been one, neither, not since I been on this run, and that's near seventeen years. Now, I can remember from when I was a boy—I'm from over D'lo way—there *used* to be a big place there. Musta been a plantation at one time, in the old days way back. Land all got sold off. Folks named . . lemme see, what was their name . . . well, anyhow, place burned sometime between when I was a boy and when I started drivin'. Maybe just before I started. Ain't nothin' there now." With that final word on the matter, it became quiet on the bus again. A mile farther down the road, the driver spoke again.

"Funny. I'as just thinkin'. Those folks had a boy went off soldierin' in the war . . . that was way back. Last war. But he got killed, or blowed up. Something. Hurt bad, I reckon he was. No, now I recall, reckon maybe he *was* killed." Nine power poles and a Brown Mule chewing tobacco sign later he confirmed it for himself: "Yep, he was killed. I 'member, now."

The glare off the white concrete highway, the flicker of amber and pale-green flashes from insulators on cross-trees atop the poles along the road had a hypnotic effect. Jeremiah Torrence felt his head swimming. He thought of pig pens again, but it was cold. He felt the cold and shivered. He saw men approaching, men with weapons, slipping stealthily between the stones and sky. He raised the barracks cap and ran his hand across his head, wiped the sweat back, then unconsciously traced the scar down from the scalp to the corner of his jaw. Emotions, tugging at his memory . . . *déjà vu*, he decided, and experienced a quick-flash vision of the big house remains.

In his mind's eye, the source of the image undefined, blackened timbers shone in the summer sun. Holding the vision mentally after it burst before his eyes, he traced patterns on a large beam, a checkered design like mud crust on a dried-up pond bottom, cracked and curling at the edges. The beams were black, deep crystalline charcoal black. Tin rusted among the fallen timbers, sienna-colored in the light. The magnolia trees were withered, sere stumps, too close to the house to survive the fire.

Frightened and confused, he scattered the dream before his eyes. And in the fright he thought of Korea again. He sought not to do so, but it was too new. Too vivid.

Memories, fragmented and fleeting.

But missing something. He could feel its absence like a loss. Something . . . to do with the old scars, the ones on his back and legs and around his side. They didn't often bother him anymore. The doctors said they . . . said something about them. The doctors! Jesus, the doctors—

He touched the scar on his face again. It had the dry, warm, smooth quality of a talisman worn around the neck. Absurdly he wondered what the odds were that he could rub it and a genie would appear.

"What's that?" Robins asked.

"Nothing. Just thinking out loud. How long until we get to my house?" He felt anticipation building, felt a knotting in his stomach as he tried to picture how they would look, tried to imagine the first words from each of them.

Mom would say, "Lord, Lord. Look who's come home. My baby."

And Paw, shy like always, he'd crush Jeremiah's hand in that big farmer's grip. Paw wasn't much for talk; his eyes said everything. If he had words for the occasion they'd likely be, "Jeremiah. Good to see you, boy."

And after some talk, when he'd walked those high, cool hallways and sat in his own room again, drinking iced tea—No! *Sweet* tea; he was back in the South—then he'd be all right. Scars would heal. And he'd get into some work clothes and help out on the farm. Big farm, Paw could use some help. He wanted to work, even with the paid hands there. But not around the pigs. Not alone. He wouldn't work around the pigs. It would be—

"I purely don't know where you're callin' home, soldier, but we're comin' to the forks now. You sure you wanna get out here?" He slowed the bus just before the road split, pulling off the floe-like slabs of highway concrete onto the shoulder, scattering gravel. His passenger did not reply. Jeremiah Torrence followed the stooped driver's lanky frame down the steps to dust.

A narrow, broken farm road, the macadam seemingly giving off more heat than it received, if that was possible, wavered off between two cornfields burned brown. Not a bird in the sky; nothing but heat risers down the road. Jeremiah stared at the corn too far gone for feed or seed, and he turned and looked across the highway to where black Angus were motionless, scattered dark mounds in a field of pale green-going-tan. He looked at Robins. He stared back down the road toward Magee and followed the driver to the baggage hold beneath the bus.

A row of dilapidated mailboxes stretched across his vision, perched on the horizon. He could barely see the tops of tiny shacks rising above the rows of withering corn, and a hedge of plum bushes and chinaberry trees. Shotgun shacks, Paw'd called them; they were built long and narrow, one room directly behind another. Joke was, you could fire a shotgun through the front door of one of those shacks and clean out everyone in the house. He couldn't remember why that had ever seemed funny.

He looked at everything, everywhere . . . except where the house had stood. He thought of the vision and he knew what it would look like without putting his eyes to it.

There were flitting images: white marble rising stark and bare out of the Johnson grass, a man in uniform in a wheelchair before the markers. The face was familiar, but he couldn't identify the man. It was someone he'd known in Korea, maybe.

Korea again! A tie to something—stock pens, maybe for pigs. Mud and snow all dead all dead.

"Here's the rest of it," Robins said, dropping the duffel bag on the gravel. "Well, gotta make schedule." He turned toward the bus but seemed reluctant to go.

Jeremiah Torrence turned, looked at the ground where the house had been.

"Say-uh, d'you get hurt?" When the soldier stared at him with no comprehension, Robins added: "In the war. You wounded in Viet Nam? I know lots of you were. Nephew of mine—"

Viet Nam! The world exploded before Jeremiah Torrance's eyes, a flash of fear, a sudden coldness. Viet Nam! Without knowing why, he felt himself caught in a flood of terror. The word . . .

He felt the word slipping out of his mind, saw momentarily a jumble of white-washed plastered huts bamboo swaying beyond and a row of trees filled with smoke and fire and then coming into focus before him. a long low wall of old sun-washed brick standing among tall weeds. There was no longer a jumble of blackened beams. Tin roofing had gone to red powder, blending back into the soil.

When he looked back, the driver was in the bus, in his seat, his hand on the door handle. "Hey, those people's name was Tolliver, I think. Tennant. Something like that. Used to have a fine big house right there, I'm told. You can still see the foundation. Yeah, lost their son in the last war. Then the house burnt down with them in it. Terrible thing. Long time ago, now, though." He tugged at the heavy door.

"Well, good luck to you, soldier. Hope you get home before dark. If you don't, see you walk toward the traffic. All them gold stripes and medals and what-all, they'll see you. Not much traffic down that road anyhow."

He waved a half salute; the door clamped shut, rubber on rubber, hissing, and the bus pulled away.

Jeremiah Torrence sat down on the duffel bag and watched the heat rising on the Magee road.

The words were there. Hazy, like the achromatic landscape. The trick lay in the ordering: the white marble slabs upright in rows, the black beams, memories of magnolia trees green and sweet with heavy blossoms, the deep red of the roof fading from the picture, flame-red bright blossoms that crowded out into the corners of his mind—a mosaic, an art form he only partly understood.

The meaning of it was just beyond him.

There was a dull, lazy, whipsawing of insects on the still air. Only that and the heat risers.

chapter twenty-one

Free Fire Zone

Cam Ranh Bay, Viet Nam: July 1969

Grange was right. A VIP was indeed coming to visit the First RR, and he would be here tonight. Not just a VIP; *the* VIP. Major General Charles Francis Langloise, Commanding General, US Army Security Agency. "Charlie Two-Star" himself.

Winter had never laid eyes on the man, though he'd been CG of ASA for several years now. Most ASA troops never saw him, unless they occupied a slot in "Confusion West"—ASA headquarters at Arlington Hall Station in Virginia. He'd seen pictures. Command photos that appeared on the walls of commanders' offices, day rooms, training halls across the world, along with photos of the chain of command from the president on down. But this senior officer held his place in that chain with aplomb, a Distinguished Service Cross from World War II valor keeping scoffing remarks within bounds.

He'd be here tonight. Grange was about to wet his pants. He'd never met the general either. Grange was an aviator, not an ASA officer; he merely worked for the general, way down the ladder. Two stars did trump oak leaves. Even if that major was a commander, a role Grange had assumed as of this morning.

The change of command was a bigger shock than Charley Two-Star's scheduled arrival. Major Nichols, pried from the Sandbag wall just after sun-up the previous day, no evidence of staples anywhere about him, had called an impromptu formation, all hands, at which he made the announcement that he had reached the end of his tour; he was going down to battalion at Sai Gon/Tan Son Nhut for a week or so, leaving today, and the new CO was . . . drum roll . . . Major Peter Porter Grange.

The shock was due to PP's colorless presence in the First. When he'd joined the unit and was named Executive Officer, no one really considered him CO material: he had as much command presence as Minnie Mouse. But the colonel down in Sai Gon had mandated his emergent position, thus implicit command presence. And he was several cuts above the next-ranking heir apparent, Major "Nat Guard" Koenigseder, Lord help us! the unit agreed. For a brief period, the First RR had sported a count of three field grade officers. But they were only a company, and with Nichols's departure, were reduced to a more workable pair.

* * *

That evening the First RR had complete and sole occupancy of the NAF Officers' Club. The only Navy officer to show up was Captain Raymond X. Carver, commander of the Naval Air Facility, who liked to be called "Bucky" by his senior officers. No one called him that, out of sheer perversity: everyone, officers and men, despised the man and called him "Captain Blye," albeit not in his presence He had alienated Army officers when he took over command and made a point of insisting that the entire NAF, grounded on sand and other insubstantial Southeast Asian waste, was to be thought of and treated as an aircraft carrier. Keel-hauling and flogging were still *de rigeur* in Carver's navy.

Winter was on the flight line when the general's U-21 taxied in and eased to a stop, the props coming to rest in precision alignment. Mandatory for a general's bird. Colonel Sizelove, battalion commander, his black face shiny with sweat even in the early morning air of Cam Ranh, was first out the door. The three-step ramp was pushed into place barely in time to prevent his first, blind step from dropping him to the tarmac. He stumbled and quickly took up a position of attention at the foot of the steps and, along with the moderate assemblage of officers and NCOs, saluted The Man when he bounced down the steps. Grange, new CO that he was, placed himself in jeopardy of never being promoted again. Immediately the toadying and arm-flapping was done, he jumped forward to shake the general's hand ahead of his boss, Sizelove.

Winter walked away before inadvertently being drawn into the show. The officers scurried about like ants on a burning log, demeaning themselves and their rank by groveling. Charley Two-Star didn't take to that kind of treatment, Winter had been told by a captain he'd known in Bad Aibling who had been on the general's staff at one time at The Hall.

Now late evening, having arrived at the great moment, the warrant officers gravitated toward a muddle at one side of the cleared area in the O Club. It might have been a dance floor in a civil venue; it could have been used for courts-martial proceedings, for promotion boards, ceremonies; for weddings, a theater club, a cattle auction, or a short-field bocci court. Here, the plentiful space was likely the result of having insufficient chairs and tables to fully equip the club. Winter was seeing the Navy O Club for the first time. When one has unhindered access to The Sandbag, why go drink with squids? was the consensus.

The command officers, led by LTC Sizelove and MAJ Grange, followed the general like a covey of quail chicks as he moved about the club floor, graciously speaking to every officer. General Langloise was a personable man, an exceptional officer, and he made a point of asking each man's title and job in the unit. If the officer was career ASA, the general wanted to know where he'd served. He was fully conversant about every ASA station, and seemed knowledgeable about aircraft, certainly about the aviation programs that ASA was engaged in, in Viet Nam. He must be on top of LAFFING EAGLE, Winter thought. They'd flown him up here from Tan Son Nhut in one of their new birds, albeit a "slick" without the installation of equipment.

Brenner, Winter, Ito, Billingsgate, and Chumley, an unpopular avionics supply warrant officer, were in one knot; others congregated in other isolated islands of indecision and expectation. As the general made his way nearer, Winter could make out the pattern of his laid-back social niceties.

Everyone was in jungle fatigues. Specifically, no flight suits. Someone had pointed out to the colonel that General Langloise had commented that the gray, Air Force-style flight suits looked like his grandchildrn's jammies, without the footing. Nice, clean, starched jungle fatigues was uniform of the day. And all felt like fools. They'd dressed in the particular style following Grange's quick order. He insisted on only "freshly starched," clean fatigues. And they'd all heard General Langloise comment, as he walked in the door to the O Club that evening, "Colonel." He nodded toward Sizelove. "Major," he added Grange to his address. "Is it really best policy to have your officers and men in starched fatigues? After a multi-million-dollar design effort to create a comfortable, practical suit of uniform clothing for troops in this terrible climate? I question if that's optimizing our assets."

The general appraised Chumley, who had overlooked the "starch and iron" portion of Grange's order, and smiled. "Now there's an officer who knows where he is." He nodded at Chumley, who looked startled. He had no idea what the general referred to. He'd just heard someone say he had to be at the O Club at eighteen-hundred hours. He presumed for drinks.

Grange stepped away from the touring general's squad and Winter saw him cross to Navy Lieutenant Ivory, the liaison Instructor Pilot assigned to the Third. Even as IP, Ivory was required also to fly regular combat missions; he had to know what the pilots faced on mission, what they demanded of the aircraft. But Ivory, husbanding his warrior tendencies, flew as seldom as possible, and consequently did not occupy a position of fond comradeship among pilots or operators in the First. But he was black; the battalion CO was black; and other officers in the command were fully cognizant of the implications. And, as an IP, he was theoretically a commendable pilot.

Colonel Sizelove escorted the general to the small gathering of warrants—*mostly* warrant officers; Lieutenant Billingsgate was in their midst. But Bimbo, it had been decided in the local WOPA ranks, was so much like a warrant officer, so devoid of commissioned officer social niceties, he was deemed an honorary warrant—and properly introduced the general, first to the one commissioned officer, and then, "Warrant Officers Brenner, Winter, and . . . uhh . . . Ito. And Chumley. Whom you've met, general."

The general shook each officer's hand. They talked briefly,

about their jobs, and three of them, about their other ASA assignments. "Sounds like you two, Mister Brenner, Chief Winter, here have been following each other around the world."

Well, Winter thought admiringly, you don't make two stars and miss many tricks.

Before the conversation could begin to drag, Major Grange swept up to the group, Lieutenant Ivory in tow, and launched into talk. "General Langloise—" Grange persisted in calling the general "Lang-loys," instead of the French pronunciation the general favored, "Lang-lwah." Winter thought he saw the general flinch with every utterance "—I'd like you to meet Navy Lieutenant Ivory. Lieutenant Ivory is with us as Instructor Pilot on the P-2V Neptune aircraft."

"Lieutenant. Good to have you with us Army folk," the general said easily, reaching to shake hands. "Our men treating you all right? Not giving you too much grief over your service affiliation, are they?" He chuckled easily, knowing they just would not dare. And probably did.

"Just fine, sir. Everything's great here: the billets, the job, the people . . ." He looked at Grange but said nothing further.

Colonel Sizelove spoke up. "Lieutenant Ivory's about to complete his tour with us. He's the second accomplished naval aviator we've had in that slot. But he's down to just under two weeks."

"Do you have a replacement lined up?" General Langloise asked straight-faced, knowing the name, flight record, and personnel file of Ivory's replacement, whom the Navy had already selected, alerted, and briefed.

"Navy's notified us of a Lieutenant Commander . . . I think the name's Kristophsen. He's in the pipeline and will be here in a week or so. They'll have overlap." The colonel—misfit, paranoid, or otherwise—did have his stuff together, Winter thought.

The general surprised him when he said, "Colonel, I trust you'll ensure the Lieutenant's fine service will be adequately recognized. Specifically an Army award, something not all Navy personnel will have." He didn't turn to the colonel when he spoke;

but Winter knew the statement was not rhetorical. Was in fact an order. The general didn't want to know specifics. Just a hint for Grange to butter up the Navy to keep the replacement pilots and parts coming.

"Uhh, yessir." Sizelove, startled, turned to Winter, but spoke to the general. "We're in process of completing his award recommendation now."

Winter cringed. He just knew it was going to mean some crawling and bullshit to write an Army Commendation Medal for Ivory. Hell, there was nothing to hang an ARCOM on; the man did nothing of commendation significance. Even that little with reluctance. And he just knew he'd probably have to contribute to the composition of this fantasy.

He heard Grange say something, but surely, had heard wrong.

Sizelove confirmed it.

"Yes, general. We're recommending Lieutenant Ivory for the Army's Legion of Merit."

Winter could have sworn he saw the general hesitate—a flaring of nostrils, a tight jaw.

"Fine. Have the paperwork completed, signed, and get it to me before we leave for Da Nang in the morning. I'll take it back to The Hall, sign it myself and put it through channels. That will speed things up by a margin of three." He turned away and moved to the next group. The general's signature was the only requirement for approval.

Colonel Sizelove nodded fiercely at Grange. Major Grange dropped out of the queue and pulled Winter to one side. "Mister Winter. I need an L.O.M. recommendation, worthy of a field grade's wording, written right now!"

"Well, sir—"

"Don't give me that 'well, sir' shit, Winter. I want that recommendation, with details, witness statements, whatever . . . and the citation. Write the citation, also. Get that done, in clean copy, six carbons, on my desk before oh-six-hundred." He huffed unnecessarily for a moment, and said, "Got that?"

There was a long moment of awkward silence.

"I'm not sure I do, Major. I can't write a Legion of Merit recommendation for this . . . pilot. Hell, I'd have no end of trouble justifying an AR-COM."

"Mister Winter, if I'd wanted . . . if the colonel had wanted An Army Commendation Medal for Lieutenant Ivory, he would have prescribed it. And don't tell me you 'can't' follow this order. I'd hate to see your career in the shithouse over something this trivial."

Prescribed? Winter, in a move toward reason, tried to recall a scenario in which he'd heard the word used, outside a doctor's office.

"Major, for the record, as your Awards and Decorations Officer, I don't consider this trivial. Is this going to be S.O.P. for awards in this company in the future? Are we going to get on the goddamned Air Force bandwagon, giving Bronze Stars for a successful bowel movement? Do we really want—"

"What I want is for you to remember who's commanding this company. What I want, junior grade Warrant Officer Winter, is for you to follow orders." He worked for a glare; it failed to come off, resulting in an unspoken and confused appeal.

Winter was on the point of bringing up the meaning of "illegal orders," those orders which were not proper and could not be enforced. This case seemed to fall square athwart the limits of that consideration. But he knew, too, that trying to get a courts-martial board to recognize and agree with this judgement—and it was strictly a judgement call on his part; hell, who knew if he was even correct—was fantasy. Winter realized with a flash of insight that he might have sought this manner of clarification anytime over an indefinite period of time . . . maybe fifteen, sixteen years.

"You got it, Major. An L.O.M. it'll be. Coming right up, sir. Hokay dokay! On the double. One L.O.M. for conspicuous misanthropy." He turned from the startled major's presence, recognizing something approaching a stare on the CO's face. He realized with a start he'd just out-word-smithed Brenner. But only in one narrow slice of invective.. He stopped, turned back and, from ten feet away entirely beyond protocol, snapped a brisk salute at his commander and held it until Grange's hand crept reluctantly into the air, approaching his wrinkled brow, but never getting there. Without waiting for fulfillment, Winter cut his salute away, then went to perform A-and-D manipulations—not duties, he insisted—acknowledging the rampant bastardization of the process.

The major had not asked if Winter required input from anyone, including himself. If he needed help with typing. Or accessing records, some of which were personal and thus secure. Grange dashed away, dragging a stunned Ivory along behind him, catching up to the procession.

Winter, returning to the gaggle of warrant officers, took a moment. He finished his beer, looked over at Brenner and Ito who still waited nearby. He hadn't said that his clerk for A-and-D purposes, SP5 Marvin O. Marsh, was probably lying in a stupor in his billet, having tried to drink the Sandbag dry earlier in the day. Marsh had ridden the mission bird yesterday, slept late, and started drinking early. Likely not much help there, Winter thought. He tossed his beer bottle to Ito. "Take care of that, my good man, will you? Take a couple of sheckels from the kitty."

He wandered off to search out Marsh, seething, determined not to show it.

* * *

Winter made a point of being at the strip when the general departed Cam Ranh Bay the following morning. The award recommendation had been finished and submitted. Signed by Major Grange. Endorsed by Lieutenant Colonel Sizelove. Winter suffered a small ripple of convulsion when he saw the colonel pass a brown envelope to the general's aide.

His own name, as creator and spiritual adviser of this work of fiction, appeared nowhere on the fabricated document. That was the only way it could happen. He had no wish—he refused—to be, in any way, associated with the bogus LOM. He would never again look at one of those lovely magenta ribbons on the chest of someone with the same feeling of respect, even envy. Just another political ass-kissing trinket.

* * *

As if it were a khaki-colored Rosetta Stone, the LOM brouhaha opened Winter's mind to shortcomings in everything around him, now and for . . . how long? The war, the actions of career and non-career personnel whose agenda was not in keeping with best government policy. The shaky military posture. Micromanagement from the Oval Office. Political posturing, craven self-interests, the usual run-of-the-mill good ol' boys skulduggery. Sensing an abyss gaping before him; he felt inclined to . . . just . . . call . . . a . . . halt . . . to all forward progress.

With a deep breath and a shake of the head, he reviewed his response to the major of the night before. Could he have done something different? Better? Was there a newfound antidote to incompetence? Toadying? Criminal complicity? With grudging acceptance, he thought not.

Likely Marsh would remember nothing of the evening. When Winter had struggled with the words, making frequent use of a dictionary and a thesaurus, and worked his way through the entire fantasy, he turned the hacked-up first draft over to Magic Marvin. The clerk, dragged drunk from his bunk, hadn't even made his usual jocular remarks about Winter's thorough editing efforts. Staring blindly through unfocused eyes, he inserted in the typewriter a series of forms and carbon paper and began typing. Winter had to wake him twice, pick him up once from the concrete floor when he'd fallen out of the chair, and had made several runs to the messhall for coffee.

The coffee was for himself; Marsh declined, insisting it would just wake him up and as a wide-awake drunk, he wouldn't be able to type.

At 0510 hours, he pulled the stack of forms from the Underwood, yanked the carbons, and handed seven pristine typed pages to Winter. Proofing it, Winter found no errors. He started to comment on the remarkable job, but Marsh was asleep with his face on the keyboard. The proper place for the little enlisted swine, Winter thought, allowing himself a tiny, affectionate smile.

When Winter had left the office with the finished recommendation, he was encouraged at least that he now could have the pleasure of awakening Major Grange. The CO, when he had last come to check on progress of the recommendation, was already three sheets to the wind.

Have to take what pleasure one can find, Winter rationalized over the pre-dawn wake-up.

Now, leaving the flightline, still up, still awake, he went to chow where he was shortly called out for a phone call. Lieutenant Lonegren at III MAF, returning his call of the day before, had things set for a visit. He'd greased the skids for Winter to accompany a combat patrol in Eye Corps. Since Winter was an old artillery hand, Lonegren hoped he appreciated that he'd put him with a Forward Observer team.

* * *

I Corps, Viet Nam: August 1969

From the OP through binoculars, Winter observed with detachment the decimation of NVA in the open paddies luxuriant with tender, green growth. Life through the glasses was one long, silent movie of muted drama or high comedy, depending upon one's relationship to those observed. He watched a wiry, middle-aged enemy officer competently pull together a scattering of dazed and wounded stragglers, disengage from the ARVN trap, and charge unexpectedly up the trail that descended from the village on the hill. Winter thought he knew that village. He had, in his earlier tour in 'Nam, in a constant quest to understand the war, accompanied a Marine CAP Team there. Or, perhaps, some place very like it. But he knew from the briefing, this was not a village friendly to the NVA. Why go up there into another trap?

Watching the engagement playing out, he was not overly concerned for the village. The briefing indicated they had integral defense forces. The enemy officer and his few survivors would soon be cast out of there, back into the arms of encircling government forces.

Winter called to the spotter, a Marine gunny who shifted his eyes away: "Make sure the guns hold their fire . . . that's a friendly ville. Tell your F.D.C."

Twenty-fourth Corps hadn't been enthusiastic about his request to spend a couple of days in the boonies with the Marines. Even inoculating babies, treating glaucoma, and teaching dental hygiene of that now-defunct CAP policy would have been unwelcome, he realized. Winter's pitch was that providing support to these III MAF Marines, in his CRAZY CAT assignment, justified any interaction that would expand understanding and improve support. With the Marines' complicity, Timid Tess Trueheart was overridden.

He wondered if having a visitor thrust upon them without explanation, the grunts would give his hold-fire request any credence. And a goddamned army pogue to boot.

Nothing happened for eight or nine minutes. The Marine Fire Direction Center was being amazingly responsive to a doggie warrant officer, Winter mused. An Air Section weenie, at that. They waited.

Then, far off he heard a dull crack. Seconds later a marking round of Willie Peter, mocking the hold-fire request, exploded on a ledge high on the cliffs above the village.

Winter waved his arms and screamed, "*Cease fire! Cease fire! Friendlies in that ville.* Get the F.D.C." The phosphorous trailed down long white ribbons against the dark hill.

It remained quiet on the OP. The gunny had absented himself. Only Winter's voice sounded across the hilltop. He heard a crackle in the earpiece of a nearby radio and looked at the RTO who, eyes gone round and questioning, said, "Sir, El Tee says the people in that ville are dead. Or done di-di-ed out?" His voice rose on the statement as a second spotting round exploded farther down the cliffs, barely on the upslope edge of the village.

"*Lieutenant's ass,*" Winter screamed. "*He lies.* The bastard is lying; he makes his living with the guns." The Lieutenant, he knew, sought a fitness report with tangible, measurable numbers, and would risk the sin of commission over the failing of omission. Like the frustration of an obscene phone call, Winter felt a powerless, undirected anger.

"He says it's double-Foxtrot Zulu, anyhow, Mister Winter." The radio-telephone operator added lamely, "A free fire zone." He listened, jerked his head around and smiled into the handset, and looked up at Winter. "But he's suspending arty, all the same. How 'bout that?" While the radio operator basked in the distant lieutenant's humanity, Winter leaned into the glasses again, recalling a strange night on Nui Ba Dinh four years ago. At once, within the village, he saw the flash and smoke of grenades, green tracers from small arms fire, and below, the ARVN infantry company, broken into maneuver units, sprinting for cover. The lieutenant's career-enhancing lie had begun a self-fulfilling truth.

"They're killing the village! Stop them! *Cease fire!* Goddammit, why isn't ARVN moving in?" Winter shouted to no one. "What's that C.O. doing? Charlie's slaughtering the village." Snapshots, memory clips of tiny forms, bird-like arms and legs, eyes tight with tears against the sting of the needle, came to him in disjointed, jerky replays. At first he heard no distinct sounds from the village—no screams or cries—a void followed only occasionally by the sharp rip of automatic weapons fire, the hollow crack of a grenade.

And then, in a rapidly blossoming crescendo of thunder, a thrust of awful beauty, Winter suddenly understood the advance stopped, the arty suspended.

The Phantoms came in a graceful parabola over the adjacent mountain, already hugging the deck on the initial pass—first the leader, then his wingman in echelon—signaling a courtesy call. A mere statement of good manners. Proposing: Here's what's coming, Charles. You poor silly bugger, you now have thirty seconds to consign your bloody little soul to Buddha or Marx, Confucius, Mao, Ho—whomever!

He could only watch. The logic was inescapable: the village . . . the NVA . . . the opportunity. And if some friendlies are still alive in there, what then? he thought. But because, and then he thought *despite* that he felt the impossibility of such devotion, he knew it was already a matter of statistics. Eye Corps chic mandated the killing-season style.

Later, he watched the play of flame across the dwindling remnants of village, napalm fusing all into one shabby, final consecration, and he felt, without understanding but also without question, a faint, elusive thrill. Of accomplishment, of identification, somehow. Of . . . love even, as if some meaningless conjoining of unrelated words in his mind had coalesced suddenly into a strophe of poetry.

chapter twenty-two

Aces, Straights, and Flushes

Bangkok, Thailand: August 1969

Brenner had first presented him the archetype of this harrowing passage, late one night three years before, in the Gasthaus Zum Braünerhof in Harmuth-Sachsen. Neither could anticipate then Winter's eventual replay of the same hapless descent from one level of hell to the next lower. And Virgil nowhere in sight.

His lone journey seemed without end, without relevance.

He looked about, unsure where he was. The back streets of Cho Lon? Kuala Lumpur? LA? Somewhere presenting urban blight at its Oriental best. He felt dazed, disconnected . . .

And the absence of grenade screening on the windows of the bus was curious, disturbing.

When finally he had chivvied his mind back into channels, the Air Force shuttle from Don Muang Air Base into Bangkok, a punishment of some 26 miles, became merely another of Lot's miseries. Disenchanted by the interminable transport, he tried seeing with tourist eyes the glamour of the Orient in jumbled and shabby Asian houses crowding the road, tried seeing them as something more than mere irritants, flanking rice paddies of inestimable ripeness and stench, luxury apartment buildings gone to seed, stands of bamboo, palms, water buffs, and commercial advertising.

Billboards, ubiquitous and invasive, lined every street, topped every building, offered everything: Seiko watches crafted from chewing gum foil; movies featuring enormous monsters and barely-clothed maidens whose buxom charms could in no way be Thai. Overt voluptuousness and garish-color echoes of low-rent Hollywood. Yamaha bikes, Kirin beer, jewelry stores, tailor shops, hotels, restaurants, temple tours, massage parlors, more tailor shops, the floating market. The works.

He should have felt more interest. He'd been here in a two-day bail-out in 1964 when 3rd RRU evacuated their aircraft from Tan Son Nhut, fleeing the annual typhoon. He'd seen little of the country then, or the city, but didn't remember a maddening trek like this to reach Bangkok.

Rebuking himself for whining, he confronted the question of how he'd gotten here. On a *second R-and-R!* Troops got no more than one break during a Warp Zone tour; some, none. He hadn't known it was happening; it had to be Brenner's doing with the CO's complicity, Magic Marvin facilitating. He understood his friends' concerns, his own state of mind, and he did appreciate their motives, but he was undeserving of a second R&R. And, he had little money. Rightfully, he should not be here, practically on the dole while shirking mission flights.

He'd had Hawaii. It was no one else's fault it had been a psychic castration.

Just being out of 'Nam however, he hoped, would make deductive thinking—if not reasoning—easier. He'd swum in dark waters of late; and if this unearned second escape for a few days could put him back mainstream, maybe it was a thing worth doing.

Disgorged from the bus in a cloud of smoke and fug when he arrived for indoctrination, he found himself already billeted in the Penang Palace Hotel, a mid-range hostelry on Chakrawat near the river. Brenner had no doubt chosen it, knowing he couldn't afford top dollar. But this trip was never about opulent digs or pricey massage parlors anyhow; this was about escape. He could do his serious thinking in an empty hangar, if need be; anonymous Bangkok would serve nicely. And the Penang Palace was as anonymous as anonymous got.

In a taxi en route to the hotel, he thought about his challenges in pri-order: first, Nickie. Nickie and the boys—package deal. He might make a life without her, but without *her* meant without *them*.

Second priority—a *close* second—Moira. They had agreed

their relationship had no future, but Winter, never one for bridge burning, retained room for maneuver.

How serious was she? About this new interest, this unnamed Captain? His own feelings vacillated in a tricky series of ricochets between love and a strong, benign affection.

First priority first—the results would dictate the second.

But then priorities three-through-ten, the enormous, looming, gray-going-black miasma of *The War!* could not be ignored. Touching everything in his career, his professional and personal life, the war might serve more reasonably as number one.

He felt the enormity of forces arrayed against him, and he with only six days—now minus some hours—to contrive a plan here away from compelling influences. Deploring the isolation in his sterile room, he left the Penang Palace. The gloomy challenges left him wandering the streets downtown, aimless, yet seeking a backwater for reflection. Time to consider—through the glass, starkly. There was no end of choices. Bangkok *was the place*, he'd been assured.

Hailing a motorized, three-wheeled *tuk-tuk* similar to *cyclo* transport in Viet Nam, he found, after a lengthy and seemingly aimless ride, a place on Sanamchi Road that billed itself a café. The Ayutthaya boasted no bargirls or other commercial enticements beyond standard café fare. No Bushmill at the western-style bar either, but Jameson: one bottle cracked, one backup. He could make do. They offered Guinness, too, though not on tap. Considering the offerings, he wondered if Gaelic seamen often made landfall here. Seemed a likely place to spend some time.

* * *

Nursing his third Irish, he gave in to bone tiredness. His watch obviously lied: only 2050 hours? Eight-fifty o'clock. PM. In the evening. And why had that occurred to him, the civilian time? His existence never ran to civilian time—two twelve-hour periods in a day were the epitome of redundancy. He functioned in a twenty-four-hour span, as did most of the world.

But Moira, bless her little civilian heart, couldn't deal with that logical process.

Staring at the face of the watch, as if it would confirm itself accurate or false, he noted the number 6 in the small box. The month had to be August. August 6th! How did he get to now? The last time he noted the date was sometime back in July. Staring at the watch, as if it needed only punishment to perform properly, he shook his arm. The Rolex timepiece Judge Monaghan had thrust upon him from his hospital bed in Cholon Navy Hospital, four years before, as thanks for saving him from an arms-dealing rap. The watch he still planned to give back, given another meeting with Jerry.

August 6.

He had less than a month to go. DEROS in sight.

Returning from the Ayutthaya's stinking relief pits, he passed along a back wall covered with bamboo plait, close by a westerner in civilian clothes who had come in shortly before and sat at a table by himself. Winter nodded.

The stranger spoke: "Hi yah!" American, all right.

"How ya doin'?" Winter replied. He stopped at the table.

"Good. Good. Didn't I see you on the R-and-R run out of Cam Ranh today? The goddamned C-One-thirty-five?"

"I came today, yes. You, too?" Not surprisingly, he hadn't noticed the man before.

With affirmation, the stranger introduced himself: CWO Emil Enright, helicopter gunship pilot from 11th Brigade, 23rd Infantry Division (Americal). Winter responded in kind and without invitation, eased into a chair. With no hint of wariness the two warrants eked out the basics on one another quickly, the major benefit being they could then discuss weightier matters without posturing and trail-covering.

It was also Enright's second sentence in 'Nam. First tour with First Air Cav, early days when bad history was written. The pilot minimized his role, and Winter found him self-effacing.

"Hell, I remember you guys." T.W.A. Teeny Weenie Airlines," back in sixty-five, sixty-six," Enright said when Winter revealed his first tour assignment. "Yeah, wore that patch sportin' a four-balled tomcat and a lightning bolt, on red. I remember that." Enright surprised Winter with his recall. "I hoisted a few at your club on . . . what was the name of your camp?"

"Davis Station. It was—"

"That's it! Davis Station. I remember. Name was on a plaque in the NCO club, named for a . . . somebody Davis, the first American killed in Viet Nam. Right?"

"At that time, it was thought so. There're rumors since, some other American, an adviser, was killed before Tom Davis. But we had to call it something. Davis Station serves." The old billet area, previously 3rd RRU ground zero, still boasted that proud provenance. Recalling it in those terms, Winter wondered why he thought of it as "proud." To be killed, *a la* Davis?

Their conversation exceeded all margins: military history and previous assignments— Enright, a rifleman in the 2nd Infantry Division in Korea, had been a kid grunt who survived Keiser's Folly almost by accident, while Winter, too late—too young—for the cold walk back from the reservoir with the First Marine Division, had to be content with later pleasures..

The conversation settled on present circumstances and became something of a contest, each man focusing on aspects of the war, changes, new developments, each example exceeding the last in the egregious nature of any meaning, all of which offered less and less hope for a successful conclusion. Laconic bar talk, solving a host of world problems. It felt good to Winter.

The pilot had thoroughly sized him up, Winter thought when, late in the evening, Enright spoke into a brief hiatus of silence. "Winter," the airplane driver glanced about for curious ears, "I'm going to tell you something. You got to promise me it won't get to the wrong place."

"Tell me what?"

"Bad stuff, friend. Ugly stuff." This was developing into a common affliction, Winter thought. What were Ratty Mac's words? His admonition . . .?

"Hell, we're in the 'Nam, aren't we? Well, not actually now, but

. . . what gets uglier?" His drinking had slowed, but he raised his glass in a tiny salute and said, "What the hell? Go."

Enright sipped his beer, staring at the bar mirror. He dragged out the moment, not for titillation, Winter realized, but edging up to some personal Rubicon. When he spoke, the pilot's voice held an elusive quality, one of near awe, Winter felt. Of wonderment.

"I've tried not even thinking about this now for weeks, since I first learned . . ." As if preparing to go into the deep end of the pool, Enright sucked in a deep breath. He spoke. "Some bad shit happened in the Americal a while back. More'n a year, now, I guess. It's not been in the news; the Army's hushed it up at every level. Probably oughtta keep my mouth shut . . . but man, I gotta tell *somebody*. It's about . . . It's gonna come out. With frigging paparazzi trailing our operations like jackals, they can't keep something like this quiet."

"Keep what quiet?" When Enright did not immediately respond, Winter began to chafe. OK, the man had come on some touchy stuff, but was he going to spill it or not?

He was . . .

"Back last year, you know, after Tet, 'bout March or April, a company of the Twentieth Infantry, Americal—my division—in the field only a short period of time, committed . . . *had* an 'incident.' They were new to 'Nam, slow learners—know what I mean? Getting picked apart by snipers, booby traps. Failed ambushes. Nobody to fight, no focus. Generally bad shit. Mostly green troops, but frustration and fear primed them to do some ass-kicking.

"Don't know exactly what started it that particular day, but during an operation the company went into a ville called My Song or My Son. In Quang Ngai Province. Took a hamlet, My Lai-Number Four. Little shithole of a place." His eyes were looking inward, the view dark.

After several tense moments, Winter said, "And . . ." He had images of Mac's evasion.

"Bottom line . . ." Enright looked around, his eyes unfathomable, "the company killed every man, woman, and child in the village.

Tried to, at least. And before you ask, No! I did *not* see it!" Enright blurted out. "I got it first hand from a Dustoff pilot in Eleventh Brigade who did see it. He was detailed to lift out casualties, and saw ditches full of bodies. Road and paths littered with little people." He went silent, looking into some dark hole.

"Who—"

"A captain was responsible, I think—that's why I said a company. But rumor has it the captain's covering for one of his platoon leaders."

Forestalling Winter's need to object, as if the thing might be undone, Enright held his hand up and ploughed on. "Talk is . . . more'n a hundred dead. Way more. And lots of people were witness. No way can they keep this under wraps forever." The pilot's voice was hollow with sepulchral overtones.

"Jee-zus! Awww . . . I really didn't want to know that shit," his hand scrabbling on the grimy bar. Winter turned away from the encroaching horror but knew it was catching up to him.

Enright looked startled, as if caught talking out of school.

"Aww, Enright . . ." Winter, looking down at the hand that gripped his glass, knuckles and fingers white. There were none but lame words. He stammered, "This is. . . ."

"I'm glad I'm 'bout finished here," Enright said soulfully. "If what Frank told me's true—and I believe him—and this is an indication of the way this bitch is going, I want no part."

"You ain't wrong," Winter said, feeling the inadequacy of his reply.

After a moment of embarrassed silence, in a measured voice Winter said, "Strange you bringing this up. I may've had a hint before. And I ran across something, just last week. Jacked me up so bad my C.O. sent me out of country, here, on a second R-and-R. I think he thought I was going to squeal on someone." He told Enright of the Marine action in Eye Corps he'd been part of. Just telling it brought it all back in living technicolor; he couldn't shake the incident.

Punishing himself, determined to don the mantle of culpability, he followed that revelation with another, that of the three officers' Jeep visit to the Koreans lager, the troubling look at their Allies' community policing.

Enright nodded. He understood. He'd bivouacked in the Land of the Morning Calm, too.

* * *

In a lull in the conversation, Winter felt a cold shadow of something familiar settle over him. It came from nowhere he could pinpoint, and it took him a moment to make the connection. Back last spring, in that terrible time when he'd just learned of his orders back to 'Nam. Back before Nickie knew. It had to have been in that passage of weird time before Van Ingen was unmasked, when Electric Man was in full fury on BA base. Those reports of midnight cyclists, strange doin's.

Nickie, the boys, and he had trundled off on a weekend in Austria. For three of them, it seemed a pleasant outing: on their way south down the *Autobahn*, past the Kufstein turn-off, past Chiemsee, past the exit for Traunstein—the litany of places was as clear in his mind as anything ever had been—south and east to Salzburg.

And his luck held; nothing gave away his urgency. Nickie was not suspicious. Without reservations, they found rooms in a small favorite hotel on the Kaigasse, directly beneath the sprawling, castellated Hohensalzburg, two blocks off the river. They left the car in the hotel lot and walked the cobbled streets for two days. Three of them in one kind of daze, he in another.

Saturday, lunch in the castle. Long, lazy delays over wine while the boys leaned over the courtyard wall and giggled in secret madness. Later, they slow-walked the narrow medieval streets at the foot of the Hohensalzburg, following the moss-gray cobbles to the Peterkirche. The *Dom*. Mozart's home followed, and graveyards, churches, gift shops. Just before dark, they stood in the square before the cathedral again, watching the play of failing light across the frescoes.

Winter had watched a lone cyclist crossing the far side of the square in near-darkness, a black rain cape descending over the back fender of the bike. He'd shivered at that sight, he remembered. And it had seemed to take the cycling Austrian forever to cross the *platz* and no one noticed him but Winter. The ubiquitous cyclist had begun to haunt him, he knew then already, and he could think of no reason why this should be so.

Walking back to the hotel later, Winter had noticed how many pedestrians—evening strollers, lovers, families, policemen—wore the traditional Loden cape-coats, black and mysteriously romantic in the night. They were, he knew, actually forest green and grey in the light. As local insurance against the chill, damp night air, they were as common as stones in the street, and nothing new. Still, for some reason he couldn't identify, the capes bothered him. As if they were a deliberate affectation sent to remind him of the masked marauder who chanted "Electric Man" and cycled for a cause that was elusive but worrisome.

That Sunday had been free from such associations, and they left at the planned time for BA and home, just ahead of a cloud front that moved down the valley over Salzburg.

* * *

"Naïve, I bet you think." Winter said, recapturing the thread of conversation with the pilot. "I mean, second tour, second war, and that kinda' shit still horrifies me."

He stared into the bar mirror, not recognizing the face staring back at him. He said, facetiously, deriding his position before the fact, "Hearken! A prediction." He knew he was drunk, and sensed he needed to apply the brakes on a runaway mouth. He could not.

Enright straightened, put on a serious face. Prepared himself for astute prescience.

"We can't win this mother!" Winter exclaimed, pounding on the bar, setting bottles and glasses at risk. Heads turned toward them. "We're losing . . . *we've lost this war*. Shit like this, we don't deserve to win. We're as bad as the bad guys. Hell, we've *become* the bad guys.

"When I watched the arty-Phantom strike on that friendly

ville, wiping out the entire community to kill a few NVA, I knew right then we couldn't win here. Just wouldn't let myself believe it. Naïve! Even our allies, our mercenaries, are right out of the Stone Age. And now this, massive killings. . . . unless it's not true," he said hopefully. Winter felt uneasy expressing such heretical opinions. He glared at the glass of Jameson as if it were somehow at fault.

After a long silence, Enright added, "That ain't naive, Chief. That's 'bout right."

* * *

After a restless night, fighting nightmares of bloody paths, littered roads, and crumpled small forms, Winter took his time in the morning: twenty-five minutes trying to get clean in the tepid shower. When he was dressed and thought to make the best of present circumstances, he went downstairs and found the dining room still serving breakfast. Fresh fruits, rolls and tortes, french breads and croissants with butter and jams. Surprisingly good coffee.

Afterward at the front desk he picked up brochures and got directions. Keeping himself uncommitted to schedules—easy, as he despised organized tours—he made his way to the docks a few blocks from the hotel, where he hired a Thai boat-woman to take him to the floating market. He wanted no part of a tour group.

When they'd traversed the broad river, and navigated a confusing network of canals, he bought a few items at Trader Joe's, a place his boat woman treated as a "must stop." He traded for fruits, nuts, and Buddhist charms with vendors in dugouts and flat-bottomed boats at the floating market. At the snake farm he couldn't get interested; convinced the cobras had had restrictive dental work. Passing up the elephant that exhibited an evil glint in his eye, he climbed on the scabrous water buffalo for an obligatory snapshot. The boys would like that.

Out of the canal complex, back along the busy river, the oddity of Thai houses built on pilings along the Chao Phrya soon grew tiresome. Too many mothers dipping too many infants into the murky sludge, washing them after each purge in lieu of diapers. Downstream, men, women, and children brushed their teeth from their own docks, using the river for both water source and sewer. Kids bathing, swimming in the limpid brown current were doomed caricatures. Spirit houses—small copies of temples—no longer caught his fancy, though some were ornate with pressed sheet gold, mounted on poles before the riverside homes, displaying various offerings of foods and gifts to ensure amiable relations with the gods. The royal barges in huge sheds along the river were magnificent, but his boat woman knew no English and he had no guidebook.

By early afternoon, the cascade of visual anomalies and alien sounds had jaded his senses; in his mind, overriding tourist sights, his personal battles never lost their damning stridency.

Long before they had reached the farthest point of the excursion, he was sick of the compost smell of the river, the dour, blank face of his guide. Nicole and Moira battled in his mind and it was a long way back to the dock while the heat and humidity replicated Viet Nam.

He wondered about the feasibility of going north to Chiang Mai for the rest of his time, seeking a bit of cool. But he'd not seen the Reclining Buddha yet, nor all the other wonders of the southern playground. And he knew, in his state of mind, he hadn't the drive. Hating the metaphor, he knew he could only go with the tide.

When his young, unsmiling boat-woman chauffeur had returned Winter to the same dock from which they had departed, he was relieved to have the experience ended. He paid her the four dollars, American, he'd agreed to, and threw in another dollar. Big spender! he thought sarcastically. Well, hell, he didn't take her to raise. He realized the expression was familiar.

Walking away, he was darkly aware of his harsh expression, although unspoken.

He returned to the same café as the previous evening, but pilot Enright was not there. The story he'd told Winter hung in his mind like a rusty bell, and like a bell tolling dirges on a laid-back morning when you wanted to sleep in, it could not be ignored.

Eating café fare, sipping hot tea, he remained long into the evening with, surprisingly, no urge for the Jameson. In the relative quiet of this small backwater establishment, he struggled to isolate, to deal with on their own level, the shibboleths and dreams and fantasies that assailed him in no discernible pattern. It was as if, suddenly, Luther's dire predictions were being borne out, all in a time of burgeoning crises.

But it cannot have been *suddenly*, he thought. He'd been asleep at the switch. Was that part of Nickie's argument? Her fear?

He reluctantly examined long-held attitudes, beliefs buttressed by history. Man's fascination with war, his predilection for it. Body counts, civilian dead, struggle, atrocities—all shaded by conflicting philosophical arguments—slid across the screen of his mind. High-sounding words; filthy reality. All things beyond his resources.

He left the café without answers, and the questions seemed no less opaque.

* * *

Dressing the following morning in his hotel bath, he heard the phone ringing. He stepped back into the room and didn't see it. By the time he found it, concealed in a compartment in the head of the bed, and jerked it up to his ear, it had stopped ringing. No one could be calling him here; must be the front desk.

"Winter," he said into the silence, anticipating a broken connection.

"Dave, it's Luther," Brenner said, still on the line.

"Well, I would ask how the hell you found me, but then, you made my reservation. How can I help you, Mister Brenner, this pristine morning from lovely, downtown Bangkok?"

"Bad cess, Dave. The Sixth Convalescent was hit last night."

"Hit? Whaddaya mean, hit?" Hell, the hospital was in an even more secure area of the peninsula than Naval Air Facility. "What, rockets? Mortars?"

"Sappers. Eight or nine of them, came ashore from small boats. Satchel charges and grenades into the wards. Plus a supply building."

"What about Moira? D'you—"

"That's why I called. Moira was wounded, Dave. She was on a ward that was blown. A couple of . . . patients, I think they were—maybe medical personnel—were killed."

"But how is she? Was it serious? I mean, was she seriously injured?" Goddammit! Brenner wouldn't drag something like this out. It had to be bad.

"She was evac-ed to Japan. Don't have any follow-up. I'll keep my ear to the ground and let you know whatever I find out, but for now, just know she's getting the best care she could possibly get."

"Oh, Jesus, Luther. D'ya have any idea where they took her? Yokusuka? Kobe—"

"Don't know, Dave. I'll call you with what I can get. You going to be all right?"

"What're my options? . . . Sorry. Delete that. Yeah, I'm OK. Let me go see if I can find a phone I can use to call the Sixth. Get back to me. If I'm not here, leave a message. Please."

"Right. Talk to you soon."

"Thanks, Luther." He gently lowered the faux 1920s phone back on its cradle and edged the small door shut in the head of the bed, his mind whirling. He left the room to find a military telephone line where he might make a call to the Sixth. An AUTOVON line, anything.

Nothing at his hotel. He took a taxi to the hotel that served as the local R&R center. They had a military phone, but use was limited to Thailand. He doubted the Air Force captain's unctuous assurance, but couldn't argue.

Returning to the Penang Palace, he packed, checked out, took a taxi to the R&R center, checked out there, and caught the round-robin Air Force bus back to Don Muang. At Flight Ops, he prevailed on an Army master sergeant to get him a seat on a flight to Viet Nam.

There was a flight direct to Cam Ranh in two hours. The

regular R&R return flight. MSG Steele said they always had open seats. GIs couldn't all be relied upon to return promptly to Viet Nam when their allotted R&R time was up.

* * *

"The night of six-seven. Night before last. Sappers came ashore from boats and blew some buildings in the Sixth. Three, I think—couple of wards and a supply hooch. Killed a couple of guys, wounded a lot more. We hope she'll be all right . . . but we haven't been able to get information about her condition. The most secure facility in country getting hit like that has the entire command shook up. Everything's in a muddle. I went down there, checked with the Bonnie Major. Nobody knows anything," Brenner assured him with concern.

"But blast damage, you said. That's what got her? Concussion? Not shrapnel or a bullet?" Winter said. He knew concussion could be as deadly as shrapnel. Internal injuries: hard to find or diagnose. "Jeezus. She's *got* to be all right." Winter's fear for Moira's condition, exacerbated by a lack of information, forced his feelings into line for her, overriding any thoughts of ambiguity that earlier might have been his. That she was in a hospital in Japan was all he could learn. All by herself. Condition unknown.

Alone. He knew what that was like.

"Not much to go on, is it?" he said to Brenner.

Harking back specifically to the sapper attack on the hospital complex, Brenner said, "It could have been worse. Only two dead that we know of, some fifty-something wounded. Most of those from wood splinters and structures collapse."

In reflex, helpless about Moira, Winter fell back on hazy horizons. He told Brenner the ugly story told him by the pilot. He wished it weren't so, but he felt compelled to believe Enright. It sounded too plausible. And why would a guy lie about his own division where they come off looking like the bad guys? *Really* bad guys. He couldn't remember the source, for sure, but he'd heard, before Thailand, vague rumblings about something like that. Probably the same thing!

Moira was in a place of no access. He needed to keep talking and strayed into innocuous areas, seeking a subject. But Brenner had Duty Officer that evening and left his friend to stew alone in his room. Shortly, above the babble from the Sandbag next door, Winter heard the rattle of poker chips somewhere. He grabbed his wallet and went out the door in search of distraction.

* * *

He had been in the game, three doors up from the Sandbag, for more than two hours, was up a full dollar-and-a-quarter, when a nearby explosion prompted the card players into the bunkers. The rocket had impacted on the opposite side of the billets from the card game and seemed not to have struck the building. Still, proximity—

In the bunker, Winter checked around him in the murky gloom lit by someone's small emergency flashlight. From the few people he could see close to the light source, and a few other voices he recognized, he could account for most of the men who lived on that other, far side of the hooch. The area he lived in.

He knew *he* was OK.

Over all, a trio of rockets fell. The latter two, impacting near the hangar, still did not find the aircraft. A low-level night stalker with a backpack of rockets typically set them up in an open paddy nearby, Winter knew, propped on a bamboo "goalpost," set a timer or lit a fuse, and di-di-ed. Results were, thankfully, reportable only for the incident, not for casualties.

When no more rounds fell, and the Korean gunners had gone to work and were well into their thing, troops began edging out of the bunker. The poker game was a wash: it wasn't a very interesting game to start with, and no one could remember whose deal it was. Plus, a quick count revealed only forty-nine cards left in the deck, including the five Winter had slid into his pocket when the first rocket fell. But it was not a hand he wanted to pursue: two pair, sixes and sevens, with a Joker. And the Joker was wasted, he thought distractedly; it was only good to pair with aces, or to fill a straight or flush. A serious poker player would lament such a waste.

Stakes had been scooped from the table by each player. Incoming prompted a civil but rigid protocol.

Winter walked back to the sand-and-scrub-grass space between his room and the Navy TDY billets. There, the next house on Elm Street, MARKET TIME, had a full push on, flying everything with wings. Leaving few pilots free, most were now on mission. No one in the Navy billet suffered, though some of their screen and batten siding was peppered with fragments. No one in the First RR on that side of the building, for that matter, seemed to have been endangered.

Winter had reached his door when Brenner and the duty NCO came through the mid-billet passage. "No point us checking your room, Dave. You're obviously not a casualty."

"Thank you for that confirmation, oh arm-banded one." He pushed open his door. The light in the space between his and Bracken's room was out, the bulb dark gray as it had been for more than a week, but even in reflected weak light from outside, something didn't look right. Winter stepped into the neutral space, reached into his room for the ceiling light string, and felt something brush his face. Something light, insubstantial, like a spider web.

He brushed flurriedly at his face, found the cord, and yanked.

He was in a snowdrift!

A blowing squall of snow. Disoriented, the world went asynchronous in an instant. The webs raked his face, tickling his nose. He sneezed. Focusing, he reached out and grasped a handful of feathers bouncing on AC currents. Glancing about at his bunk, he could only stare at the unlikely source of the blizzard. His knees went wobbly.

The remains of his pillow, a flat remnant of ripped cotton, lay carelessly over the head of his bunk in a display the hooch maid would deplore.

He leaned over the bunk. The army-issue, olive-drab blanket appeared divided, though essentially still in place. Confirmed with close scrutiny, the blanket *was* in two pieces, except for about three inches intact near the head of the bed. What?

Who'd been in his room while he played poker?

Who would pull such shit? Couldn't be the inconstant Captain Warren. He was living the high life in Alabama. He heard a voice behind him.

"D'ja see this, Mister Winter?" the Duty NCO asked.

Winter turned to stare blindly at Brenner who stood near the NCO. What the hell was his sergeant going on about? His mouth was moving but Winter heard zilch.

He followed Brenner's pointing finger and saw where some creature, large and angry, had flown through the screen designed to keep out such invaders. The screen was pooched in and ripped for about three inches. Splinters from the sheet of outside plywood protruded through the screen wire. The fuzzy picture snapped sharply into focus.

Stepping to the foot of his bed, he pulled the scraps of blanket, pillow case, and top sheet up from the bed. When he'd moved the detritus, the lower sheet, mattress sack, and mattress appeared untouched. Beyond the head of his bunk, just at pillow height, a dark object protruded from the wall. Without thinking, he reached for it.

"*Don't!* Brenner yelled, too late.

Winter jerked his hand back from the jagged shard of metal that stuck from the two-by-four wall stud, blew on his fingers, leaned close and looked. He touched his forefinger gingerly onto the metal. "Goddamn, that sucker's still warm."

"Right from the dragon's mouth. I thought it might still be hot. You O.K.?" Brenner was looking away from the shrapnel, staring at the bed, less interested in an answer as understanding broke over him.

"Yeah. Not to worry. I wasn't, as you say, 'abed'." Winter grabbed a flashlight off his shelf and stepped out through the door, his lower stomach performing a fandango. Flashing the light in arcs, starting close to his feet and working outward, he quickly found the ragged eruption of soil some twenty feet out from his room, directly across from his door. He walked over, played the light into the hole, and saw it was larger than he'd thought, perhaps five feet across. Deep enough to drown a mule. Scattered about the hole were torn pieces of steel, ugly scraps, twisted and sharp from the force and fire of explosion. Two pieces of tail fin several feet long lay against the wall of the Navy billet. They would be finding missile residue for days, he knew. A 122-millimeter rocket was no small munition.

Back in his room, Winter worked the piece of shrapnel from the wall stud using his Kabar. The killing sample was an ugly thing, about two-and-a-half inches by an inch-and-a-half, irregularly shaped. The sharp, brittle edges of the steel looked rusted. He slipped it in his pocket, looked back to where it had ripped through the wall and screen and, dropping to one knee, eyed the path it had taken, precisely at bed-surface height, ripping its way straight up his bed, splitting the blanket and top sheet, exploding his pillow, and ending its destructive flight in the wall stud behind.

Winter stood, the movement a kind of agony. His knees, still weak, began a tremor as full realization flooded him. He sat on the bed that threatened to toss him off.

He felt a visceral contraction in his crotch. Felt his testicles withdraw up into his body cavity. His stomach spasmed. Staring at his friend, he suspected Brenner experienced the same.

* * *

Brenner returned to the Orderly Room and wrote up an After-Action Report, accounting for damages he could assess during the hours of darkness, including Winter's bedding. Someone from the Pentagon or White House would doubtless intervene and replace that issue, sometime after reveille.

He couldn't still a churning quiver in his lower stomach, thinking of his friend's close call. Brenner would have stayed with him, talked him through it, somehow . . . but Winter was flying later that day and had to get some sleep. Brenner wondered if he could sleep on that bunk, blanket or no.

Irony at play here, he judged. Again. Winter was flying today. He was, by rule, to have had eight hours of sleep before takeoff at 1100 hours. Yet, he was on the far side of the building, playing poker, at four in the AM. Didn't compute, for Winter was not a soldier who flaunted the rules. Normally, he would have been asleep. At least, in his bunk—no one knew how much sleep he was getting these days as crises congregated about him.

But if Winter had been in his bunk, Brenner knew he'd be inventorying his friend's gear later today, and writing a letter. Following up Grange's command actions because the casualty was a personal friend.

Not a subject to deliberate upon.

chapter twenty-three

Green on Green

Cam Ranh Bay, Viet Nam: August 1969

A couple of days went by before I saw Dave again. He flew the day after my OD duty; I flew the next day, slept in late, and missed him. The following day I saw on the sked board in Ops that he was on the manifest again for the next day and figured I'd better make an effort. Cohorts cannot afford to go so long without communal grousing.

After work I caught up with him and Ito on their way to the chow hall. I wasn't hungry, and suggested we get a brew and think about dining out. We headed to the Sandbag. The watering hole was open to the world, but no one manned the bar at this hour. Ito grabbed a cold San Miguel and stuffed a handful of small-change—brightly colored MPC scrip notes—into the coffee can without counting. We drank cheaply enough anytime. Fred was making up some slack, likely, from a time of thirst when he found himself without purchasing power.

Talk was slow in coming. I made a point—Fred did the same—of avoiding discussion of home or family. Moira was another subject we knew was best left alone, for there was still no word on her. Her friends and co-workers were unable to get any news; and the hospital authorities put out the word that unless you were in her chain of command—and above the hospital CO—or you were legally related to Moira, they felt unobliged to divulge whatever they may or may not have known. Information, for whatever elusive reason, was apparently not to be forthcoming. Those restrictions on our conversational choices left only the body of gossip about our prolific social calendar. When that was disposed of, in about eight seconds, talk drifted across schedules, replacements, weather, other pointless drivel. Pointless, because schedules would be what they would be, as would weather; replacements would not, but they were a myth anyhow.

Still, the question mark of the enchanting young nurse hung over the conversation, try as we might to go elsewhere. Winter, none of us even with the CO's intervention, had been able to satisfy ourselves about Moira. Dave was pushy of course, leaning on every possible source, but got little information. What he did hear from the 6th Convalescent was uncertain, with a tinge of hush-hush. He commented on that when I was able to work the subject around to Moira. It was inevitable: however we tried to avoid the subject, it remained the gorilla at the birthday ball.

"Those goddmaned people act as if . . . Hell, she's not even in country anymore, not their responsibility," Dave ranted. "The assholes act like it's classified information, how bad she's hurt. Where she is. I don't even have a military address to write her or send flowers. Here we are, in the middle of a war; we got barbecue grills, dancing girls, FTD florist service, and I can't send a damned bouquet." After a moment spent in frustrated silence, he added, "It must be bad. Otherwise, somebody would talk. There's no reason, even so, to keep it from us. From me."

I edged the conversation into other channels following time to vent. I did my best to bring up the subject of the recent rocket attack without getting into hot water there. I didn't know how he felt about that, how he'd reacted. And I needed to know. Dave could be a soul-searching sonuvabitch at times, but I thought if he could talk about it, it wasn't all that bad.

Rationalization 101.

"Yeah," Winter said in response, almost playful, "Really spooky, were it not? The way I wasn't there. Illogical. Not even kosher, according to flight rules. But being outside the bounds saved my life. Gotta be worth something."

Ito made noises of assurance and agreement between long draughts of San Miguel. I had nothing to offer but triteness, so I said nothing.

"How many more times, Luther?" Winter turned to stare at me as he spoke, and I looked into bottomless wells. The allusion to "many more" bothered me for reasons I couldn't divine.

"Hell, Dave, you're just lucky. The Zips on that rocket squad are rank amateurs. Just out of basic. They never hit anything. Made glass of some beach sand a couple of times. Blew—"

"Not just this time, though this one was . . . uughh." He shivered.

"What are you saying?"

"*You know* this is my third near miss. You were involved or present for all of them."

My face must have reflected blank ignorance.

"Late 'sixty-four?" he said, ticking off on his fingers, reminding me of the time he let Krebs take his mission flight, and Stoetzel, Krebs, and Beaver aircraft One-five-one took out two rows of rubber trees near Tay Ninh.

Winter's eyes flickered about while talking, as if to catch something sneaking up on him.

Hey, when he's right, he's right. I had no trouble remembering that episode.

I felt his dialogue, like an ungoverned motor, gathering speed, his voice increasingly urgent, ticking off details on fingers that trembled. Number two was the booby trap blast at the airport grill when, he insisted, by all rights he should have been with Lessor, Monaghan, Lieutenant Chaldano, and me at noon when the mine blew. We four Operations sergeants and our Ops Officer ate lunch together in that airport restaurant every day. Had done for weeks, because the lieutenant had a Jeep, but per command directive, as an officer wasn't allowed to drive. I wasn't likely to forget that: the four of us who did go had the Purple Heart special for lunch that day. His point was, by rights, he should have been the fifth.

"I was walking up the flight line from early chow at Davis Station mess when the sky fell." Winter said. Ito and I exchanged glances. But Winter got ahead of us.

"And since I'm thinking on strange doin's, another occurs to me. Counting the other night, a fourth. In February 'sixty-five, the month before I DEROS-ed, I came down sick."

Yes, I remembered that too. A veritable archive was I.

Winter had awoken one morning, complaining of being dizzy,

feverish, light-headed. Couldn't think clearly, he said. I insisted that was not a new ailment. But Dave was seriously serious. Red Tubberman and I drove him to the Sixty-eighth's dispensary down the dirt road from Davis Station.

They didn't know what his problem was and sent us over to the Air Force Thirty-second Dispensary.

They were redundantly clueless. Doctor called it FUO—fever of undetermined origin. Hell, that was my diagnosis. And I didn't charge.

"I went back and crashed, slept through the day and night," Dave reminded me, thinking I might have trouble remembering. All the time my friend talked, and he was talking as if he had a fever now; compulsive, almost . . . *frantic*, I remembered well the time he spoke of, but couldn't imagine where he was headed with it.

Red and Judge and I had probably kept Dave alive, bringing sodas and water, Kool-Aid, beer . . . waking him, forcing him to drink to avoid dehydration. No room in the dispensary due to an unusual spike in casualties, First Shirt had extended his buck slip because Dave still couldn't make it to work the third day. He slept twenty-three out of twenty-four.

"So? I remember," I said. "but it wasn't exactly the sort of close calls you're talking about. You were just sick." I was willing to give him the benefit of the doubt, but Dave was bordering on weird territory. I felt the strangeness.

"Wrong, Mister Brenner. The fourth day—four days after I first got sick—I woke up and knew I had to get off my ass. I forced myself out of the bunk, wringing wet, my sheets soaked, and headed for the showers. When I stepped out into the sun, and Wilmot walked by, he pointed out I was covered in red spots. I'd broken out in a rash, all over my body. First Shirt himself drove me to the dispensary—you other guys were all working—and when I walked in the door, there was that same Air Force doctor. He took one look at me and said, 'Ah-hah! Now I know what you got.'"

"You had dengué."

"Yeah, I thought that the weirdest diagnosis. He said I had dengué fever. I argued with the damned doctor, so sure dengué was something out of history, a plague from the Pacific in World War Twice. Marines and soldiers on Guadalcanal, Pelilieu, other swampy islands got it." Winter reflected briefly. "Damned if that major wasn't right."

The three of us sat for long moments, all staring at different segments of the horizon. Finally, I had to ask. "So what's that to do with the price of spring onions?"

"It was while I was on bed rest. Couldn't do my job. Captain Pyburn drafted Caddell to take over V-NAF tasking. Now you remember? You understand?"

Caddell had been on a courier run, driving the mission tasking sheet over to the Zips' flight ops, when he got caught in the ARVN Seventh Division coup shootout and was killed.

"Well, just goddammit it, Dave. You aren't responsible for Caddell and Zip coups. Besides, it wasn't legitimate combat killed him." I did see where he was going; I had to put a stop to it. But David Winter was, in no less degree, David Winter yet.

"Caddell's still dead. Seems sufficiently legitimate to me."

"And so, you're saying—" I began, but he hadn't run out his string yet.

"I'm saying nothing. Just, counting this last, four times when I should have bought it, been hit, or at least been in harm's way like others, I skated. You other guys been paying my tab."

If it hadn't posed a serious risk of rupturing a treasured friendship, I would have said something to him then about his affected Joan-of-Arc image of beatific piety.

* * *

Winter felt Brenner's disdain; nothing he could do about that. Luther had his own devils. But why, Winter thought, why didn't I see this coming? There were signs. Not just the wound on the LZ—that was an alert, not just a sign—but other guys, friends and otherwise, had read so much more into what they saw building. He'd sat, a silenced observer one night late in 1964, and listened to Judge Monaghan and Lessor in a free-for-all on policy. It never occurred to him that either of them could be right.

* * *

Tan Son Nut, Viet Nam: November 1964

Monaghan was explaining to Lessor, who had been on emergency leave to the states for the previous two weeks, the cascading effect of increasing activity while he'd been absent.

"Picture this: October thirty. Halloween tomorrow. Night time. A company of Viet Cong, carrying mortars and rocket-propelled grenades, filters through the countryside some twenty miles northeast of here. They situate themselves into firing positions—probably sites they'd already prepared—about the base at Bien Hoa. No one sounds the alarm, though locals are standing around, watching charlie set up. Same ol' shit." Monaghan held a dim view of the political probity of the Vietnamese.

"Picture this. On the airfield, arrayed like toys in nice, neat rows, is a squadron of B-57s. These old bombers aren't a verifiable threat in anybody's war, but the VC have their hackles raised. The transfer of the jets from the Philippines into Viet Nam has crossed some political No-Man's Land, and the VC feel obliged to respond to their unwelcome presence. The perfection of this line-up is a perfect echo of General Martin's deployment of B-17s at Hickam Field, Hawaii, in December 1941. That had led to their efficient decimation by Japanese airmen when they struck Pearl Harbor."

"Where you going with this shit, Judge? I know about Pearl Harbor," Lessor demanded impatiently. He wanted to get to the club for a beer so he could once again, as a matter of daily observance, begin to forget this place.

"No! Now listen. At Bien Hoa, in the present 1964, these little people attack the base. In the ensuing bombardment that lasts several hours without, I am forced to believe, any effective response or defense, American troops, Vietnamese civilian workers and other hangers-on rage and dash about pointlessly while the mortars pour seemingly endless fire on the nicely arrayed aircraft." Monaghan held up his hand imperiously, forestalling further interruption.

"Six B-57s are completely destroyed and some twenty other aircraft, including additional B-57s, damaged, with a loss of five American and two South Vietnamese military personnel killed, a number more wounded." This time, Monaghan's monologue was not interrupted.

"It's a slap in the face for our government, who still has, apparently, no cohesive policy in place regarding American intentions and goals in this wayward, backward country. But it's also the stimulus that enables American Ambassador to South Vietnam, U.S. Army Retired General Maxwell Taylor, to urge President Johnson to bomb North Vietnam in retaliation. You'll recall how the President has avoided making decisions, anguishing over political, career implications of such a move. But Bien Hoa apparently finally establishes a mindset that may provide, in the future, a basis for some serious bombing of North Vietnam. Despite L.B.J.'s misgivings.

"I wouldn't be surprised if the intelligence needs to support such a strategy should drive Third RRU's efforts for the rest of this short conflict. I think we may find ourselves in the role of key players."

Monaghan concluded his lecture with what might have been a bombshell, if anyone had thought he might be, not necessarily on the right page, but at least in the right book. But no one believed such, and he and Lessor went for a beer and talked baseball. Winter had stayed behind.

* * *

Sai Gon/Cho Lon, Viet Nam: August 1969

Winter, vacationing in the south according to Brenner, was in fact in Sai Gon/Tan Son Nhut completing necessary paperwork for his impending reassignment. He was, after all, a short-timer, though his mind couldn't seem to linger on those positive attributes. Only one night, hot-bedding in the Newport BOQ, and he awoke sick at the stench of *nuoc mam*, a plague still visited upon the inhabitants of the building. His head pounded; he knew it was not merely a headache, not just the pungent fish sauce. His head did more than ache. In full revolt, it reverberated at the instigation of any external noise. Absent outside threats, he felt internal eruptions add to the terrible din in his head.

He did the rounds, trying first the 3rd Field Hospital next door; nobody but surgeons and death-watch harridans on duty. He wandered on, trying the Air Force dispensary on Tan Son Nhut. Duty doctor there could not abide the upstart warrant officer diagnosing his own malady as something more than a headache. He smilingly referred him to Walter Reed Army Hospital in Washington. Winter smilingly told him to go fuck himself. They parted in a consensual huff.

Catching the duty bus which ran to the 509th Transient Billets in Cho Lon, he dropped off and went into the Navy Hospital, where he was seen, examined, diagnosed with something inexplicable and un-spellable, and prescribed. Standing in the line at the Rx pickup window, he felt a nudge from behind. He didn't even turn around. Some unstable deck ape, he presumed.

The next nudge pushed him 30 degrees off plumb and two feet out of line. Winter swung about, whatever the un-spellable malady that was his prompting him to do some ass-kicking. In the face of a broadly grinning SFC Bernie Glasgow, he pulled up short, snorted, and said nothing. It had been four years, he thought. More. He'd last seen him when, as a staff sergeant in Third Herd, Glasgow'd lost his Top Secret security clearance and ASA dumped him back on the warrior market. The loss of clearance was initiated by the discovery that Glasgow's foreign-born wife, to whom he had been married for seven years, a Korean, was not kosher, under the circumstances.

After an exhaustive background check—which initially had cleared the woman to be the wife of a serving ASA soldier—it was later determined, by a particularly aggressive-minded clerk, that the part of Korea she came from was called The Democratic

Republic of Korea, not because it was democratic in theory and practice; rather, the opposite. The misinformed agent who had initially signed off on Kim Lee Glasgow's bondfides had assumed that bearing the Democratic buzzword meant that segment of Korea fell south of the 38th Parallel. In fact, Kim Lee's antecedents were hardcore communists before it was political necessity. The fact that Kim Lee bore no such allegiance meant nothing to the recidivist investigator. And the fact that Glasgow had divorced the woman, what, six years ago? That fact did not bear on the investigation, its findings, nor its determinations.

SFC Bernard Glasgow, back on the job market, was quickly relegated back to an earlier livelihood, transforming into a grunt. The fact that he had been a damned good infantryman at some earlier time in an earlier war served him well in the surprising transition.

All this flashed through Winter's mind as he stared at the old familiar face with that haunting smile, and he had the quick recall that he'd heard, after the fact, that Glasgow's squad had fallen in the shit during the same enemy offensive that had caught Winter, out of place, out of time, on that hated LZ in 1965. He felt a sympathetic twinge in that leg when he thought it. But Glasgow had been wounded four times that same day. And here he was.

"Well no shit, Sam Spade." Winter's hand shot out, gripped Glasgow's jacket sleeve, and tugged him forward into a crushing embrace. Glasgow must have seen it coming, or sensed it, for he responded in kind, enveloping Winter equally.

"Winter-Man. How's it to go? Man, you are a sight for bloodshot eyes. Look at you, a weenie warrant." He glanced up. "Sorry, I know you're from a different environment, but in the Army, we don't salute indoors." There was an awkward silence, and just as Winter might have commented to the contrary, Glasgow guffawed and said, "No. Not right. It's in that bad-ass Corps where you don't salute indoors." He stepped back, disentangled himself, and popped a sordid approximation of military propriety at the startled warrant officer.

When the social niceties had been assuaged, while the two

stood, inching forward in the pill line, Winter explained his presence. He looked the question at Glasgow.

He said laconically, as if admitting to being late for church, "Had to come to town for paperwork. El tee asked me to pick up a couple of F.N.G.s, and I'm gathering up some supplies for our medic. You know, A.P.C.s; good for everything from greenstick fractures to sucking chest wounds. When we finish here, let's go grab a *Ba-mui-ba* and bullshit one another."

He turned away to the window as the second class hospital corpsman impatiently called, for the second time, "Next!"

* * *

The soiree was taking on overtones of uniqueness. It was not Vietnamese bar practice to let empty bottles stand on a table when others were waiting to be emptied, as might happen in more parochial watering holes. An unseemly number of empties crowded the tiny, round table inside the grenade screening in the Fellows Bar. Initially reluctant to take their trade inside, as the intimation in the name indicated it might be the province of persons "light in the loafers," a passing MP assured the sergeant and warrant officer that their chastity was safe; they might get their throats cut or at least lose their wallet, but their sexual orientation would not be an issue.

Four-plus years of history gone over, by-passed or done away with, the two sat in mutual satisfaction. Glasgow, though he'd known Winter in a couple of earlier assignments, had never met his wife; so Winter felt no compunction to dump his troubles on the other.

"So how's the outfit you're with? They good troops or what?" Winter asked.

Glasgow did a wiggle-waggle with his hand. "So-so. Not bad, I guess. But even back in the real Army after years in—" He cut off his speech, looked about. Sniffed. Said, "—Radio Research, it sure'n hell ain't like it was in the old Army."

"Yeah, I know. I've had that point driven home. Forcefully. Several times of late," Winter acknowleged.

"Weird people, they take in now. Weird people they keep. I guess it's the hard-up grab for troops keeps 'em holding onto some of these strange birds. But, man. I gotta tell you . . ."

And he did.

* * *

II Corps, Viet Nam: June 1967

PELETIER was stenciled on his gear. PELETIER, M., with no middle name. No one in the platoon ever knew his first name; records showed only an initial. He came to Delta Company from a recovery ward at the 6th Convalescent at Cam Ranh-South, and some old timers—elderly nineteen- and twenty-year-olds who had come in country with the 133rd and had managed to remain vertical and warm because they looked quicker, moved faster, and learned without question—remembered him from earlier existence of a Charlie Company. Before Charlie Company took Operation JUNCTION CITY into the Tay Ninh AO. Before a diet of realism— hard truths, bad country, and the 391st NVA Battalion— had slimmed them down from a hundred sixty-three men to just Pelletier and two other fragile remnants in the 45-hour doodah that shaped the Brigade forever after.

Back then, in the days of Charlie extant, Peletier was just a draftee infantryman, designated sniper, doing his 365 in the jungle for failing Calculus III. Fashionably hip, strung out on whatever he could find, whenever: beads, peace symbols, numbers on his helmet cover in a descending arrogance, as if they were some kind of holy promise of making it all the way down to zero, some kind of magic-marker mantra. His record photos showed nothing extraordinary. He was near cross-section height and weight, and his coloring was white or pink or green, depending upon whether you saw him in the shade, the sun, or the light of flares. Just a kid grunt.

He was competent as a sniper, nothing special, though he once joked he suffered because he wasn't a country-bred, squirrel-hunting natural like Alvin York of the Three Forks of the Valley of the Wolf. Peletier, a product of river-front New Orleans, had acquired what skill he had by practice, reasonable dedication to the mystique of the craft, and slightly more than a passing interest in surviving his involuntary tour in 'Nam.

But that was before.

When he left the burn ward at Cam Ranh-South, the skin on his hands was still candy pink and glossy, and the hair had not come in evenly. But he was total billboard soldier: the sparse hair high and tight, the patchy skin clean-shaven, decked-out in shiny brand new pressed green ripstop jungle fatigues with that quartermaster sheen still on them that marked the wearer as a new guy or some kind of career freak. The spitshine on his boots was a measure of how out of place he was on the firebase. For their sins, Second Platoon got Peletier while the battalion was in stand-down in a semi-secure zone near a ville without a name, appearing only as a dirty pink smudge on the 25,000:1 tactical map.

Snipers are never run-of-the-mill, since often they are the only ones who have a chance to see whom they're killing, the only ones usually who know for sure they *have* killed. The mechanized, depersonalized, managed-rather-than-commanded killing and dying in a hail of automatic fire so far removed the average soldier from any identity with moral objectives that personal motivation was not even vigorously sought, and was looked upon with mild cynicism and surprise when encountered in a soldier. Still, Peletier's second coming was no more than a ripple on the pond that was the 133rd's area of operations.

Something about him, though—actually, everything about him—discouraged familiarity. The new troops, the replacements who were Peletier's civilian life contemporaries, the FNGs who stumbled in through the dust of chopper pads wherever in Two Corps they could catch up with the brigade, walked a wide circle about him from the start. Young troops conditioned by a generation of John Wayne, filtered through Freudian overlays, thought it was merely that Peletier was a sniper; they imagined the personal facing off with verified kills, seeing the faces through the friendliness of the scope, provoked isolation. Captain Crunch knew the young convert's particular job, albeit a labor of love, had nothing to do with it: *how* Peletier killed was only incidental to *why*.

But it was never complicated. JUNCTION CITY, Peletier's rite of passage, was sterner perhaps than that of most nineteen-year-olds, and it left him, with regard to his craft, devoid of the tangential impedimenta of compassion. In III Corps, he'd left behind not only a lot of friends, but all he had of naïvete and innocence. The bloods said he had no Soul, but even the humorless skeptics in the Recon Squad knew he had no soul. And then there were the eyes.

Black, like marbles, like there was no iris, just a large pupil. And no lustre. Writers of hardcore adventure tales would have him with cold eyes. Not this Cajun. Those flat black shark's eyes burned as with fever, day and night, happy or sad, little opportunity though there was to see Peletier happy. The only times when his eyes did not have that burning, possessed look was when he snuggled into the stock of the Model 70 and found the rim of the scope. Then there was a sort of vagueness about his entire expression, a relaxing of rigid lines. At least the left eye, the one free of the scope, was blank. Not cold, not burning then—simply blank.

But the real kicker, what defined him as the cynosure he became, was the paint. Peletier wore LRRP mascara, camouflage grease paint on the face and hands for patrolling and skulking about in someone else's real estate. But Peletier wore the camouflage inside the wire, too. At first the standard broken pattern of black and brown and green; then later, as his devotion to the world outside the wire grew, there came a subtle shift toward two or three shades of green only. He slept and ate in the anonymity of this mask. He put it on the day he joined Charlie Company and he was never without it after that, a sad, surprisingly green Pagliacci in a bad production.

The first time the platoon watched him at what he did best, they realized it wasn't as if he got any pleasure from it. And that evening, even as the members of his squad watched and knew he was setting up shop for the first time since Tay Ninh Province, they saw nothing that looked like sloppy work.

He came on line in the early dusk, the delineations between shades of green on his face faded to insignificance. He walked bent-over to the corner of the berm where the sandbags projected out over a little draw that ran down into the bush. The sun was already below the jungle crown to the west, and the sky had that fading luminescence that makes scope work tricky. He just stood in the corner, staring off across the ravine for a while at the hill line behind the ville some 900 meters away. Then he crawled into a tight corner of the sandbags and pulled from a canvas bag an old, scarred spotting scope, wrapped in Ace bandage. He lay staring through the scope for a long time.

He never spoke when he worked.

Dusk was the time, all right. There was a lot of movement in and around the village as the resident farmers shifted gears and became the resident Viet Cong. Through the scope Peletier had a clear picture of anyone with a weapon or acting compromisingly military. Finally, he unwarapped the long strip of green, cotton bandaging from the Model 70, mounted the scope, slid it into place, worked the bolt slowly and silently to load a round, and lay still.

Lieutenant Franconi sat by the command APC and watched Peletier for almost an hour. Sergeant Glasgow came and waited with him awhile, neither speaking, the sniper acknowledging neither of them. It was like scrutinizing a still life painting, waiting for it to declare itself in some unlikely enlivement.

Peletier lay, hunkered into the corner of the sandbags. The long taped-up rifle barrel stuck out through the firing enclosure over no-man's land. Everyone on the firebase knew by then of the sniper's opening act, and they waited.

Everything slowed down.

Stopped.

After more than an hour of increasing tension, just before stark dark, there was a sudden, single explosion. One shot. Beyond the wire everything was beset with the commonality of deep shadow. Peletier lay where he was, hunched into the scope, for another ten minutes. Then he straightened, stood up and stepped carefully back down off the ammo box, unthreaded the scope, slung his piece, and slipped on down the line in the dark.

After that, from the vantage point of the firebase, he selected just one target in a day's time, never more. Sometimes none at all, as the VC presence went subliminal. Occasionally, a hit was made in the opposite quadrant, into what was supposedly a secure and friendly area, but if it was questionable how valid his target was, no one voiced the query.

When Peletier began disappearing from the firebase, it was assumed he was out hunting on his own with no spotter or backup, a violation of sniper orders but within the bounds of acceptable performance. Then a captain visiting from Brigade took a round through the head on the edge of the berm one rainy dawn. The round was from an SKS Soviet sniper's rifle, but the shot came from out of range of the VC snipers the brigade had previously encountered. The Delta XO remembered afterward the kill had occurred while Peletier was beyond the wire. By the time he was sought out, the Cajun sniper was found asleep in his bunker.

No one from the battalion was ever fired on in such circumstances, but when a brigade major on an inspection visit was grazed by a shot, just missing him, when he unexpectedly bent over, brigade visits stopped. Soldiers began to remember rumors of staff ineptness, brigade waffling, that led to the JUNCTION CITY dust-up. Peletier was had before the CO and later some CID people, but he came back to his bunker in a placid state, almost smiling.

That all happened in the first month or so after Pelletier joined Delta Company, and was distinctly separate from what happened when he began to recognize his targets beyond the wire, his rare comments relating sightings of soldiers known to have bought it on JUNCTION CITY; people wasted, stuffed in body bags, and rotated.

And then Peletier went away, the sergeant said with no inflection.

"But, Bernie. JUNCTION CITY was back in 'sixty-seven. More than two years ago. You'd come back here then? After your tour in 'sixty-five?" Winter asked, surprised.

"I never left. Been here sixty-three months, next week. Straight, in this shit hole."

Glasgow stood, swept the bottles off the table, reached with a tentative hand and touched Winter's face, staring at him with deeply recessed eyes.

Then Glasgow went away.

chapter twenty-four

Bad Cess Rising

Cam Ranh Bay, Viet Nam: August 1969

Back at Cam Ranh, Winter had found relief from his evasive medical threat but found no joy in the passing days though nearing the end of his Viet Nam tour—the Holy Grail of current military service. He fully realized his mental and emotional state had become a subject of concern for his friends, but he knew no way to mitigate that.

Defying logic, Moira's state was still a cipher. The rare letter from his wife offered no relief. He flew missions, wrote awards recommendations, taught training classes, and counted days. Major Grange relieved him of teaching aircrews, griping to Brenner, as Brenner later told Winter, "Your friend exudes a fatalism that's depressing the troops. I don't want him doing it anymore." Brenner did not want that either, but did not echo the major's judgement.

Beyond crumpling the copy of orders which he found in his mailbox the morning of fifteen August relieving him of instructor duties, Winter didn't seem to notice. A measure of his declining interest in the world about him was his lack of comment when Brenner, that same day, finally became the proud tenant of a room in the Crazy Cathouse following Captain Lamb's transfer out. From his open door across the way Winter, sitting in his unlighted room with the AC off, watched as Brenner put his gypsy existence once more in gear, moving from the open Navy billets to a semi-private room in three rapid trips, carrying everything he owned without help. And still without his footlocker.

Later, Winter imagined the leap to judgement Brenner would make when he came in that evening to his new quarters and found a collection of books he would recognize as Winter's, stacked on his table. Several military classics: inspired reading. A note he'd scribbled on a scrap of teletype paper read, "Yours now. Dave."

Brenner would recognize those standards of the oeuevre: Sun Tzu, Clausewitz, Schirer, Churchill. One curiosity entitled *Letters on Artillery*, by Prince Kraft Zu Hohenlohe Ingelfingen, third edition, London,1889, translated by one Colonel Walford, Royal Artillery, would likely catch his eye. Faded red coverboards, brittle pages. Winter hadn't been an artilleryman now for sixteen years. "Man kept his eye on the ball," Brenner would marvel, Winter knew. He also knew Brenner had never doubted that.

* * *

The morning of the sixteenth dawned cloudy and blustery. An early mission takeoff was delayed. With time on his hands in stand-down, Ito left the chow hall for the Orderly Room to check his box. He was standing by the water jug, reading a letter from crazy Uncle Michimoro while the work day crept into being. The door squeaked open behind him. No one but Magic Marvin paid the newcomer much attention—for fully ten seconds, until a soldier grabbed Ito by the arm and swung him around, bellowing threats.

"You fuckin' little Gook, I'm gonna kick your ass."

Specialist-4 Beard, a malcontent on his best day, an ineffective linguist, a waste as a soldier, had just been informed he was pulled from today's flight manifest—mission or no—and was being stricken from the flight crew roster. Ito had had enough of Beard's scrambled translations, his lame excuses for tardiness at every assigned responsibility: missing training, pre-flight briefs, and mission launches. He'd boogered up two entire missions and was on everybody's shit list. Ito, linguist guru, tripped his switch thinking to let the man market his questionable talents as a translator to some less-discerning grunt outfit.

But now, in Beard's tight grasp, Ito was terrified. Small of stature, the warrant did not enjoy the feistiness accompanying a Napoleon complex, or any of the other phobias of his size. He was not a battler. No moral coward, his physical limits were simply easily exceeded. So it was with the brutish, alcohol-reeking specialist who enveloped him now, crushing him to his chest..

Ito watched in mild surprise the only thing he could see past Beard's bulk: Magic Marvin springing from his desk chair in one swift move. The diminutive warrant officer lost track after that, the epicanthic folds of his eyes disappearing in a distended stare that made him resemble, in Marsh's later terms, a bushbaby.

Magic Marvin had noticed and followed Beard's entrance into the Orderly Room with suspicion. The soldier's demeanor telegraphed danger, his scowl manifesting a mission. In the few seconds before it was declared, Marsh considered something preemptive. And suddenly, with Ito's officerly untouchableness in tatters, he thought no further, reacting instinctively. Marsh grabbed Beard around the throat from behind and threw him to the concrete floor, freeing Ito. The warrant backed away, looking about for help. Another clerk sat frozen in his chair, eyes wide, hands poised above the keyboard. He was not the help sought.

Beard's bitter cries increased in volume and vehemence as he climbed to his feet. His focus of rage shifted from the small officer to the interfering specialist. The fact that Marsh was known as a lifer—a pejorative term for career military personnel, disdained by draftees and various slackers—facilitated Beard's transfer of anger. He yanked a .45 Colt service automatic from his beltline where it had been hidden under his filthy fatigue jacket.

Waving the gun, trying to cock back the hammer, Beard screamed hysterically, prophesying a mean but garbled list of terrible things he was going to do to Marsh, beginning with shooting him, followed by hurting him.

Marsh did not wait for Beard to fulfill his promises, but attacked, punching the linguist in the throat. The angry soldier, charged with adrenalin like a cokehead on the wing, seemed not to feel the blow, though his movements became slowed by a strangling cough. He still struggled with the .45 hammer until Marsh slammed into his body, threw an arm about his neck, and began pulling him down again. Marsh's head was tight in the tangle of Beard's arms and gun and, suddenly thrust against the specialist's bulk, he found his footing unstable. Beard's size inured him to normal threats.

Marsh felt his feet go out from under him as the screen door burst open. The First Sergeant launched in with a bellow, and Beard, reacting to this new threat, jerked his head about, managing finally, almost inadvertently, to thumb back the hammer on the pistol—not quite far enough to lock. The hammer snapped forward.

An explosion filled the small room with thunder.

Marsh fell back with a cry as Beard's arms flew wide..

The First Sergeant, as big as Beard and twenty-eight years-in-the-Army-and-three-wars meaner, grabbed the armed specialist by the same hand that held the gun and twisting, flung him into a row of file cabinets. The gun came away in the First Sergeant's hand.

Ito lurched forward to where Marsh lay on the floor, his face covered with his hands. In the background, the other clerk scrambled for the phone.

"Marve, you hit?" Ito shouted. He couldn't see any blood.

There was no response. Only a low groaning sound from Marsh.

"Marve, where're you hit? Did he get you?" Ito's hands scrabbled over Marsh's uniform, seeking blood, ruptures, burned holes. Something.

"My eyes!" the clerk grated. "Got my eyes."

"He shot you in the eye?" Ito immediately tried pulling Marsh's hands away.

"No. Burned, I think. Burned my eyes. They're on fire." He writhed momentarily; then, as if realizing the unseemliness of giving in to pain, went still.

"Move your hands. Lemme see," Ito ordered. "Pull your hands away, man. Now!"

"I can't. I can't take the pressure off—" he sighed, pulled in a vicious intake of breath as he tried to obey "—it burns like a bitch." Marsh went quiet, his hands clamped over his eyes.

"OK. OK. Doc'll be here in a minute. We'll get you to the hospital." Ito, trying to materialize a medic, looked frantically to the First Sergeant. That old soldier was busy tying Beard's hands together behind his back with a web belt.

Ito, watching a few seconds, said "Should we wash out his eyes, Top? With water, or—"

"No. Don't do anything. Medics been called," he grunted, breathing hard. "Let me take care-a this piece-a shit and I'll check on 'em." He looked up at a sound, out through the screen. "Never mind. They're here."

An Air Force ambulance squealed to a halt before the walkway into the Orderly Room.

"Don't let them take me to the Sixth," Marsh grated. "Sappers'll finish me." Weeks after, the startling attack on the hospital down south still dominated mindsets on the peninsula.

A medic asked a half dozen questions, while Marsh was laid on a stretcher by two other medics. Marsh complained every breath that he wasn't crippled; there was no need for a stretcher. "Get me a cane . . . and a German Shepherd," he said. Intending a quip, it came out as a nervous plea; striving for a WC Fields voice, unable to achieve it.

When they departed, Marsh had the medics in stitches. Ito knew that was fear; Marsh was not the funniest of people.

* * *

I woke Winter, who was sleeping in after mission. I told him what Ito had told me of Marsh's blinding. If I'd thought he looked bad before, this latest catastrophe seemed to bow him down beyond recovery. Tears came into his eyes as he dressed; his hands trembled, fumbling with buttons. Dave's close friends were being whittled down. I'd better watch my ass.

We borrowed Grange's Jeep and drove across the field to the Air Force dispensary. Sitting on metal stools, we watched through a glass wall as several doctors and nurses moved about Marsh on an examining table under bright lights. One doctor, wearing futuristic headgear comprising mirrors and tiny lights and titanium rods, stayed bent over him for a long time. He used a series of tweezers and tiny picks working over Marsh's face. When the doctor finally straightened, I saw no body language that augered well.

Winter looked away as if to dispel the reality of what he was seeing. In a spectral voice he said something that held little meaning at the time; something, though, that's stayed with me. "You remember The Perpetual P.F.C.? A mechanic named Foreman. From 'sixty-four, 'sixty-five flight ops? Don't know what his M.O.S. was. They used him as the firewatch on the flight line. The guy who was supposed to stand by with the fire extinguisher when the pilot went into start-up. Just in case . . . but the extinguisher was always somewhere else. Not important. What I remember, though, is something he used to say. And he said it more than once, almost like a mantra spoken to each flight. He'd call out, 'Mister whoever-was-flying, don't sail your ship out there. The world is flat. You'll fall off.'"

I had a vague notion of the guy he meant, but it didn't set me ablaze. Marvin looked like hell and for once, no metaphorical connect leaped to my mind.

Dave, heeding my stumped silence, said, "I think . . . we may've gone over that edge."

I was distracted, heard him but didn't pay attention, as a nurse bent and began applying something from a tube onto Marsh's face, using Q-Tips and small squares of surgical gauze. Another nurse followed with a wide swathe of white gauze about his head as the Q-Tip nurse held him up off the table.

Show over, someone off stage flipped the bright operating lights off. An orderly moved a wheelchair to the table. Marsh sat up from the steel table awkwardly, assisted by a sensationally ugly nurse with a gentle touch. The clerk resembled a geriatric Ichabod Crane.

Watching Marsh in his first moves in darkness, I could not imagine being unable to see. Relying on others for everything. But considering the ugly nurse, I thought, hating the blasphemy, being blind wasn't all bad. Dave would divorce me if I'd spoken that aloud.

The orderly helped Marsh into the wheeled chair and pushed him forward, through the swinging doors into the hallway where we waited.

"How is he?" "What's the word on his injuries?" we asked the medic, as if the patient were unconscious.

"Marve, are you OK? How do you feel?" There were insufficient words for Winter to ask all the questions he needed answers to. I was stunned by the rapid events; but I knew that Winter must be devastated. It hadn't even fully settled on him, and already he was a basket case. Marsh, only seven or eight years younger than Winter, was the warrant officer's child in every sense but genetics. I, too, was wrung out with the damage this was doing, not just to Marsh, but to Winter as well.

The orderly stopped. "Can't tell you gentlemen anything. Doctor will be out soon, but I don't believe he can say how much of the damage is permanent, or how much might come back. You know, how much he'll be able to see when the eyes heal. Burned, of course; the flash of the gunpowder. The doctor picked a lot of grainy black shit out of the flesh around his eyes. Some from the eyes. The trauma, the concussion and flaring effect, account for most loss of vision right now. Likely for some time yet. Doctor's coming," he added, looking behind him into the exam room. "Ask him."

Marsh had said nothing. But as the orderly pushed him away, I thought I heard the blinded clerk say, "Sorry 'bout that!"

My ass!

The medic was a smokescreen for the doctor who didn't make housecalls.

When the doctor did emerge, he lost no time in emphasizing that he was just *The Doctor on Duty*, a dermatologist by trade. Trying to answer our barrage of questions, he said, "I think his problem is two-fold. And I emphasize, I say it as other than an eye specialist. The Navy has an opthamologist at the Cho Lon hospital, and he'll be up to check Specialist Marsh when he can get free. Or we may send him down there. But, I think, two significant problems.

"One, there is debris from the gunshot residue, most of which was outside the eye itself, mostly about his face in the area of the eyes—the eye sockets. I removed most of that, and some of the material which got into the eye ball, the larger pieces. I want an eye man to go for the smaller stuff. But that debris, and the searing from the heat of the blast—the burn effect, the powder flash—affected primarily the cornea. From what I know, the cornea's pretty resilient. I think that element will heal somewhat, even in the next five or six days; even more downstream. Any probing to remove the remainder of the gunshot residue from the cornea will be done A-SAP, in order to let that healing process begin."

I saw the doctor could tell that Winter had questions backed up that were keeping him in a state of vibration, almost, but the dermatologist held up his hand, imperiously, and went on.

"That delicate work may require more skill than we have in-country, and we're suggesting he be scheduled out for the P.I. Air Force has a prime eye care facility at Clark Air Force Base."

He could wait no longer; Winter pushed in: "So, in a week or so, he should pretty much get his sight back?" Dave wanted a signed warranty.

"There'll be improvement, no doubt but . . ."

After long seconds of open-ended, incomplete-diagnosis quiet, Dave pushed again.

"You said two things; the burn and powder residue in the . . . what? the cornea? What else is not good. What's number two?"

"I can't tell—maybe a specialist can—how much damage might have been done by the force of the shot itself, the explosion, that near his eyes. There's certainly a risk of percussive damage to the optic nerve. The concussion of the explosion when the gun went off. That close to his eyes, could have . . . lasting effects. For now, that's an unknown."

Winter tried to protest. The doctor gave that imperial hand signal in the air again, and said, "You're just going to have to wait for him to go further through the examination and evaluation process by eye specialists." As if to reiterate his non-involvement, he insisted, "Hey, I do actinic keratoses, chloracne, and remove warts, for the most part. You'll have to wait, at least, until the docs in Cho Lon get a look, and maybe the guys in Clark. Sorry." He turned away and was gone before Winter could react. Superman couldn't have caught up with him.

End of prognosis.

Winter reluctantly left the hospital. I followed and drove us back across to NAF.

Everyone wanted to know Marsh's condition and, tired of explaining that no one really knew, we wandered back to Winter's room. I grabbed a couple of Tuborgs from the fridge and we sat, making small talk. If body language could really speak, and I never doubted it, right now his was saying that CW2 David D. Winter was inches—seconds, degrees, something microscopically small—away from collapse. All the chaos, the angst, the losses— all the shit, was finally coming together for him: critical mass. I felt helpless and sat quietly, watching Dave openly, not disguising my concern. I might not have been there, for all the response this got me.

In a quirky move that might have saved the day momentarily, Bracken suddenly came rushing in, all a-dither, and switched on the TV. Waiting for it to warm, he said he'd caught part of a radio simulcast that Winter needed to know about. He wouldn't say what. "Wait. Wait."

Reception wasn't great—a lot of aural white noise—but watchable. Bobbie, the weather girl, was eminently watchable. One could always make out Bobbie among electronic clutter: great cumulus build-ups. I was ogling, not paying attention to what she was saying, when Dave sat up straight, glaring at the set. He jumped up, turned the volume up, and stood watching just inches from the screen.

Bobbie was reporting a storm making in the Gulf of Mexico. A big storm. A hurricane, detected initially on the fourteenth near Grand Cayman, it had now moved across Cuba with high winds, dumped ten inches of rain, and was on its way to the Gulf. Miami Center predicted a Gulf Coast landfall from Biloxi to St. Mark's, Florida—too early for specifics—on the seventeenth.

Late tomorrow!

Biloxi, Mississippi, was some twenty miles or so from Long Beach and Dave's family.

AFRTS inserted an override weather broadcast from a grim-visaged, rain- and wind-swept prognosticator who told us more than we wanted to know about a hurricane swirling through the southern seas toward the Gulf coast. Third of the season, alpha-gender named Camille.

I didn't know how old the broadcast was, but the time codes, allowing for different time zones, indicated the pictures might be live. Images of blowing palm trees and rippling tin roofs on shotgun shacks, fast food stores, and service stations. Steeple-less churches. Roofless houses. And the storm was still more than a day away, still at sea. Official notices and warnings were read from state and federal authorities. All residents, with the exception of specified emergency personnel, were advised to close up homes and businesses, get in a vehicle, and drive inland.

Did people really do that? I wondered. Just pack some grits, hop in the pickup, and head north. Logical, though; from the Gulf Coast bottom of Mississippi there was a lot of north up there to go to.

I felt Dave's concerns: two children and a sometime-wife—not to mention a home—in the path of ruin. But Mississippi was home ground for Nickie and Dave; he had talked of going to the Gulf beaches while growing up in Jackson. Though Dave's birfh family were all dead except for the occasional cousin, Nickie's mother still lived there, 160 miles north of Long Beach. Nickie had plenty of warning, was not stupid. Surely she'd bundle the kids into the wagon and drive to mama's. Of course that obvious, simple solution wasn't occurring to Winter right now.

* * *

Winter bled the broadcast of every bit of storm news for most of that day, which put it late into the night on the Gulf Coast. It did not sound good. There had been monster storms over the years along that coast, but they were predicting this one might be the most powerful blow of all. Already, winds up to 150 mph were observed in the Gulf, over water, by hurricane hunters flying into the eye. August had been exceptionally hot; water temps were high and fed the greedy gale over the Gulf. It would likely get worse, and projected landfall had shifted west, effectively targeting Mississippi, maybe even Louisiana, leaving Florida to get on with vacationers.

Winter realized Brenner was talking and, focusing on what he said, felt somewhat relieved. Luther was right! Whatever Nickie was, she wasn't stupid. She *would* pack it in, load the kids, and go to Mrs. Jay's house. Wind damage might extend inshore for a couple of miles, even more, but not to mid-state. He felt a sense of gratitude: to the gods, to the weather people who provided the alert, and to his friend who made him aware of an obvious truth.

Later, doubts swirling about him as he watched weather predictions through the day with assessments worsening; his concern built again. He had to know. Though communications were not as good in late afternoon, with the atmosphere superheated and sun spots active, he could not wait for night schedules at the MARS station. Once more he begged loan of the CO's Jeep to go to South Beach to make a stateside call. Grange would start charging him rental car fees soon.

Driving down the peninsula, he was jarred by the return of concerns for Moira. He felt a sense of guilt that he'd momentarily lost sight of her, her status still in a limbo he couldn't penetrate. But whatever those concerns, Camille's entry into the equation had shifted the balance.

The MARS facility was almost empty. A medic sergeant slept in a chair in the corner, making hawking noises through his nose. A 1st Log Command PFC paced back and forth, glancing repeatedly at a photo in his hand, then at his watch. Winter got a booth after a few minutes, he too watching the time.

As he held the old black, hard-rubber Bell System phone, he realized he had it in a death grip. He tried, without success, to relax. His hands were not listening to his mind. Or perhaps they were.

When he'd waited some ten minutes, his fist tightly about the phone, the MARS op spoke into his ear. "Sorry, Chief. I can get several Hams, but phone circuits to the coastal region are out. No calls gettng through at all."

"Can I try another number?"

"Sure, but if it's in the same area, it'll be the same."

"I understand," Winter said, exasperated. "This would be farther inland."

"Okay. What's the number?"

The operator was back in only a few minutes: "You're connected, Mr. Winter."

The line sounded like a long, echoing tunnel. "Hello, Mrs. Jay. This is David, calling from Viet Nam. I can't get through to Nicole. I thought you might have some news, or is she there with you? And Mrs. Jay, don't forget, after you speak, you have to say 'over' in order to let me speak. O.K.? Over." He knew she'd been instructed in the procedure by the connecting Ham op, but neither technology nor details were simple issues with his mother-in-law.

There was a succession of clicks and scufflings on the line, and suddenly her voice came through clearly. "Hello, David. I'm so glad to hear from you, son. Are you okay?" There was a long pause. She said, "David . . . Oh. Over."

"I'm fine, Mrs. Jay.. I'm calling to find out about Nicole and the boys. Are they there in Jackson with you? Or on their way there? Over."

Clickety-clack. "Hello, David? Oh, no, dear. Nicole is not here, nor the boys. She's at home." Long pause. "In Long Beach." Longer pause. "Over."

"Mrs. Jay, are you aware of the hurricane threatening the coast? Isn't that on the news there? Have you heard from Nickie at all?" He began shaking his head. "Over." The damned woman, persistently dotty, was disconnected from the real world. His spirits spiraled south.

"Hello, David? Oh, no dear. I've not heard from her since this morning. She's in Long Beach. A storm? I think she said something. You know, I don't watch the news on television; it's so depressing, all you young men over there in danger. I just don't watch it. They're all well in Long Beach. But they have storms there as regular as clockwork. And they're not on the beach, of course. She did say she would call me in a day or so, when things got better. Now what do you suppose . . . ? So thoughtful." Long, long pause. "Oh, my goodness. Over."

"Mrs. Jay, is Nicole planning to come to Jackson with the children? Over." His last word was nearly shouted. It did not improve communications.

"Of course not, David, dear. She and the boys were just up here two weeks ago. You know what the price of gas is like; she can't afford to be running back and forth on a whim. I expect I'll hear from her in a day or so. Over." Had she somehow found the formula?

"Mrs. Jay, you should advise her to come to Jackson. Urge her. Hell, *demand* she come, bring your grandsons. This is going to be a monster storm, by all accounts. Over."

"Oh, David. You know Nicole's determination. I can't force her. Never could," she said distractedly. "They'll be fine. And—oh, yes. Over."

There was nothing to be done. "I have to go now, Mrs. Jay. You be well. If you talk to her, tell Nicole and the boys I love them." A curious wrenching. "Goodbye! Over." He felt his emotions plummet.

"Yes, well, goodbye, David. 'bye . . ." He waited several minutes for an "Over," an "Out." But she struggled with the first instruction; proper termination was unknown to her. He placed the phone back on the hook, no doubt leaving some Ham operator in Nacogdoches or Canton hanging on an open link..

* * *

Late the following day, the *Day of Camille* as he thought of it, when he had debriefed following an aborted mission, Winter tried for news. AFRTS was off the air. He pushed his luck, borrowed the Jeep, and drove again to the MARS facility. This time, he did not have to wait in line. The signals people were giving priority to anyone with family or loved ones in the region where the storm had finally come ashore, leaving behind massive death and destruction. There were a number of Air Force personnel with connections to Keesler Air Force Base and the Biloxi area, and several SeaBees waiting in the room, hoping to reach loved ones near where their battalion headquarters was located at Gulfport.

The phone lines to the coast were still out, and he could no longer reach Jackson. The only information he got, from some of the waiting Seabees, was that the eye of the hurricane had passed approximately through the Long Beach-Pass Christian stretch of coastline, and spread disaster fifty miles either side.

Long Beach! Jeremy. Adam. Nickie . . . .

chapter twenty five

Goodbye to All That

Cam Ranh Bay, Viet Nam: August 1969

Brenner and Ito awaited Winter's return from South Beach. As he pulled up before the Orderly Room in the dark, Lieutenant Billingsgate and CW3 Mapes joined them. A chorus greeted Winter, wanting news, seeking to help him cope.

Fending off questions and solemn good wishes, he made his way to his room where he found Bracken in the mid-space, drinking beer and watching a televised weather report from the states. Winter stared at him for a few moments, question nuancing his posture, but not speaking.

"Looks bad, Dave," Bracken said. "Pictures from helicopters, flying along the beach, nothing but Pick-Up Sticks." The warrant hesitated, than said, "The death toll is reported high. They don't know how bad; they can't get into a lot of areas due to debris in the roads. Trees and powerlines and poles down everywhere, destroyed structures in the streets . . ."

"Anything about Long Beach, in particular?"

"The TV just came back on. Heard nothing on Long Beach, but Pass Christian is effectively gone—"

"Oh, Jeez-us. That's only a coupla' miles." Winter unconsciously dry-washed his hands.

"Bad shit in Gulfport and Biloxi. Winds over two hundred; tidal surge over thirty feet. There are ocean-going tankers astride the coast highway in Gulfport—What's that? Interstate 10? —and fishing boats two city blocks inland, on top of houses and in trees. A jungle of trees down. Pascagoula took some hits. Here, let me get the sound back on . . ." He reached and twisted a knob and an excited newscaster's voice boomed out in the tiny space. He twisted the knob partly back.

"—Force weather reconnaissance aircraft, who have flown into and tracked the eye of the storm which wreaked such destruction on Long Beach and Pass Christian, say it continues to move east and north. It is already being felt in the Carolinas, and Virginia is under alert. Here on the Gulf Coast, survivors are only just beginning to emerge, and it is to a scene of almost total devastation they're introduced. It is this reporter's judgement that the Mississippi Gulf Coast has ceased to exist." The announcer's voice fluctuated along the edge of panic.

"Damage beyond the state border with Louisiana indicates several parishes there with significant damage: loss of homes and businesses, injuries, and some unconfirmed deaths. But from beyond Pass Christian in the west, back through Long Beach and Gulfport, practically every structure along the seafront is gone and damage continues inland, in places more than five miles."

"My home's less than two miles from the water," Winter murmured.

Bad news continued from the same reporter, and from other commentators, Air Force, SeaBee, and Coast Guard rescue workers, Red Cross reps, and local authorities. The Hamilton County Sheriff's Office warned residents to keep off the streets. Looting had already been reported, and there was considerable danger of disease due to the number of animal carcasses and human bodies floating off the beach, in waterways, and in swampy areas along rivers and creeks. Public water was shut down.

Military personnel from Keesler Air Force Base were drafted as emergency workers, as were the SeaBees from their Gulfport home base. Both military organizations had integral heavy-duty equipment, and they were working the critical problem areas, clearing.

When he'd heard all he could take, Winter dashed out the door into the knot of men gathered there, leaning in the door to hear the broadcast. Ito said, "It's always the worst when the eye's just passed. In Hawaii, every time a hurricane or typhoon blows through—"

"That asshole just said Long Beach is wiped out. Wiped out! Jeez, what the goddamned hell does that mean. Wiped out? The business district? The shopping mall, service stations . . . or does he mean every living soul in Long Beach?"

"Dave, come on. It's still likely Nickie and the boys got away to her mom's. They said the roads north were open until the storm struck. Crowded . . . but open. Nickie had several days' notice about the storm. You have to know she's gone to Jackson," Brenner encouraged.

"No. I don't think so, Luther. Her mom talked as if that was something unheard of. I don't know why—she's not a longtime resident on the coast; and I can't imagine she's got ties there, this quickly—but for some goddamned illogical, unreasoned reason, she chose to ride out the storm. With the boys. I just know it. They could be dead, Luther. All dead." Winter caught himself. He wanted to thrash something; he wanted to wail and scream and pound his fists on something.

He would never forgive her for this, alive or dead.

No, he couldn't think about that. They had to be alive. He described his conversation with Mrs. Jay. When he'd told them the frustrating results of his efforts, Billingsgate said, "Come on," grabbed Winter's shirt, and turned away toward the mid-billets passage to the Sandbag.

"Bimbo, I don't want a drink," Winter said.

"We're gonna see the major."

Winter lifted an eyebrow at the others; they all followed the Can-Do officer.

The Bonnie Major was with Grange in his room. Timing was good; both were dressed. All four officers crowded in, making crowd noise. Bonnie smiled ruefully, as if she recognized, and accepted, a ruined evening.

Billingsgate laid out the problem as he knew it, glancing at Winter for confirmation. He was essentially correct in all respects; still he deferred to Winter, who said nothing.

"What can we do?" Grange asked, bumped unwillingly up to the role of Commander in front of his woman.

"I don't know, sir. Seems almost hopeless to get something done at this late stage. I can't get through to my home," Winter said. "I've no idea of their circumstances."

The Bonnie Major was sympathetic. "We saw the storm

reports on TV; looks like it's smacked the Mississippi coast pretty hard."

She looked suddenly to Major Grange, motioned with her head, and drew him aside, talking softly and rapidly. The CO glanced back at Winter, looked at Brenner, turned back to Bonnie and nodded. He moved back into the center of the cluttered room.

"Major Hirschi has an inspiration. She thinks you should go home. To Mississippi. Even with the storm over, you'll be needed. Two kids, right?" The CO said nothing trite.

Silence hung over the room, like a bell glass clapped over a boombox. The idea had not occurred to anyone else. And who the hell was Major Hirschi? Winter stared at Bonnie, suddenly aware, realizing he'd never known her last name. She was always in civvies when he'd seen her, and when he first met her, she'd said, "Call me Bonnie."

"But how can we do that?" Grange asked, seemingly to himself.

Billingsgate spoke up: "We'll get on it, sir. If we can find a way, will you support it?"

"Sure. Find me a reasonable action, a wrinkle in the regs or something, and I'll go the distance." The major suddenly sounded decisive, almost like a commander.

* * *

Dawn was no longer new. Sounds of life stirred from every azimuth. Somewhere, a small aircraft engine buzzed angrily, restrained. Motor vehicle noises came from the Motor Pool. In brief interstices between the noises of saturated civilization, the slurp of tidal-change waves on the beach sounded a soothing panacea. The crimping of aluminum cans in the quiet of early morning advertised at least one late or early drinker in the Sandbag. The hours crept by.

Winter returned mid-morning to the Orderly Room from the latrine to find an excited Ito, who said, "Dave, we got it!" His eyes behind thick eyeglass lenses were wide with excitement.

"What?" Winter demanded, staring at him, turning to the First Sergeant who had his finger in the pages of a book of regulations.

The First Sergeant let Ito tell it. "Emergency leave," Ito said.

"That's no good, Fred. Top already went through that," Winter replied. "Early on . . ."

"Well, I missed something," the First Sergeant said. "Never had occasion to use the reg this way. We always associate emergency leave with a death or serious illness in the family. This paragraph says, in essence, cases involving emergency situations, like storms, earthquakes, et-cetera, in a service member's home area or involving his direct relations, are circumstances under which a commander is encouraged to be, and I quote, 'extremely liberal in granting Emergency Leave.'" He looked pleased. "Now does that, or does that not, fit your situation?"

When Major Grange entered the Orderly Room, he'd already been informed a potential crease had been found in the regs. "Top, see if you can get Mister Winter a seat on anything going to Sai Gon. He'll be leaving today," he said.

"Already in hand, sir," said First Sergeant. "Mister Bracken will fly him down in a U-eight on loan from the One-forty-fourth." His eyes held an unaccustomed twinkle. "I need your O.K. to request an order number for the Emergency Leave orders."

"How much time you got left here, Winter?" the CO asked.

"Eleven days, sir. And a wakeup. DE-ROS twenty-nine August."

"Emergency leave will put you reporting to your next duty station," the First Sergeant spoke up. "You won't come back here. You understand that?" the First Sergeant asked.

"Yeah, Top. Got it. Thanks. Appreciate all you guys' help. And you, sir," Winter said, ensuring Grange came in for accolades not included in *you guys*.

"No problem," the CO said. "Talking with the Ops Officer, we've already designated Mister Brenner as your replacement; he's on site and flying. You got any problem with any of that,

Mister Brenner?" he said, turning to the WO1. This was not the CO that any of them had known to this point.

"No, sir. Not a thing. I can hardly wait to get this clown out of my hair so I can shape up the criminals in his crews." Brenner became all business. "Sir, if we can borrow your Jeep later, after Mister Winter packs his gear, we'll drive down to Shipping, get his hold baggage in the pipeline. And he'll have to clear his Crypto and Classified Documents accounts. I'll help him with all that, if we can use your vehicle." Brenner was pushing everything into high gear.

Winter, moving in a daze with all the things that required doing, could not dwell on the unknown circumstances of his family. Several times in the following couple of hours, he went for at least five seconds without thinking of them and worrying.

He packed quickly, sending the hooch maid to pick up his laundry, ready or not. Two-thirds of his uniform clothing—most of the skivvies and tee-shirts, two old sets of jungle fatigues, socks without a future, and a hodgepodge of assorted items he could live without—went in the trash can. He gave Brenner two almost new Air Force gray flight suits. After packing, and with binoculars, Kabar, and a few other select items fitted into a carry-on bag, he went to supply. He turned in bed linen and pillow, and had the clerk sign off on his locker and mattress.

Winter walked through the pointless exercise of clearance, getting signatures on the form, firmly and irrevocably relinquishing his pistol, emergency kit, and blood chit, all of which were in the hands of supply already. There was no accounting for a parachute, a daily draw item. He left his old, non-issue Gothic flight helmet in the chair outside the beaded entrance to his room. Free for the taking! His owner's interest in the AC, TV, and fridge went, by convention, to Bracken.

From Supply to Operations. The S-2 clerk was waiting with his records. They located everything on the list after some tricky shuffling, investigating a few illogical hidey-holes where they should not have been, and then sent for Brenner. When he came, they set up a chain operation: Winter initialed the log, indicating turn-in of a document; the clerk signed, acknowledging receipt of it, turned it over to Brenner; Brenner signed for the document, and the clerk made a corresponding entry in his records indicating disposition. Winter was surprised when, after forty-five minutes, the clerk said with relief, "That's it, sir. All done."

"Thanks, Bailey." Winter turned to Brenner, "Let's get to Shipping. We can stop and see Marvin on the way back." He walked quickly down the length of the building for the last time, and out the door.

* * *

When the two warrants had disposed of Winter's hold baggage, drove back up the peninsula, and entered the Air Force hospital, Brenner said, "Wish Ito could have come. But Marsh'll remain here a couple of days yet, I think. Ito can come anytime."

Marsh was in a room with one other patient. It was semi-dark and they assumed it was due to the SP5's eye damage. Glare. But the other patient, bandaged over his entire lower body, spoke out, "Don't turn on that light. Hurts my eyes." Winter glanced at the chart on the foot of the bed: an airman third class. Hardly in position to be issuing directives.

"Marve, you awake under there? You want light?" Brenner asked facetiously, taking the decision out of junior birdman's hands.

Winter said, "Jeez-us, Luther. You gotta nerve."

"That's O.K., Mister Winter. That's gotta be Mister Brenner. And what f—what good would a light do me? I'm too tired to read. Leave Chuckles—" he nodded his bandaged head toward his fellow patient "—in the dark. He might Zoomie right out of here in protest."

"Asshole," Brenner confirmed, glancing at the airman-in-white.

When Winter had explained the hurry-up departure being arranged, Marsh wrenched himself up straighter in his bed. "Damn, I'm glad about that, sir. Glad you could make it. I know Mrs. Winter will be fine, her and the boys. It's chaos right now, if she's still on the coast." He made no comment when his boss told him of Nickie's likely imponderable lack of good sense. "Where I live in southern Illinois, we have a lot of tornadoes, and it always turns the phones and public services into nightmares." If it was meant to placate Winter, it failed.

Marsh still had no word from his doctors. Too soon. But the pain was controlled by a narcotic salve and a salad of colored pills, and he was grateful for that.

When they'd said what was to be said—in Winter's case, what he could say without choking up, and he didn't know if it was the kid who lay before him, or those two kids and a wife who were lately in the path of destruction, and whom he didn't know were alive or dead, that caused the choking—Winter promised to write, flinching when he heard his own words. He knew that nurses or care providers would read the letters aloud. Marsh promised to write back, though he admitted he'd never been good at that. Brenner told the clerk he would return and visit and asked if Marsh needed anything. Marsh made one valiant effort, asking for Army regs in Braille.

The two officers said a rapid goodbye and departed. Back on NAF, Winter double-checked his room, said goodby to several pilots, ops, and one mechanic hanging around The Sandbag. In addition to the appliances, he willed his beer ration in the fridge in their room to Bracken. He then carried his B-4 and overnight bags and briefcase across to the Orderly Room.

"Top, Bracken tells me the bird's here, being refueled. You got my orders?"

First Sergeant shook his head, "Change of plan, sir. You don't get 'em here. Personnel office at the Two-Two-Four, Tan Son Nhut, will issue. They said they 'want to be sure details are right.' I think they wanted time to confirm the Regs on this . . . bastards probably had the 509th wire the Hall to ensure they wouldn't get their butts kicked. It's a first for me, too, though. Never seen that Reg implemented this way. But absolutely legal."

"I never knew, either." Winter didn't make light of it; he was grateful for his friends' persistence that identified the reg.

"If you're on your way, Major said tell you goodbye. He's still over on mainside, but he got his Jeep back. Wanted you to know, thinking you might be concerned." His eyebrows raised. "Man's not a total write-off as a commander, maybe," and for the first time in his experience, Winter saw a hint of smile on the NCO's whiskery face. He held out his hand. "Good luck to ya, Mister Winter. I wish the best, f'r you and yours. Take care." He returned to paperwork.

* * *

The flight lasted forever; the end came too soon. When the twin runways of Tan Son Nhut came into view and Winter checked his watch, he was amazed to find they'd been in the air little more than three-quarters of an hour. But the runways could be seen for a long way. Bracken finally slipped into the landing pattern between an Australian Caribou and a tandem pair of VNAF A-1Es. Smooth landing, not a Bracken specialty, and within five minutes Winter climbed out onto the starboard wing. He reached back, pulled his bags after him, saluted his former roomie, an dropped to the ground. Bracken flipped him the bird and grinned. Revving the port engine, swinging the U-8 in a tight circle, he moved the Seminole forward to join the takeoff queue.

Winter had walked only a few yards when he heard a horn and saw a Jeep flashing its lights at the edge of the apron. He walked over and greeted Mister Travaglia, the last in-country, charter member of the International Brigade, still in the Warp Zone after four years. A resident. Homesteading. Avoiding the *Carabinieri commandante* in his Italian home province. As Winter threw the bags into the back and climbed in the passenger seat, his eyes flicked over Travaglia's person in a casual inspection. He reached his hand again across to the Italian expatriate and said, "Congratulations on the promotion. Double-u three suits you."

"The pay suits me, you are right. Otherwise, I still drive the airplanes." But he smiled to show he was pleased. "I am sorry to hear your . . . problem. The storm."

"Yeah, I think the family's probably all right, but I can't find out anything. Television says the hurricane's beat hell out of that whole area."

"*Non te la prendere! Sai bene che le dichiarazioni di television vonno sempre prese con beneficio d'inventario.* You know that." The Italian pilot grinned at Winter as if he did.

"Sure, whatever," Winter muttered.

The short drive ended at the steel front door of the 224th Aviation Battalion (RR). Winter got out, dragged his bags from the back, and leaned over to shake Travaglia's hand again.

"*Ey—Attenzione! Buona fortuna* and *ciao*," he said, and drove away.

Winter was met in the hallway inside by CW4 Wally Stegner, Personnel Officer. Stegner handed him a sheaf of orders, saying, "Don't rub those fuckers hard. Ink's not dry. Come on, Davey, me lad." Stegner was the officer who'd placed the brown scarf about Winter's neck the day he was commissioned a warrant officer, in Rothwesten two years before. The old man turned and hobbled down the hall toward the front door. Turning back he asked, "You want to say your bye-byes to anybody here? We're not in a big hurry—you're not gonna get a flight this time of day, anyhow—but I want to get you over to Group for final debrief and check-out. You could come back here after." He walked on as if it was a given.

Winter thought of Ratty Mac, working Days now, but decided he didn't have it in him to keep up a front with Mac. He said nothing.

After a ride to the 509th in the front seat of a three-quarter-ton truck with a bed full of new, unfilled sandbags and enough privates to fill them, Winter began working his way down the abbreviated clearance form Stegner had given him. His primary clearance was behind him at Cam Ranh Bay. Some persons signed in more than one space, saying, "You'll never find him this time of day," or "He's on TDY. Don't bother to come back. I'll sign for him."

He found a few men he'd known, worked with, said good-bye

after quick explanations, and rode the same three-quarter back to the 224th. There were many more men here whom he wanted to say farewell to, and he was making his way through another list, this one in his head, when something out of that memory chain touched him, and he felt as if he'd been slammed by a fast ball. He looked about, a stunned look on his face.

He was leaving!

He was really leaving. All these guys. The work, the job where it's at, he thought. The war. And in phase with his deliberations, the overwhelming fears for his family rushed back in, dominating his thoughts. He felt bad later, not remembering the last few soldiers he spoke to.

Wally Stegner drove him to the terminal across the field. The combined civilian-military air terminal teemed with both categories, heavily civilian. The military flights mostly came and went in the morning. It was now almost 1800 hours. A few decrepit transports, two CIA commuters, and several French-owned civilian aircraft from rubber plantations in the interior might keep the terminal open, but outgoing tactical strikes would keep the strip operable all night. Wally waved good bye, called "Keep your pecker up, kid," and drove away, waving.

It was all Winter could do to lift the B-4 bag in one hand, the two smaller ones in the other, and make his way to the main passenger area. Any physical drive he'd started the day with was exhausted. He made his way in the semi-gloom of evening across the scarred and pitted tile floor. Something, large and dark, back in his mind behind Camille, nagged at him.

He set his B-4 bag down, propped the overnight bag and briefcase alongside, and looked at his watch. He'd not eaten since breakfast, right after Ito had announced the miracle of the emergency leave reg. He made his way through the diminishing crowd to the little restaurant where he'd eaten many a lunchtime meal. That venue—where the booby-trapped mine planted in the ceiling had wounded four friends, and should have gotten him in 1965, he was convinced—was closed. The security flex was pulled across and the interior coldly empty.

He returned, realigned his bags, wondered why, and walked outside still hungry. A young, crippled Vietnamese girl on the curbside was hawking fruit. He bought two oranges and a tiny Vietnamese banana while avoiding staring at her distorted cleft palate and withered left arm. Back in the cavernous departure area the crowds had dispersed. Tan Son Nhut terminal did not run to the elegance of chairs. But as one of a half-dozen men in Army uniform, he alone in fatigues and sartorially deprived, he had no hesitation in sitting on the filthy floor to eat.

Flights to the world prohibited travel in fatigues; only summer dress khakis or greens would serve. But he'd thrown away the last of his frayed, smelly khakis back at Cam Ranh. And his greens were mildewed and unlikely to be resurrected even by stateside cleaners. He would plead ignorance and flash the Emergency Leave orders.

Nothing to do but wait. Stegner had directed him to the departure area for whatever transport might happen to touch down at Tan Son Nhut in the coming hours. A check with military flight booking confirmed that nothing further was scheduled that night. The Air Force clerk added that, though unlikely, something unscheduled *might* show up; but Winter would, for sure, be on the first morning flight. His Emergency Leave orders guaranteed him a seat, even if it meant bumping some other GI who likely had pulled his full tour. Winter felt only slightly cheapened for curtailing ten days of his tour.

With no trash receptacle visible—he cringed, remembering Ratty Mac's assessment that ". . . the entire fuckin' country is a joint sewer-landfill."—Winter piled the orange peels and tiny banana skin in a small heap next to the tiled column. He stared closely at the yellow skin of the banana, urging focus, consciously seeking distance from a subliminal memory. His mind, curious and roving, would mpt have done the same at anytime in the past, but he instinctively knew this impinging memory was devastating. Like an overhung student, he could not keep focus.

What the hell was the question, professor?

Memories, bright and brittle, alternately corniced with

darkness, flashed through his mind, asserting their influences on disproportionate scales. The flow of pictures and sounds, random smells and feelings, mostly pain, coalesced into one swirling rush.

Ditches and dirt roads littered with bloody corpses, all sizes, all ages, all persuasions and politicies and sex and education and alliances—all moot, while damaged youths played out their fantasies. Right makes might and vice-versa and so forth and oops-a-daisy . . .

A Phantom pulls out of a beautifully arced dive, deadly container detaching from its belly, tumbling over and over erratically, nothing graceful about it, until it plashes a sheath of fire indiscriminately over the village on the mountainside; and through smoke and flames, quick flashes he couldn't quite isolate, each on its own, framed a mere impression of tiny children's faces, grimacing, eyes wide, fearful, lost in an instant. Electric Man sits quietly in a cell-like treatment center, despairing of treatment, his intellect fractured against an implacable wall of violence and bureaucratic indifference. Human heads grace the spikes of bamboo stakes, eyes wide against the blasphemy or closed in a benign acceptance of lives in conflict. Troughs filled to a towering improbability with unmatched body parts, the liquids of their congested gathering trickling with a crashing roar while in the background, engines roared in futility. Four implacable instances of catastrophe avoidance—that bill due!

Swimming haphazardly along the edges, inducing incandescent impressions—a windmill. A painting by Goya. An empty, following sea so silent he could count piston strokes of the carrier engines five decks below.

Wooden structures of human habitation fired, blown into litter. Suddenly, there loomed the subject avoided: Moira! He couldn't deal with that; there was the detritus of coastal storms.

He was nudged from coruscating chaos, memories both salving and scarifying, by the sound of a soul hosting a broken heart, penetrating the background noise of occasional aircraft and the hum of diesel generators. Someone sobbed with the forlorn assurance of a lost being. Winter looked about in the gloomy terminal and located another figure in fatigues, seated, hunched against another pillar, his knees drawn up, his face buried in his hands. He wore a KP hat and old-style fatigues. A huge mound of boxes and bags, luggage, packs, and saddle bags were piled about him. He sobbed without awareness of any other presence.

Winter got up, went over. Standing before the slick-sleeved private, he took in the man's short, chunky body and the nature of his outdated uniform.

He knew this private. He'd encountered him before. Several times. Now he thought of it, going back to his first 'Nam tour. He was half of the pair whom Winter had thought of as Spanish, though he couldn't remember why he had thought so. As players, they were on the same circuit. He should know more about this soldier. He bent down before the private.

"Soldier! Soldier!"

The suffering EM continued his private despair.

"Soldier! *Hey, soldier, goddammit!*" Rising impatience freed him to overcome the erratic disturbance of the choppy, freeze-frame visuals looming in his concscious mind. *"Hey, private!"*

The man jerked his hands down. Seeing the officer's bar, he tried scrambling to his feet; but his corporeal self was unequal to the task. He was inundated with gear and belongings, certainly beyond his own. Winter looked about, seeking the second of the pair. The tall dude who dressed and talked funny, and who was never far from this soldier.

"Where's your officer, soldier? Where's . . . the lieutenant?" He felt strange, fixing the older man with such an unexalted label, but it was the only rank by which he knew him.

"Oh, sir, gone," the private answered quickly. "He's go-go-gone."

"Has he abandoned you?" Winter somehow thought that an unreasonable assumption.

"Yes, sir, he has. He left me in this sad and angry land without assistance, with no money, no orders, or even a mule or any means to make my way home." As if suddenly inspired, he reached toward one of the many pockets about his supplemented fatigues, scratching to retrieve something. "He did honor his word," he snuffled. "He did honor me with title to the island he promised me. I have the deed here somewhere, signed and witnessed . . ."

Winter could not imagine what that was all about. "Where do you think he's gone, soldier?" It was unlikely the wretch would be lying here, sniveling, if he had any idea.

"Oh, sir. He has abandoned me and the rest of this wicked world for the final time. He has passed, sir. Gone west. Died." From his tone, it might have been evident.

"Died. Died?" Winter felt stupid, echoing a vision he wanted to avoid. "Was he killed in combat?"

"No, sir, though he might have been in any one of a thousand mistaken efforts to be the world's keeper." With that, he broke into a new, more vehement spouting of grief.

"Hush, man. Hush," Winter urged, looking around. "What happened to him?"

When he had caught his breath, the private rolled onto the right side of his ample cheeks and managed to get his right leg under him. Using the column, he pushed himself erect. He saluted, so startling Winter with the ludicrous proprieties he couldn't respond. "What happened?" he repeated.

"Oh, sir, my master—my officer, whose honorable name was Daniel Dewey, and whose honorable title was Senior Lieutenant, with ties to . . .," he halted, confused. He added, without benefit of the question, "Of insignificance, I am Private Samuel Fellows. My officer and I had been together for many years. Many, many years. Since he found me in my village," he murmured, his voice trailing off. "What happened, you ask. Indeed, what did happen?" He stared into the distance, appearing totally at sea.

"The world, sir . . . the world betrayed, destroyed, and finally killed my officer. The world broke his heart. He was an old man, his mind besieged with fantasies and romance and he could not live when he finally was forced to face the facts of those beliefs as fantasies. He had spent his years and capacities to do good, to aid the weak, to help the poor, to defend the virgin, to right all wrongs. You can well imagine," he looked up at Winter with a knowing leer, "what it would be like to suddenly know that all you had believed in was a shopworn joke."

There was a message behind his look. The warrant officer felt a visceral response . . . to the words. The message. He forced himself to confront only the soldier, though he thought . . . he *could* imagine. He felt . . . *crowded*, sudden claustrophobia a thing he'd never suffered from.

Winter realized with a growing fascination that during the few moments he had listened to the rotund private, the man's diction and pronunciation, even his vocabulary, had grown in scope, in confidence. Somewhere, in the recesses of his experience, deep within himself, Winter felt a corresponding uplift in his psychic acuity. He felt *deeper*, somehow more knowledgeable, less . . . ephemeral. More emotional, perhaps, but.less sure . . .

The private saluted again, his stained, gnarled fingers barely touching the brim of the boonie hat, as if their relationship was now less formal. More on a personal level. He smiled wryly, but wiped away real tears and said, "I must go. My transport is here—" though Winter had heard no aircraft sounds, no noise of ground vehicles "—and it is expected of me to fulfill the wishes of my mast—my officer. I must take control of the island to ensure the circumstances he valued. Sir!" He began lifting, slinging, bundling the large number of containers and while Winter watched, silent, the private, looking more like a packmule with each added burden, lumbered off into the gloom of the terminal.

Winter walked slowly in the same direction, knowing he would never catch up enough to learn the private's objective. He did not need to, he thought. There was something more than slightly skewed in the man's attitude. The lieutenant, though— that lieutenant had style.

He walked back and slumped by the column. The night, stretching long before him until first transport departure, offered nothing of solace. Visions of waste and sunlight, drunken revels and death kaleidoscoped before his eyes, closed or open. David Winter waited, frozen in a vast welter of ambiguous loss.

Epilogue

October 1973; Rome, Italy

> "In the fall the war was always there, but
> we did not go to it any more."
> The opening line from "In Another Country"
> in the collection *Men Without Women*.
>
> Ernest Hemingway, 1927

Tourist shills tout the attractions of the Eternal City in spring. And summer, a mecca for visitors and lovers—until August when *Ferragusto* produces a ghost town. Then, even the redoubtable Romans flee the city's heat for Lago Bracciano or the mountains around L'Aquila and Frascati.

Though it has, to some tastes, its own warm-weather charm, I am besotted with the Rome of autumn. The air of the parks and piazzas and on the banks along the Tiber fragrant with the blue-smoke aroma of roasting chestnuts, their prickly shells broken and cast aside beneath the trees. I would prefer the bittersweet pang of painfully azure skies to contrast the bite of autumn, but today's pervasive bow to season's end under gray masses seems compelling.

Now, in October, the first discernible sense of chill winter winds sweeping down out of the Appenines is in the air, presaging an end to street society. Not a bad thing if you've other purposes to your life beyond people-watching.

Via Vittorio Veneto, a short street of societal ambitions, beginning at Piazza Barberini, climbs past the Church of the Bones, the American Embassy and Consulate, and continues on past my streetside table at Doney's before the Hotel Excelsior, on beyond the furniture emporium and Wimpy's hamburger heaven to breach the two-thousand-year-old wall leading into the park.

Seated facing south, I spotted him strolling up the broad sidewalk. Better dressed, and his infamous tangle of mustache brought into acceptable limits, no doubt under directives of his current bureaucratic master—a thing the Army had never been able to manage. I could not have mistaken Algernon MacGantry's shambling gait in an actors' cattle call of imposters.

When he had picked me out of the *cappuccino e apéritivo* drinkers, I saw that slow, taunting grin crack across sunburn. I thought the Burberry a touch overdone for the mild Rome weather, but at the time I didn't know where he'd come from. The phone call late the evening before only informed me he was in Rome for a day, passing through from somewhere to somewhere else. Could we meet for a drink?

He stood by my table without speaking, as if awaiting my drink order. Obstinate enough to go on standing there, speechless, forcing me to make overtures. Ratty Mac, Burberry or no, still fit the mold.

"Discreet, my ass!" I said, rising with my hand out. "You're a recruiting poster boy for The Spooks."

"'The Company,' Chief," he facetiously corrected me. "That's my employer. The Company. And how's by you, *boychik?*" His hand, as ever rough and abrasive as dried boar's hide, crushed mine; and though I feared habits of old, he restrained himself from clenching me in a bear hug. Had he—*we*— finally reached some long-sought plane in the maturation process? I sincerely hoped not.

Mac glanced about, effecting tourist curiosity, but I saw in those red, ferret eyes the cataloguing process that took in everything and everybody near us, including the early-stroll, fifty-dollar whores.

Watching his eyes, I said, "Nice to see some things don't change, isn't it?"

"I wouldn't know," he replied laconically, unlike the Mac I knew. "My first time here."

"Coming from where?" I asked, and turned, signaling the waiter.

He hesitated. "Djakarta. Place full of Indonesians. More Gooks!"

The waiter took my order for another *vino rosso*, made two

hashmarks on his pad when Mac indicated the same, and shuffled off to some private serenade. When the waiter was out of earshot, Mac pulled a chair around and sat beside me, his back to a stretch of Doney's solid wall.

Its not that Mac deliberately exhibited drama; it had been four years, and this was a different player. And Djakarta can't have been all fun and games. But within moments, I noted a mellowing as the fact of being in another time zone settled on him. He smiled that old lazy, disarming grin that, if you read sign, meant potential for mayhem was present. It was a quieter Mac, though, and we were content to sit silently, awaiting the wine.

"Where you off to next?" I asked, though it was clear his agenda was to avoid mention of plans or destination. But, despite the fact his assignment was likely covert, and he directed not to discuss it with anyone, even old friends, Mac, well . . . I tried to imagine how that Yale-Princeton-Harvard crowd would respond to Ratty Mac's different drummer's strut.

"Got a few weeks leave coming. Going home, to Illinois. Then, I got to get on my Hebrew studies," he murmured quietly.

"Tel Aviv?" I mouthed silently. I said, "*Sao-o-o!* They don't lavish assignment gems on you, do they? Couldn't have been one of my EERs that got you two plum assignments, back-to-back, do you think?" I asked facetiously. I'd only ever written one enlisted evaluation report on Mac, late in my first tour in Viet Nam when his rater, SFC Michilak, was wounded in a little friendly fire and unable to fulfil his duties. But I knew his assignments reflected no matter of choice. It was how The Company processed careers: take a new recruit, steep him in shit for two or three tours, see if he floats. Mac would manage.

"Well, enough small talk, Herr Brenner. I gotta catch up on Hall doin's," he said, briskly washing his dry hands in that old anxiety motion of his.

"You can expect short shrift in that department. Except for the five days I spent there, early 'seventy when I left 'Nam graced with this assignment, transitioned through there for briefings, I haven't been back. And we don't communicate much, Arlington

Hall and I, beyond directives for ass kicking and such." Mac could read between the lines as well as I could delve into that intuitive realm.

"You know what I mean. Our main men. What's to know?" Mac effected a casual, almost disinterested air, but his eyes were darting again. "Startin' with you. What's with this cushy, downtown-Europe gig? How'd you rate?"

"I suspect I cribbed Winter's tour. Remember, he'd figured out that his request for special assignment, early 'sixty-eight, was what got him on a bird back to 'Nam for a second tour. And he told me once, at Cam Ranh, mid-'sixty-nine in sworn confidence, that he had advance notice of assignment to Rome. This job."

"Then why're you here instead of Dave?"

"In a minute. When he wasn't . . . available, after his 'Nam tour, they must have skimmed down the roster and found the next available warrant officer, oh-five-one, coming out of 'Nam." I let my thumb to my chest answer for Himself. "I had no idea, no advance notice, until I received my orders. I never applied for the assignment. Sergeant Major at The Hall explained it to me."

"What exactly is your assignment?" He seemed only marginally interested.

"I command a small office attached to the Defense Attaché at the embassy. Civilian clothes. Living on the economy. Separate rats, et cetera. An unimaginably different world."

"Nice. Really nice. I could've used Rome, instead of that cesspool." Though he said it with emotion, I knew Mac to be a simple tool for bureaucrats, a man who flourished in adversity.

"Not available? Dave?" Mac said, falling behind the conversational curve.

I ignored the question. "You know about Magic Marvin," I reminded him. Surely he knew.

"Blinded by some asshole at Cam Ranh, I heard. Guy name a' Beard. I remember because I thought it might have been a Beard I knew. But I didn't know this guy. I was down south in the S-3, two-two-four. Marve was shipped to Valley Forge, that's all I ever heard."

"Transferred to a hospital at Fort Sheridan later, nearer home, and he did recover partial vision. Something like twenty percent. I mean, how do you measure something like that? He's still legally blind. He was on his second enlistment, proving career intentions, so he got a hundred percent medical retirement . He's in school at Southern Illinois."

Mac glowered into space for a moment. "I think I'd rather be dead," he said with conviction. "Maybe I'll see him while I'm home."

"He'd like that. I've had a couple of cassette tapes from him. He uses them instead of letters. And I've responded in kind." It was a fact that when Winter had adopted Magic Marvin, the clerk had become the ward of our full circle—of whatever and whomever that was considered to consist.

"Yeah. And Ito?" Mac played along.

"Korea. He was—"

"Yeah. 'kay."

"Haven't heard from him." I had written once, but Fred didn't even write his parents in Honolulu.

A quick burst of flak from a northern wind sent loose menus and drink doilies and streetwalkers' skirts flying. Winter season might not be here yet, but the preface was building in the mountains. Mac's topcoat began to look a good choice to me.

"I saw Hewitt in . . . a stopover in one of our embassies," Mac said evasively.

"The El Tee from Commo Mountain? Talbot Hewitt? Doing what there?"

"Some kind of personal assistant to the ambassador. I heard he was hand-picked, right out of Dip school," Mac said.

"Sharp guy. Had a Master's in something odd . . . French Lit or something. That would fit. I didn't know about him; he was still on the mountain when I left."

"Yeah. Uhhh, Luther," with some force, "I think we've danced about this social network bullshit long enough."

Yeah, classic Mac.

"You know who I want to know about," he said pointedly.

"Dave Winter. When he left on emergency leave, he never came back to 'Nam, and I didn't hear anything before I got out. If anyone knows, you do."

Mac was right, and that was my cross.

"He's in Maine. "

"Maine! Him and Moira?"

"No. Family."

"Family? As in . . . Nickie? The boys?"

"That would be the family."

"What about Moira? The Sweetheart of Sigma Cat? Didn't work out?"

Fantasies dispelled. "Moira died in the hospital. In Japan."

Mac had an economical way of conveying sadness with silence. He demonstrated that covert skill then, looking off with hooded eyes, down the curving Via Veneto. "Yeah, sure," he murmured after a bit.

I felt as if my face were carved in chalk.

After a black moment, Mac surprised me. "You were in love with her, too, weren't you?"

What's the point? Can't lie to comrades and nuns. "Not too much. What couldn't be avoided. Nominal lust. She belonged to my friend."

"How'd Dave take it? Her death."

"That's the thing. I don't think he knows. Everything to do with 'Nam was pretty much kept from him while he was in the straight-jacket ward. But maybe . . ." It was hard, hiding my anger.

"Straight jacket? Really?"

"No. Not really, you simple shit. But he *was* incommunicado for more than a year." I didn't want to go there and turned to an end run. "But you're right, Mac, he never came back. Not to Cam Ranh. To 'Nam." Not to reality.

"He got home to Mississippi, found his wife and children had foolishly *not* evacuated their home on the coast, and Camille had bitched it all. Oddly, his family and home were safe. But pretty much everything else in the region was wiped out. Widespread, massive destruction. They stayed with Nickie's mom in Jackson while the clean-up was going on, until they could get back to the house in Long Beach. By the time his thirty-day leave was up, his tour in 'Nam was over. The Hall called him, told him to sit tight, wait for orders."

"So where'd he go? How'd he wind up in a rubber room?" Mac really had heard nothing. I tried to frame an answer he could accept, as I'd had to compromise; something avuncular.

"Awaiting orders, Dave had some kind of—my take is, that goddamned bleeding heart of his reared up and bit him in the ass." I didn't know how else to put it. Then I thought, trying to divorce myself from a judgement: God will get you, Brenner, mixing metaphors like that!

"He had a heart attack?" Mac seemed startled.

"No, nothing physical."

"He went Asiatic!" For Mac, it was the logical fallback—an involuntary condition, its symptoms described as *a ten-thousand meter stare in a ten-foot bunker*, the charming vets' depiction of one who'd been too long in the Orient, or one whom Asian service had affected to an unnatural degree—and he was closer than he knew. Joseph Conrad had dealt with that once and got it pretty much right, though that was in another country.

"Not exactly. Simply and un-medically put, he had a breakdown. He just . . . What the brass euphemistically would label a retrograde movement. Retreat. Everything he believed in went south on him, left him bare ass to the elements. It had to be the war that did him in. What he encountered there, alien to what he stood for. I don't believe he ever knew about Moira. He might. But he quit dealing with it. All of it. He just stepped back from it. Checked out."

I felt the words woefully trite, trying to label something as poorly-defined as Dave's renouncement of reality. I understood it, I thought; I just couldn't explain it. Only if you'd known him as I had could you hope to ride that wavelength. Mac almost did, I would have thought at one time; but Mac went away and lived now in another elusive, shadowy world.

"I can't believe he wouldn't know about her dyin'," he scoffed.

"Well, *you* didn't know."

"Yeah, but . . . Where was he? In Walter Reed, or some Veterans Admin?"

"Bethesda. Been out a couple years now. Medically retired. Nickie stayed with him . . . took him in tow. They bought a house on the Naskeag Peninsula, up near Brooklin." Dave finally got to the coast of Maine after all the years I'd heard him longingly fantasize, expecting nothing.

"Is he working? What's he doing?" Mac was going to do the biography.

"He's got a small boat. Pots a few lobster, digs a few clams, catches some fish. Dropped most other interests. He just . . . lives there. But he has the boys."

"I thought his marriage was over. Him and Nicole split up."

"Apparently not. She pretty much has him now where I guess she always wanted him— dependent on her." Cutting through what had once been a fondness between Nickie and me was a hot flare of bitterness. "But maybe that's just me. At least he has the boys. And he's finished with the Army; won't be pulling any more short tours." Maybe that was all Nickie had wanted from day one. I'd never have suspected that when I first knew her. "All I know for a fact is, the David Winter she got—to care for, share with, to be with—he's not the same David Winter who started out in that role. The guy we went to war with—went to see the elephant with."

"Did you see him?" Mac snapped.

"Saw him once. In Bethesda. He wasn't a happy trooper, I don't care what the resident witch doctor said. But as to his mental state . . ." I wasn't going there.

That's all? You didn't follow up?" Incredulous.

"Mac, I had a small window coming out of Viet Nam, en route here, briefings and the Spanish Inquisition at The Hall. I only had time for the one visit." How could I make him see it wasn't for lack of effort. "He was essentially non-communicative then. And he didn't ask me back."

Mac fumed but said nothing.

"I did fly up when I came home on emergency leave to bury my grandfather. Nickie said he would see *no*-one. She even pretended to go ask him, in the next room. Came back, said it was a no-go. I don't know if she asked him or not, or whether he was even in the next room. But I wasn't going to force the issue. She exudes *kamp Kommandant* attitude. But there was no reason, either, to think it was all down to her. I haven't been back. Not even to the states. And I won't be back there soon. My tour here's about up. Moving on to Oslo."

"Well, shit!"

"I believe I expressed something similar on that final occasion."

Mac was silent a long time, watching the bizarre parade of freaks, skeptical at the unlikely personalities passing on the Veneto. He sipped his wine, twirling the stem between his fingers as he spoke. "I heard Mister Surtain got the Distinguished Flying Cross for saving that aircraft and crew, back in 'sixty-nine. Dave's flight," he said pointedly, in case I didn't remember.

"Yeah. I heard that. He deserved a DFC, minimum. Saved a lot of bods." A DFC was way down on Surtain's Christmas list. "And Dave turned down his Bronze Star. Said it was chickenshit and he'd have nothing to do with it."

No comment from Mac.

"You going to be around awhile?" I asked, though I knew different.

"Got a flight out of Fumicino tomorrow night." He stood, nodded up the street. "Gotta *di-di*, Luther. Best go have a little chat with that redhead who's sashayed past us a dozen-or-so times. She looks like she could use a little Christian guidance." He shrugged the topcoat tighter, gave me that raggedy-ass Ratty Mac grin, waved two fingers, and started away.

He turned back before he'd gone ten steps; his stance was awkward on the edge of the sidewalk. He said, "You're wrong, though. He knew!"

I waited, completely without a clue. I was probably staring like some simp.

"He knew . . . about Moira. You probably knew Dave better than me, Luther. Better than anyone, probably. But I knew him. And Dave had to know. If not, they'd have never had a rubber room that could hold him. And he wouldn't be puttering around now with fishes and squids and shit. No, Dave Winter knew about Moira Burke." He nodded in affirmation, and walked away.

I sat a while, feeling the cold seeping through me as the evening advanced, my wine glass unforgivingly empty. The lights along the Veneto were garish, oppressive even: inside and outside hotel lobbies, street lights, guttering candles on tabletops, car headlights in the constant traffic surge. I blinked and squeezed out a few sacrificial tears to ease tired eyes and got up from the table. I reached for my wallet, then saw Mac had left a ten-thousand-lire note under the Cinzano ashtray.

The redhead was nowhere in sight, nor the Burberry.

Somewhere nearby a crackle of Spanish *flamenco* rent the air. I felt a fleeting kinship with the music, but walked on back to the embassy parking lot for the Fiat without staying to listen. Like Chinese food, nothing Spanish seemed to sustain me for long anymore.

Journey's end:
Ganslhof
Salzburg, Austria
September 25, 2007